Danica Winters is a multiple-award-winning, bestselling author who writes books that grip readers with their ability to drive emotion through suspense and occasionally a touch of magic. When she's not working, she can be found in the wilds of Montana, testing her patience while she tries to hone her skills at various crafts—quilting, pottery and painting are not her areas of expertise. She believes the cup is neither half-full nor half-empty, but it better be filled with wine. Visit her website at danicawinters.net

By day **Maggie Wells** is buried in spreadsheets. At night she pens tales of intrigue and people tangling up the sheets. She has a weakness for hot heroes and happy endings. She is the product of a charming rogue and a shameless flirt, and you only have to scratch the surface of this mild-mannered married lady to find a naughty streak a mile wide.

K-9 RECOVERY

DANICA WINTERS

FOR THE DEFENCE

MAGGIE WELLS

MILLS & BOON

First Published in Great Britain 2021
by Mills & Boon, an imprint of HarperCollins*Publishers* Ltd
1 London Bridge Street, London, SE1 9GF

www.harpercollins.co.uk

HarperCollins*Publishers*
1st Floor, Watermarque Building,
Ringsend Road, Dublin 4, Ireland

K-9 Recovery © 2021 Danica Winters
For the Defence © 2021 Margaret Ethridge

ISBN: 978-0-263-28349-5

0821

MIX
Paper from
responsible sources
FSC™ C007454

This book is produced from independently certified FSC™ paper to ensure responsible forest management.

For more information visit: www.harpercollins.co.uk/green

Printed and bound in Spain
by CPI, Barcelona

K-9 RECOVERY

DANICA WINTERS

To the men and women in blue who serve our great nation. Thank you and your families for your sacrifices.

Chapter One

Love was a language everyone spoke, but few were fluent. Elle was definitely one of those who struggled.

It wasn't the concept of love that she found difficult to embrace—a union of souls so enmeshed that nothing and no one could come between them. At least, that was what the fairy tales that had been spoon-fed to her as a child and adolescent had told her. Perhaps it was these insipid stories that had set her up for failure in the relationship department. According to those stories, love was built on a foundation of ball gowns, champagne and whispers of forever, while reality peppered her with missed dates, drunken late-night phone calls and broken promises. As far as she could tell, love was all a lie.

The three-year-old girl standing before her was just another reminder of the consequences to the innocent when lies and love went too far.

"Ms. Elle?" she said, her voice high and pleading, though she had asked no real question.

"What is it, Lily babe?" Elle smiled down at the little blonde whose hands were covered with the remnants of cotton candy and pocket lint. She reached into her purse and pulled out a packet of baby wipes.

She was really starting to get this whole caretaker thing down.

"No," Lily said, pouting as she put her hands behind her back and stuffed her cherubic cheeks into the shoulder of her jacket.

Or maybe Elle wasn't doing quite as well as she thought.

"Just a quick wipe and then you can head back out to the swings. Okay?"

"I want juice." Lily smiled, her eyes big and bright. It reminded Elle of her dog, Daisy.

She put the wipes back and handed her a box of apple juice from her bag. "Only one, okay?"

Lily didn't say anything as she took the juice box, walked over to the sandbox and plopped down, already chatting with a new friend.

She had just been worked over by a toddler. *Damn.*

Before long, and after a series of carefully constructed arguments on Lily's side, they found themselves headed back to the Clark house. They walked up the steps to the front door of the colonial-style home, a throwback to the type of residence built by people who'd come to the wilderness of Montana to make their fortunes—and succeeded. The house was hardly the only sign of generational wealth. Everything, down to the three-year-old's shoes, wing tips she would likely only wear once, spoke of what old money could buy.

When Elle had been three, she had been running barefoot through the sands of Liberia while her parents were taking contracts and acting as spooks for the United States government. Though they had been gone for several years now, she missed them.

The door swung open before they even reached it, and

Catherine stepped out. She sent Elle a composed smile, the woman's trademark—a look of benevolence and influence all wrapped into one.

"She was perfect, as per usual," Elle said, watching as Lily slipped behind her mother's legs and disappeared into the belly of the house without so much as a backward wave. "Bye, little one!" she called after Lily.

It was a good thing she wasn't a sensitive soul or the little girl's apathy at her leaving would have broken her heart. Actually, it did hurt a little, but she would never let it show.

Catherine looked after her daughter but didn't say anything as the girl shuffled up the stairs.

Watching Lily's toddling steps up made Elle's skin prickle. She couldn't believe Catherine was letting the girl ascend to the second floor without a helping hand. One little slip, one poorly planted foot and Lily could have been lost to them all—and that girl was a gift. Everywhere she went she left the glitter of laughter.

"Do you want me to help her up to her room?" Elle said, stepping into the parlor.

"No," Catherine said, waving her off.

In the living room to her left, there was a group of men standing around and talking. They were all wearing suits and ties, except one, who was dressed in khakis and had a stinking cigar wedged into the corner of his mouth and a tumbler of scotch in his hand. The men looked like models for a fraternity's alum party or a political gathering.

"Thank you for taking her. It is appreciated." Catherine reached over for her purse, like she was going to pay Elle as if she was nothing more than a teenage babysitter.

She stopped her with a wave of her hand. "No, ma'am, please don't."

"I know I pay your company, but you need a tip at the very least."

She wasn't an hourly charge kind of woman, and the only reason she had agreed to take this security position was because she was the most temperate of the Spades. The boys would have handled the little girl like she was an egg, especially given the fact that Lily's father was a senator.

Elle couldn't give two shakes who the girl's parents were, except right now, when she was forced to face the fact that Catherine's focus was on her friends and not on her baby. Elle hadn't even seen the senator since she had taken the security position three months ago.

She had to reserve her judgments about the family. Her interactions were limited to drop-offs, pickups and little else. Catherine had made a point of not letting her interact with Lily when she was around.

Catherine stuffed a $100 bill into her hand. Part of her wanted to throw it on the ground and tell her to screw off, but instead she slipped it into her pocket. As she did, Catherine closed the door in her face.

It was no wonder the woman's daughter wasn't the kind for long goodbyes.

Maybe she didn't have to reserve judgments after all— Catherine was a brat.

That would make it easier to say goodbye when this security detail came to an end. But it was going to be tough to say goodbye to Lily.

As she walked to her truck, she took one long look back at the house. Lily was sitting in her bedroom window looking out. When she spotted her, the little girl waved.

Yes, saying goodbye would be hard.

As she got into her truck, she sighed and then rolled out toward the ranch. The miles drifted by as she forced herself to think about something other than the little girl. Tonight, she was supposed to have Daisy work with members of the local sheriff's department, who had graciously offered up their Search and Rescue and training warehouse as well as give assistance in running hides.

Daisy had come so far in just a couple of years; from a crazy little rottweiler puppy, she had turned into a dog that was capable of finding a castaway shoe in a rainstorm from a half mile away. She wasn't perfect—there would always be off days—but she was better than even Elle could have hoped.

When she made it home to the Widow Maker Ranch, Daisy was waiting for her at her little cabin. Her nubby black tail whipped back and forth violently as Elle walked in. The dog spun in excited circles, prancing, her face as close to a human smile as it could get.

Yes, she loved that dog. So had Lily, until her mother had put a stop to her bringing Daisy onto the property—even when only in her vehicle.

Loading Daisy and the gear up into the truck, she made her way over to the training warehouse. They hadn't worked there before; mostly she had worked with the K-9 units from the city police department, so this would be a fun, new experience.

Arriving, she found a tall, brooding sheriff's officer standing beside the bay doors. He was doing something on his phone, and he looked put out that he was standing in the icy near dark of the late winter night. Most people she worked with forgot any apprehensions the moment they saw Daisy. She was beautiful, with her gleaming black coat and buckskin-colored face and paws, and a blaze mark on her chest. And she loved everyone.

The man looked up from his phone, and his eyes flashed bright green in the thin light. He was stocky, and he wore a knit cap. When he gazed at her, he smiled for a split second, but as quickly as the sexy smile came, it disappeared and was replaced with what she assumed was a trademark scowl.

"You were supposed to be here ten minutes ago." He stuffed his phone away.

She wasn't late, she was never late, and the accusation made her hackles raise. She wanted to growl back at him and tell him to look at his watch, but she resisted the urge. They were here at the sheriff's invitation. Clearly this man wasn't here of his own volition.

"There must have been a miscommunication. Sorry about that." She was careful not to put the apology on herself or her mistake. If anything, he should be apologizing for the lack of a professional and warm welcome.

He said something under his breath.

It was a good thing he was handsome and she wanted this hour to train with Daisy, or she would have told him to pound sand then and there. She hated not having the upper hand. If he was sexist, too…she would be out of here in no time. Daisy could train somewhere else.

"If you like, I can come back another time." When someone else wanted to work with her and Daisy.

He sighed, the sound resigned. "We're both here."

She flipped her keys in her hand, thinking about how easy it would be to get in her truck and start the engine.

"Look," she said, her frustration finally threatening to come to a full boil, "if you don't want to do this, it's okay. I can promise you that I'm trustworthy and Daisy and I can use the training warehouse without supervision. You can just unlock the door and go. I will lock up when we're done. No big deal," she said, giving him the out he appeared to want.

His whole body shifted, like he suddenly must have realized how he was coming off to her. "No, no. As one of the search and rescue coordinators, I'm more than happy to help." He turned to the door and entered the code. The garage door ground open, exposing the interior of the building.

One side of the warehouse kept a variety of trucks, rafts, snowmobiles and mobile command units marked with the Missoula County Search and Rescue badge. The other half of the warehouse had been set up to look like a makeshift house.

She led Daisy out of the back seat of the truck and clicked her onto her lead. He had his back turned to them and didn't seem to notice the dog.

It was silly, but Elle was a bit crestfallen. No one ignored Daisy's beautiful face. She was always the star of the show. How dare he snub her baby dog?

Today really wasn't having any pity on her ego.

She followed behind him as he walked into the makeshift rooms built around the facility, making the interior of the warehouse look like something out of a movie set.

"We were just using this place for room clearing today," he said, pointing at a spent flash-bang on the floor in the staged living room. "I was going to clean up but decided to wait until you were done."

She nodded. "The more scents, the better. I like to make it hard on her."

He smiled, a *real* full-toothed smile, and he finally looked down at Daisy. "May I touch her?"

Finally, they were getting somewhere.

"Sure," she said, looking at the nameplate on his chest. "Sergeant Anders."

He glanced up at her and looked surprised before connecting the dots with how she would have known his name. "Sorry about being a little short with you," he said, bending the knee to Daisy and petting her.

The animal leaned into him, her bulletproof vest pressing against his. They made quite the pair.

Daisy's butt jiggled as she tried to wag her tail. "She likes you."

At least one of them did. If nothing else, Daisy's endorsement of the man was something to like him for.

"I'm a huge dog guy—it's why I offered to stay behind and help you out."

He had *offered*?

"Well, I appreciate your helping me." She felt suddenly embarrassed that she had taken an instant disliking to him. Maybe she really was too fast to judge.

She would need to focus on her self-improvement for a while.

"What do you need me to do?" he asked, motioning around the place.

She reached into her tactical bag and took out a Ziploc. "This bait has a scent on it. I'll take Daisy outside and make her wait. Then I'm going to need you to take this out of the bag and plant the cloth somewhere in the facility. I don't want to touch it. She knows what I smell like and can use that."

He threw his head back with a laugh. "We'd hate for her to cheat."

"She is smarter than I am sometimes." She smiled.

He looked at her as he stood up, studying her. "I find

that hard to believe. The handler is just as important as the dog in K-9 work."

She pushed the bait into his hands and moved to step out the side door before he could read anything on her face. "I'll wait out here."

She felt something in her chest shift as she walked away from him. Was he hitting on her? Or was she just seeing something that wasn't there because she had been without a man for too long?

Yeah, there was nothing there. She had just witnessed a mirage in the desert of her love life. All she needed was to go on a date with a man, leave in the morning and forget about feelings. Relationships were for people who had the time and patience to deal with them; she had better things to do.

She shifted her weight, like she was readjusting her nonexistent, feelings-proof vest.

"Daisy, you are not a good influence," she said, scratching behind the dog's ears as Daisy looked up at her and gave her a doggie grin. "Like I said. You know what you did, didn't you? You're devious."

Daisy wiggled. "If you want a man in our lives, we can get you a cute dog to run with. Don't you dare look at me and get any kind of silly ideas."

Chapter Two

What a long damned day. He loved training with the special response team, or SRT, but going from 6:00 a.m. until 6:00 p.m. had drained him. When he'd agreed to take care of the K-9 handler, he'd had no idea it was going to be a woman. As soon as she had stepped out of that truck, he'd hated his decision to volunteer even more.

She was way too good-looking, with her long brunette hair pulled back into a loose ponytail and her skintight tactical pants. Looking at her, and the way she moved, he instantly wondered if this woman was here to train or to flirt. He had a history with women who fell in the latter category. He'd met his ex when she had signed up for a ride-along. Things had seemed normal during the ride, but the next day the texting had started, and quicker than he realized, he was in it deep.

Amber had been great—things had been easy between them—but that had led to most of their problems. She would bow to anything he wanted, with no counterpoints, no opinions of her own and always acquiescence. He had needed a woman who challenged him.

Breaking up with her had been murder. She was nice enough and there was no concrete moment that had torn them apart after two years. It just was...*time*.

She hadn't taken it well and had begged him to stay. He had been tempted to give in—she wasn't a bad girlfriend in any way—but if he was honest, he didn't want to settle for happy enough. He wanted more than that in his life. He wanted a woman who made his heart race when she walked into the room. It sounded stupid, but he wanted a woman who could speak to his soul even in moments when he knew he was wrong and then she could make him right.

But what he was looking for, what he needed, wasn't something he would ever find.

He'd damned well given up looking. And until he figured out what he really wanted, something that made some sense, he wasn't about to jump into a relationship again. He didn't want to hurt anyone because he didn't know what he needed—he was a better man than that, or at least he would have liked to think he was.

Grant walked around the facility, running scent for Elle and her dog before planting the T-shirt behind a cushion on the floral-patterned couch in the makeshift den. There was probably a better place to hide the smelly thing, but it would have to work. The quicker the dog found what it was looking for and the quicker the beautiful woman and her cute dog were gone, the better.

As he walked back, he reminded himself not to look her in the eyes. If he did, if the little niggle of excitement he felt upon seeing her was truly going to be some kind of feeling, staring into her eyes wasn't going to help. Better to avoid trouble than to walk headfirst into it.

She looked up as he opened the door leading outside. Blue. Her eyes weren't just plain old blue; rather, they were the color of the sky on a summer day—crystal clear and bright, full of spirit.

Damn it. Error. Major error.

"Did you plant the shirt somewhere?" she asked, the question sounding as awkward as he felt.

He nodded. "What else you need me to do?" He squirmed as he stood there, holding the heavy metal door open for her.

"If you want to watch, you can follow us through. But I've got it all from here, or rather... Daisy does," she said, sending him a sexy smile.

Daisy looked up at her, like she realized they were talking about her, and her entire body vibrated with joy. It was as if the dog knew what was going to come and was loving her job. If only everyone on his teams loved their jobs the same way this dog seemed to.

He watched as the woman gave the dog a command in what sounded like Russian.

Though he had worked with K-9 units during SWAT calls, this was one of the few times he had a chance to see what it took to teach the dogs he often saw in action.

He walked behind them as she followed the dog. She wove back and forth, locating the scent. It struck him how different the dog looked from the bouncing, wiggling beast Daisy had been outside to this focused task-driven animal that was now working the room in front of him.

It was impressive.

"I thought most K-9s were German shepherds?"

"Most are, or Belgian Malinois." She didn't look away from Daisy as they worked. "Rotties are somewhat rare in the SRT game, but more common in search and rescue. They are a breed with a peppered track record in the court of public opinion, but they are having a resurgence in popularity."

He heard the words she was saying, but all he could

focus on was the sound of her voice and the way her words were flecked with an accent he couldn't quite put his finger on. She sounded like she was from somewhere farther north, but it wasn't quite Canadian. There was also the twang and hard *A* sounds of the Midwest. Where had she grown up?

Maybe she was a corn-fed girl out of Iowa. Hard raised and strong as hell. It would definitely explain how she had gotten into such a male-dominated field. However, maybe he was wrong—there were more and more women getting into search and rescue, and they were all better for it. The next commander was likely even going to be a woman, Melody Warner. She was as badass as they came in SAR. She could pull together a swift-water rigging quicker and better than any man he knew.

His phone buzzed, and he ignored it, though he knew it was likely something to do with work.

"How did you get involved with rottweilers?" he asked, trying to ignore the pull to answer his work phone—it should have been priority number one, but all he could focus on was her and this place and how she smelled like floral perfumes and rubber dog toys.

"My best friend runs Big Sky Rottweiler Rescue. They focus on rehoming rotts who have been surrendered or abandoned to shelters." She rushed after Daisy, who was pulling hard on the leather lead as they made their way down the hall. "Daisy came to me after living in a cage for over a year."

He looked at the beautiful, healthy dog who was sniffing the ground like it held all the answers.

His phone buzzed again, an angry bee just looking to lance his flesh. "Excuse me for a minute." He lifted a finger, knowing she would go about her business though all he wanted her to do was stay by his side and continue his time with her. Being here, watching her work and just learning the steps was the break he needed from his day.

And yet, life called.

"Hello?" he asked, turning away for a moment and walking toward the main door.

"You're working with Elle Spade right now, correct?" He instinctively glanced in her direction as the sheriff spoke.

"Yeah, why?"

"Tell her that there has been an incident…involving one Lily Clark and her family." The sheriff paused, clearing his throat. "I have also approved your volunteer SAR team to act on this one."

"What are you talking about? What happened?" And why would he be asked to tell Elle about it? He was having a hard time pulling the real meaning together behind the sheriff's cryptic instructions.

"A three-year-old girl, Lily Clark, and her mother, Catherine, have gone missing. It looks as though there was some kind of altercation inside the residence, but the team is still sorting through everything. I have yet to get the full report from the crime scene." Grant heard the clink of ice in a glass, but he wouldn't dare ask the sheriff if he had been drinking—such questions only led to lies or trouble. "We aren't sure what happened to the mother, but we have reason to believe the little girl slipped out of her house and may be lost in the national forest service land that abuts their property. Both are, as of yet, unaccounted for."

"I'll pull together my team, and we will head out there as soon as possible."

"Sooner than that. I need you out there now. Go grab

Elle and get in your truck. Head straight there and let your team take care of everything else. If you need me to call in one of the coordinators to help, I can."

That wasn't procedure, and he couldn't make sense of why the sheriff would be pushing him like this when he damned well knew that everything SAR did was done as quickly and safely as possible—not only for those they were sent to rescue or recover but also for all members of the unit.

"Yeah, call in Commander Warner. She is the best team leader we've got. But can I ask why the push?"

The sheriff sighed. "Lily Clark isn't just an average kid. She is United States Senator Dean Clark's daughter. If we don't get that girl back..." The sheriff trailed off.

He didn't need to explain that the senator controlled much of their funding—or lack thereof. If a senator turned against them, they would be limited to nothing more than donations and fundraising events.

Basically, if they failed...so did their program.

As awful as that might be, though, it didn't compare to the situation at hand—a missing girl, probably frightened beyond imagining.

"I'll be there as quickly as I can. Text me the address. You make the call to Warner. Get her up to speed. Out." He hung up his phone, remembering that he hadn't even asked the sheriff why he was supposed to tell Elle about the girl's disappearance. Hell, it was probably so she could bring the dog.

He ran down the hall. "Hey, Elle, SAR got a call!"

She stepped out of the makeshift den, Daisy holding a rubber ball in her mouth and wiggling while Elle pushed the T-shirt he'd hidden back into the Ziploc bag.

"Do whatever you need to. I can lock up here. Seriously, and thank you for letting us train with you."

His face puckered. "Actually, the sheriff just called personally. He knew you were here and asked that you go with me on this one."

"Really? Why?" She cocked her head, an oddly canine mannerism, but it fit the woman.

"Do you know the Clarks?" he asked, his stomach clenching, though he wasn't sure exactly why. "Lily and Catherine?"

She stared at him, unmoving and unblinking, as though her world had just come crashing down. Daisy stopped moving and looked up at Elle like she could feel the change in the energy around the woman just as abruptly as he did. The dog sank to the floor, laying her head on Elle's feet and letting the ball fall from her mouth and roll haphazardly over the concrete.

"What happened to her?" Elle asked, her voice sounding breathless as all the color drained from her features.

It was strange, but he could understand the dog's sudden need to touch her, to comfort her in the only way possible. And yet he barely knew this woman or why this news would affect her so dramatically. "Something has happened up at their place, some kind of altercation."

"What kind of *altercation*?" She spat the word.

"I can't tell you." He moved to touch her, but she jerked away. "Are you going to be okay?"

She rushed past him, bumping hard against him like she had somehow forgotten he was there even though he had been speaking to her.

Daisy ran behind her as they sprinted outside.

As he stood there, he could make out the sound of her truck revving to life and her tires squealing on the asphalt. As quickly as the woman nosed her way into his life, she had sprinted out of it—and he was far more confused than ever. In a matter of minutes, he'd gone from safely contained and tired from a long day, to geared up and having his and his team's asses on the chopping block…and it seemed highly likely it was all because of her and secrets he was yet to discover.

Chapter Three

The entire ride back to the Clarks', Elle couldn't think of anything except Lily. She'd only been missing a matter of hours, and already things had gone haywire. She should never have left the little girl.

Hopefully the altercation Grant had alluded to was nothing more than a fistfight, nothing involving weapons. She should have asked Grant more questions. If only she had been thinking. That was always one of her biggest and most profound faults—emotions and actions first, questions later. It wasn't a recipe for success in her personal or professional life.

She grabbed her phone. She could call him. But as she looked at the screen, she realized she didn't have his number. *Damn it.*

No doubt, if she had been able to talk to him, he would be unlikely to give her much. He'd been pretty vague with providing any sort of details, and when it came to law enforcement and anyone in special operations, she had learned long ago that when they kept silent, it was for a reason.

That silence was always chilling.

Her mind went to all the dark places as she sped down the road. Lily had to be okay. Catherine could fend for herself—well, so long as the altercation was as minor as she hoped. Yet why would the sheriff ask for her to come if it was something inconsequential?

Perhaps it was so she could act as a witness. Or maybe they needed her there to help Lily calm down. Maybe the little girl was asking for her.

She smiled faintly at the thought. Of course, that was probably it. Otherwise the sheriff would probably not even know Elle existed.

Then again, Grant had first told her that *SAR had a call.* That meant search and rescue teams were involved. Which meant that one or both of the Clark ladies were missing. It was probably Lily. Maybe Lily was just playing, hiding away in some closet in the house and Catherine couldn't find her.

Yes, this was probably all blown out of proportion and Elle was just jumping to the darkness out of habit—she and her military contracting teams had spent far too many nights planted in the tumultuous and dangerous world of war-ravaged countries.

Her mind drifted to Afghanistan. They had been running an operation for the military-contracted agency, or MCA, she'd been working for at the time, taking her dog into the mud houses and working to clear them of explosives. In the Pashtun region, none of the dwellings were for single families. Rather, extended family groups crowded into them, and they normally held between twelve and twenty people. Most of the residents hated dogs and Americans and, with her having both strikes against her, she was never a welcome sight—not to mention she was a woman working in an area heavy with Taliban forces.

On her last trip, she had been operating in a building

that had already had one IED detonation in the court-yard. When she'd arrived on scene, the team before her had pulled out all the remaining living members of the family. The complex had taken on an eerie, disquieting feel that spoke of the horror that had filled it only hours before her arrival.

It wasn't the first time she had been to a place like that, where the acrid scent of spent explosives still mixed with the tang of freshly spilled blood and lingered in the air like a eulogy, yet when she got to the courtyard, she hadn't been prepared for the scene that had unfolded.

She had to work through a number of bodies, most so thoroughly peppered with shrapnel that if it weren't for their clothes, it would have been hard to tell if they were women or men. There was a small crater where the initial blast had happened. There, at the edge, was a well-worn pair of children's Adidas sneakers. One was tipped on its side, as if the kid who had been wearing them had been blown out of them.

She later learned that, according to eyewitnesses, the child had picked up the bomb and had been playing with it when it detonated.

She'd been shipped out later that week and had never been happier to get out of a country.

It had taken her a long time after her feet had arrived on American soil for her soul to come home, as well. No matter how many debriefings or offers to speak to chaplains happened, she would never again go to sleep without the image of those shoes popping into the front of her mind.

Ever since that day, she'd been on a mission to be on the front line when it came to children and her job. Most would have backed away, put distance between themselves and the possible horrors that would hurt them the most, but not her. It was odd, but seeing those horrors made her want to do everything in her power to never have those tragedies or hellscapes happen again—and therefore witnessed by anyone else.

She could be the whipping girl so others wouldn't have to endure the same traumas.

Trauma. Her past. All of it was swirling into her mind and masking the reality of her present. She couldn't let that happen. Not now. Not when Lily was likely in trouble.

Maybe it was the trauma that scared her the most, nothing more than the ghosts of the past haunting the present. More than likely, Lily was probably just being Lily and hiding in the house somewhere, she reminded herself. Maybe her father had called in the cavalry when really only patience and steadiness were all that were needed.

Maybe this was nothing more than the senator pulling strings in order to bring the media to their knees at his beck and call—attention to him and his family, especially in their time of need, would likely be helpful in any sort of political campaign. Hell, he was known for pandering to the media.

If this was some kind of political move, she was going to have to quit the job on the spot. Then again, she couldn't leave Lily alone and unsupervised with two such toxic people.

As she crested the top of the hill, she turned down the driveway that led to the Clarks'. The place was lit up with a collection of red and blue lights. The image made her stomach drop. In the evening shadows, the lights reflected off the snow and made it look like some sort of scene out of a murder documentary.

Murder.

No.

There was no way Lily could be dead.

Yet the scene made it clear that this situation was far more serious than what she had been hoping to find.

As she pulled up the driveway, her thoughts moved to the men who had been standing around in the living room like frat boys when she had been here earlier.

Was she here because of something they did? It wouldn't have surprised her if things had escalated into a full-blown altercation with that kind of crowd. When there was a room full of self-important and power-hungry men drinking and smoking cigars, no doubt they would have been trying to one-up each other. They were probably playing at the hierarchy of asshats.

For now, she just needed to get the information she required and go to work in helping Lily. She couldn't go down the road of what-ifs and hows. She was here to help, first and foremost. The rest of the professionals on-site could help her make sense of everything else. It was the reason they had teams. And, in her case, she not only had the crew that was already swarming around the house, but her family, as well.

Whatever the police couldn't handle—or were limited in what they could legally do—her family and teams at STEALTH could step in and take care of. It was one of the best things about her job and family. She was always surrounded by badasses. In fact, some could have even said she was one, but if she was, it was because of her dog. If she had to pick the biggest badass in her family, the title would have to go to her sister, Kendra.

She parked, got out of her truck and walked to the back door to check on Daisy. Grant pulled in behind her, a sour expression on his face. As he exited his truck, the look on his face deepened. "Don't you think you were driving a little fast?" From the tone of his voice, she would have thought he was kidding, but from his expression he was clearly annoyed.

"If Lily is in trouble, there's no speed limit in the world that's going to keep me from getting to her." She gave Daisy a scratch behind the ears as the dog stared at her and attempted to make sense of everything that was happening.

"So, you do know this girl?" Grant asked. "I mean, I assumed you did…given the fact you ran away from me like your ass was on fire. But you could have at least let me give you the lay of the land before you tore out."

She huffed. He wasn't wrong. "Yes, I know Lily. I was hired as her guard by her family. I only left here a few hours ago." She clicked Daisy's lead onto her collar, readying her for whatever their next steps may be. "What's happened to her?"

His sour, annoyed expression was quickly replaced with one of a pained empathy. "From what I was able to glean on the ride over, the mother and her child have gone missing. They initially believed the little girl may have slipped out of the house sometime after you left… but the scene's—"

"Lily didn't sneak out of the house," she said, interrupting him. "Lily isn't that kind of girl." Her thoughts came in a mad dash.

"I know, but—"

"If anyone is at fault here, it isn't Lily. Her parents are…" She glanced up at the front door of the house. The senator was nowhere to be seen. "They are not as *attentive* to Lily as parents should be. In fact, I'm surprised they didn't have a nanny on staff. They should have."

Catherine and Dean hadn't been especially forthcoming with why they had hired Elle and her team to watch over Lily, but if they thought there was enough of a security threat that they needed to call in private VIP teams, then obviously there was something going on.

She should have pushed for more answers before taking this job. She should have gotten all the details. And yet, they had been vague. In a world of shadows, she hadn't found it surprising at the time. Maybe it had been their hubris or hers, but as long as she was around, she hadn't been overly concerned that anything bad would happen to Lily. But that had been on the condition that she was around. This had happened after her watch had ended. She should have been adamant about making sure that Lily had around-the-clock coverage. Or at least that they had boots on the ground outside the house.

She looked at Grant. He'd crossed his arms over his chest and was looking down at his feet, and she realized that she had once again spoken over him. When would she just start listening instead of pushing her way through life?

"Sorry. So, both Catherine and Lily are missing?" Elle asked, more focused on the child than the mother. At least Catherine could look out for herself.

He nodded. "No one knows where they went, but there was a sign of a struggle inside the residence. A table is broken and, from what the deputy on the inside said, there were shots fired within the house, and a gun registered to Catherine was found under a sofa. It was a .38 Special, and they believe it is the same caliber as that which left the holes in the walls."

"So you believe Catherine was shooting at someone?"

Grant shrugged. "Hard to say how this played out as of now. We are pretty early on in our investigation. You know how these things have a way of distorting under first impressions."

He spoke to her as though someone had filled him in on some key details of her life, but she couldn't imagine who or when. She had always been insistent about keeping herself to herself, but then again, this was Montana.

"One of the neighbors said they saw you leaving the house this afternoon," he continued. "It is believed you were one of the last people in or out of the house."

"What? No. I wasn't the last one here by any means. There were quite a few men in the living room, socializing with Mrs. Clark, when I left. But, wait…"

He didn't call her here to help in the search. No. He'd called her here because she was one of their possible suspects.

"Am I a suspect in their disappearance?" she asked.

If she had been the lead working this case, she would have been her first stop, too. And it had been one hell of a play for Grant to bring her right to this place and put her on the spot, when, in fact, he was really questioning her. She had fallen for his game hook, line and sinker.

But she wasn't afraid—she had nothing to hide.

"I didn't say anything of the sort," he said. "However, what time did you leave here?" Grant asked, careful to phrase his questions in a way that if she hadn't been aware she was being interrogated, she wouldn't have picked up on it.

"I left about thirty minutes before I met up with you."

She scowled. "I know what you're thinking, but I'm telling you right now that if there was anything or any information I could give you about this little girl's disappearance, I'd be the first to do it."

Grant twitched. "You're always two steps ahead, aren't you?"

"I just live in this world, one of law enforcement and carefully constructed realities."

He chuckled. "I do appreciate that we have the ability to speak the same language on this." He seemed to relax, whatever suspicions he held about her momentarily falling to the wayside.

He was trying to play her again, to make her feel comfortable around him in an attempt to get more information. Little did he know, she was a master at that stupid game. However, it was odd and uncomfortable for her to be sitting on the receiving end.

"Do your guys know how long they've been missing? Who called this in?"

He leaned against the front of her truck. Daisy whined at her, and she stroked her head.

"Again, I don't have all the details, but I think it was a neighbor who reported hearing gunshots."

"Any blood?" She clicked off Daisy's lead and closed the back door of the truck, leaving the dog safely tucked inside. "Did your guys look everywhere for Lily? That girl won't just answer to anyone. If she's hiding in there, she's probably not going to come out for anyone other than someone she knows." She took a step toward the house.

"Stop," Grant said, putting his hands up to keep her from advancing. "I know what you are thinking, but you can't just barge into that house and start yelling for Lily.

This is potentially an active crime scene. Whatever we do, we have to be careful. We have to follow procedure, at least as much as we can."

Her hands were balled into tight fists, almost like her body wanted to strike out and take down anything and anyone who stood between her and Lily's safety—or lack thereof—even if that someone was the sergeant.

She tried to control her impulses to run into the house and flip open every cabinet and overturn every drawer in her search for Lily, but it was a struggle. Daisy whined from the back seat, and when Elle glanced over at her, Daisy barked.

I know. I screwed up, Daisy, she thought. *I never should have left today. I knew something wasn't right. I effing knew it.*

Daisy's nose pressed on the glass, and she whined again.

She should have trusted her gut and not left when she had seen the men in the house alone with Catherine. She should have taken Lily and gone somewhere...anywhere. And yet, she hadn't listened to the little voice, and now her ward and her mother were missing.

She thought about Gavin de Becker's *The Gift of Fear*. Like so many other self-help and self-defense–themed books, it spoke of a person's intuition being their greatest weapon in their defense arsenal. There was nothing more effective to defer crime and injuries than to avoid situations that put a person at risk. Yet the only person who had avoided anything was Elle—she had wanted to avoid a confrontation with Catherine, and in the end...

Her boss was nowhere to be found.

One confrontation and she could have saved a woman and a child from disappearing.

Elle had avoided conflict and walked them straight into danger.

Maybe she needed to read that book again. Then again, she didn't need a book to tell her to be afraid. She knew all too much about that on her own.

"Would you mind taking me through the house? I won't touch anything, but if we are going to look for Lily, I'm going to need to know where we are going to have to start." *And whether or not she is still alive.*

"Why don't we leave Daisy for now? I want to do a quick walk-through and then, if you feel it necessary, we can have her do a sweep. Okay?" Grant asked, giving her a pinched, pleading look.

She opened the back door and clicked Daisy's lead in place and then helped her step out of the back. "Dog goes. In a case like this, I can promise you that she is likely to pull more information than we ever could. Humans are always at the dumb end of the lead."

Chapter Four

The house still smelled like it had when she left, a strange mix of whiskey, expensive women's perfume and cigar smoke. Now, however, beneath the familiar odors was the distinct scent that came with the police—disinfectant, sweat, leather and gun powder.

She lifted her shirt, taking a quick sniff to see which world she smelled of after being in the training warehouse, but all she could smell was this morning's shower, fresh air and Daisy.

Careful to slip under the tape, she walked into the foyer and glanced into the living room. The various law officers were in other parts of the house now, so the room was empty. "When I left, Catherine was here with a group of about eight men." Daisy sat down beside her, leaning against her, her body tight and ready for action.

"Do you happen to know the identity of any of those men? Or what they were doing here?" Sergeant Anders asked.

She shook her head. "This family has a lot of foot traffic in and out of the place. It's why I normally take Lily out of the house when she is under my care. It is easier to control the variables."

"Are you saying that the type of people who came

through this place weren't who you would call reliable and safe?" he asked, reaching for his pocket like he wanted to take notes, but then he stopped and dropped his hands back down to his sides.

"It's not that they were drugged-out meth heads, or people who you would look at and think they were dangerous—actually, far from it. These people weren't the kind to keep themselves in bad company. Their lives were completely taken up by their image and the public's opinion of that image. Especially right now, as the senator is up for reelection and is behind in the polls."

She looked at the spot where she had last seen the stranger in khakis who had been smoking the cigar. Aside from the broken side table and three bullet holes in the wall to her right, nothing was out of place. If anything, it was too clean. Had someone staged this?

Grant bent over slightly and pointed toward the couch. "Right there, see the gun?" He pointed in the direction he was looking.

She crouched down. There, on the floor under the couch, was the .38 Special. She didn't recognize the gun, but she hadn't even been aware that Catherine owned a gun, let alone kept it at the ready.

"This room is ridiculously clean," Grant said, standing up. "Do the Clarks hire a cleaning staff?"

The question seemed kind of out of place, but she assumed he must have been thinking the same about the lack of detritus and debris in what they had been told was the site of an altercation that may or may not have led to Lily and Catherine going missing.

"Yes, but they only come in once a week," she said.

"Did Mrs. Clark always keep house in such a way?"

She stood up and chuckled. "Everything about the

Clarks was always picture-perfect. I agree that this isn't much to work with for investigators, but... Who knows?" She shrugged, trying to dispel some of her nerves. "This whole thing may not be as bad as we first assumed. Did your people try and call Catherine? Dean?"

Grant gave her a look that would have crumbled a lesser woman. "Yes, we tried to contact Catherine and Dean. Dean is unavailable. We have the Washington, DC, police department looking for him in order to notify him about what has happened. And Catherine's phone was found in the backyard—its screen was cracked, but we have bagged it for evidence and our teams will see if they can pull any information." He started to walk again, and she followed after, Daisy close at her heels.

"Were you and Mrs. Clark close?" Grant asked, looking over at her with a sidelong glance.

She shook her head as they made their way toward the back of the house. "Hardly. I'm nothing more than an employee. In fact, today she tried to give me a hundred-dollar tip. It was her way of reminding me that I'm nothing to Lily other than paid help—not a friend, not a parent and definitely not someone irreplaceable."

Grant reached up and touched her shoulder, the motion far too real and sympathetic than she was prepared for. He didn't need to say he was sorry; she could see it on him, and she didn't like it.

"It's okay. Sometimes it is good to be reminded to keep a little emotional distance from your work. And, regardless of how much I enjoyed Lily, I needed to keep in mind that the care of her was a job." Yet, even talking about what the girl *shouldn't* have meant to her made her ache with concern.

"Do you feel like you failed at that job?" he asked, almost as though he could read her truths on her features.

A lump formed in her throat, and she knew if she spoke, her voice would crack with pain. She simply shrugged.

"No matter what, Elle, you didn't fail this girl. You did exactly what you were paid to do during your working hours."

Had she? Her gaze moved to the travertine floor and the beige-and-gray speckling of its glistening surface; in her few months here she had never noticed the way it flowed like water.

He sighed. "I can see you are just like me. When you're off the clock, you struggle to leave the job at the doorstep. I know what that's like. And I know what you're likely struggling with. But you can't do this to yourself."

"My guilt will subside when I know that Lily is safe—and her mother."

He opened his mouth and then shut it, but she knew what he was going to say…that they both needed to be prepared for any possible outcomes.

As they walked by the stairs, she pointed in the direction of the living quarters. "Do you want me to show you Lily's room? Maybe there is something there." Really, though, she was just hoping that as soon as she stepped into the room, Lily would come bounding out from inside her closet or from under her bed; she loved to play hide-and-seek.

Even as she considered it, she could feel in her gut that such a thing wasn't going to happen. Lily wasn't in this house. There were at least twenty different law enforcement personnel circulating through the residence, taking pictures and documenting the scene. Several were talking on their phones, and their voices mixed into an odd cacophony of stoic babble and garbled calls from dispatch on handsets.

He started up the stairs, and she stepped around him, leading him down the long white-carpeted hallway toward the girl's bedroom. "I could never understand why anyone in their right mind would have carpet this color when they have children. Since I've been here, they've already had to replace the carpet in Lily's bedroom once after she spilled a glass of grape juice—organic, of course."

He smirked. "I can't profess to understand or comprehend the thought processes of the extremely wealthy."

"It's wasteful." As she spoke, she realized that she had completely unleashed all of the opinions and judgments she had been withholding. Yet, with the sergeant, it may not have been the wisest of choices.

She needed to shut up. All he needed to know were facts that would help them locate Lily and Catherine. Everything else was frivolous.

The window where she had last seen Lily was open, and the cold winter air crept through the little girl's bedroom. It sent a chill down Elle's back, but she wasn't sure if it was because of the cold or the fear of what the window being open could have meant.

By the window, on the corner of the ledge, was a Barbie doll, her hair half-shorn and the other colored pink with Magic Marker. If Catherine had seen such a doll, it would have been pitched in the garbage and replaced with a new doll, hair intact.

"Lily was sitting there," she said, pointing at the ledge. "She waved at me when I left, then I came to see you."

"After Catherine gave you the tip?" Grant asked.

She gave him the side-eye.

"I'm just making sure that I'm tracking all of this correctly."

"Yes, after Catherine slipped me the money. I still have it." She reached down toward her pocket, but he waved her off. "Why do I get the feeling you are struggling to trust me?"

"I don't rush into anything, especially trusting people I just met—even in law enforcement. Don't be offended. It's not a reflection on you."

Was that this guy's way of telling her he was all kinds of screwed up? He'd hardly be the first LEO she'd met with a chip on his shoulder and a need for therapy. In fact, it was so normal, that she was forced to wonder if it was a chicken-or-the-egg kind of conundrum. On the other hand, perhaps the same could be said of her.

Beside the bed she spotted the wing-tip shoes, the ones with the black around the tops, that Lily had been wearing when she'd left. They were askew, pitched exactly where the little girl must have taken them off. No other shoes were missing, making her wonder what Lily was wearing. She couldn't have been out of the house. Not in this weather, not without shoes.

Then again, that was assuming she had been taken out willingly. If that little girl was out there in the cold, whoever had her would have hell to pay. *If* someone had her.

GRANT'S HANDSET CRACKLED to life. "Officer 466, we have blood. Requesting backup." He recognized Deputy Terrill's voice.

Pressing the button on his handset, he leaned into the mic. "Ten-four, location?"

"Four sixty-six, we've located it just outside the property line to the south," Deputy Terrill said.

Grant glanced over at Elle, whose eyes were wide and filled with fear. Blood was never a positive sign, but at least they had something to help them find the missing Clarks. Yet, he couldn't help but wonder if including Elle on this one was going to be too much for the woman. "Elle, if you don't want to come with me, you don't have to. You are welcome to stick around here with one of the other officers and help them look around the house and see if you can pull more evidence."

Elle shook her head violently. "There's no way I'm not going to be involved on this. But let me get Daisy ready. She knows Lily's scent." She patted the dog's head.

He smiled. She was right. This dog was probably their best bet in tracking down the woman and child. "Go for it. I'll meet you around back." Her jaw was set, and where there had once been fear in her eyes, the look was now replaced with rage. He could understand it. "Again, Elle, if you change your mind about going along, all you have to do is let me know—we can get another handler in here. Sometimes when we're too close to a case, it can take a lot out of us."

"It's far harder on me knowing that Lily and Catherine are out there somewhere, possibly hurt, and I'm doing nothing about it. There's not a chance in hell I'm going to change my mind."

ELLE AND HER dog walked out of the bedroom, but she looked back one more time as if she hoped that she would spot the little girl hiding somewhere in a corner or behind a drape, when they both knew all too well what the likely outcome was in a case like this.

He waited a few minutes, looking for anything out of place—a hair band, blood spatter, even an empty glass. But the only thing that seemed slightly out of place was the little girl's shoes. Clearly Lily had been in a hurry when she'd removed them. Just from the way they were strewn on the floor, he could almost tell the child's personality—it was the only part of the room that really spoke of the little girl and not her mother.

Elle had made a point of telling him that the family was definitely the kind who would keep everything in line. Which made him wonder exactly how the Clarks had found themselves in this kind of predicament. Then again, sometimes when people held on too tight, it was because they were the ones who had the most to fear if they lost control. He knew a little bit about that—he always felt as if he was one hairbreadth away from disaster, both in his personal life and his professional one.

As he made his way out of Lily's bedroom, he walked past the master bedroom. From inside, he could hear a few officers talking about the senator in colorful language. As their sergeant, he should have stuck his head into the room and reminded the team that it was more than possible that one of them had their cameras rolling and everything they were saying was likely being recorded, but he didn't bother. They had already been warned they were always being monitored. At this point, if they wanted to talk smack about the senator, he wasn't going to be the one who put his ass on the line to stop them.

Then again, crap always rolled downhill, and if he didn't speak up, this could well end up with him standing at attention in the chief's office and taking a tongue-lashing for not keeping his team in line during a high-priority call.

He opened the door without announcing his presence. The three officers standing near the end of the bed glanced up at him with guilty looks, and the deputy on the left put his hand up in a slight wave. "How's it going, Sarge? You find anything?"

The deputy next to him had a slight redness to his cheeks. They all knew they had been caught.

"I'm sure I don't need to tell you how important this case could be for our department. I recommend you guys get your asses in gear and do everything in our power to find these missing females and all while not running our mouths." He pointed at the camera that he had attached to his vest.

All nodded, reminding him of three little monkeys—no see, no hear, no speak. He didn't care if they had to tap the message on the floor to one another, just so long as they fully understood that it was truly all their asses on the line here.

If they didn't get the Clarks back into their custody quick, fast and in a hurry, the media would blow this all up and they would be the ones taking the most flak. No doubt, as team leader, he would be made out to be a Barney Fife—some bumbling cop from a bygone era who didn't always know his ass from his elbow.

Yeah, he couldn't run the risk of those girls being gone for any more time than absolutely necessary.

Without so much as a backhanded wave, he rushed out of the bedroom and downstairs, nearly jogging as he made it outside.

A group of team members was standing outside the white vinyl fence, the kind that looked beautiful but was brittle and prone to shattering in the cold. The snow was deeper in the back of the house, and it crunched under his feet as he was careful to walk in areas not taped off. Perpetrators' footprints could be on the ground.

Deputy Terrill looked over at him and gave him a tip of the head in acknowledgment as he said something to the other two officers he was standing with.

Daisy popped out from around the side of the house, her nose already to the ground as she wove back and forth, working over the scene. Her black tail stood at attention as she moved toward him and Elle came into view.

He stood watching the dog move right and left, huffing as she took in the cold winter air and picked apart the medley of odors that must have been peppering it. He'd always heard a dog's sense of smell was at least a thousand times keener than a human's, which meant Daisy could probably pick up everything that had happened in the house today…all the people who had walked through its doors and even the cars they had driven in. Hell, she probably could make out the scent of the discarded fast-food wrappers and chewed gum that were in the garbage bags inside the people's cars.

Having that kind of ability to make out scents was an incredible superpower, but what made it even more incredible was that these dogs and their handlers had also managed to create a system of communication through training that enabled them to understand what the other was looking for and when it was found. He had seen the K-9 units work before. He'd even been asked to take a bite during training—and he would only do that once. He had tremendous respect for the human-animal bonds that allowed these teams to do their jobs effectively.

Elle finally looked up from Daisy as the dog slowed.

He met her gaze, and there was an intensity in her eyes that made it clear she was just as on-task as the dog. Yet, as he looked at her, he couldn't manage the same level of professionalism—all he could think about was the brunette hair that had fallen free of her messy bun and was cascading down her neck. She had a slender neck that curved delicately into the arch of her shoulder. The notch at the base of her throat was exposed, and sitting at its center was a diamond on a gold chain.

The place where her necklace rested looked soft, kissably soft. If he kissed her there, was she the kind of woman who would tip her head back and moan, or was she the type to pull in a breath and tighten in anticipation? If he had to guess, she held her breath. She didn't seem like the kind of woman who would melt easily under a man's touch.

The thought of another man touching her made the hairs on the back of his neck rise.

He turned away from them, forcing himself to work. This wasn't the time. Actually, it was never going to be a good time to think about her the way he was thinking about her and all the things he would like to do to her body.

"Sergeant Anders, over here," Terrill said, motioning toward something on the ground.

He made his way over to Terrill as Daisy worked a weaving path across the backyard. He didn't know what scent Elle had put her on, but from the way the dog moved, he couldn't help but wonder if it was some small, skittish mammal—the scent path moved like a rabbit.

Careful to keep in the trail the officers had already created in the snow, he slipped between the rails of the fence and came to a stop beside Terrill. "What's going on? You found blood?"

Terrill pointed at the ground a few feet out from where the men stood. There, the snow had been trampled down and there was a mess of small footprints. It looked as though someone had lain in the snow and rolled around, but it was hard to tell the size of the individual—even if it was an adult or a child. Yet, at the edge of the compressed snow was a splatter of blood. The holes the warm blood had created in the snow were dime sized, and if the holes hadn't been edged in the pinkish-red stain, it would have been almost impossible to see. It definitely wasn't a quantity of blood that would mean whomever it had belonged to was close to death, but that was the only good news.

Daisy whined from behind him, and he turned and watched as she slipped under the fence and moved toward them. She pulled on her lead, the muscles in her shoulders pressing out hard as she tried to force Elle to come where she wanted her. Elle stopped, holding Daisy back.

"Sidet," Elle commanded in Russian.

Daisy dropped to her haunches, sitting. There was no moment of hesitation, no pause between command and obedient action.

When he'd been a kid, they'd had a chocolate Lab. The dog, Duke, would only listen to him when and if it was beneficial to the dog. He couldn't even begin to imagine how much these two must have worked and trained to get to the perfection of that simple command.

She was definitely capable of a level of dedication that he envied. He had always thought himself good at his job, but the officers under his command weren't nearly as well trained.

Maybe he needed to start giving them treats and praise.

He smirked, but it disappeared as he noticed the terror in Elle's eyes as she looked at the droplets of blood in the snow.

"Can you tell us whose blood that is?" he asked, afraid that he knew the answer before he had even asked the question.

She chewed on her bottom lip for a quick second. "I had Daisy on Lily's scent, but that doesn't necessarily mean that blood belongs to her. If there was someone out here with her, it could be theirs," she said, but he could hear the feeble hope in her tone.

Elle stepped around the bloodstain and moved toward the timber. He followed a few feet behind her, letting her and the dog do their work. There were two sets of tracks in the snow, what looked like a man's and a woman's. Their footfalls were wide apart, as if they had been running.

She stopped after about twenty yards and turned to him. "Look."

The footsteps in the snow appeared to grow closer, like the man and woman had slowed down and then come to a full stop. Where they had stopped was another set of small footprints—complete with toe marks. At the center of one of the child's footprints was a pink smudge, as though she had blood on her barefooted step.

Lily was in far more danger than either of them had assumed.

Chapter Five

The wind had kicked up as the sun was touching the tips of the mountains to the west; snow was fluttering down, and with each passing minute it seemed to be coming down faster in plump, wet flakes. If they didn't work quickly, soon the easy trail would be obscured and they would have to rely solely on Daisy's nose.

She tried to quell her disgust as she looked at the marks in the snow where Lily had been dragging her bare feet.

Who in their right mind would have brought a three-year-old out into the cold and then made her walk bare-footed in the snow?

When she found the kidnapper, she would personally make sure they hiked twice as far without their god-damned shoes—and that was *if* Lily was okay. If she was hurt, or if her little feet were frostbitten, there would be more than hell to pay.

Is there something worse than hell? She paused at the thought but followed Daisy as the dog moved ahead.

All she knew was that anyone who hurt Lily would suffer pain at her hands that would be real and unbear-able. It was more than possible that she would be the one who ended up in jail, but if she got justice for Lily, it would be worth it.

Her jaw ached as she jogged with Daisy, and she realized that she had been gritting her teeth, though for how long, she didn't know.

There was another long drag mark in the snow where it appeared as though Lily had literally stopped walking and had been pulled ahead.

That a girl. At least her friend was putting up a fight.

Since she had been taking care of Lily, she had been spending time having the kiddo do simple exercises—jumping jacks and push-ups, squats and lunges. At the time, Elle had been using the exercise as something to do to keep Lily busy, but now she was glad she had helped the girl gain strength. Though, never in her wildest dreams had she thought the child would need the stamina and strength they had been working to build for surviving the elements.

Thankfully, she hadn't spotted any more blood in the snow. If it was Lily who had been bleeding, she was going to survive…probably.

If only she had some kind of idea why they were out here, what had made them disappear into the woods. Was the man with them keeping guard, or had he taken them? Were they running or being forced to run?

Her mind went wild with a million different theories, playing them out from start to finish. Though it was good for her to be prepared and to try to make sense of what had happened, she wasn't a detective; she was merely a private security contractor, and she couldn't rush to any conclusions. If she assumed anything, it could adversely affect their tracking and Grant's team's investigation.

Well, *her* opinions and assumptions wouldn't affect them, or at least she didn't think they would; they seemed like a team that had their roles and expectations dialed in.

She could make out the sounds of his footfalls crunching in the snow beside her, and she glanced over at him. The red light on Grant's body camera was on, indicating he was recording everything they were doing. *Good.*

If they missed anything, or if something unexpected happened, he would have a record of it. Maybe they could find things after the fact when they were back in their warm offices and reviewing the recordings. Though, if she had her way, there would be no need. She wouldn't be stopping her search until Lily was safely back in her care and out of harm's way.

The mountain grew steeper and, as the sun slipped behind the peaks and cast them in the cold, wintery shade of impending night, the trail they had been following became harder and harder to see. As she wove around a bend in what must have been a game trail under the snow, the footsteps they'd been following disappeared. For a moment, she stopped and waited for Grant to catch up. He was saying something into his handset, and as he stopped beside her, he struggled to catch his breath.

She would have assumed a sergeant would be in better shape—he must have spent his entire adult life getting to the position he was in within the department. Yet he probably was more of a paper pusher than a boots-on-the-ground kind of guy. It was one of the benefits from moving up in any organization—manual labor grew lighter while mental fortitude became more pivotal.

"You okay?" he asked, letting out a long breath as though he was forcing his body to fall back in line with his hard-edged spirit.

She nodded. "The trail just disappeared."

He looked down at the ground, seeming to notice it for the first time in at least a mile. "You're right." He glanced up at the sky, and a fat snowflake landed on his cheek. As he looked back toward her, she watched as the flake disappeared into nothing more than a droplet of water, which he wiped away with the back of his hand.

Even in the gray, she could see his cheeks were cherry red from the cold and exertion. She considered slowing down for him, allowing him time to recover, but there was no time for rest. Not when it came to Lily. They had to go.

"Hasn't Daisy been leading us, not you?" he asked.

She shook her head. "Yeah, but no. We've mostly been just following the tracks. The problem with snow and cold is that in this kind of weather, especially with the wind, the scents she uses to track can disappear pretty rapidly. The wind alone can really make the odors drift off course. That being said, I'll put her on this, but if they got off this trail, it could really slow down our progress."

He gave a dip of the head, and though she thought he would have been secretly relieved to slow down, he looked as frustrated as she felt. "We won't stop, Elle, I promise. I will do everything and put every resource I can behind finding Lily." His handset crackled, and she could make out a woman's voice but couldn't hear what she was saying. A thin smile moved over his lips and he looked up at her. "Search and rescue is on the ground. They just arrived at the house."

She glanced down at her watch. They had been on the trail now for a little under an hour. At the pace they had been moving, that made them just less than three miles from where Lily had last been seen.

"They are putting together their plan, but for now it sounds like they are going to bring up their four-wheelers, then send hikers out to catch up with us, maybe even get Two Bear helicopter to fly them in, but they are still working on that. I let them know we are still running tracks, but that the tracks may have given out."

A thin wave of relief washed over her. At the very least, they wouldn't be the only two on the mountain searching.

She gave Daisy her command, and the dog got on scent. Daisy pulled at the leather lead, glad to finally be back in control of the situation. The rocks under the slick pack of snow made travel slippery as they moved higher and deeper into the timber. The snow went from a few inches deep to now nearly touching her ankles over her hiking boots.

Hopefully when the trio had made it to this point in the trail, Lily was no longer being forced to hike without her shoes. She could imagine Lily now; she'd never been one for long walks, and especially not any that involved her being scared and uncomfortable. Lily had to have been crying the moment she had left the house, and by this point she was probably exhausted and in an overwhelmed flurry of hiccups and sobs.

Elle's chest ached as she thought of Lily and how scared she must have been.

Lily, baby girl, it's going to be okay. She sent up a silent prayer to the universe. Hopefully Lily knew that she was going to come out here looking for her, that she would never let her get hurt… And yet, hadn't she done just that?

She tried to swallow back the guilt that welled in her throat. Guilt would do nothing to make things better; all it would do was obscure her focus on the goal of getting Lily back and into safety.

Daisy pulled harder as they moved up a switchback.

The world was almost pitch-black, and between the falling snow and the enveloping timber, she couldn't even make out light from the stars. Luckily, the city lights from below were reflecting off the clouds and giving her just enough illumination to find her next step.

Lily would have hated this. She hated the dark. On the rare occasions she had been there to put Lily to bed, Lily had always asked for a night-light and for Elle to promise to stand in her room until she had fallen asleep. The first night had taken two hours, three bedtime stories and nearly one million glasses of water and trips to the restroom.

She smiled at the memory and how it brought with it the faint scent of baby powder and new dolls.

Lily would be okay. She had to be okay. *I'm coming for you, baby.*

She sped up.

Maybe the trio had stopped for the night. If they were out here on their own volition, they would have likely called it a night and put down a place for a camp—along with a fire to keep them warm. If they were kidnapped, if the perpetrator wanted to keep them alive and relatively unscathed, he would have needed to let them rest soon.

Which meant all they had to do to catch up with the trio was keep pushing forward.

The wind pressed against her cheeks, blowing down hard from the top of the mountain. Elle pulled in a long breath, hoping to catch the tarry scent of burning pine and a campfire, but she couldn't smell anything but the biting scent of ice.

Without a fire it was unlikely that anyone could survive a night out here, not at the mercy of the elements. Without shoes and drained from miles of hiking, Lily would be especially at risk. She didn't have the body mass or the gear to be out here like she was for any extended period of time, let alone the night hours when the temperature was expected to drop at least another twenty degrees.

Daisy paused.

"What is it, Daisy? *Poshli.*" She took a step, urging the dog forward.

Instead, Daisy sat down and looked up the mountain, signaling.

"What did you find, girl?" She walked to Daisy and searched the ground; she couldn't see anything, and she was forced to flip on the light on her cell phone to illuminate the ground. There, barely poking up from the snow, was a purple mitten.

Lily's mitten.

The lump returned to her throat. Not only did Lily not have shoes, but now she was missing a glove.

Why hadn't they stopped to pick up her glove?

They must have been moving fast. Catherine wasn't the best mother Elle had ever seen, but she was hardly the worst. She had seen terrorists use children in ways that she would have never thought of or expected, but Catherine wasn't the type who would just let her daughter freeze. Catherine loved her.

Elle had to assume she would fight for her daughter. Perhaps that was where the blood they had found had come from. Perhaps it was Catherine's. If she had been in the mother's shoes, she would have fought tooth and nail until they were safe.

Then again, from the trail they had followed so far, there hadn't been any more areas where it looked as though there had been an altercation—at least not when they could make out the tracks in the snow. Did that mean that Catherine had just gone along with the man? Had she allowed herself to be pliable? Or had the man been threatening them? Or was Catherine out here for some purpose that they didn't yet understand?

Grant stopped beside her, taking pictures with his cell phone and noting the mitten for the camera.

The wind washed through the timber, making the branches rub against each other and creating an eerie melody from nature's cello. The sound made chills run down her spine.

It's nothing. I can't be afraid. There's no time for fear. Not for myself.

Clearly, she had watched too many horror flicks, but she couldn't let them seep into this search.

Grant slipped on a pair of nitrile gloves and took out a plastic bag from his pocket. Ever so meticulously, he leaned down and picked up the mitten and glided it into the bag, careful to keep it as pristine as he could, no doubt in an effort to protect any evidence they acquired should they need to take this to court or be judged for their actions later.

They both stared at the glove for a long moment. There was a faint red stain on the seam near the fingertips of the mitten, almost as if Lily had touched a wound with the edge of her glove.

"Does it seem odd to you that they would have remembered to bring her gloves but not boots?" Grant asked.

"If I know anything from my experience with kids, it's that they can never find their shoes when you're in a hurry." There was a wisp of a smile at the corners of her lips, but it was overtaken by the gravity of the moment.

She pointed the light of her phone up the mountain. It was hard to tell how far they were from the peak, or how much farther they would go from here. How far could Lily have gone if she was bloodied and cold?

Not much farther.

"I bet that blood isn't from her. It's probably Catherine's," she said, her voice sounding hollow and dampened by the snowy world around them.

Grant frowned, shrugging. He turned on the light of his phone and illuminated the bagged glove as if doing so would give him the answers they were seeking. "It's possible. But hell, anything is." He clamped his mouth shut like he was refusing to say another damned word on the subject, always the cop. There was nothing they were better at than being unflappable.

She both loved and hated that calm in the face of chaos. Why couldn't he just say what he thought, what he feared? Then again, she had enough fears and imagined outcomes; if he laid his upon her, she wasn't sure she was strong enough to bear the weight.

Why couldn't she be stronger?

Hopefully Lily was proving to be far more formidable. Lily's smiling face floated to the front of her mind, making tears well in her eyes.

The wind rustled through the pines, hard and faster, and there was the drop of snow from branches, the sound reminiscent of footfalls. Just like the answers, even the forest was attempting to run away from them.

There was a thud and a crack of a branch, and she shined her light in the direction of the sound. She wasn't entirely sure whether or not it was more snow falling or something else, maybe an animal. This time of year, bears were in hibernation, but it could've been something large like an elk or even possibly a mountain lion.

Wouldn't that be crazy, them coming up the mountain looking for the missing Clarks and their possible kidnapper and then she and Grant falling victim to another kind of predator? The darkness in her heart made her laugh at the sick humor.

She looked at Daisy, but the dog was sniffing the ground around where they'd found the mitten and seemed oblivious to the noise coming from the woods. Daisy was good, but just like her, the dog had a habit of being almost myopic when it came to the task at hand.

She moved the beam of her light right to left, and as she was about to look away, she made out the unmistakable glow of two eyes from her peripheral vision. Instinctively, she stepped closer to Daisy and in front of Grant as though she was his shield. She moved the light in the direction of the eyes, but as she did, they disappeared into the thick stand of timber. Though she searched the area where she thought the animal had gone, she didn't see it again.

Daisy wasn't the only animal who seemed to be drawn to Lily—or rather, the scent of blood.

If the scavengers were starting to descend, she and Grant were likely walking into something far more sinister than simply two missing people.

Her stomach roiled at the thought.

She looked to the place where they had found the glove and then up at Grant. She thought about telling him of the eyes in the darkness, but she held back. There were plenty of things to be frightened of, but eyes staring out of the darkness seemed like the most innocuous of the dangers they faced. Whatever animal had been staring at them had been skittish. It was likely more curious than anything else.

Like people, there were different kinds of predators—those who preyed upon weakness and were opportunistic killers, almost scavengers in their selection of their weak quarry, and then there were those predators who sought more challenging prey in order to test their killing abilities. The animal in the woods was likely more the scavenger type and less the stalker... Or perhaps it was situationally dependent. Perhaps the predator in the woods was seeking an easy meal because of the spent blood and wouldn't waste its energy stalking them.

"You okay?" Grant asked. He put his hand on the side of her waist, and the action was so unexpected that she allowed his hand to remain.

She didn't like to be touched.

"Yeah, just thought I saw something, but it was nothing." It was strange how she wanted to protect this man. Instead of stepping away, she wanted to reach out, to shield him.

Or maybe it wasn't about the man at all. Maybe she was just acting this way in an effort to protect herself from feeling more fear. But now wasn't the time for some deep introspection; no, this was the time for Lily.

He motioned up the hill. "Do you see that up there?"

She had no idea what he was talking about. "What?"

He pointed his finger more vehemently as if his simple action would clarify the entire situation for her. "Up there, see that line in the snow? There, under the tree." He shined the beam of his flashlight near the base of a large fir tree.

She finally spotted what appeared to be a drag mark

in the snow. Though they were at least a dozen yards from the spot, it appeared to be the approximate width of a body.

Carefully, they picked their way straight up the hillside, moving through deadfall. There was the snap of sticks and the crunch of the snow as they slowly struggled upward. It was steep, and as they neared the tree, Grant grunted. She glanced in his direction in time to watch him slip, then catch and right himself.

If that mark in the snow was a drag mark, how could anyone move a body through this? They could barely walk through it on their own even without a three-year-old.

When she was growing up, her father had taught her to hunt. When he wasn't jetting around the world and taking down bad guys for the US government, he had taken her and her siblings out into the woods. They had spent time every fall and early winter in the woods, tracking and learning the patterns of animals. Her father had always told her it was so they could be more in touch with nature, but as she grew older, she realized it was just as much about human nature as it was about flora and fauna.

One of the things that her father had drilled into her was that when animals and humans were injured, they would look for areas of cover. Most animals would run downhill toward water sources—creek beds and rivers. If water wasn't close by or if they were significantly injured, they would seek shelter from trees.

As she stopped to catch her breath, she realized that what they were looking at wasn't likely to be a drag mark from someone being pulled up the hill, but it was more likely whoever had been hiding had slid down. They were, simply put, injured prey hiding from the predator. Little had they known, but predators and scavengers were everywhere around them.

Daisy whined, pulling hard at the lead and nosing in the direction of the tree.

"I know, Daisy." She tried to control her heavy breathing; until now she hadn't realized how much the hike had taken out of her. "Hello?" she called, hoping that if there was someone at the base of the tree, someone they couldn't yet see, that they would call out an answer... anything, even a grunt that could act as a sign of life.

Grant was a few steps ahead of her and stopped as she called out, but there was nothing, only the cascading sounds of the winter wind. Somehow, the world around them felt colder.

Ascending the last few yards, in the thin light she could make out the edge of a bench beneath the tree, a flattened area that sometimes naturally occurred under large, aged trees thanks to years of deadfall accumulation, which then became alcoves.

She silently prayed she was wrong, that her years of wilderness training were making her jump to the wrong conclusions. For all she knew, the animal they had run into below had made a kill and was actually watching them to make sure they didn't find its quarry.

Goose bumps rose on her skin.

It was strange how a person's sixth sense could pique and the mind could usher it away with a million different reasons to not pay it heed. Yet, when it came down to the critical moment, it was usually the sixth sense that would be proven right.

Daisy leaped up and over the edge of the bench and

immediately sat down, indicating something. Grant stood beside her, holding out his hand and helping Elle up the last step so she could be beside the dog.

The bench under the tree was larger than she had thought it would have been—it was approximately as wide as the widest point of the tree's canopy, and as she stepped up, the dead limbs of the tree tore at her hair and scraped against her cheeks, forcing her to push the limbs away. It was really no wonder animals would have chosen this alcove to tuck in and away from the world.

Grant grunted as he stepped up. She held back the branches so he could move beside her without being ripped to shreds by the gnarled fingers of the protective sentry. The dry twig in her hand snapped, the sound making her jump.

"You're okay," Grant whispered, as though he was just as at odds with the fear in his gut as she was. His hand found its way to her waist again, and this time instead of merely allowing his touch, she moved into it ever so slightly.

"I'm fine," she lied.

He moved the beam of his flashlight in the direction of the base of the tree, but there were so many branches that he was forced to crouch down. As he moved, he sucked in a breath.

She dropped to her knees in the snow and dirt beside him. There, slumped against the gray bark, was a woman. Her hands were palm up in her lap. She listed to the right, and her face and shoulder were pressed into the brackish moss and bark. Her face was down, but thanks to the bottled, platinum-blond color of her hair, Elle knew she was staring at Catherine.

She glanced at Catherine's fingers. The tips were purple, but her skin was the gray-white that only came with death.

Chapter Six

The Two Bear helo touched down at the top of the mountain just short of midnight on one of the longest days of Grant's life. He had thought he had been in good shape, but apparently a six-plus-mile hike straight up the face of a mountain wasn't something his body was adequately prepared for. He waited as the coroner stepped out of the helicopter, followed by a few more members of the search and rescue team.

The members of the team who had come up from the bottom of the mountain had finally caught up with them, and those volunteers were now in a holding pattern, sitting and resting while they waited for the helo team.

The commander, Melody, stepped out and made her way toward him, holding her head and crouching down to protect herself from the rotor's wash. "Any new information?" she called over the noise of the blades.

He shook his head and motioned for her to follow him toward the rest of their waiting team. The helicopter took off, dipping its nose as it turned and descended back down toward the valley and the city at its heart.

Part of him wished he was on the bird, having completed the task and having found Lily and the man who was still at large. Unfortunately, he had fallen short.

The coroner followed in Melody's wake, looking down at his phone like he was deep into reading something on the screen. As they stopped, the coroner bumped into her. "Whoa, sorry," he said, finally looking up. "How long has it been since you found the deceased?"

Well, at least he wasn't one for screwing around.

"It's been about two hours."

"And you said she was limp when you found her? No signs of rigor mortis setting in?" The coroner made a note on his phone.

"We only touched her to try and get a pulse, but her neck was soft to the touch."

The coroner nodded. He was all about getting straight to the point. If only Grant had more people in his life who ran on that kind of a timeline. Elle was just starting a campfire as he glanced over at her. As if feeling his gaze, she looked at him. Their eyes connected for a moment, and he could see that hers were red and tired.

She needed to get off this mountain, or at the very least take a rest and then start fresh in the morning. Yet he was sure that no matter what he said to her, or how hard he tried to convince her, there was nothing he could do to pull her away from this. She wasn't going to stop until Lily was safe.

Unfortunately, their trail had run dry. No matter how much Daisy had sniffed and searched, it seemed as if where Catherine's body had been found was also the last place there had been any active scent. They had spent at least an hour while they had waited for the teams, looking for any leads. Nothing. It was almost as if Lily and the presumed man had disappeared the moment Catherine died.

As the flames took hold and enveloped the logs in

the fire, Elle made her way over to them. Melody and the SAR team who had just arrived sat down next to the four already around the fire, and they all started talking, something about maps and directions. A few were checking their radios and getting ready for the dog and pony show.

The coroner looked up from his notes. "From the temperature out here currently and from what information you have given me, I think it is fair to assume that our victim has been dead for no more than four to six hours based on the primary indicators. The cold has kept her from going into full rigor mortis, but I would expect, given her glycogen output hiking up the hill, if my math is correct, the victim will probably start having the onset of rigor mortis within the next hour. But first I must see the vic."

He wasn't sure what to make of the information. Did that mean that the coroner wanted to get her off the mountain before she was completely immobilized?

"Can you take me to her?" the coroner asked, holding on to the strap of the satchel that was crossed over his chest.

Elle looked at him, asking for an invitation though she said nothing aloud. "Yeah," Grant said, "Elle, why don't you join us?"

She gave him a tip of the head in thanks, but the coroner gave her a quick side-eye before sighing and shrugging her presence off.

"Let's go," the coroner said, pointing vaguely downhill. "It is colder than the backside of the moon up here, and I have a hot cup of coffee with my name on it sitting in my living room."

Was that the sand in this man's craw? That he was having to come out to the woods in the cold in the middle of the night in order to retrieve a body?

He had met the deputy coroner a few times—he worked in the same office, but the deputy coroner was on the other side and they rarely shared more than a few words socially. Now, he wasn't too upset that his time had been limited with the officer. They were definitely cut from different cloth. When he'd been acting as coroner a few years ago, he was always jonesing to go on a call—not that he wished anyone an ill fate—he just found the work fascinating. It was a small thing, helping the dead find rest. Yet it brought solace to the victims' families, and someone had to do it.

If Grant hadn't become a cop, he wouldn't have minded going to work as a medical examiner. He always loved working through a good mystery, and nothing was more confusing than people—though the living were far more confusing than the dead.

Elle led the way down the hill, taking the broken trail until they were standing just above the ledge and the tree where Catherine could be found.

The coroner looked over his shoulder at him, like he found it a nuisance that he was going to have to crawl down over the ledge and onto the bench to get to the deceased woman. Yep, this coroner would need some more hours on this job. It was a great learning opportunity, but it seemed as though the kid was not quite realizing that just yet. Until he did, Grant would make sure to make a few calls when he got back to the office.

Grant and Elle climbed down onto the bench, carefully working around the limbs of the tree until they once again found themselves face-to-face—well, rather face to *head*—with Catherine. The coroner took a series of photographs, making sure that they were holding up lights to help illuminate the scene.

The coroner clicked his tongue a few times before reaching into his satchel and taking out a pair of nitrile gloves. He set to work taking more pictures and then going over the body. He took measurements of the scene, documenting everything in his phone before finally touching Catherine's head. He moved her chin up and peered under her neck. There, beneath the base of her chin, was a large abrasion. "Hmm."

He took another picture and made a note.

The coroner's movements were slow, methodical as he started at the top of the woman's body and worked his way down. He unzipped her jacket. Her white silk blouse was stained deep crimson red, some areas so dark that it was almost black with blood. At the center of the blackness were slits in the cloth and the flesh beneath.

Grant sucked in a breath.

"Yep," the coroner said, sounding unsurprised, "looks like we have found the most likely cause of death. Looks like we have at least ten or fifteen puncture wounds here, but the medical examiner will have to open her up for the official count—and the weapon used, but from what I can see… I'd guess it was a large fixed-blade knife. There are some wide, deep punctures here." He moved back a bit of the woman's stained shirt to expose what looked like a two-inch-long stab wound.

As he moved the shirt slightly, Elle let out a thin wheezing sound, making Grant turn.

Tears were streaming down her face, and Daisy was licking her hand. He hadn't been thinking. If he had been, he would have never put her in the position to watch her former employer being poked and prodded.

He wrapped his arm around her shoulder and led her away. Whatever the coroner found, he could tell them later. For now, Grant needed get her the hell out of there.

Elle's body was rigid under his arm, but she didn't resist as he led her away. Daisy followed in their footsteps, watching warily as her mistress slowly picked her way back up the hill. It took twenty minutes to climb to the top of the mountain, where the SAR team had moved out, leaving the campfire gently flickering in the darkness. To the north, he could make out the thin lights of their flashlights as they started to make their way over to the other side of the mountain saddle.

As he stood with Elle in the thin firelight, watching the beams of flashlights bounce around and move between the smattering of trees at the top of the mountain, he couldn't help but feel the futility in their situation. If their kidnapper was capable of such a brutal murder, one with possibly dozens of stab wounds, they had to be angry. And when a killer was so filled with rage, there was no telling what they might do—and not even a child would be considered out of bounds when it came to murder.

Chapter Seven

Elle didn't know when she fell asleep—she sure as hell hadn't meant to, not with everything happening. Yet, at some point when she had been sitting beside the fire wrapped in Grant's warm embrace with Daisy on her feet, she must have succumbed to her exhaustion. As she woke, she looked out at the fire. During the night, someone must have kept it fed, as it was in full roar, a trio of large blackened logs at its heart.

She was lying on a bed of pine boughs, and there was a thin Mylar blanket over her. It surprised her that she had been sleeping so hard that someone could have moved her in such a way, but at the same time, exhaustion had that effect on her. Honestly, she couldn't recall a time she had been more physically or emotionally drained.

She had been in some real pits of hell before—her thoughts drifted back to the empty pair of shoes at the bomb site—but even then, she had struggled to find sleep. During that time in her life, she had turned to sleeping pills and vodka. Her body never allowed her to sleep like she had last night.

There was the crunch of footsteps in the snow behind her, and she considered pretending she was still asleep.

Yet, no matter how much she wanted to hide from the reality that she was confronted with, Lily depended on her.

She turned. Grant was standing with his back to her, looking out at the sun as it peeked over the top of the mountains to the east. Daisy was seated on the ground beside him, and he was scratching behind her ears. Of course, Daisy would be amenable to a good-looking man who wanted to give her attention. And yet, Elle couldn't help but be a little bit jealous that the dog had given herself so freely over to the man.

"Where is everyone?" she asked, sitting up.

"After you fell asleep, I helped the coroner bag Catherine's remains. Two Bear dropped the line from the helo, and we got her on board." He took out his phone and peered down at the screen. "Catherine's remains were transported to the medical examiner's office, where they are already performing an autopsy. They found hair samples on her body, and they have started performing DNA analysis in hope we can find the identity of the murderer."

She nodded, wishing she was slightly more awake so she could make sense of everything that Grant was trying to tell her without the fuzziness of having just woken. "I'm sorry I fell asleep. You should've woken me. I could've been out there helping you guys." She was suddenly embarrassed that he had witnessed her inability to keep pace with what the situation required. "Where's the SAR team? Have they found anything, any idea as to Lily's location? Has there been a ransom call?"

He looked down at his hands as he scratched Daisy's head slightly more vigorously. "No calls. Yet. They have started working their way down the mountain. This morning, actually about an hour ago, on the other side of the mountain saddle, they found evidence that a helicopter had been on-site."

"Another helicopter, as in one besides Two Bear?" She was confused.

"When Two Bear airlifted the SAR team out, we talked to them, and they said they hadn't been in that specific area—we are thinking someone picked up Lily and her kidnapper before you and I made it to Catherine."

"How do they know it was Lily?" She heard the frantic note in her voice.

"They found a child's tracks near the pickup site. They were covered by last night's snowfall. Lily is gone, airlifted out. If nothing else, at least we know she is still alive and didn't have to spend the night on the mountain."

Thank goodness. "Is there any way we can track her helicopter? There has to be some kind of flight record, right?"

"I have my teams working on that, but whoever this kidnapper is, they have resources that up until now we weren't aware of."

She put her hands over her face and rubbed at her temples. "We were so close. We had a chance to save her…"

He put his hands up in surrender. "It's okay, we will find her. She's relatively unharmed. She's going to be okay."

"You can't tell me any of that." She stood up, the motion so fast that her head swam. She reached out, but there was nothing to support her and Grant rushed to her side. "I don't believe you." She tried to pull away from his touch, but her body was unsteady and he gripped her harder to keep her from falling.

"You need to sit down for a minute. You're probably really dehydrated after yesterday. Did you even drink any water?" He reached behind him and grabbed a water bottle that had been clipped to his utility belt. He opened up the lid with a squeak and handed it over.

Though she was upset, she allowed him to help her to sit and took the water. She hadn't realized how thirsty she was until the ice-cold liquid hit her parched lips. She closed the bottle and handed it back to him with a nod. Logically she knew she wasn't angry with the man who was trying his very best to help her, yet all she wanted to do was snarl and bite at him. Why did he have to be so perfect, having everything she needed before she even knew she needed it—all while looking sexy?

She took another swig of water and reached up to touch her hair, forgetting she was wearing a knit cap. Her hair poked out from under the edge of the hat above her ears, and she could instantly envision what a mess she must have looked like. Running her fingers over her cheek, she could feel the indentations made by the pine boughs; there was even a small pine needle stuck to the side of her cheek, and she had to scratch to free it from her skin.

Though, what did it really matter what she looked like right now?

The fact she cared about that at all concerned her more than her actual appearance. She wasn't one to get too wrapped up in vanity, but when she was, under these circumstances, it made her wonder what she wasn't admitting to herself when it came to her feelings toward Grant. His hand was on her shoulder, and she found herself enjoying the warmth of his touch.

He barely knew her, and he had gone out of his way last night to make sure that she was comfortable and warm. Taking care of her in her moment of greatest weakness. Did that mean that he also felt something, or did it just fall under the scope of him being the nearly picture-perfect hero he seemed to be?

No. She almost shook her head. *If he is perfect, we would have Lily back in our custody. She would have never had the time to get away.*

As quickly as the angry thoughts came to her, she batted them away. It wasn't Grant's fault she had allowed the little girl to fall into the wrong hands. This was all her fault...everything could be pinned down to her and her error in judgments.

"What's the matter? Are you okay? Do you need anything?" Grant asked, sitting down on the ground beside her.

Daisy trotted over and gave her a quick lick to the face as if she, too, could tell that Elle was struggling. She wrapped her arm around the dog's neck, and Daisy perched against her, nuzzling her snout under Elle's chin and snuggling in as she hugged her. "I love you, angel," she whispered into the dog's fur.

There was nothing like a dog's touch to calm the most turbulent storms in the soul. Hopefully Lily had an animal with her, something that she could touch that would help her stay calm—that was, if she was still alive.

A sob threatened to escape from her throat, but she tried to bite it back. She was too slow, and the sound rattled from her, far too loud.

Grant's hand moved to her knee, and he put his other arm around her, surrounding her with his stupidly perfect body. Didn't he realize that he was making this all so much worse by being kind? If he would just stop helping her, she could control some of the weakness and stonewall it with her normal aplomb and resolve. What was it about this man that made her break down and actually *feel*?

His thumb gently stroked her inner thigh, and she felt what little control she still had drift from her. Didn't he realize what he was doing to her? He was going to make her totally melt down. There would be tears. No woman in the world wanted to wake up and just go straight to fear and crying over the things that were outside her control.

There was only one way she was going to get out of this moment by not breaking down and just crying in front of him again. She had to do it if she wanted to save what little pride she had left.

Before she had a chance to reconsider her impulsive thought, she leaned over and pushed her lips to his. He hadn't been ready, but neither was she, and his lips were pulled into a thin smile, making it so she kissed the cool slickness of his teeth.

What was I thinking? Gah, I can be so stupid sometimes.

Embarrassment filled her and she started to move, but before she could pull away, he took her face in his hands and closed his mouth and kissed her back. The tip of his tongue darted out, and he moved it gently against her bottom lip; she followed, tasting the lingering sweetness of his gum and the bite of the cold mountain air. He caressed her cheeks with his thumbs, and his lips slowed, moving her starved, hurried action into a sultry, deep kiss. It was like he could read her mind, follow her thoughts… thoughts and desires she didn't even know she had…and yet that he could satisfy.

If she hadn't gone through so many emotions, she would have called this her very best first kiss. What if this was her last first kiss?

What if she had screwed up her best first kiss by stealing it in the wrong moment but with the right man?

Worse, what if she had just had her first and last kiss with Grant? What if he was once again just trying to save her feelings by doing what he thought she wanted him to do and once they got back down into the valley and back to their lives, he would let her down gracefully? What if none of this was real? Or what if he was only kissing her because she was kissing him—was it just some kiss of opportunity?

As his tongue flicked against hers, she tried to force herself back in the moment, to stop thinking about all the things that were flipping through her mind. Daisy plopped down on her foot and let out a long sigh. The sound made her smile, and as she did, Grant let his hands move from her face and he sat back.

"Was my kiss that bad?"

"What?" she asked, finally opening her eyes and looking at him. "No...that's not it." He had the best eyes—they were green around the outsides and brown in the middle, and in the thin morning light they even picked up bits of gray and purple from the sky.

His eyes, just like the man to which they belonged, were perfect. They were everything, every color...he was the embodiment of all the things she wanted to see and feel, and damn it if he didn't make every part of her body spark with want. But she couldn't have him.

She stood up, carefully away from Daisy, and Grant moved to reach for her, but she noted how he stopped himself. Maybe he realized they were wrong, too. Maybe he had seen her kiss for what she had intended it to be—a stopgap in the moment, anything to make her stop feeling. And then...well, and then it screwed everything up.

She turned her back to him, afraid if she looked into that perfect face and those perfect eyes she would sink back down to the ground and beg for him to take her into his arms. Closing her eyes, she reached up and touched the place on her lip where his tongue had brushed against her. It was still wet from their kiss, and she gently licked the residue.

She tasted like him, and she wished she could keep that flavor on her lips forever—it could be the one part of him that she could keep. The rest of him, she had to let go. Not only was she far too big of a dumpster fire to think having a relationship was a good idea, but she needed to get Lily back and make sure that she would still have a job with STEALTH after this major screwup.

"Elle, you don't need to run away from me."

Oh yes, she did. But unless she and Daisy were about to jog down a damned mountain by themselves, there weren't a whole lot of places she could run to.

"I'm not running away." *Not a lie.* "I just…" *Can't get caught up in falling for someone right now, or ever.* "I don't want to…"

"It's okay," he said, sounding dejected. "You don't need to tell me that you think it was a mistake to kiss me. You're hardly the first woman to kiss and run."

Now that sounded like a story from his past that she wanted to hear, but if she stopped and asked him about it, he might get the wrong idea.

"What is wrong with women?" he countered.

Every hair on the back of her neck stood up. "What in the hell is that supposed to mean?"

His face fell, and he gave her an apologetic stare; he looked like Lily did when she knew she had said something she wasn't supposed to and had been overheard.

Unlike Lily, she couldn't send Grant to the corner for a timeout and a moment to reflect on his mistake.

"I... I don't mean you... I just meant..."

"You most certainly did mean me," she seethed. "Have you men ever stopped to think that maybe it isn't the women who *have something wrong* with them? Have you ever considered that maybe it's men and their failure to actually talk to women? Maybe if you could actually take a moment and express yourself carefully and with accurate language, maybe we could work together?"

"Whoa," he said, sitting back like she had just thrown mud at him. "I... I'm sorry."

She turned to the fire and kicked a pile of snow atop the flames; the logs sizzled as the ice hit them and instantly evaporated into the dry air. She kicked again and again as Grant tried to talk to her, but she blocked him out with the manic kicking and her heaving breaths as she fought the fire, choking it out.

As she worked herself down off the edge of anger, she realized her mistake. Grant hadn't meant to be misogynistic, not the now not-quite-as-perfect specimen of man. He had definitely misspoken, but he wasn't guilty of the things that she had called him out for being.

Just like his statement about kissing and running, it was easy to tell that her own baggage had come back to be hauled out and strewn into the open.

"Elle," he whispered her name, begging, "please listen to me."

Exhausted by her fury, she took a deep breath and released it into the steam rising from the fire. Finally, she turned but said nothing as she looked at him. She didn't know what she wanted him to say to her, or what she should say to him. If anything, she should have apologized for her outburst. She was embarrassed by her over-reaction, but at the same time, she had found something cathartic in the meltdown. Maybe Lily and her toddler tantrums had worn off on her, but if they had, there was something to be said for their efficacy in bringing her back to an internal stasis.

She dropped her hands to her sides, releasing the tension from her shoulders as she finally met his pleading gaze. "I'm listening," she said plaintively.

He reached up and took her hands in his, squeezing them. "I think you are so beautiful. I kissed you because I wanted to kiss you. And damn it, if you'd let me, I'd kiss you again—"

"But," she said, interrupting. It was only what he said after the *but* that would really matter. Those words would be the ones he truly meant, the ones that weren't said to assuage the pain but instead would do the tearing.

"*But* you aren't in a good place right now."

She opened her mouth to speak, or perhaps it was from the shock of his words. Did he mean that she was too big of a mess to give love to? Or did he mean that he thought she would never be in a place where they could be together?

Well, if he felt even remotely close to either of those things, she didn't need him. Her anger threatened to boil back up thanks to the salt he had thrown.

She closed her mouth. Maybe he wasn't wrong; she had already admitted to herself that she was a dumpster fire right now. But how dare he actually call her out for it?

Could she really be upset with him for saying what she had clearly been unable to hide?

No. She couldn't be. It wasn't his fault for the way she was feeling. It was only hers.

All she could really do was try to find the stasis she had thought she had brought into her life only moments before. It sucked, feeling this unbalanced. If only there was some simple fix—if only his kiss could have been that for her.

Though it had led to nothing more than a few extra hurt feelings, at least she had tried. For a moment, he had given her an escape from her thoughts, but it was her responsibility to set things right.

She squeezed his hands as she closed her eyes, taking in the smell of the campfire and the world around them.

He was a sweet man. He was trying to do the right thing. No matter how badly she wanted to push him away and tell him he was wrong in his assessment of her, she couldn't deny the nearly perfect man hadn't missed the mark.

He stood up and let go of her hands so he could wrap his arms around her. He pulled her into his embrace and held her there. She went rigid for a moment, at odds with all the feelings and thoughts inside her, but as his breath caressed her cheek and warmed her, she fell into the rhythm of him. She wished he wasn't wearing a heavy coat so she could hear his heart. It was strange how listening to another person's heartbeat could bring calm. More than calm—she couldn't help but wonder if that in this instance listening to his heartbeat would also bring some semblance of love.

She needed to press herself away at the mere consideration or fluttering of the word *love* from within her. That was the real fire. That word, that sensation, had the power to burn down everything, including the feeble foundation of self-control she was teetering upon.

"You're okay." He whispered the words into her hair,

but as he spoke, she could hear the thumping of a helicopter moving toward them in the distance.

As relieved as she was to hear the chopper coming, she couldn't help feeling disappointment, as well. She needed this moment, one only his embrace could provide.

Chapter Eight

His father had always told him that the key to a good life was to live for today and prepare for tomorrow. It had been two days since he had spoken to Elle, and he couldn't help the feeling that if he had heeded his father's advice, his life could have been going in an entirely different direction. If only he had given in to more than just her kiss, if only he had told her that he wanted her...all of her.

Sure, they didn't need to act on it, but if he had just told her all the things that had been roiling inside him at least she could have known, and he could have been free from going over the what-ifs.

He'd had no excuse to contact her, which made it worse. The case wasn't moving, and the trail seemed cold. No ransom calls had come in. No new information. He knew there were others in DC working it—with a US senator involved, FBI and Secret Service were in the mix—but they weren't sharing information in anything approaching a fulsome way. No one on his team had even been able to get to the senator for an interview. Two days after his wife's murder and daughter's disappearance.

Luckily, it was only in his downtime, the hours after he came home and was standing in the shower, that his mind had been allowed to wander to that night spent on the mountain beside Elle. She had been so sexy, lying there in the campfire light, the oranges and reds picking up the bits of copper in her dark locks and making them shimmer in the night.

He couldn't think of any other woman who'd stayed in his mind that way, where he remembered those kinds of details about her. It made him almost feel bad. He had been with his ex-girlfriend for two years. He had loved her, but he could barely even remember the feel of her hair in his fingers or the color of it in the moonlight. Yet he had spent one night with Elle—probably one of the hardest nights she had ever experienced—and he couldn't get the thoughts of her out of his mind.

Had he really ever loved his ex like he had thought he had? Or were time and absence making those little details, the ones he was noticing about Elle, disappear from his memory? He hoped it was time, because every woman he professed to love deserved to be loved with as much energy and feeling as he could muster. What was love if not given in its entirety?

Any man worth his weight should give his woman every ounce of himself. It was why he couldn't understand cheating. While he could understand the ability to love more than one person in life, he couldn't understand how a person could have enough love to give two people everything they had at the same time. It was impossible. And if a person wasn't giving all of their love to the person they were with, and had the capacity to spill the same romantic love out to others, then they had to have been with the wrong person.

That was what had happened with his ex. He hadn't cheated, but he found that he could suddenly look at other women and think about wanting them. In that moment, he had known his relationship with her was over. She was a good woman, a lawyer, but he couldn't be with anyone whom he couldn't give himself fully to. She deserved better, a love that would keep them both up at night. And he loved her enough to give that to her, even if that meant it was another man who gave her all she deserved.

It had hurt to let her go, even more when he explained that he didn't think he was enough for her, and she hadn't wanted to accept his rationale. Yet, in the end they had gone their separate ways as friends. She had married a doctor a year later, and Grant couldn't have been happier for her.

Sometimes, like now, he found he was jealous of her ability to move on and find the right man for her while he was still single, but he was happy for her. She deserved the best things in life, and if life wasn't ready to bring him the same grace of happiness…well, he had to just accept the things it did have to offer.

As he turned off the shower and stepped out and started drying off, his thoughts moved back to Elle. Was she the one he was supposed to have in his life? Was that why every thought he had came back to her? Or was it that he was addicted to her because in that moment on the hillside he got to be her knight in shining armor?

He nearly groaned at the thought. He did not just think that.

Yep. There had to be something wrong with him. Maybe he needed to just have a few more minutes alone in the shower in order to clear his mind. Yeah, that could have been it.

She wasn't interested in him. If she had been, she would have called him by now. As it was, he was surprised she hadn't called him to check in on the case. Two days was a hell of a long time when there was a little girl missing.

So far, they had managed to track down the helicopter that had picked up the man and Lily. It had come from the Neptune airfield and was owned by a private party who was hard to track. It was registered to an LLC out of Nevada called NightGens, and when he had tried to call the company it was registered to, he had only come to voice mails and dead ends. Even their address was just some lawyer's office in Las Vegas, and that fellow had been close-mouthed, not even willing to admit he handled the business. Grant had reached out to LVPD, and they'd done him a solid by scoping out the airfield only to come up empty. It had looked abandoned.

Whoever owned that helicopter must have loved their anonymity, or else the person who had hired them had known they needed a company and a team that could keep them from being found. Either way, it made his investigation and search for the little girl that much harder.

Luckily, Deputy Terrill had taken the lead on Lily's disappearance and had been putting boots on the ground when Grant was off shift. His phone had been pinging nonstop with updates from the teams, but so far everyone had been coming up empty-handed.

The little girl's father, Dean Clark, was set to return to the state today, and Grant would be at the airport waiting to pick him up the minute his plane touched down. The senator had been informed of his wife's death and his daughter's disappearance but had been playing on the stage in Washington, DC, and some office assistant had informed him Senator Clark was working with federal authorities and would talk to him when he returned.

Grant had a hard time not being angry with the man. In this day and age, when information availability was nearly immediate, he couldn't believe that the senator hadn't bothered to check in with the law enforcement who'd first been on the scene. Then, there was nothing about this case that hadn't been a goat rope. If things started to go smoothly and things just easily clicked into place, Grant wasn't sure if he would have trusted it.

From what Grant had been told, the senator hadn't received the news well, which was to be expected. One of the members of the team who had been tasked with tracking him down had managed to talk to the agent who'd first given Clark the news. The senator had actually begun to cry. It was the man's one saving grace in being nearly inaccessible.

In an investigation with a wife and child involved, normally the first suspect on any list for a disappearance or death was the spouse. They were usually the ones with the motive and opportunity. However, from the limited number of interviews they had been doing with household staff and neighbors, including the one who had reported the crime, the senator and his wife appeared to be the picture-perfect couple.

He had even been able to pull the phone records for both Catherine and Dean, and neither had seemed to have any dastardly texts or phone calls from lovers. Really, on paper, they were just as picturesque as everyone had touted them to be. Then again, Elle had made a point of telling him how everything would be exactly that way with this family.

No one on his teams had yet to figure out who the other people had been in the house the day of the kidnapping, the ones Elle had seen. They'd reached out to neighbors, friends, business associates. And fingerprints had been smudged or nonexistent. If those men had been involved, they were smart enough to wipe things down.

After putting on his shoes and grabbing his phone, Grant headed out to his department-issued truck. His phone pinged, and he considered not looking at it while he got settled into his driver's seat.

But it could be Elle. He couldn't gain control of the thought, and if he was honest with himself, it was the only thought he had every time his phone had gone off since he had left her.

She had almost run away from him when they had come down from the mountain. Unfortunately, he had been forced to go in and write up his report about what had happened up there and then give it to the oncoming teams. He had told her to call him and given her his card, but…yeah, nothing.

Maybe she had lost his card. Maybe she'd left it in her pants pocket and then washed it, making it into the little crispy white ball of paper that he so often found when doing his own laundry.

He took out his phone and looked down at the screen. It was another of the deputies who had been on last night. Apparently, they'd had just about as much luck as he and his team had in tracking down any leads.

If they didn't find something soon, anything that could point to Lily's location, he feared that the little girl would get lost to the system. Sure, no one would ever just say they would stop looking, but the everyday grind of what they did, answering calls and serving warrants, had a way of pulling attention away from the crimes that he truly wished he could solve.

If he never found Lily, he would never forgive himself. Elle would never forgive him. From the look on her face when he had told her about Lily going missing from the mountain, he couldn't help but feel like she was already blaming him for not having found her. If only they had hiked faster, if he hadn't slowed them down, maybe they would have made it to Catherine before she had been murdered... And if they hadn't focused so much on Catherine's body, maybe they could have made it to Lily before she had been swept off the mountain.

There had to be answers, something he was missing.

For now, though, he had to call Elle. He had to know she was okay. Hopefully she was doing better than the last time he had seen her. She had been such a mess; her emotions were all over the map and all he could do was be there. It hadn't been enough. Not when all he wanted to do was set things right and be the hero whom she had so desperately needed and yet he had been unable to become.

He had let her down.

He pulled her information up on his computer and found her phone number. Hopefully she wouldn't be too freaked out that he was taking the lead and calling her first. If she was, he would play it off like he was doing his job and nothing more. Hell, he *was* just doing his job by making sure that she was home and well cared for. He could even pull the Daisy card and ask about how the pup was doing; a hike like that could be hard on a dog.

He punched in her number, and after the third ring he was just about to hang up when he heard the distinct click of her picking up the call. "Hello?" she asked. Her voice sounded tired.

Hopefully she had been taking care of herself.

"Hey, Ms. Spade? This is Sergeant Anders from the

Missoula County Sheriff's Office. How are you doing today?" What was wrong with him? Why did he go into full professional mode even though all he wanted to do was be himself and ask her all about herself?

It was no wonder she hadn't reached out to him.

"Hello, Sergeant," she said, but she sounded slightly confused. "I'm doing…okay."

He read into the silence of her answer—no doubt she was worried about Lily. How could he have been so stupid as to ask her how she was doing—she wouldn't be all right.

"Did you find her?" she asked, fear flecking her voice.

Of course that would be why she would think he was calling. The pit in his stomach deepened. For once, he wished he could be the hero. "Unfortunately, no. I was calling to check in on you."

There was a prolonged silence, so long that for a moment he wondered if the call had been dropped. He was going to say her name, but then he heard her breath.

"Like I said, I'm okay." She cleared her throat. "But what has happened…it shouldn't matter how I'm feeling. The only thing that matters to me is Lily. If you want me to be okay, I need her to be found and be safe."

He felt like he was on the stand in the courtroom, every action he took or would take being called into question. If he was in her shoes, though, he would be just as adamant about what needed to be done…and if anything, if things weren't being handled as he wanted them to be, he'd be taking matters into his own hands.

Given who her family was, he had to wonder if she was doing the same. Yet he wasn't sure how he could bring it up. She and her crew weren't the normal armchair quarterbacks; they knew what they were doing and had resources that even he and the department didn't have—on top of it all, they didn't have to adhere to the same set of rules and standards that he and his teams did. STEALTH group had lateral freedoms that he envied. It was really no wonder that when it came to international matters, one of the best weapons the government had was military contractors.

From what he knew about their group and others like it, they worked under the UN and had some immunity and leeway others didn't.

"Elle, about your team and your family..." he started.

"What about us?"

"Have you guys made any progress on the case, gotten anything my teams haven't?" He didn't even bother to ask her *if* they were working on this.

She gave a thin chuckle. "I don't know everything your team has pulled, but we have been running into roadblocks. You find the LLC, the one that owns the helo and airport?"

"Is that why you haven't called me? You didn't need me to get answers?" And did she not miss him at all? He tried to make it sound cute, his insecurities, by giving a little laugh, but even to his own ears it sounded false.

She mustn't have been thinking about him like he had been thinking about her. If she had, there wasn't a chance she had gone this long without reaching out. He had waited as long as he humanly could.

"I was actually planning on calling you later today. I was hoping you had gotten farther ahead." There was a tension in her voice that he wanted to assume was her own attraction and pull to him, one that matched his own. "Do you want to meet up today? There are a few things that I wanted to look into, and I was hoping you could give me some of the findings, if there are any, about Catherine's autopsy."

Though he was more than aware he shouldn't have been excited about seeing her and discussing the dead and missing, he couldn't help himself. He would take every second he could get with Elle, even if it wasn't in date form.

"Sure, they are supposed to be wrapping things up and getting the last toxicology findings today. I'll give the medical examiner a call and see if I can pull the full reports. In the meantime, I'm heading to my office. Meet me there."

WHEN HE ARRIVED at the courthouse and headed up the stairs to headquarters, she was already standing outside the nondescript door that led to the back offices. It made him wonder if she had been inside his world before. Most people didn't know anything about his department or their sanctum aside from it being on the third floor. It constantly surprised him how well his world of law enforcement was masked from the public eye just by being hidden in plain sight.

When she saw him walking up the steps, she smiled, and it was so real that it hit her eyes. He loved that smile, the way it lit her up even though their lives were dark and heavy. Did he have the same lightness? With all the things he had witnessed and been a part of—the lives that had ended in his hands and the worlds he had watched collapse—it wouldn't have surprised him if that part of him had died.

"Hi," she said, giving him a small wave.

He swallowed, trying to keep control of the emotions that were working through him. "Hey. No Daisy today?"

She shook her head as he walked by her and keyed in the code to open the office door.

"She is back at the ranch, hanging with the pack."

"The ranch?" he asked.

Elle nodded as he opened the door and motioned for her to walk ahead.

"Yeah, my team stays at the group's headquarters at the Widow Maker. They have quite a spread, and each year it is getting bigger." She slipped by him as she spoke, and he couldn't help but look at how her black, firehouse-cloth pants hugged her curves.

She did have some great curves. From the lines on her ass, she liked bikini-style underwear. Probably red. No. Blue. She seemed like the kind of woman who wanted relaxed, easygoing lovemaking. In his limited experience, it was the women who wore red panties who were the wild things and those who leaned more toward blue who were more of his speed.

He couldn't look away from the way her hips swayed as they made their way down the hall toward his office until she turned around and looked at him. He jerked, hoping she didn't notice him looking at her like he had been. She didn't need to think he was some kind of pervert. He wasn't like many of the other cops, guys who were all about their dicks. Sure, he could pull any number of women, but he didn't want just anyone. He was looking for a whole lot more than just sex.

She said something about the case, bringing his thoughts back to work and he turned away and pretended to read a flyer someone had tacked to the corkboard until he could regain his composure.

"Did you hear me?" she asked, walking back to stand beside him.

"No, what?" He shook his foot ever so slightly.

"Were you able to get the toxicology reports you told me about?" she asked.

Sure his body was not going to give his thoughts away, he turned back to her. "I haven't gotten a chance to look yet. We just got done with our report." He motioned down the hall. "My office is this way. If you're going to ride with me today, I need you to fill out some forms. And to be honest, it's been so long since I've had a rider with me—I assume you'd want to tag along on the case—that I don't even know where the forms are. It may take me a minute to get everything together for you."

He actually couldn't remember the last time he'd had someone outside law enforcement ride with him. It had to have been when he was working patrol, but that had been almost three years ago.

She blushed. "I'm glad you thought enough of me to want to let me join you, then. I thought that what we were doing...it was something you did. You know, joint task force–style."

He gave her a half grin. She wasn't wrong—he did work with a variety of people, but normally they didn't hang out while doing their jobs. "I do work with others, but working with private contracting groups is a new one for me. Trained with you guys before at the Special Operations Association for the state, but that's about it. We don't often cross paths." He walked into his office and she followed behind. "Feel free to take a seat."

She cleared her throat, like she was trying to dispel some of her nervous energy, or that could have just been his wishful thinking.

Landing on his email, he found the latest from the medical examiner. Clicking on the file, he opened up the complete autopsy reports. "Yep. Looks like we got everything back on Catherine," he said, looking over at Elle. "And, by the way, just to cover our bases…whatever I tell you, it needs to stay between us."

She frowned. "That shouldn't be a problem, just so long as I can let my team in as well—at least, if need requires. Will that be okay?"

"As this is an open investigation, I'm afraid there may be things that I can't tell you. But what I do tell you, you can give to your team…if need requires."

She nodded, but from the tight expression on her face, he could tell that she was slightly annoyed that he couldn't just give her all the answers. He wished he could, if it would make things easier on her. Yet, in his world, there were too many prying eyes and ears and few people he could trust. If something got leaked about this case, something that he had told her, and the kidnapper got off on a murder charge because of Grant's misstep, he wouldn't be able to forgive himself.

Though he was certain that Elle wouldn't do anything or say anything to intentionally cause problems, it was the littlest cracks in a case that could cause them to crumble or implode. And there were few things worse than watching a person he knew was guilty walk for a crime they had committed.

And that was *if* they got their hands on the person or people responsible for Catherine's death and Lily's disappearance. Right now, it was one hell of an *if*, and it just kept getting more precariously unattainable with every passing hour.

He clicked open the file and stared at the pictures the ME had sent over. Catherine's body was exposed. In the woods, he could tell she had been stabbed repeatedly.

Yet, seeing her cleaned up and naked, the savagery took on a whole new level. There wasn't any part of her that hadn't been touched by a blade. Whoever had come after her had even sliced at the back of her ankle.

Had they been trying to cut her so she couldn't run away? Had she been trying to run?

From the multitude of wounds, the killer had to have been full of rage—as he had first assumed. Yet who could have been this angry with the woman?

He looked at the picture of Catherine on her side, her back exposed. She had at least fifteen stab wounds to her torso, one just where her kidney was located and another over her heart. Either of them would have been enough to end her life.

One thing most people didn't realize was how slowly a person died. There were only four things that could instantly end a person—a stabbing wasn't one of them. Which meant that, for at least a few moments, Catherine had to have known what was happening to her and that she was likely experiencing her last moments.

The thought made a chill run over his skin.

Maybe she had been fighting, and that was what had caused the rage. It made sense. She had been off the trail when they found her. Maybe she had broken free and the attacker had tried to catch her, cut her Achilles tendon to slow her down. Maybe she had run and hidden under the tree, but the killer knew she wasn't long for the world. That order of events, that made sense…finally. He had an answer as to how she had ended up where they had found her.

He clicked on the picture of Catherine's arms. On the back of the forearms were the bruises and slashes consistent with defensive wounds. She had been fighting.

Good for her.

It was a strange relief to know that this woman hadn't gone down easily. She hadn't won, but she hadn't just given up, either. There was an incredible amount of bravery in her end, one that he appreciated. If only her fight could have been enough, at least enough for them to have found her before she passed.

Unfortunately, he hadn't made it to her in time.

And that, that inability to save everyone who needed his help, was one of the hardest parts of his job.

"Are you okay?" Elle asked, and he realized she was staring at him. He had no idea how long she had been watching.

He pinched his lips. "Yeah. I'm fine. From the looks of things, Catherine fought hard."

Elle sent him a tired smile. "That doesn't surprise me. I just hope that we can work fast enough that her daughter doesn't have to."

He nodded, unable to look her in the eyes. Scanning the document, he paused as he spotted something in the section about Catherine's clothing. There, it read:

Blood located on upper arm of gray coat. Two-square-inch sample removed and analyzed. Using a precipitin test, it was found blood was human. Blood was type O pos. Deceased was found to be AB positive. As such, blood was not that of the deceased. Further DNA testing is required. Sample sent to state crime lab in Billings.

He wasn't sure whether or not he could give the information to Elle. On one hand, it was intriguing; clearly there were multiple people injured. But what if the injured party wasn't the attacker, but was Lily?

Such information could set Elle over the edge.

"Do you happen to know Lily's blood type?" he asked.

Elle frowned. "No, why?"

"Just curious." He could probably get his hands on that information by the end of the day. At the very least, perhaps he could find out if the other blood was the same type. If it wasn't, they could still hang on to the hopes that the little girl was still alive.

Chapter Nine

She couldn't handle sitting there in his office and doing nothing. Elle had never been one for inaction, and ever since she had gotten off the mountain, she had been working on finding Lily. Her boss at STEALTH, Zoey Martin, had put all their tech gurus on task, running drones, LIDAR and every other thing they could to scour the mountain. Then she had them go over every flight record in hopes that they could track down the child.

Unfortunately, even with all of the professionals on their team and their abundant resources, they had come up empty-handed and Elle had ended up sitting here, as hobbled by the sheriff's department and the crime lab's response time as she was by her team's lack of information.

Grant's face was stoic, but she noticed him read something and then move in closer to the screen, making her wonder if he was having a hard time seeing something and needed readers or if he was just focusing hard on something she couldn't see. He was too young for readers, so he had to be focusing. Was it to do with Lily's blood type?

After he had asked her about it, everything in him had seemed to shift. It was like watching Daisy. When she was looking for a scent, she would weave right and left, working the area. Yet when she picked it up, her whole body shifted; she went rigid and the weaving stopped.

Just by watching him read, she could see his weaving had stopped. Grant had picked up a scent.

Unfortunately, he had made it clear that he was only going to give her information on a need-to-know basis. She wished he would trust her and open up, but at the same time she could completely understand the nature of his job. His inability to give her information wasn't really about her, or any of her failings. There were parts of her job that she wouldn't have shared with him, either. Yet it didn't change the fact that it sucked. Lily's life was on the line, and here they were having to play the game of politics and secrets.

She sent a text to Zoey. If anyone could get their hands on Lily's blood type, it was Zoey. She could probably either personally hack a hospital's records system or have one of her team members do it before they even left the office. What that woman could do with a computer was impressive.

In fact, she could probably get into Grant's computer right now. Sure, law enforcement and the courthouse likely had several layers of cybersecurity, but that didn't make them impenetrable. As quickly as the option came to mind, she brushed it away. Whatever was in that report, she would come to learn it on her own. Zoey didn't need to get into more trouble than absolutely necessary.

In fact, she had an idea, and better, she wouldn't have to call in the big guns.

"How do you feel about HIPAA guidelines?" she asked, giving Grant a mischievous grin.

He scowled, but the action was sexy and only partially judgmental. "Why?"

"How badly do we need to know Lily's blood type? Is it critical or just a curiosity?" She silently begged for it to be the latter, just some potentially inconsequential detail that had only a minor bearing on their case.

A pain filled his eyes and moved straight into her core. "It could be pretty important."

She nodded, looking away from him out of fear that if she continued to meet his gaze, what little control she had over her fluxing emotions would collapse. "Then I'm on it."

She picked up her phone and pulled up the email Catherine had first sent her when she had agreed to take on Lily's security detail. There, she found the numbers and information she was looking for. She dialed the pediatrician's office, and a secretary answered. The woman sounded cloying and chipper, at odds with every part of Elle's current existence.

"Hi, Mary," she said, regurgitating the woman's name in the same chipper tone in hopes it would soften the woman up to the ask she was about to make. "My name is Catherine Clark, and I'm calling about my daughter, Lily Clark."

"Hello, Mrs. Clark, so great to hear from you. How can I help? Is Lily doing okay?"

Grant's eyes were wide with surprise, and her mischievous grin widened into a dark smile. Sometimes the best part of living in small communities was the inherent trust that came with it; fortunately for them today it could be used to their benefit—hopefully.

"Lily is just fine," she lied. "I was just filling out some paperwork for an upcoming summer camp, and I was wondering if you could provide me with some information I have missing from my records. Would you be able to do that?"

"Hmm." The secretary paused, as if she was considering what information she was willing to give. "What kind of info do you need?"

"First, we would need her vaccination records," she lied, trying to think of what reasonable things a camp would need in order to sell her real ask. "Also, it looks like they have a question about blood type, as well. Would that be on record?"

The woman tapped away on a keyboard in the background. "Can you give me her date of birth?"

Elle rattled it off, thanking the real Mrs. Clark for being the ever-so-uptight mother—at least when it came to hiring the help—and also thanking law enforcement for not yet releasing the information about the murder and kidnapping to the media. Otherwise, Mary wouldn't be dealing with her.

"If you like I'd be more than happy to email this information over to you," the secretary said.

"That would be great," she said, giving the woman her encrypted email address that she used for STEALTH. "By chance, did we have her typed and crossed?"

"Yep," the woman said, "looks like she is O positive. Don't worry, I will go ahead and attach those results to the email, as well."

Elle smiled as she thanked the woman and hung up the phone. She looked over at Grant, her smile so wide that it was actually starting to pinch at her cheeks. "It is amazing what a mom can accomplish in five minutes. I don't know if you are aware, but being a mom may actually be kind of magic."

He nodded, but there was something wrong about him. Her smile disappeared.

"What's wrong, Grant?" She slipped her phone back into her purse.

"She's O positive?" he asked, a strange pleading tone to his voice almost as if he was hoping that he had heard the secretary wrong.

"Yeah, why?" There was a long pause, and with each passing second, her body clenched harder and harder, threatening to collapse in upon itself. What wasn't he telling her? What did he know? "You have to tell me what is going on here, Grant. You can't leave me in the dark."

He looked up at her, and she could have sworn there were tears in the corners of his eyes, but as quickly as she noticed them, he blinked them back. "The examiner found some blood on Catherine's sleeve. Blood that didn't match. It came back as O positive." His voice thinned as he spoke, becoming almost unintelligible.

She swallowed, hard. Lily had been injured…

Elle slumped back into the chair as the news flooded through her senses. She brought her hands to her mouth, chewing on the edge of her fingernail.

Lily was out there, hurt somewhere. She was sitting here and doing nothing. Yet, what could they do? Who could they talk to that would know anything, that could lead them to her?

Futility. This was pure hell.

Grant moved to come closer to her, like he wanted to somehow take back the words he had said to her, but the findings weren't something he could control. This wasn't his fault. None of this was his fault—it was all hers. She put her hand up to stop him from moving closer, and he sat back down in his chair across the desk from her.

He looked dejected. Had he needed to be consoled just as she did? Or was his need to comfort her for her alone?

Right now, it didn't matter. Nothing mattered but getting Lily back.

"Grant," she said, her voice hoarse from the silence and stress.

"Hmm?" he asked, watching her.

"I can't just sit here and hope to find answers."

He nodded, sadness marking his features. "I know. But there are only so many doors we can knock on to get answers. This case, it's proving to be far more complex than what we had initially assumed it would be, especially with federal law enforcement involved. It's been hard getting anyone to answer our calls in DC, let alone share much beyond what we already know. According to the feds, the senator has had the usual string of death threats, and he'll share those with us when we see him. I hope you know I have been stopping at nothing to get Lily home."

He grabbed some papers as they spit out of the printer and handed them over to her, waivers for her to ride along. She signed them and slid them across his desk. "Can you print out the autopsy findings, too?"

His eyes darkened, and he shook his head. "I can answer questions and give you information, but that could get me into some hot water."

She sighed, but she couldn't pretend that she didn't understand the whys and hows of his thinking. "Fair. But what else did they find? Is there anything? Did they ever manage to get into her phone?"

"iPhones are known for being ridiculously hard to get into without a password. I was hoping that when we meet up with Senator Clark he would give us that." As he spoke, he glanced down at his watch. He picked up her signed forms and stuffed them into the basket on his desk. "In fact, we need to head his way."

She didn't want to stay here and be helpless, but she didn't really want to go and question the senator, either. The good news was that he probably wouldn't even know who she was, as they'd never met each other in person, but that wouldn't stop the growing dislike she held for the man.

How could it have taken him so long to get back to the state when his *daughter* was missing? She would have taken advantage of every possible resource—hell, she *had been already*, to help Lily.

Grant stood up and pulled on his jacket. "His plane, if it's on time, should be arriving in fifteen minutes."

"Do you really think he is going to freely give us information? And you know whatever he has to say, it will be nothing but lies." She felt the fire on her tongue as she spoke.

Grant glanced over at her, his eyes widening. "I take it you don't like Dean Clark?"

She shrugged. "I don't like him or his political ads, but in reality, I don't even know him. He is never with his daughter. In the months I have been working there, I have not once actually seen him in person, let alone heard Lily talk about him. I honestly couldn't tell you one time that she said the word *Daddy*."

He checked his utility belt and then stepped toward the door, motioning for her to walk ahead of him. "That's interesting. You ever have any idea why he is so distant?"

"From the family or from Lily?" she asked, walking into the hall as he closed up and locked the office behind them.

"Both, either… I'm curious. I don't have any kids, but if they didn't talk about me, I would take it pretty hard. I would like to think most men want their children to love them." They made their way out as they spoke.

"Not all men want to be fathers, and I think it's fair to assume he is one only because then he can pull constituents from the suburbs. If he is anything like Catherine, you know what he is focused on—and it most certainly isn't actually being the person he pretends to be." As she spoke, all of her secret and pent-up feelings about the family came boiling to the surface.

In fact, she hadn't even realized she had been thinking such things, and yet there they all were coming out of her mouth like she had opened up some kind of fire hose full of unspoken opinions.

Grant was silent as they made their way outside and to his truck. He opened up the door for her, and as she climbed in, she couldn't help feeling as though she had perhaps said too much and had come off as something and someone she wasn't. She didn't hate Dean or even wish him ill; she just couldn't understand him.

As Grant closed the door and walked around the other side, she watched him move. His coat was stretched tight over his shoulders, and for the first time she noticed how wide they were and how his body was the perfect V-shape of a man who worked out. He stopped and picked something up, and as he moved, she couldn't help but stare at his round ass. That ass. Damn. He must have been the master of squats.

The animalistic part of her brain, the part she wished she could control, made her wonder how it would feel to have him in between her legs. She could almost feel his ass in her hands as he made a few of her wilder fantasies come true.

Maybe it was the tension of the case that turned her thoughts to carnal pleasures and away from the grimness of reality.

What would it be like to feel his breath mix with hers? To have him whispering all the things he wanted to do to her in her ear?

She shifted in the seat, trying not to let her thoughts reach her body but already knowing that there were some things—just like her thoughts about Grant—that she could not control.

It had been incredible just to kiss that man. Yet things had gone all kinds of wrong when they had. It was up in the air as to what would happen if they were ever to try again, but damn if she didn't want to.

She licked her lips as he got in, and she sucked at her bottom lip before letting it pop out of her mouth as she gave him one more sidelong glance. He started to look over at her, and she quickly glanced away. He didn't need to know the thoughts she was experiencing about him right at this moment. If he did…well, she didn't want to know where it would lead. At least not yet, not right now.

Maybe if they finally found Lily and put Catherine's killer behind bars, then she could focus on getting back into the dating world. Her loneliness could have been the driving force behind everything she was feeling when it came to Grant.

There were a million reasons they couldn't be together. First and foremost, that they worked together—but that wouldn't be a permanent thing. And well, for all intents and purposes, she didn't really *know* him. She wasn't the kind of woman, or at least she didn't think she was the kind, who fell head over heels for a man after having just met him. She was far too methodical for that kind of nonsense. Then again, Daisy had approved, and that spoke volumes about what kind of man he was.

"Lily is going to be okay. It's all going to be okay," he said, looking as though he wanted to reach over and touch her once again.

He kept doing that. "Why don't you want to touch me?" she asked, looking down at his hand.

He balled his fingers into a fist and then extended them toward her. "I want to. Believe me, I *really* want to touch you, but I have to be careful. In my job, if we lay hands on someone, those folks are going to jail."

She tilted her head back as she laughed. "Well, then don't touch me. I have shit to do."

Now he was the one laughing, and she ate up the rich, baritone sound of him cutting up. That would be an amazing way to spend a day, in his arms and listening to that sound.

She reached over and extended her hand to him, palm up. "If you promise not to arrest me, I think we can try this thing."

He slipped his hand into hers, pulling their palms tight. It felt secure there in his grasp, and the image of him bending over and all the things she wanted him to do to her body flashed through her mind.

"I'm glad you wanted to touch me again. I was afraid that I had scared you away." He smiled at her.

That smile...she wasn't sure which part of him she liked best. His eyes pulled her into their medley of colors and lines, but then he spoke. Even his voice...oh, his voice.

"You are something special, Ms. Spade." He lifted her hands and gave her a soft kiss to the back of her knuckles.

Her legs tightened together, giving away all the places her body was responding to his lips on her skin. She didn't know what to say to him. Did she compliment him back, or would it be too forced and inauthentic? But she couldn't just say nothing—maybe she should say thank you, but if she did that, would she seem like a narcissist?

"Thank you," she said, smiling at him. Self-love and knowing her self-worth wasn't narcissism, it was power. And damn it, she wasn't a doormat.

It felt strange and wonderful to claim her power and go against so many of the life lessons that had been thrust down her throat as she had grown up. Her mother had been a powerhouse and her father had been supportive of having a wild child as a daughter, but it was ridiculous how the world worked to stuff a woman in the submissive patriarchal box. If a woman didn't cook for her man, she was lazy. If she liked sex, she was a whore who must have been with hundreds of men. And if she could see the power in herself, the fire within her, she was a stuck-up brat.

His smile widened. "It's nice to hear a woman accept a compliment for once."

She forced herself to look over at him instead of coyly looking down at her hands. "Well, I appreciate you telling me what you are thinking and feeling. Seriously, it is amazing what two people can accomplish if they actually just say what they are thinking and feeling to one another—at least in the way they can."

His grip loosened. "I'm sorry about that. That I can't give you everything you want in the investigation."

Crap.

"That's not what I meant, not at all. I just meant in life." She squeezed his hands in hopes it would reassure him. She wanted to explain it more, to tell him all the things she was thinking and how she wasn't the kind to be intentionally rude or cruel, but they were pulling up to the terminals.

"It's fine," he said, letting go of her and putting the truck into Park. "I'm just glad I get to touch you, at least once in a while."

She felt the heat rising into her cheeks, but she wasn't sure what had caused it, his sweetness or the thought of his skin pressed against her again.

How could this hard-edged, stoic man who had intimidated her when they first met be such a soft-hearted guy when they were alone? He was full of contradictions, but damned if she didn't have a growing need for what he was offering.

Like a true gentleman, he came around and helped her out of his truck. She cleared her throat as she tried her damnedest to stay cool. It was possible that his being a gentleman was a result of his job, and likely a habit of cuffing and stuffing. The thought made her giggle lightly.

"What are you laughing about?" he asked, closing the door behind her.

"Nothing." *And everything.* How had she found herself holding hands with a man she could have sworn was hotter than the surface of the sun?

If he knew all the things she had done and seen, she had a feeling he would accept her for them. And yet, the thought of being with someone in their field—door kicking, so to speak—made her somewhat uncomfortable. Could two people in their world really work? She could be a bit manic about her job, and she had a feeling he could, too.

He hadn't even called her for two days after their night in the woods. That had to mean something, didn't it?

The doors at the front of the terminal opened, and a good-looking man with graying hair at his temples came sauntering out in a barely mussed Armani suit.

Though she had never met the man, she would have known Dean Clark anywhere. She had seen his picture over the fireplace every morning since she had started this job, and his photo ran in campaign ads. And damned if he didn't look exactly like the oil painting of him and his family.

As though he could feel her staring at him, he glanced over at her and their eyes met. In the cold steel blue of his, she could see she may have finally found answers.

Chapter Ten

Senator Clark was exactly the man Grant would have expected him to be after having watched him on the news over the years. He'd once heard gossip that the senator had opposed a Veterans Affairs funding bill for a new hospital, but then when the bill passed and funding was granted, he made sure to show up on the day they broke ground—nothing like a photo op at the expense of truth.

The senator swept back his pomaded hair as he spoke to a woman who was beaming up at him when they walked out of the terminal together. He smiled, and Grant wasn't sure he had ever seen a more lustful, flirtatious gaze on any woman. If only the woman knew the truth—that the man she was talking to had come back to Montana because his wife had been murdered.

If anything, at least the senator had just moved himself firmly into the number one position on Grant's list of suspects.

Grant gritted his teeth but smiled as he made his way over to the man. "Senator Clark, I'm Sergeant Anders. We spoke on the phone." He normally would have extended his hand in a show of respect to those he was working with, but he had a hard time acting congenial when the senator had been so damned hard to get in touch with.

The senator kissed the woman on the cheek and slipped something into her purse as he bade her farewell, then he finally turned to Grant. "Hello, Anders. I thought we were going to meet at my hotel?"

His hackles rose and he started to say something, but the man cut him off.

"Regardless, I do appreciate just getting this all taken care of as quickly and as efficiently as we can. I need to get Lily back and find justice for my wife," the man said, a look of concern finally flickering over his features.

Grant wondered if his reaction was nothing more than a staged response and a canned script. He hated to have hope this man was genuinely concerned for his wife and child.

"I'm glad you feel that way, sir," he said. "If you wouldn't mind, perhaps we can find a quiet corner in the airport and we can chat." He motioned back inside.

The man was wheeling a small carry-on bag, and as Grant spoke, he looked down at it as if he was put out that he would have to be seen dragging around a suitcase for any amount of extra time. "Do you mind if I put this in my vehicle?"

He wasn't sure that he could trust the senator to come back, so instead of merely letting him go, he motioned toward Elle. "Sure thing. I could certainly stretch my legs, as well. Nothing quite like sitting in a truck or behind a desk and making phone calls all day." He tried to sound jovial, nonescalatory in any way.

Dean looked over at him and smiled, but it was just as fake as the man it belonged to.

Insincere people, especially those like politicians who

used phony concern as a campaign tactic, were hard to read. It made getting information incredibly challenging—and this case would be no exception. The honey and the wax would be inseparable.

Elle walked closer and looked to him. As she did, he realized the senator and Elle didn't actually know one another. How could the man not even know whom he had hired to take care of his child?

"Senator, this is Elle Spade. She is the woman who was hired to help protect your family." As he spoke, Grant nearly bit off his tongue as he realized what he had said and the unintentional burn his words may have left. "She works for STEALTH."

The senator stopped and looked her up and down, like he was taking her all in before choosing his words. If only Grant had taken the same time. He mouthed "I'm sorry" to Elle, but she just shrugged. Her simple action only made him feel that much worse. Of course she was probably beating herself up for what had happened, and then he had gone ahead and made it all that much worse.

"I'm sorry about what has happened, Senator Clark. Please know that I offer my most sincere condolences. Your wife was a remarkable woman," Elle said, bowing her head in sympathy. "I would have never left your home that day if I had known what was going to take place after I had gone."

The senator put his hand on Elle's shoulder, and she tensed under the man's grip. Though the action looked as if it was meant to ease her guilt, there was something insincere about the gesture. Or perhaps Grant was just picking up on what he wanted to see. He didn't like the senator, but that didn't necessarily mean that at his core the man was a monster—or at least more of a monster than any other human being.

Grant's mind wandered to all the things he had seen on the job and the saintlike people who turned out to be the greatest monsters of all and the dangerous-looking biker types who went out of their way to work with law enforcement to stop crimes from happening. Assumptions could be obstacles when it came to finding the truth.

"Thank you, Ms. Spade." The senator squeezed her shoulder. "Know that I don't hold you or your team responsible for what has happened. This was my own mistake. I wish I had told Catherine she required twenty-four-hour protection."

Elle looked even more surprised than Grant felt. The man couldn't have been this kind or understanding. Yet, there he was. Was Grant wrong about him?

Grant watched the senator's features, hoping to read any kind of details the man might give away in his body language. "Why *did* you hire protection?"

"I had been receiving threats. The Secret Service was aware and offered to protect my wife as well as myself, but she refused. She found my job and all these things, safety hazards included, to be invasive." The senator started walking again.

Elle nodded as she walked beside the senator. "She had mentioned that to me on occasion."

The senator gave a thin smile, but it quickly disappeared. "Catherine has always been a stubborn woman. No amount of my talking could convince her to take these threats seriously. She wasn't naive, but she really felt that by living in Montana we would be kept away from the big-city dangers."

Grant nodded. "Do you have a record of any of these threats? Any you think are more credible than others?"

Senator Clark took out his phone as they walked. "What's your email address? I can send you exactly what I sent the Secret Service. I'm surprised they haven't shared it with your team."

Grant wasn't surprised. Federal agencies often had communications and turf issues. It would have been nice if the senator had greased the skids on that.

He handed the man his card. "You can send the information here."

"Great. Just give me a moment." The senator didn't even slow down as he typed away on his phone. "There you go, will be to you in a moment."

They came to the long-term parking, and Grant stopped walking. "I'll wait here for you while you put your bag away." He lifted his phone slightly.

"I'll be right back. I'm happy to give you as much time as you need to go over all the details. However, I do have some other meetings this evening." He glanced down at his watch. "Actually, I have one with the local media outlets starting in just an hour, and I was hoping to clean up before I met them."

"Sir, I mean this in the most professional way, but I would like to think that should I need you to answer questions about your wife's murder and your daughter's disappearance, I will take priority."

The senator smirked. "Oh, they are my number one priority. They always have been and Lily always will be. However...my job doesn't stop because of events in my personal life. This state and the people within it depend on me and my delegation. I must be able to perform to my greatest abilities. I may only be in this job a few more months before the election is over, and I have people breathing down my neck to make certain things happen."

"People who would use your wife and your family's safety as a card to get you to do what they wanted?"

"Perhaps this is me being as naive as my wife, but when it comes to my world, there are certain things that good, moral people won't do. As you will see in that email, the people who have threatened me are not the kind of people you would call *upstanding*. These are folks who have issues." The senator twisted his bag, clearly annoyed at being held back from being able to do exactly as he wanted.

"Hmm," Grant said, but Elle was giving him the side-eye and he didn't have a clue what it meant. "Let me look things over."

The senator dipped his head in acknowledgment. "I'm parked not far from here."

As he walked away, the only sounds were of the fellow travelers who were chatting away in the parking lots mixed with the scraping sound of plastic suitcase wheels as they ground against the pavement. Oh, he knew that sound entirely too well.

Elle stood beside him as he pulled up the senator's email. "You watch him, make sure he doesn't get lost."

She nodded.

"Did you know about the death threats?" he asked.

"Catherine didn't mention them, but I assumed there had to be something going on—why else would they have called STEALTH? We aren't cheap, and we don't take contracts for people who don't have legitimate safety concerns." Her head was on a swivel, as she must have been monitoring the senator.

He scrolled through the email, which read as though

it had been drafted by a lawyer even though it had been sent from the senator's personal account. In the email, he mentioned three possible threats, and with each person of interest he had provided a picture and evidence of the direct threats. One was an audio recording of a voice mail left on the senator's personal phone by a man who called himself Jazz Garner.

He wished he was in his truck so he could listen to the audio and run the names through the database, but it would have to wait.

The next was an email sent by one Philip Crenshaw. He was wearing desert tac gear and a shemagh wrapped around his neck. There was a gun in his hands, but he wasn't displaying a flag or patches on his gear. He was standing next to a mud house, similar to those Grant had seen in pictures of the Middle East. If he had to guess, the guy looked like a contractor. But what contractor would send a senator a death threat? They weren't the kind to threaten, they were the kinds to kill—with no one being the wiser.

Strange.

He pulled up the email. The spelling was poor and the grammar was worse, but the message was clear—if Senator Clark didn't vote for the bill SB 102, there would be hell to pay. Grant had heard of the bill, but he couldn't recall what it was about.

Regardless, he wasn't sure why this had been deemed a credible threat. Yeah, the guy looked intimidating, but without seeing the man's picture it wasn't an email that would have made the hair rise on his arms.

The last threat was from one Steve Rubbick. Another email. In this one, the man had cited neo-Nazi propaganda before writing, "…you and your wife will feel my wrath. I will cut you down like the sheep you are and mutilate your corpse while I make her watch…"

The man went into details, listing things he planned to do to Catherine that made Grant's skin crawl. This man had put time, thought and rage into his threat. Grant could understand why the senator would have taken note. The only thing that wasn't listed was where the man intended to kill them or the senator's home address. Either the man hadn't known it or perhaps his letter was nothing more than a rant by a madman.

More than the details or even the diatribe of whys, it was the rage that drew Grant's ire the most. Catherine had been stabbed more than seventy-three times in total. That kind of overkill was something that was only done in a heightened stage of emotional turmoil.

With murderers he had interviewed in the past, when they committed homicides like this, they talked about going into an almost trancelike state. They found pleasure in the method, pulling the trigger and focusing on the muscles in their fingers and the smell of the spent gunpowder, or when stabbing, they found a rhythm in their motion and lusted after the sensation of the point piercing the skin, slicing through muscle and glancing off bone.

"Anything?" Elle asked.

"Definitely some things to go off." He pulled the picture of the contractor on his phone. "How long have you been active in the contracting world?"

She shrugged as she stared out into the parking lot. "I dunno, more than five years now, why?"

"One of our possible suspects is a contractor, or was one." Asking her if she knew this guy was like asking someone from New York if they knew another New Yorker; the chances were almost nil. Yet, he had to check.

He lifted his phone for her to see. "Do you recognize this guy?"

Elle reached over for his phone, not letting her watch on the senator down. She glanced at the photograph on his phone. Her gaze flicked over the image and she looked up, but a second later she looked back at it and stared.

"So, you do know him?" he asked, surprised.

"I didn't know he was a contractor." She frowned. "But he is one of the guys who was with Catherine the day she was killed."

Holy shit.

It couldn't have been that easy. No way. Yet, these stars aligned. Finally, they had gotten their break. They would have gotten it earlier if the senator had bothered to work with the locals.

She flipped to the next photo on Grant's phone. Elle's breath caught in her throat. This man in the photo collage from the senator had also been standing in Catherine's living room the day she had disappeared. The photo of the third man, who was identified as Jazz, was the only one of the group she didn't recognize.

The contractor, Philip, was the man she'd seen smoking a cigar. She closed her eyes, trying to recreate the last image she could recall of the living room and where the men had been standing when she'd last seen them. Steve had been across the room with the group of men, but she couldn't recall what he had been wearing or if he had said anything to her.

There was the sound of footsteps approaching in the distance, and she looked up and watched as the senator returned. He had a smile on his face and gave them a small wave. "The email help at all?" he asked.

Grant returned the man's smile and gave him a stiff nod. "Interesting. We will definitely look into things." He reached into his pocket and withdrew Catherine's cell phone; it was bagged and tagged for evidence. "I was actually hoping you could help me with one more thing before I hit you with too many questions. Do you know the passcode for your wife's mobile device?"

The senator reached up and ran his hand over his neck, unintentionally covering his weak point. He was stressed. Daisy would do the same thing—cower and cover her neck—if she was upset or concerned for her safety. It was an instinctual move, and Elle had even caught herself doing it sometimes. Yet the senator doing it in this moment struck her as odd. Why would opening up his wife's phone make him uncomfortable?

"I don't know if I can get you in, but I guess I could try." He held out his hand. "You think there's anything on there that could help point you in the right direction, as far as possible suspects go?"

"Don't take it out of the bag." Grant handed the phone over. "As you well know, we're just trying to put some pieces together here. We are trying our hardest to get to the bottom of this case and find justice for your wife as well as locate Lily."

Taking the phone, the senator tapped in a series of numbers. He opened it on his third try and, as it opened, he chuckled and handed the phone back to Grant. "The code is 062510. I'm sorry. I thought the feds already gave this to you."

"What is that?"

"Our wedding anniversary." The senator smiled. "Catherine was always a wonderful wife." As he spoke, his voice cracked with emotion.

Grant nodded. "From everything I've heard about your wife from the witnesses we all have interviewed, it sounds as though you were a very lucky man. I am sorry for your loss."

The senator nodded, clearing his throat. "You guys have anything on Lily yet? The last I'd heard your teams hadn't managed to locate anything that could point us in her direction. Is that still true?"

Elle twitched.

Grant put his phone away and rested his hands on his utility belt, masking his badge. "Unfortunately, we are still struggling to find where she could be located. Again, we are looking."

The senator's eyes darkened, and she could tell he was angry. For the first time, she liked the man. But it had taken talking about Lily before she had seen any genuine emotion.

"Would Lily have known any of the men that were referenced in your email?"

The senator balked. "No, what would make you ask that?"

This time, she wasn't sure if the reaction was real. "I was just wondering if you know of anyone who she would have felt comfortable going with. For a while, on the trail, we found her tracks. She had been walking side by side with her kidnapper for almost a mile."

The senator closed his eyes, and his head dropped low. He ran his hands over his face as they stood there in the cold. When he lifted his head, there were tears in his eyes. "You of all people have to know that I've been a shitty father when it came to Lily. I haven't been with her nearly enough. The truth is, I didn't know you—and I should have. If I tell you I know who was coming and going in her life, that would be a lie. And that, that is something I'm not proud of."

She wouldn't have expected those words to come out of the senator's mouth in a thousand years. He was a seasoned politician, and even for a person in that role, the level of candor and humility in his words stunned her.

Grant nodded, and he also seemed to appear to soften to the man. "Senator, we have all made mistakes in our lives. And as much as I wish you could give me the right answers to our questions, I prefer the honest ones."

The senator dabbed at the corner of his eye, collecting himself. "Do you know when they will be releasing my wife's body? I was hoping to take care of her funeral arrangements while I'm in Montana."

"The medical examiner has filed their reports, but there are a few more tests before everything is finalized. However, I think that you can now claim her remains at any time."

"I will let the funeral home know," he said. "In the meantime, if we are done here, I need to see the rest of my family and take care of some business. If you need to ask me more questions, or if things arise that need my attention, please do not hesitate to reach out."

Elle was sure Grant had more questions for the man, and he had to be as put out by his dismissal of them as she was, but Grant didn't say anything.

The senator turned to her and extended his hand. "And I want to say thank you. I appreciate you coming out and working with the local law enforcement in helping to find my daughter. I didn't fail to notice that you are going above and beyond the call of duty."

She appreciated the flattery. "You are welcome, sir.

And I promise I won't stop looking for Lily until I have her in my arms."

"I'm sure that is true." The senator gave her a double pat to her shoulder. "Good evening, and again. Thank you both." He turned and walked away, leaving them standing there at the entrance of the lot.

If she had to explain the situation to someone who hadn't been there, she would have had to admit they had just been worked over by the senator. He was definitely a power player in the world of communication. The old adage of "could sell ketchup Popsicles to a woman in a white dress" came to mind.

They watched him pull out of the lot and make his way to the toll booth before Grant finally turned to her. "What do you make of that?"

She shook her head. "I think that if he's who we need to talk to in order to get answers, then this investigation is going to take a while."

Chapter Eleven

Grant tapped away on his computer inside the truck. Elle had gone quiet, but he couldn't tell if it was because she was relieved or upset. She was softhearted, and surely the senator had thrown her for a loop, yet she wasn't giving her thoughts away.

If anything, she looked *okay*. Maybe the senator's words had helped to mollify the guilt she must have been feeling about Lily falling to the family's enemies.

Grant opened the audio file. The sound was poor and the man who was speaking was slurring as he spewed hate for the senator. He didn't mention Catherine.

"Do you want me to look through Catherine's phone?" Elle asked, finally breaking the silence between them. "Maybe I can pull something."

He reached into his pocket and handed it over to her. "Have at it."

They had gotten a warrant after they had sent a preservation letter to request that the phone company save the data from the phone as well as from the senator's, but so far, he hadn't received the device's text message and call history. With it open, they might not have to wait for the company to get on the ball.

She tapped in the unlock code and flipped through the screens while he turned back to his computer.

He started by running Jazz through the database. The man came up known, but clean. Next, he turned to the contractor, Philip. Nothing came up when he typed the man's name in the database. As a contractor, the man might be using a false name, Grant thought. He ran the name as an alias, but no matter how deeply he searched, he couldn't even pull this guy's driver's license or known address.

His thoughts moved to Elle. Was she the same way? Was her name even Elle? What if she was working under an alias and just couldn't tell him? If she was, so was the rest of her family. The Spades were well-known in the small, local law enforcement community. They and the rest of the STEALTH group were always more than willing to lend a hand or get information when they were in a pinch.

Yet that didn't make what he knew about her any more real or accurate than what he knew about the senator. The realization bothered him, deeply. At the same time, he couldn't condemn her or judge her because of her lifestyle. There were innumerable details that he couldn't give her about himself. Besides, what was really in a name or background information...even in a past? He liked the woman who sat beside him, the woman who wasn't afraid to show her emotions, who worked harder than most people he knew and lived to make the world a better place.

He sat there thinking about everything as he stared at the screen and pretended to read through the list of ongoing and open calls coming from dispatch. "Elle," he said, finally unable to hold back any longer, "do you use an alias?"

She jerked as she looked up from Catherine's phone. "Huh?"

"Is your name really Elle?" He felt sheepish for even asking.

She chuckled. "You finally going to ask? I was wondering if you would."

He shrugged.

"Yes, my name really is Elle. But when I'm not home, I work under any number of names depending on where in the world I will be. Why?"

He was secretly thankful she had trusted him enough to give him her real name.

"The guy you recognized, do you think he's working an alias right now?" Grant lifted the phone so she could look at the man again.

"If he is on a contract right now, he probably is using a false name." Elle paused for a moment. "And if he was working under an alias, it makes me think he is definitely the man that we should be looking for."

Grant nodded, but he hadn't needed her to point him in the man's direction; he was already there. He typed in the next suspect's name and waited as the computer ground through the data. Several different Steve Rubbicks popped up; they were a variety of ages ranging from eighteen to eighty-four. From the picture, he guessed the guy they were looking for had to be in his late thirties to early forties. Three off the list fit the demographic.

He clicked on the second one, and the man who popped up was a ringer. Same dark eyes and cleft chin. According to arrest records, the man had been locked up for a PFMA, or partner/family member assault, five years ago. Since then, he'd been free of trouble, but in his booking photo there was a swastika tattooed at the base of his throat.

According to his arrest record, his last known address was just outside city limits.

"I have a hit." Grant smiled. "Buckle up. Let's take a ride out to Steve's place. See if we can find him."

Elle buckled her seat belt, but she barely looked up from the phone. It surprised him that she wasn't more excited, but even he was feeling like this very well could be an ill-fated run. The man had been at the right place at the right time to fall well within their list of suspects, but he seemed like the kind who wasn't about to just roll over and give them the information they wanted. If anything, he looked entirely antigovernment in the way he sneered back from his booking photo.

How had such a man ever even stood in the same room as the senator's wife? STEALTH had been tasked with personal security for Lily, but apparently they didn't have any active roles in monitoring who came and went from the property. And if Catherine wasn't taking the death threats seriously, it definitely made sense that she wouldn't have pushed the security team for that kind of vetting.

It all came back to being from a sparsely populated and isolated state. Around here, there was an inherent trust. And that naive trust had come back to bite the Clarks squarely in the ass. On the heels of his thoughts was his pity for Elle. What a mess she had found herself in—the scandal would undoubtedly mark her career if the public ever caught word of what had led up to Catherine's death and Lily's disappearance.

Even though STEALTH wasn't responsible for the

breech, they would be the ones who would find themselves being scrutinized by the court of public opinion. Luckily, the news hadn't really broken too wide. The only thing he'd seen mentioned was that the sheriff's department was investigating a possible homicide. No word of Lily.

But when and if it came out that a senator's wife had been murdered, it was possible that all hell would break loose. He would be getting calls from every Tom, Dick and Harry who would swear they saw something and knew all the answers. And then there would be the mix of people who wanted to both commend or condemn him and his fellow officers for the work they did. It was an understatement to say his hands would be full.

"Do you have any idea what the men were doing with Catherine? Anything at all?" he asked as they drove toward Steve's place.

Elle shook her head. "I have no idea. Besides myself, Catherine was the only woman there and I thought that was strange, but I didn't pay it too much mind given the nature of her husband's job."

"But you didn't hear anything?"

She nibbled at the inside of her cheek. "They were just acting like frat boys, laughing and joking. I don't remember anything that was said, but I would assume that based on how they acted with one another, they likely knew one another fairly well."

"Do you think the men worked together? That they could all be contractors or in the same crew?"

She nodded. "Maybe, but before any are hired, they have to go through a rigorous background check. This Steve guy isn't someone STEALTH would ever consider hiring, not given his radical leanings—that kind of person makes for a hell of a liability."

"I thought you all lived above the law? No offense intended," he added, but she didn't give any indication that she had taken it as anything more than a legitimate question.

"No one is above the law, not even us." She sent him a knowing smile. "Though we do get to run with a looser set of guidelines."

He could imagine, but he'd also seen innumerable headlines about black ops crews that had run afoul of the law—and changed their names and continued on taking care of the business that would always keep them employed. The only people or organizations he had actually heard of being shuttered were the ones who actually did hire people like Steve—the wild cards who got lost in the bloodlust.

If this guy was a contractor by trade and not merely some radical, then they very well could have been walking into a hornet's nest. This guy looked like the kind who would be solidly antigovernment and loaded for bear. He probably was the kind who had a target range in his basement and a bug-out tunnel coming out of a panic room.

Grant had no doubt that if he looked up the man's ATF records, he would find a list of gun serial numbers that would make any revolutionary proud. And that was what the man had bought legally. Who knew how many guns and incendiary devices he had bought from gun shows and out of the back of people's cars? Gun trades were a common thing in all rural communities, but in Montana it was well-known that a person could buy or trade for an unregistered gun within the hour if they felt the need.

In most cases, those kinds of trades and purchases weren't something to be overconcerned about; it was just like any other flea market or garage sale purchase. See a need, fill a need kind of thing. Yet, when it came to radicals, they were the reason that it was frowned upon. In all of his years in law enforcement, there were only a small number of cases in which they had solved a homicide by using a gun's serial number. Most of the time, serial numbers were only used to return stolen guns to their original owners.

As they drove up to the house, there were signs on the trees along Steve's dirt driveway that read Trespassers Will Be Shot in dripping red spray paint on plywood.

"Nothing like feeling welcome," Elle said with a dry laugh.

"It may not be a bad idea for you to stay in the car while I introduce myself to this guy."

Her mouth pinched closed.

"I just want you to be safe. You're only a rider. If you were on duty, I'm sure that you would be more than capable of dealing with this guy," he added, trying to tiptoe around her.

Her scowl disappeared, and he was pretty sure he had even seen her dip her head slightly, as if she was thinking, *damn right*. She was something. He liked that she was soft and hard, lace and leather. He had always wanted a woman like that, one who had the power to take control and face the enemy, and who knew she was a badass who could save herself—but one who still occasionally needed saving.

Right now, she didn't need to be saved, but he could still give her some level of protection against the unknown and potentially dangerous.

The road leading to the house was scattered with pot-holes and cobbles that made the truck bounce and jump, working his suspension. Why was it that all these societal outliers couldn't take care of their property? Or was it some kind of thing that they wanted to slow any intrud-er's advance to their front door? In this case, he would have believed the man capable of that kind of thinking. If he was watching them on a closed-circuit camera, then he was probably already grabbing his mags and getting himself ready for a shootout.

Luckily, Grant's pickup wasn't easily identifiable as a police vehicle. It wasn't until a person was up close and personal that they could see the light bar in the wind-shield that really gave it away. To the layman, it was just another truck, but to this guy... Grant was glad to be locked and loaded.

They came around a bend in the driveway, and the small, boxy house came into view. The place had a cor-rugated steel roof that was covered in a red patina of rust. The sides of the house were covered with rotting gray wooden siding a few feet up from the ground and then above was torn and faded plastic construction wrap. One of the front windows had been broken, and instead of fixing the glass, the occupants had covered the bro-ken seams with silvery duct tape.

The driveway obviously wasn't some plan to slow; rather, it appeared as though it was neglected out of hard-ship—just like the rest of the place.

The state of the place was a bit of a shock. Some mili-tary contractors made more than $100,000 a year. There were a lot of things a person could do with that kind of money. This man's property didn't give off the scent of prosperity in any way. Maybe he wasn't a contractor after all. Then again, it was also a known thing that when it came to contractors, many had the attitude "earn it to burn it," and that could certainly have been the case here.

It would be smart to look bedraggled from the outside if a person was keeping a gun warehouse behind the walls. Robberies could happen anywhere, but most criminals who were after large hauls weren't going to target a place like this. Then, that could have been thanks to the spray-painted signs, as well.

If he had been on patrol, this would have been one call he would have loved to take. With something like this, at a place that put off the don't-screw-with-me vibe, it was always because there was something interesting and usually dangerous to find.

"I don't feel good about this. Did you let dispatch know that we were heading out here?" Elle asked, running her hands over her hair.

"Don't worry. We will be just fine. Dispatch knows where we are. And you know what to do and how to do it if anything unexpected goes down." He tried to sound unconcerned but wasn't sure he had sold it.

Not to mention the fact that he hadn't actually told dispatch where they would be located. This had been a last-minute, seat-of-the-pants decision to come out here, but dispatch could find him via his phone if they needed to. His phone, just like everyone else's in America, could be tracked with little more than a few clicks of a button.

He pulled the truck to a stop and, with a quick check of his utility belt, stepped out.

"Don't go in the house," she said, still on guard.

The last thing he would do was enter that house, unless things went sideways. "Don't worry, babe, this will be okay."

Though there was no way he could promise anything other than that the future was unknown, she appeared to relax a tiny bit.

He closed his door behind him and looked back at her one more time before he walked up the steps and knocked on the front door. There weren't any visible cameras, but there easily could have been pinhole cameras carefully placed out of sight.

Grant could hear footsteps coming from inside the house. His heart picked up its pace, and he could feel a thin layer of sweat forming on his lower back, but he couldn't allow his central nervous system to kick in right now. He was the one who had to be in control, even in the midst of an adrenaline jolt.

He tensed to listen, hoping that from somewhere inside he would hear the pitter-patter of small footfalls and Lily's little voice calling out to him. Good God, it would feel so good to get this case buttoned up, and then he could think about all the things he wanted to do to Elle.

Beneath the *bomp, bomp* of an adult's footfalls was a strange pattering *click, click, click*.

He had to have been losing his mind or willing things into existence. There was no way in the world that just because he had been hoping to hear Lily's footfalls at that exact moment that he actually was, but then again, fact could be stranger than fiction.

"Hello?" he called, putting his hand on his sidearm.

"I'll be there in a goddamned minute. Hold your goddamned horses. I'm just putting on my pants." A man's voice, raspy and tired, sounded from inside.

The man could take all the time he needed; the last thing that Grant wanted to see was some guy's tally-wacker wiggling about while he asked him some questions. Unless it was like Pinocchio and grew any time he told a lie.

That was terrible.

Yet, he found himself chuckling. At the same time, he couldn't help the little voice in his head that wondered if that man wasn't actually in there putting pants on, but was instead loading a gun and getting ready to shoot him. A push of adrenaline ran through him, making his hands tremble ever so slightly. He squeezed them into tight balls, willing them to come back to fully being under his control.

Control. He breathed out as he knocked on the door again.

This time instead of the man yelling at him, the door flung open. He gripped his pistol, hard. At knee level, a black-and-white goat wearing a hand-knitted purple sweater with a large yellow *A* on it came bounding outside. It bleated at him, and he was sure it was as close to an expletive as a goat could muster.

He had seen some strange shit, but this was a new one. When he looked back, a man was standing in the doorway and smirking out at him. "What in the hell do ya want?" the man asked, spitting on the ground beside Grant's black boot.

Any hopes of getting this on the right foot were now shot.

He paused, taking in the man who was leaning against the door frame and sneering at him. He was balding, with a comb-over, fortysomething, and wore a torn flannel shirt. His hands were beat-up and his knuckles were bruised, but they seemed right at home on the fellow.

"Are you Steve Rubbick?" Grant asked, ever so

slightly angling so he was sure that the other man could see the badge attached to his utility belt.

The man's gaze flittered downward to his tin star, and the smirk disappeared. "What the hell do you want?"

"My name is Sergeant Anders from the Missoula County Sheriff's Office, and I was just hoping to ask you a few questions. Nothing too major," he said, trying to put the man a little more at ease.

The man bristled. "We don't need no law out here. You ain't welcome."

He wasn't sure what the man meant by "out here"—they were hardly off the grid, being only a few minutes outside the city, but he didn't dare press that issue. "I can understand you not wanting to talk to me today. I get that you weren't expecting this kind of visit during your day." He spoke unassumingly, trying his best to mirror the man and his speech. "I know when I get a day off from work, the last thing I wanna do is deal with all kinds of nonsense."

The man chuffed. "That ain't no shit." He leaned his body more against the frame, putting his hands over his chest.

At least he wasn't coming at him armed and ready for a showdown. "That's a nice little goat you got there. What's its name?"

The man smiled. He had all his teeth, but as he smiled his neck muscles shifted and exposed the tattoo at the base of his throat. Dollars for doughnuts, the goat's name was Adolf.

"He's Arnie and he's a real dumbass, and yeah, I'm Steve." He didn't extend his hand, but some of the steeliness that he had greeted Grant with had melted off. "That dumbass loves to eat all my goddamned flowers in the spring. Last year, I spent a buncha money on petunias at the store and he ate every damned one of 'em. He's lucky he ain't goat burger."

It was working; the man was letting his guard down and he wasn't even really aware he was doing it. This was one of Grant's favorite aspects of his job—figuring out how to relate to people to get them to open up. People, by and large, were creatures of habit. They ran by a system of social mores and cues that dictated their behaviors until drugs, alcohol or stress affected their judgment.

"I ain't owned a goat. I bet they're a lot of work." He smiled at the man, the action easy and coated with the proverbial butter. "I was always more of a dog person, myself."

The man laughed. "Oh, dogs are good, man. I always had 'em around as a kid, but goats… They best watchdogs I ever owned. Ain't no one gonna sneak up on me at night with ol' Arnie around."

This just kept getting stranger and stranger, but he wasn't sure he wanted to dig a whole lot more into the man's way of thinking, or else it might dirty his boots. He could empathize all day with odd thinking, but he had to remain objective in order to get this job done.

"I can't imagine who would be sneaking up on you. You got one nice little spread here."

The man puffed up with pride. "I worked real hard getting this place together. I worked for every dime I ever earned, and there ain't no one that is gonna think they're gonna step foot on here and take it away from me."

Though he didn't completely understand the man's ramblings, Grant got the general idea he didn't want to be screwed with. "I bet. What kind of work you do?"

"A little of this and that. I'm telling you, I worked harder than an ugly stripper for each and every dime."

He didn't doubt that for a minute; money was hard to come by for those who weren't born into it in this state. "You look like the security type. You workin' at the mall?" he asked, playing dumb.

The man huffed, clearly a bit put out by his assumption. "Damn, man, what kind of weekend Rambo do you think I am?" He snickered. "I just got back from spending the last six months overseas."

"Overseas, huh? So you've not been around here long? Know anyone named Clark? A girl named Lily?"

The man's eyes narrowed. "Clark's a pretty common name, and like I said, I ain't been back home long. Had a gig in the sandbox."

So, he was likely a contractor. But somehow it just didn't jibe. This man wasn't like any of the other contractors he had ever met. He was more like something out of an FBI video about who not to trust.

"What were you doing over there?" He leaned back a bit, flashing his badge like it had the same effect as truth serum.

The man glanced down, his eyes drawn by his reflexive action. "Well, I ain't supposed to be talkin' about it, but I've been cleaning up a few governmental messes here and there. You know, taking care of business that needs seein' to. That kind of thing."

"You've been contracting for the government, eh?"

The man beamed like he couldn't have been prouder if he had won a gold medal at the dumbass Olympics.

"Which outfit you work for?" Grant asked, giving the man an attaboy bump to the shoulder. "That's some cool shit right there. I got a couple of buddies who have spent some time over there in the sandbox, doing that kind of thing. Good money in it."

The man couldn't have puffed up any bigger or else the buttons on his shirt would have popped open. "Yeah, real good money. But ain't no picnic. You gotta be tough. I seen shit over there...man, there just ain't nothing like it." He stared off into space like he was picking up some memory, likely one that had the power to keep him up at night. That, or he was thinking of a woman. Either way, this man wasn't sleeping anytime soon.

As Rubbick spoke, Grant couldn't help but notice that he had carefully maneuvered around his pressing question. He was probably used to not giving answers, which was something Grant knew a little about himself.

"Who's the woman ya got out there?" the man asked, waving his hand in the general direction of his truck. "She a rider?"

He was a bit surprised Rubbick didn't at least recognize Elle if this was the same person who had been at the Clarks' house. Then, she had said that they had only briefly seen one another, and it was as she had been making her way out of the house. It was more than possible that she had just been a blip on Steve's radar.

"She is a friend of mine," Grant said, trying to sound relaxed and as if her presence was just a normal thing. "I know you can't tell me a whole lot, thanks to the NDAs in your life, but I need to get a few answers to my questions in order to cross you off my list in a murder investigation. You tell me the crew you're working with, and I'd be more than happy to give your boss a call and get you approvals to talk."

The man's eyes narrowed as though he was studying

Grant for signs of weakness, but he wasn't about to find any that Steve hadn't already inadvertently pointed out.

"Me and my brother, we're with STEALTH. They are out of Montana here."

The blood drained from his face and Grant had to put his hand against the house and pretend to lean in order to keep himself from swaying. The man had to be screwing with him. "Excuse me, you and your brother work for STEALTH? What's your brother's name?"

"My brother goes by Ace." The man nodded, sending him a crooked smile. "And yeah, STEALTH's a great crew."

He swallowed back the frog in his throat and tried to keep his gaze from skirting over to Elle. He didn't think the STEALTH crew was large enough to have members, especially in the same town, who didn't know each other. So, one of them had to have been lying to him, but who was it, Elle or this man?

"How long you guys been with that group?"

The man tapped his chin. "I guess it's been about a year now."

"Hmm." He couldn't remember how long Elle had been working with them, but he assumed she had been there for a long time. Maybe he had assumed incorrectly.

Or maybe they were both working for STEALTH but were intentionally kept away from one another and used as a system of checks and balances by their superiors. He'd heard of other organizations, the military usually, that used counterspies as a way to keep their troops accountable and from swaying in the wrong directions.

All the possible explanations he could come up with seemed unlikely, but for the life of him he couldn't wrap his head around everything the man's admission had just done to complicate his case—and Grant and Elle's burgeoning relationship.

Chapter Twelve

When Grant came back to the truck, he was oddly quiet. His eyes were shadowy, and he avoided meeting her gaze as he got in and buckled up. She wanted to ask him what was wrong, but she doubted Grant would tell her.

He slammed the door shut and rolled out of the driveway and onto the main road without a word.

"How did it go?" she asked, already somewhat knowing the answer, but not sure what else to say in order to alleviate the tension which was reverberating around inside the cab of the pickup.

"Fine." He scowled.

Oh shit.

She hated that word. *Fine* could mean a million different things—from calling out a hot woman on Venice Boulevard all the way to being the last word spoken at the end of a relationship.

In this moment, she had a feeling it was the end of something, and she hated the word even more.

"Did he admit to being at the Clarks' place the day Lily disappeared?"

"No." His jaw was set into a hard line.

"Did he know anything about Lily's current whereabouts?" She tried to unlock his jaw with another question.

He shook his head.

She chewed on the inside of her cheek, trying to think of a way to stop whatever it was that was happening between them. What could Steve have said that would have upset Grant like this? Grant hadn't arrested him, so that had to mean that he didn't believe, or at least couldn't prove, the man had anything to do with the crimes.

"Where are we going now?" she asked, hoping what he needed most was just a change of focus and then they could get back to being where they had been with one another before he had gone up to that damned house.

"I'm going to take you to your place. What's your address?" His words were short and hard, and they hit her like stones.

The air in her lungs escaped her as his words struck her. "I… You…" She motioned back toward the man's place. "What in the hell happened back there? We were doing good. We were a team, and now you come in here and act like I'm your enemy."

He let out a long sigh, and it reminded her of Daisy when she was trying to relieve her body of stress. It was funny how people liked to pretend they weren't animals. In all actuality, Daisy was a far better soul than either of them could ever hope to be. All Daisy cared about was loving and pleasing her, through her work and through her play. There were no complications, no games—only love.

"I'm sorry. I didn't mean to be an ass with you. Not my intention. I'm just… I guess I'm trying to sort through some new information. That's all." He put his hand out, palm side up and open and closed his hand like he wanted to hold her hand.

Was that where they were now? Could she hold his

hand? Five seconds before he had been furious. Did he think he could just give her his hand and everything between them would go back to being all good?

She couldn't help herself. There were all kinds of pains that could be healed with the complexity that came with a lover's touch. Not that he was her lover—not yet, anyway. And even if his touch didn't fix the weirdness that had come between them, at the very least she wouldn't feel quite as alone. They could navigate this as long as they were in it together, no matter what the world had in store for them.

She slipped her hand into his, and he wrapped his fingers around hers. His hand was so much bigger than hers that he nearly encompassed her completely. She liked that feeling of solidity that came with being touched by a man who was so much bigger than her; he made her feel as if he could protect her from almost anything.

"I know you don't want to tell me what happened, but I hope you know that I'm here if you need anything—even just someone to listen and help you sort through your thoughts."

He twitched as he looked over at her. There was something in the way he stared at her that made her feel as if he was trying to read her for secrets and lies. The warmth and sense of protection in his touch began to dissipate and be replaced with the bitterness of distrust. She tried to swallow back the flavor of it from her mouth, but it lingered on her lips.

He finally looked away. "Where are you staying?"

She tried to pull her hand back, but his grip tightened ever so slightly. "Why do you want to get rid of me?" she asked, trying to say the words lightly when all she really wanted to do was yell at him to just open up and tell her exactly what it was that was bothering him so much about her. "Why won't you tell me anything about your conversation? Did he tell you something about Lily? Something bad?" This wasn't merely new information—this had to be something to do with them. She could feel it. It couldn't be about Lily.

He let go of her hand. "Seriously, it's not about Lily. He…he didn't have anything valuable to give us. There hasn't been anything you've lied to me about, is there?"

"What?" she asked, frowning. "No, why? Did the guy tell you something, something that is making you question me?"

He stared out at the road like it was all he could focus on, but he wasn't blinking. She had hit on something.

"He did, didn't he?" she continued. "What did he tell you?"

"I just need to talk to your bosses. That's all." Finally, he let go of her hand, as though he was getting as frustrated as she was.

"Why? Please, Grant, talk to me." It felt weak having to beg him like she was, but she was out of ideas.

He ran his hand down the back of his neck and pulled his truck over to the side of the road.

What terrible thing had Steve told him that it required Grant to pull over in order to talk to her about it? She had seen cops talk on the phone, text and work on their computer, all while driving. She couldn't imagine anything that would have made him respond as he was.

"How long have you been working with your team?"

"The Shadow team or STEALTH?"

He shrugged. "Both."

She looked up and to the left as she tried to pull numbers from her memory. "My family and I have been working together, in some facet or another, for the last ten years. We are the only members of the Shadow team right now. As for STEALTH, we've been working for them for a couple of years. Why?"

"Do you know everyone who is employed with them?" he asked, staring over at her as he clenched the steering wheel.

"I know most, but they have contractors that work for them all over the world." She wasn't sure what he was getting after.

"Ah," he said, and his grip loosened on the steering wheel. "So, it's possible that there could be someone working out of here that you didn't know." He huffed. "I gotta say I'm relieved. I thought for sure that you would know everyone working here."

"I do. Or at least I think I do," she said, as what he was implicitly telling her sank in. "Wait, did Steve say he works for STEALTH?"

"Both him and his brother... Ace." He nodded. "I have to wonder if he was trying to screw with me." He chuckled and ran his fingers through his hair. "Not gonna lie, I'm not quite sure what the hell was going on back there. He threw me. I was worried you were hiding something from me. Something that could have screwed this investigation."

A pit formed in her stomach. She wasn't intentionally keeping anything from him, but that didn't mean anything. There could be any number of things he could have needed to know that she had at her fingertips and yet he was just failing to ask.

"I'm not going to hold anything back from you, Grant. I told you, you can trust me."

A smile finally flickered over his features. "You don't

know how much that means to me. Seriously. I have to admit, it freaked me out...the thought of you keeping something like that intentionally from me. I guess, without meaning to, I have come to trust you without you ever telling me it was okay. I felt a bit like a fool."

She smiled back. "There are only a few people in this world that I would say I trust with my life, but you are one of them. I feel lucky to have met you." She looked down at her hands, wishing she was still touching him. "But I have to say, you freaked me out, too. I want you to know that whatever you are thinking, just ask. I can't stand the thought of you thinking I'm something I'm not. And sure, I have a lot of secrets and I have made more mistakes and done things others would judge me for, but I don't want to ever have to hide anything from you."

She wanted him to be hers and for her to be his. She didn't know if he wanted the same, but if she didn't put herself out there and take advantage of these quiet and raw moments that seemed so scarce between them, she would regret it later.

"Why didn't you call me after the night in the woods?" he asked, and she couldn't ignore the faint hurt that flecked his voice.

She pressed her palms together as she tried to find the words. "I... I didn't know how to handle that—you. I just was such a mess. And to be completely honest with you, my team and I had been working hard to locate Lily."

"If you had found her, would you have even called me? Or would your team leaders have made the phone call to the department?" There was a note of insecurity in his words, and it made her chest ache.

"I would have called you. I just... I was a mess."

"But you aren't now?" he asked.

Though she was aware he was just trying to feel her out and measure what she was feeling toward him, she couldn't help but be a little hurt. "I know we've only just started hanging out. But being with you—" she paused, finding her words "—actually, just being *near* you is incredible. You drive me wild. I never, in my wildest dreams, imagined that I would kiss a man in the middle of a job."

He laughed.

"You can laugh all you want," she said, sending him a little smirk, "but I'm serious. I'm normally all business when I'm working. Especially when I have Daisy with me. And with Lily and Catherine, I needed to give them my solid focus, but up there on the mountain, sitting with you... I don't know how to explain it."

"But it felt *right*?" he asked, finishing her thought.

"Yes. *Right*." She smiled as he reached over and took her hand. He drew their entwined hands to his lips and gave her knuckles a kiss. "But it's something more than that. I just can't even—"

"I know exactly what you mean," he said, pulling his truck back on the road.

She wasn't sure that he did, but she was glad they were at least on the same page, a page that could serve as the first of many in building their full story together.

"If you want to talk to Zoey, I'm sure she would be happy to answer any questions you have," Elle said, glad to take some of the pressure off the emotions she and Grant were feeling and trying to navigate together.

She had never completely understood why love had to be so hard. In the history of her relationships, love had never been easy. She had felt love before, but it was something that was so fleeting in her life. If anything, love was a weakness. And maybe that was why she didn't want to talk about it, why they both wanted to push it away and simply focus on the task at hand.

But if they were going to make a go of this thing between them and try and strive for a real relationship, then they needed to talk about the feelings and the weaknesses that came with them. Yet she wasn't sure either of them was ready for that kind of thing. Like they had said, they had only known each other for a short time. In those limited days, love and lust had one hell of a way of looking like each other's identical twins.

After okaying exposing the location of their headquarters to him with Zoey, she pointed Grant in the direction of the Widow Maker Ranch. Sarge, the beloved black gelding who lived at the ranch, was running along the fence line as they made their way to the main house.

Zoey's office was offset from the house in a separate building not far from the stables. In the distance were a series of cabins and row houses. Leading to them was a dirt road, and at the end of it was a flatbed full of trusses, as if they were planning on building yet more cabins or houses.

"I live back there," she said, pointing to the cabin that sat second from the end closest to them. "It's a two-bedroom with one bath, but it fits me perfectly. I was just glad to have my own cabin. A couple of my siblings have chosen to take rooms in the house instead of private cabins." She didn't know why she was telling him all the superfluous details, but she would do anything to make things comfortable between them.

She had no idea why she was feeling so nervous with him—even with their hands intertwined and the acknowledgment that there were mutual feelings between them, she couldn't make her nerves recede. Part of her wondered if it was because of the lingering feeling of his lips on her skin and how badly she wished to feel them again.

"Zoey is probably over there," she said, pointing at the office. "That's our main headquarters. It's where we take reports and have our meetings."

Grant nodded. "But not everyone who works with STEALTH is allowed to be present?"

She shrugged. "No. The main team leaders are normally at most meetings, but folks like me—the grunts—are normally kept out. AJ or Zoey are normally the ones I get my information from."

He nodded and seemed far more at ease.

They parked and made their way over to the ranch's main office. The enormous room was newly constructed and still had the smell of fresh lumber, and it mixed with the ozone smell of the electronics that filled the main area. Zoey was sitting at the far end of the office and swiveled around in her chair as they walked inside. Her hair was purple today, and she had a fresh black tattoo on her neck. "Hey, guys, how's it going?"

Elle smiled. She'd always liked her boss; Zoey was the kind of woman who would not only take no crap from anyone, but she would also make sure that she protected all those around her. If Elle had a choice, she would be just like her when she grew up.

She chuckled at the thought.

"Sorry to bug you," Elle said. "This is Sergeant Grant Anders. He works over at the sheriff's office, and he is helping with the Clark case."

"Ah, I see." The small smile on Zoey's face disappeared, and she searched Elle's face like she was wondering what she had told Grant.

"He has some questions for you."

"Nice to meet you, Mrs.—"

Zoey stood up and stuck out her hand. "Just call me Zoey. I'm not about the patriarchal crap. I may be married and a mom, but no one owns me. My husband and I are partners."

Grant shook her proffered hand. "Nice to meet you. I appreciate you seeing me."

She crossed her arms over her chest, and as she moved, Elle could make out new ink on the top of her breasts, as well. The woman was so cool. Elle had never been one for getting tattoos, but Zoey had her questioning her stalemate on skin art.

"Most of the surveillance team is out for the day, but I should be able to get whatever it is you need," Zoey said, motioning vaguely at the computer screens lining the walls.

"That's great. Right now, though, we were just out talking to one of the men Elle pointed out from the Clarks' place before Catherine disappeared." He glanced over at Elle. "He mentioned that he was working for STEALTH."

Zoey nodded, turning away and making her way back to her workstation at the far end of the windowless room. "What did you say his name was?"

"Steve Rubbick. You heard of him?"

"Hmm. I don't know that name, but you know how it is. These guys could be working under any number of names." Zoey kept her face turned away from them as she tapped away on the computer. "What did he look like?" Finally, she glanced over her shoulder at them.

From the blank expression on Zoey's face, Elle would have said that Zoey was telling the truth about not knowing the man.

"He looks a bit like an extremist. Swastika right here on his neck," Grant said, pointing to the base of his throat.

"Ah," Zoey said. "Well, I don't have to search shit, then. While you can see I'm a fan of ink, I'm not about to hire anyone with gang tats or who are of a questionable moral character." She turned to face them. "I'm proud to say that we only hire contractors who have exceeded our standards and perform at a high ethical level both personally and professionally. We don't want to hire folks we have to monitor."

"Do you know a Philip Crenshaw?" Elle asked, thinking about the frat boy.

"I don't know the name. You have a picture?" Zoey asked.

Grant pulled up a picture of the man from his phone and showed it to Zoey. Zoey choked out a thin laugh. "Yeah, now him...him, I know. He tried to get hired on with us. I handled his interview process. Couldn't have recalled his name, though."

"But he doesn't work for you, I take it?" Grant asked.

Zoey pointed at him. "He had the credentials, but that man was a wild card. He'd had some things in his past that ran a little too far into the legal and ethical gray. I wasn't there and couldn't say if he was right or wrong in making the decisions he did in the heat of the moment, but let's just say I wouldn't have been pleased if he was working for us."

"Do you know where we could locate him?" Grant asked. "I couldn't pull anything up about his last known whereabouts."

"I can see what I can find on him. I will probably have

to use the facial recognition software. It may take me a while," Zoey said, pointing at the screens. "You guys have a few hours to burn?"

Elle wasn't sure about what Grant had on his docket, but she hated the thought of not actively searching for Lily. Yet there was little they could physically do without more information—info that was at the mercy of Zoey's tech skills.

"We can hang out for a bit." Grant nodded.

Elle smiled. "I'll just text you their pictures. Maybe you can see if you can pull up anything on Philip."

Grant looked over at Elle. "In the meantime, I'd love to take a look around your place."

That was the last thing she had expected Grant to say, and she could feel her cheeks burning at the thought of being alone with him in her house. At the same time, he hadn't said anything even slightly suggestive.

"Uh, yeah. I'd be happy to show you," Elle said, walking toward the office door with Grant following close behind her.

As they made their way outside, Zoey let out a belly laugh. "You guys have fun. I'll text when I find something. I won't come knocking."

Elle's face burned. Yeah, Zoey definitely worked on a whole different wavelength than she did; she was far bolder.

Their feet crunched on the frozen snow as they made their way across the parking area and toward the row houses. Her arm brushed against her pocket, and she felt the familiar bump of a phone and realized she still had Catherine's cell phone. "Wait." She pulled the phone out of her pocket and showed it to Grant, then held up her finger, motioning for him to wait for her there. "I'll bet she can make something out of this. I'll be right back."

Though she had started to go through the phone, she had found little usable information. The woman had a million contacts and got more texts and phone calls than a retail pharmacy. Elle had gone through what she could in the time she'd had, but given just the volume of information held in the iPhone, it could have taken her days to find anything—let alone anything that would point them toward the killer or Lily.

Zoey was already tapping away when she made her way back into the office. "'Sup? You guys done already? Girl, you work fast." She sent Elle a devious smile.

"We aren't that kind of friends," Elle said, but the burn returned to her cheeks. Just because they weren't those kinds of friends yet didn't mean that she didn't want to see him naked and underneath her.

"Yeah, right." Zoey laughed. "You do know I'm in intelligence, right? Even if I wasn't, I can see the way the two of you look at each other. Remind me not to put you into an undercover role. You can't lie for shit."

"You've put me in all kinds of undercover roles. I did great." She stuck her tongue out at Zoey.

"True as that may be, you can't lie to me about that man," Zoey teased. "Is there something you needed?"

"I forgot," she said with a nod, holding up the bagged phone for Zoey to see. "Here's Catherine's phone. I wrote the unlock code there on the bag." She handed over the phone, pointing at the numbers scrawled in black Sharpie.

"Sweet. I can definitely use this." Zoey gave her a wide smile. "In the meantime, seriously, go and have some fun."

Zoey stood up and shooed her out of the office, but

as Elle took one more look back at the computers, she saw Philip's face staring out at her from the screen. His eyes were dark and brooding, far from the jovial man she had last seen smoking a cigar while laughing with Catherine. The man staring out at her looked like a true, cold-blooded killer.

Chapter Thirteen

The little cabin was even smaller on the inside than it appeared on the outside, and Grant could understand why several of Elle's siblings had chosen to take rooms in the main house over these tiny dwellings. It was smart of the STEALTH company to keep their contractors on-site, especially given the nature of their work and the security risks.

Elle's hands were trembling as she pressed the numbers and unlocked the door. He wanted to tell her not to be nervous, that he didn't have anything less than completely honorable intentions on his mind. Yet he was as nervous as she was, and, well, the rest would have been a lie. He had wanted to press her down and make love to her from the moment their hands had touched. But he wouldn't pressure her for anything. If she wanted to be with him, she could lead the show.

Then, she didn't really seem like an aggressive kind of woman. He doubted she would take the lead and make the first moves.

She opened the door and flipped on the lights as Daisy came barreling down the hallway toward them. "Daisy girl!" she said, clearly as happy to see the dog as the dog was to see her.

Daisy dropped down and rolled over in front of them, her tail wagging so hard that her whole entire butt moved right and left on the vinyl flooring. Elle squatted down and loved on the animal as he chuckled. There was nothing sexier than a woman playing with and loving on her dog.

Daisy stood up and finally seemed to notice him; she lunged toward him and rubbed herself around his legs, almost catlike in her excitement. He was slightly taken aback by the dog's warm reaction to his being there, but they had spent a night together taking care of Elle. "Hi, Daisy," he said, squatting down and giving the dog a vigorous scratch behind the ears. "I missed ya, pupper dog."

He caught Elle smiling out of the corner of his eye.

Daisy gave him a big, slobbering kiss to the side of his cheek. Daisy's breath smelled like dog food.

"Oh," Elle said, covering her mouth with her hands. "She's not much of a licker. Sorry about that. If it makes you feel better, she is the ranch dog who is the least addicted to eating horse manure."

"I'm glad." He laughed, but as Elle must have realized what she said, her face turned crimson.

"I, uh…" She ran her hand down the back of her neck and looked toward the main living area. "Obviously, I don't have people out to my place very often. I'm sorry if it's a mess. In fact, I can't say that anyone other than my family has been here." She cringed as she looked at her couch, where a basket full of folded laundry sat ready to be put away.

"Your place is cleaner than mine," he said. "I get two days off a week, and I have to say that I don't really enjoy spending my downtime doing chores. I can't even tell you the last time I mopped a floor. Don't feel bad."

"With Daisy around, if I didn't mop the place, it would be covered in muddy paw prints." She let Daisy outside. The dog bounded away, and Elle looked about, making sure she was safe, then closed the door. "She should be good outside for a little while. She sticks around. Want a drink or something?" She rushed away from him toward the kitchen, as if being close to him was making her even more nervous than she had first seemed when they arrived.

He followed her toward the kitchen. "I'd take some water, but I can get it." He wasn't sure who was more on edge, her or him. It was as if all the feelings he'd been having for her had culminated into this single moment and he couldn't quite sift through them all.

He walked to the small cabinet by the sink and grabbed a glass out of the cupboard, but before he could fill it with water, he turned around toward her and put the glass down on the counter. "Are you sure you are okay with my being here? We could just go back to my truck or—"

She moved toward him and threw her arms around his neck, and her lips pressed against his. For a second, he couldn't quite make sense of what was happening, but then he wrapped his arms around her and pulled her body against his as he kissed her back. She nibbled at his lower lip, and her tongue flicked against his.

He hadn't pegged her as the dominant type, but he had never been more excited to be wrong. She leaned into him, and though he couldn't tell, it felt like she was even lifting her leg as she tiptoed to kiss him. He slid his hands down from her back and took her ass into his hands. It felt even better in his palms than he thought it would. She had to work out, but not so much that there wasn't the softness that he loved on a woman.

She was the perfect combination of soft and toned, feminine but strong.

He laced his lips down her neck, and her breath caressed his skin in a moan. His body awakened at the sound. He could listen to that sound, the weak moan of a woman in want, forever. His lips found the base of her throat, and he traced his tongue along the hard edges of the little V-shape. She sucked in her breath and held it.

He stopped, taking a moment to look at her. Her eyes were the color of the sky in the middle of a storm, promising a temporary break for the sunshine. "You are so damned beautiful. You know that, don't you?"

She tried to avoid his gaze, but he drew her back with his finger until she was staring at him again. "Don't look away. You don't need to. I want to look at you, all of you." Her gaze drifted to his chest, but he didn't know exactly what she was thinking. "If you're not ready for this, or if you are rethinking things with me, don't worry, you can tell me. We can stop this right here and now. We can just go back to being friends."

Elle reached up and took his hands in hers and finally looked up into his eyes. "No. That's not it. I want you. I want this. I want to do things with you that I've never done with anyone else. I just…"

"You don't feel it?"

She frowned. "What? No."

"Then what is bothering you?" He kissed her hands but kept looking into her eyes.

"I haven't had sex in a long time. I just don't want to be bad." Her hand tensed in his.

He started to laugh but checked himself as she began to pull away. "No, don't go. I didn't mean to laugh. You surprised me, that's all. I thought you didn't want me—I didn't even think you could possibly be feeling insecure about anything. You are the most beautiful woman I've ever known."

"You don't need to lie to me. I know I'm not ugly or anything, but I'm hardly anything special." She looked away again.

He leaned in close and whispered into her ear, "You are something incredibly special to me." He kissed the top of her ear ever so gently. "And I am not concerned about how you are in bed. I think that as long as we are together and we talk, we can be amazing together. You just have to talk to me. Okay?"

She looked up at him and smiled, and there was a new light in her eyes. "It's funny, you telling me that, when that's all I've wanted from you from the very beginning."

"We both have a lot to learn. I will never be perfect—"

"And you know I'm not," she said, giggling.

"You are much closer than I am, but regardless, we can be imperfect together." He kissed her forehead and ran his hands through her hair, pushing it behind her ears and cupping her face. "Well, you can be perfect and I can try to keep up." He kissed her lips gently. "And I promise I will try to talk to you, to tell you what I'm thinking."

She reached up and unbuttoned the top of his shirt. "Right now, all I'm thinking about is how badly I've wanted you."

He smiled wildly. "What do you want me to do to you?"

She looked at him with wide eyes, leaning back in mock surprise. A cute smirk took over her lips. "Take off your shirt." She let go of him and stepped back.

He felt silly, but Elle telling him what to do was so damned sexy, he could have eaten it all up. "As you command," he said, slipping the buttons clear of the holes and leaving his shirt open and loose.

"All the way off," she said.

"Elle." He whispered her name in surprise as he slipped his shirt off his shoulders and let it drop to the floor. He reached for her, but she stepped back playfully.

"What?" she asked, giving him an innocent look. "Vest, too."

He peeled the Velcro straps open and pulled the vest over his head. Then he stripped off the white T-shirt that he always wore underneath.

She sucked in a breath as she watched him, making him smile. That was one hell of a reaction, a reaction he would never get enough of hearing.

"I thought you were feeling out of practice?" he teased.

"That doesn't keep me from knowing exactly what and how I want it. It just means I've had plenty of time to think of all the ways I want to be pleased."

He pressed hard against his zipper. There was just something so sexy about a woman who could talk openly and honestly about sex. If they could say what their hearts desired, then they were probably more than happy to do all the things they wanted to do with their body, as well. And that, that freedom, was something he had always found a great quality in a lover.

She may have been out of practice, but he had no doubts that she was going to be the greatest lover he had ever been with. Then, he had to be grateful for any woman who wanted to give him the gift of allowing him to enter her body.

The thought of slipping inside her, slowly…so slowly… and watching her face made him feel as if he was going to drip.

"Now what do you want me to do?" he asked, opening his arms and exposing his naked chest to her.

She stepped closer and ran her fingers over the tattoo on his left pec. "What was this for?" she asked, tracing the edges of the black bear paw.

Her fingertips moved slowly along the paw; in their tenderness it reminded him of the pain and reasons he'd chosen to get the tattoo. "One of my best friends was killed in the line of duty. He was shot while performing a routine traffic stop that turned ugly. I got it in his memory, over my heart—I never want to forget that in my world, every day is a gift."

She moved in closer, pressing her body hard against him. "That is beautiful and so true." Her hands slipped down his chest, running over the lines of his stomach and toward his utility belt.

He reached down and unclicked his belt, carefully taking it off so it didn't bump against her. There was nothing worse than dropping that heavy-ass thing on a toe. He threw it on the couch behind them. Before turning back, he glanced at the front windows and made sure the drapes were pulled closed. The last thing they needed was someone walking by and peeking in on what he hoped was about to happen. He needed to protect her privacy as much as he did his own.

"We should take this to the bedroom." He reached for her hand, and she nodded, leading him down the short hallway.

The place was simple, two bedrooms and a bathroom, kitchen and a living area. For his life it would have been perfect. He had to imagine it was for hers, as well.

She slipped the door closed behind them and clicked on a bedside lamp, casting her purple bedroom in a thin light that made everything in the room seem like something out of a burlesque club. He hadn't imagined her bedroom being anything like it was, though he had to admit he had never thought of anything in her bedroom besides her.

There were black satin sheets on her bed, and just like the woman they belonged to, they whispered of fantasies so close to being realized that he was forced to reach down and unzip his pants.

"Take them off," she said, motioning to his pants.

He slid the zipper all the way down and then let them fall to the floor, exposing his gray boxer briefs. She smiled as she glanced at his package, and her expression made his heart leap with joy as he took pride in knowing she liked what he had to offer.

Yet she had no idea. If there was one thing he prided himself on, it was knowing how to please a woman. There was nothing that he would rather do than bring the woman he was with pleasure. He'd heard about men being selfish lovers, only caring about getting theirs, but what was the point of such behavior? He would get his, that wasn't a question, so why not take joy in the journey of pleasure that two people could experience together?

He'd never understand a woman who stayed with a man who wouldn't try to make sure she enjoyed herself to the fullest. If he wasn't selfless in the bedroom, what made a woman think he would try to make her happy outside the bedroom?

"Where is your mind right now?" she asked, looking up at him with an inquisitive look on her face.

He smiled. "I was thinking about all the ways I want to pleasure you." Reaching over to her, he slipped his hands under the edges of her shirt and slowly pulled it up and over her head, exposing her hot-pink lace bra. He felt stupid for thinking she was a blue underwear kind of girl when she stood there wearing this.

If he wasn't already hard enough to cut glass, the sight of her luscious curves would have done it. If he wasn't careful, he was going to have to apologize for losing control.

"It's your turn." He motioned to her pants.

Instead of listening, she turned to her phone and clicked a few buttons. As impatient as he was for things to continue, he was glad for the reprieve. Chris Stapleton started to play from a Bluetooth speaker she had set up in the corner of the room. This was a girl who knew how to set a mood.

With the beat of the music, she unbuttoned her pants and slipped them down her thighs, pulled them off and threw them on the footboard of her bed. She was wearing hot-pink panties that matched her bra. He'd once heard that if a woman was wearing matching underwear, then they had chosen to have sex when they'd gotten dressed that day. Had she known this was going to happen all along, that they were going to find themselves in a position to share their bodies?

The thought alone turned him on, and in combination with her standing in front of him…*damn.*

A growl rippled from his throat, and he pulled her into his body. He wanted to rip those panties off her with his teeth and then gently kiss every part of her body that the lace had touched.

She gasped as his mouth found her throat, and he cupped her breast in one hand and the small of her back with the other. Every part of her was about to become his.

"Tell me you want me, Elle." He sounded raspy as he spoke her name, and she shivered under his touch.

"Grant, I've wanted you...since the first time we met." She was breathless with want.

"I know that's not true, but I appreciate it anyways," he said with a slight laugh. "I was a dick when we first met, and I'm sorry. But I'm glad you saw past that... that you were patient with me while I found my way to you." He kissed the lace at the top of her bra, taking in the soft scent of flowers on her skin. "To here. To now." He pushed the lace away, exposing her nipple and pulling it into his mouth.

She threw her head back and arched her back as he sucked. He popped it out of his mouth and licked the sensitive nub, then rubbed it gently with his thumb as if thanking it for allowing him the honor of tasting her.

She gasped as he repeated himself on her other side.

He moved his hand between her legs, over her panties, and traced her wet, round mounds until he found what he was looking for. Dropping down to his knees, he pulled off her panties, not wanting to destroy his new favorite article of clothing—one he hoped to see again in the future.

He lifted her leg over his shoulder and pulled her into his wide-open mouth. He grabbed her, holding her upright even though her body threatened to collapse. He licked her like she was a Popsicle, not just some damned little lollipop. He wanted her all in his mouth and he wouldn't stop until she was either dripping down his chin or begging for something else.

He was her plaything, and they were both going to love every second of it.

Her body moved in tandem with his tongue, rolling

and pressing, pulling and sucking. It could have been minutes or hours, he had no idea. He was lost in her.

"Grant…" She moaned his name as he felt her clench around his tongue and gasp. "Oh my…" She moved, and he didn't miss a beat as she fell back against the wall and gave herself fully to her release.

She panted his name as she pulled him up to his feet. "You…are fantastic," she whispered, taking his lips and licking herself from them.

Reaching down, she slipped him inside her, and as she did, he knew that without a single doubt, he had found the woman and the place that could be his forever.

Chapter Fourteen

She was shocked Zoey hadn't texted or come and knocked on her door by now; she was normally super quick at pulling information from a multitude of sources even when on her own. Elle looked down at her watch. It was getting late.

The last thing Elle wanted to do was to move from her place on Grant's chest to pick up her phone and send Zoey a text, but now that she could think about something other than him, she needed to refocus on their case.

Lily was still missing, and Elle had to believe she was alive somewhere, just waiting for them to find her. Maybe Zoey had come up with something by now.

With a groan, she moved off his chest, and he finally looked up. "Where are you going?" he asked, touching her back as she sat up.

"Have you heard from anyone?" she asked, nudging her chin in the direction of his phone that was hanging haphazardly out of the back pocket of his pants. "I can't believe we actually got to be alone for this long. Normally one of our phones is going off." She frowned. Was something happening, something that was keeping everyone so busy that they had forgotten to inform them? Her anxiety rose.

He sat up, grabbing his phone as she did the same. "All I have is the regular thing—texts from my guys at the department and a few emails. Nothing to do with the case. You?"

She picked up her phone, and it vibrated in her hand. There was a text from Zoey.

Shit. What did we miss?

If something had happened while they had been making love and their temporary reprieve from reality had affected their case and finding Lily, she wasn't sure she would forgive herself—even though the sex with Grant had been absolutely breathtaking.

Zoey's text was vague, nothing more than Give me a call.

Did that mean she had found nothing? That all the information they had given her had proven to be of little use and they were really going to be starting from square one once again?

They shouldn't have waited. They shouldn't have taken any downtime. Why did the needs of their bodies, to feel one another, have to be so extreme?

She glanced over at Grant, who was leaning back in the bed and had one hand under his head against the headboard. His tattoo was stretched over his pec and she found herself staring at him again, wondering how she had gotten so lucky to find him in her bed.

If she wasn't careful, and if she didn't have such a personal connection to the case at hand, she could have easily found herself falling back into those arms and going for several more rounds. She could have made love to him every day for the rest of her life, if the fates would allow.

Yet she couldn't help but worry that now he had been with her, he was going to wake up from whatever lust trance she had managed to cast on him and realize he was out of her league.

She was an empowered woman in a male-dominated field, and logically she knew that what she felt was non-sensical, but she couldn't help the dark voice in the back of her mind that told her she wasn't enough for Grant. Unfortunately, this wasn't the first time she had felt this way around a man. The last time, she had tried to make the guy happy, telling him what he wanted to hear at the expense of being herself and living her truth. In the end, she had morphed into someone she had thought he wanted instead of her authentic self, the one he had said he had once loved.

She couldn't overthink this if she wanted to keep Grant. Well, if he wanted to keep her.

Running her hands over her face, she tried to wipe away the thoughts that were haunting her. She stood up and put on her clothes, slipping her phone into her pocket. She was almost afraid to face Grant in the event he would see she was already starting to feel insecure.

Though she was sure she could feel safe with him, and as soon as he pulled her back into his arms she would feel right at home, she feared it. To fall in love, to be her authentic self with this man was to make herself truly vulnerable. And any time she had ever been vulnerable with a man—well, with anyone, really—she ended up hurting.

Until she was sure he was worth suffering for, completely, she needed to protect her heart. And she wouldn't protect it by giving herself to him again, or by giving away any more of her power in what relationship they did have.

"I'll take by you getting dressed that Zoey must have texted you?" he asked, making her realize she had never really answered his question and had just had an entire fight with him without ever saying a word.

Or was it a fight? Maybe it was just her being self-conscious.

If he took her in his arms and kissed away all the feelings she was having right now, he was the one—the man she could love, the man who could read her body and just solve all of her problems.

"She wants to see us." He picked up his clothes and started to get dressed, too.

She'd hoped for a sign, maybe something in neon, that suggested they had a future together—she would have liked for him to be her forever—but she shrugged off the sentiment. She wasn't a teen crushing on her idol. There was work to do.

Making her way out to the kitchen, she grabbed a bottle of water and a second one for Grant, putting his on the counter while she waited.

Hoping for a sign might have been too much to ask for, but there had to be something that told her he was the one…something he did or said that could prove he wanted her for something besides her body and that thing that had happened between them hadn't occurred just because it had been a possibility. She just needed some kind of solid proof that this was *real* and not just another lover—as much for herself as for him.

Her phone rang, and she pulled it from her pocket. It was Zoey. "Hello?"

She was met with the muffled sound of a phone being moved around and Zoey yelling things in the background. Though she wasn't sure what she was listening to, Zoey's voice made her blood run cold as she screamed for help.

The line went dead.

"Grant!" She dropped her water bottle.

He came running down the hall, his shoes untied. "What? Are you okay?"

"We have to go." She grabbed her coat and slipped her gun into her waistband as she moved outside.

He followed behind her as he readjusted his utility belt. "What's going on?"

"Zoey needs us." She motioned her chin in the direction of the office.

He tied his shoe and quickly caught up to her as she sprinted toward headquarters. There weren't any cars she didn't recognize in the ranch's parking lot, but that didn't mean anything. This ranch had been infiltrated by enemies before. It had happened before she was hired, but there was still talk about it to this day—normally after a night centered around campfires and whiskey, like the former attacks were some kind of horror story that were used to scare them at night.

It worked.

She shoved open the door to the office, and it slammed against the wall behind it. She expected to find Zoey mid-swing in some kind of fistfight. Instead, Daisy was on the ground wrestling with a stray dog Elle didn't recognize. The stray was bloodied and its ear was half hanging on, and as it jumped up to its feet, it snarled at her as though it was going to attack.

"Daisy!" Elle screamed, watching as her dog lunged, taking down the dark brown mutt-looking dog.

She wasn't upset with her dog, but she was afraid. Daisy was her baby. Nothing could happen to her baby. And yet, there was nothing she could do.

The dogs tore at each other, ripping with the teeth and diving for each other's throats. Daisy seemed to be winning, standing over the dog and having it pinned down to the ground between her front legs. But the brown dog broke free and grabbed Daisy's front leg and swept it out from underneath her, dropping her to the ground and taking the top.

Elle's throat threatened to close as she watched the dog tear away at Daisy's fur, throwing black hair every which way around the office.

She looked up at Zoey, who was standing there, looking as at a loss as Elle felt. What had happened that had caused the fight? Then, what did it matter? All that mattered was that Daisy came away from this unharmed. She couldn't stand the thought of losing her baby.

Just like everything else that had gone wrong, this was her fault, too. She had been so stupid. She should have been focusing on her case instead of taking Grant to her bed. If she had just kept her head in her work, Daisy wouldn't have found herself in the position she was.

It was no wonder Elle couldn't keep Lily safe when she couldn't even keep her own dog from being hurt.

What would have ever possessed Zoey or the Clarks to ever entrust her with a damned child?

"Daisy, come!" she yelled, hoping the dog could hear her over the melee, but Daisy only looked at her with the white-eyed stress eyes of a dog in trouble.

She had to do something. There was no way she could stand here any longer and just watch as her dog was hurt.

Picking up an office chair, she jabbed at the snarling stray, pressing against it with the wheels until the dog unlatched from Daisy's throat. Elle's fingers pressed into the coarse carpet-like fabric as she lunged, using the chair like it was a door-breaching ram.

"Get out of here, dog!" she screamed.

Grant held open the door as she pushed at it with the chair until the brown dog stepped outside, its hackles raised and its teeth bared. When it realized it was no longer cornered in the office and had found its way back outside, the dog looked around wildly and took off in the direction of the mountains.

"What happened? How'd the fight start?" She turned on Zoey.

Zoey shook her head. "I think Daisy was trying to defend me, but I don't know. The dog just showed up and there was a snarl and..." She trailed off.

Daisy laid her head down on the ground and whimpered, and Elle ran over, sliding on her knees on the tile floor as she neared the animal. "Are you okay, baby? Mama is here," she said, careful to reach down and touch the dog gently in case she was still scared.

Daisy looked up at her with a sad, pained expression. "Let me look you over, honey. I promise I won't hurt you. I just need to check that everything is okay."

She looked back over her shoulder at Grant as she touched Daisy's shoulder. "You need to go find the other dog. Make sure it's okay. And it'll have to be tested for rabies."

He nodded, but he didn't look nearly as worried or upset as she did, and the thought irritated her. "And hurry about it. If that dog is hurt and heading to the mountains, we may never find it again if you don't move fast. I don't want to have any other lives on my hands." She spat the words, feeling the hurt in them but not allowing it to register.

Though she wasn't looking, she could feel the unspoken conversation that was happening between Zoey and Grant right over her head, and it pissed her off even more.

She had every right to be angry—at the situation, at her choices and at the fact she had once again fallen short.

She was so goddamned tired of not being enough and of doing something for herself for once and instantly having to pay the price in a pound of her best friend's flesh.

She leaned into Daisy and put her forehead against the dog. "I'm so sorry, honey. I've got you, Daisy. I shouldn't have left you outside. I'm so, so sorry."

The dog leaned in and gave her a sweet lick to the side of the face, like she was accepting the apology, even though Elle was nowhere near deserving of the dog's mercy.

That, this bond between her and Daisy, was what true love was. Pain and misery, injury and assault, and then forgiveness and love beyond all that agony. It was seeing a being at its worst and in its most vulnerable state and yet staying by their side.

It was endless faithfulness. No matter what.

No man, not even Grant, could offer her the same love as Daisy.

She had been a fool to be so selfish. Never again.

There was a growing pool of blood around Daisy's neck and chest. It stained the white tile floor, and Elle tried not to panic. Ever so gently, she ran her hands down the dog's body over the lumps and welts caused by the dog's bites and then around her thoracic area until her fingers felt the warm, wet tear just below her throat and at the front edge of her right shoulder.

"Baby..." she cooed, tears welling in her eyes and forcing her to blink them back. "Zoey, grab me some towels."

Zoey ran past her and headed toward the bathroom, coming out with a stack of hand towels and a roll of pink vet wrap. "Will this work?" she asked, handing it all over to her.

"Just press that towel right here, keep your pressure." Elle stood up and ran toward the back room where they kept all of their tactical gear in case they needed to bug out.

She pulled open her locker, exposing her black tactical bag, and pulled out a QuikClot kit she kept in it all the time in case of emergencies. She didn't know if the clotting agents would work on her dog, but she couldn't think of a reason they wouldn't. And, at the very least, it would slow the bleeding enough that she could hopefully get Daisy to the vet's office.

Elle made her way out to the main office and ripped open the kit. Zoey moved back, and she pressed the pad to the dog's exposed muscle. Daisy whimpered, trying to lick at the wound and pull off the gauze, but Elle kept her from getting to the pad. "Hold the pad there for a second," she said, motioning for Zoey to take over.

"It's going to be okay," she said to Daisy, repeating it over and over while she made sure the dressing stayed on the wound by wrapping it in the pink vet wrap.

From the look of the wound, it wasn't too bad as long as they got the bleeding stopped. After that, she would just need stitches and time to heal. Hopefully.

Elle pulled a shirt off the hook by the door and slipped it over the dog's head and covered up the wound and the dressing. "That's my good dog, Daisy. Mama has got you."

She stood up and, lifting with her knees, picked the rottweiler up. She held her against her chest as she looked over at Zoey. "Grab the door, will you?"

Zoey rushed by, holding open the office door and then

jogging ahead of Elle to open up the back door of one of the ranch trucks. She put down a blanket and then helped lift Daisy inside. The dog's eyes were still wide, but now it appeared as if it was more the pain and most of the adrenaline had started to wear off.

Zoey ran back to the office and quickly locked up; when she came back, she was carrying the truck's keys.

Daisy let out a long, breathy moan and laid her head down on the blanket and gave Elle one more look before closing her eyes. The look made Elle's stomach pitch. Daisy was going to be all right. She had made her pup a promise, a promise she intended on keeping no matter what.

Clicking the back door shut gently, she made her way around to the passenger's side of the truck and moved to get inside. She looked toward the mountain, and as she did, she caught a movement out of the corner of her eye. Walking out of the woods, carrying the brown dog, was Grant. He'd wrapped the dog in a blanket, but it was looking up at him like he was some kind of hero.

She ran toward his truck and flung open the doors as he approached, carrying the other pup. Though she was upset about what had happened, it was terrible to ever see an animal in distress. "Is she okay?" Elle asked, motioning toward the dog as Grant moved to set her in the back.

"She is banged up, needs a few stitches. How's Daisy?" He ran his hand down the dog's head and scratched her gently behind the ears. The dog was panting but otherwise seemed to have fared better.

"Same, but seems to be hurting." She looked back over at Zoey. "We are heading to the vet's office. Follow us over." She started to jog back to the ranch truck but stopped and looked back at Grant. Her heart pulled her back to him, but if forced to choose, she couldn't leave Daisy alone. Not again.

"Grant?" she called, and he looked in her direction. "Thank you. I appreciate you finding the dog. You're a good man." She gave him a sweet, delicate smile and a tip of the head.

It had been a long time since she'd been around a man who wasn't on the Shadow team who could actually be trusted. It hurt her deeply to turn away from him and go to the ranch truck, to her waiting boss and her dog, but she knew she had to focus on the sure things in her life, and they included Daisy, Zoey and the STEALTH team. When she allowed herself to get distracted, she let them all down.

Chapter Fifteen

With the dogs back in surgery at the after-hours emergency vet clinic, Grant was left standing in the waiting room with Zoey and Elle. He had a sinking feeling that Elle felt this was partially his fault, that if they had been focusing on the things they had been hired to focus on, that none of this would have happened to her dog. He couldn't blame her.

Though he didn't own an animal, he understood the bond that came with owning one. He and his dog Duke had been inseparable until Grant had gone off to college. Duke crossed the rainbow bridge when he was away, and when he'd come home, it had never again felt the same. A part of him had gone over that bridge with his best friend.

If Elle was feeling even a small percentage of that same kind of pain, it was crazy to him that she was even allowing him to stand in the same room with her. The lady at the desk disappeared into the back, and Zoey finally turned to them. "This is probably going to take a while."

Elle nodded, and as he looked at her, he noticed how tired she looked. It wasn't just the kind of tired that was in the eyes. Instead, it appeared as though it was all the way down in her bones. He wanted to hold her and comfort her, but here in front of her boss seemed like one hell of a piss-poor place. She needed to keep it together in front of her boss, at least as much as she could, given the circumstances, and if he pulled her into his embrace, he had a feeling he would have to take her back to bed and hold her until her tears ran dry.

"I know you don't want to leave Daisy," Zoey said, looking down at her hands and then flipping her purple hair back and out of her face. "Did you ever get my text?"

Elle nodded.

"Did you manage to pull something?" Grant asked, hoping for the best.

Zoey pushed her hands over her chest and looked around as though making sure that they were alone and couldn't be overheard. "I had a phone call. It wasn't *great.*"

His heart rate spiked. "What is that supposed to mean?"

Zoey looked over at Elle and then at him. "Senator Clark called me not long after you left my office." She cleared her throat like trying to remove the discomfort that was reverberating between them. "He made it clear that he will be pursuing a lawsuit against our group for negligence in the death of his wife and disappearance of his daughter. He is going to try and ruin us."

Holy shit.

Elle opened her mouth then closed it several times, and a single tear slowly escaped her eye and trembled down her cheek. "I... I'm so sorry." Elle sounded choked, like Zoey's statement was gripping her throat and threatening to kill the last parts of her soul that had, up until now, remained unscathed.

This was all his doing. Clark hadn't been gunning for Elle until they had pulled him off the woman admirer outside the airport. He should have known better than to publicly embarrass the senator, especially in front of a woman he might have been trying to get into his bed. The man was a narcissist, and while Grant was sure that he was hurting after his wife's death and the loss of his daughter, for a man like the senator, the worst kind of pain was always going to be the pain to his ego. He was nothing if he wasn't being pedestaled and revered—especially by the opposite sex.

"He is just looking for someone to blame," Grant said.

Elle looked at him, and there were more tears in her eyes. He could tell there were a million things she wanted to say, but in her current broken state he would take this on for her. If this was the only way he could show how much he cared about her, how much he secretly *loved* her, he was going to protect her. He was her man, even if only in his heart and only until the end of this case. She needed him, though she would never say it aloud.

"I know you're right," Zoey said, careful to avert her gaze from Elle in what he assumed was an attempt to allow Elle a moment to collect herself and keep her dignity intact.

He always hated losing his edge in front of a superior officer. That kind of thing had the power to kill a career, or at least throw a major hurdle in front of advancement. Maybe it was different for women, he didn't know, but he didn't think it would be good for her, either.

He stepped in front of Elle, shielding her with his body even though he was sure that Zoey cared for her. There was a bond between the two women, he could see it in the way they treated one another. No doubt, it was a saving grace in their line of work. It probably even provided them with some additional level of protection, to have a fellow woman at her side, but that didn't mean that weakness would be perceived as anything other than just that. And in teams like theirs, weaknesses could bring harm.

Elle exhaled, and he could feel her move behind him like she was brushing the tear from her face and shaking off the display of emotions. She stepped out and took her place beside him. "So, if you know it is just misplaced anger and this really isn't my fault—"

Zoey stopped her with a raise of her hand. "Whoa. I didn't say it wasn't our fault."

"You mean *my* fault," Elle said.

Zoey looked away. "All I'm saying is that things could have gone differently. There were definitely some aspects of our handling of our security duties that could have been better. Perhaps better communication from both sides of the desk would have stopped this from ever happening. Regardless, we are going to walk away from this incident with a large black eye and an even larger hit to our bankroll."

"Don't worry about your bankroll," Grant said. "I'm sure that we will make things right here. We will get Lily back and find whoever was responsible for Catherine's death."

"Even if you do, I don't know if that is going to stop the senator from gunning for us," Zoey said. "And as such, I can only do one thing to protect our company. It's something I don't want to do, Elle. Especially not here and now, but my hands are tied…at least until and *if* you guys can get the senator off our ass. Elle, I need you off the team."

Elle nodded. He expected her to cry, but instead her jaw was set and anger sparked in her eyes. She pushed past Zoey and made her way outside.

"What in the hell, Zoey?" he growled. "You don't move against your team members when they need you the most. She did her goddamned job, she did exactly what she was told and now you are taking this out on her? You are wrong right now in how you are handling this, and I think you know it. She was already hurting, and you just took her out at the knees."

Zoey started to say something, but he didn't want to hear it.

"I have been a part of this investigation from day one, and let me tell you, from everything I can see, she isn't the one in STEALTH who was the problem." He looked her up and down and then, without waiting for her to speak, he charged out of the office.

Elle was sitting in his pickup staring out through the passenger-side window and into space. He had no idea how he was going to fix this. Even if he could, he wasn't sure that the damage to her career would be repairable. While STEALTH would likely recover, it was doubtful that Elle could say the same.

He still just couldn't believe that Zoey would have moved against one of her own like this, but going against a senator could be deadly if she and her team weren't careful. It was one of those situations in which it was live by the sword, die by the sword. They had chosen to work with vipers, now they would have to take the teeth.

Unfortunately, the teeth had pierced the neck of the mother of the child she had promised to protect.

As he got in and they hit the road, there was an impenetrable silence between them. He didn't know if he should tell her he was sorry or unleash a diatribe about how stupid her boss was, so he remained quiet. She and Zoey had been friends, but that probably only made what had just happened that much worse. She had been wounded by someone she trusted.

Her phone pinged, and he looked over and saw a text from Zoey flash over the screen. "What does she want?" he asked.

"I'm sure it's not to apologize and beg me to come back. And even if it was…" Elle sighed as she clicked the message off without reading it.

Grant touched her knee. "If you don't like your job, if you want to follow another path in life, you have my support. I will do whatever you need to help you out."

She chuffed. "I have no idea what to do right now. I don't have any damned answers. If you didn't notice, my entire life just came crashing down. The last thing I want or need is some guy who is only going to make things worse."

Was that what he had become, just *some guy*?

He wanted to argue with her, to tell her what she had just done to him and to his feelings. He wanted to tell her how all he wanted to do was be the man she needed and not like the men in her past who must have let her down. He loved her. But she mustn't have felt the same way.

In that case, he just needed to button his feelings up and cinch them down. He wasn't a fan of self-inflicted pain, and that's what he'd be doing to himself if he kept after her when it was clear she was dismissing him.

Though he was more than aware she was likely striking at him out of her own pain, he hadn't been prepared.

Yet, what did it matter? He had his answer as to her feelings toward him one way or another. At least it was a solid, unwavering rejection. A clear rejection was far better than half-assed feelings and empty promises.

"Stop," Elle said, touching his hand on her knee as she stared down at her phone. "Pull over."

"What?" he said, jerking the wheel to the right and pulling the truck to the side of the road. "Are you okay?" he asked, forgetting he was hurt and angry at the mere thought that she needed him.

"I'm okay," she said, not really paying his question any mind. "Zoey said that she just managed to find another phone that was linked to the Clarks. She sent me the phone number, but said she is going to have her people dig into it, as well. Hoping to get the phone records as soon as she can."

He smiled; information like that was right in his wheelhouse. Opening up the computer that sat atop the truck's middle-seat console, he started it up. "What's the number?"

She rattled it off as he typed it into NexTx, a cellular tracking program used by law enforcement. He laughed wildly as the phone pinged. "You are going to love this," he said, turning the computer for her to see it.

"What am I looking at?"

"Right now, the phone is located near the Blackfoot River, just down I-90. Twenty minutes ago, it was moving. And five hours before that, it was in Mineral County."

"So what?" She frowned. "There is nothing tying it to our case other than the fact it is a phone on the Clarks' account. For all we know, they had given one of their other employees a work phone."

He couldn't deny that she might be right. There were any number of reasons a senator and his wife would have needed a phone, but that didn't squash the feeling in her stomach that they had just stumbled on something;

whether it would prove to be helpful or hurtful was up to time to tell, but at least it brought them something they needed most—hope in the time of darkness.

Chapter Sixteen

Elle looked down at her phone, half hoping that Zoey would send her another text and tell her that she was sorry, but she knew that it would never come. Even if Zoey was wrong, she wasn't the kind to apologize—ever.

Unlike her, Zoey was unflappable. She could stare into the fire and let the world burn down around her without ever blinking, even if she wasn't the one who threw the match.

Though she was incredibly angry, she couldn't hold a grudge against Zoey. Her boss had taken her on and allowed her to pursue her passion for K-9 work without even the tiniest of pressure to rush her dog's training. If anything, Zoey had been incredibly understanding about the kind of work she did and the benefit it was for the team. The only real mistake Zoey had made was allowing her to be assigned to the care of a senator's child.

It was Elle's failure that had brought them here; Zoey was right. And she had been justified, actually *forced*, into letting her go. If Elle had been thrust into Zoey's position, she probably would have made the same choice.

The road zipped by them as they drove down the interstate in the direction of the Blackfoot River, where Grant had gotten the ping on the phone. He kept looking over at the computer, checking to make sure that the phone's location was relatively unchanging.

She couldn't believe his reaction to this minor piece of evidence. It was like he saw this as their saving grace, when there was no saving anyone here. Her career was over, her dog was hurt and they were on the rocks. And Lily was still missing. If this wasn't a last-ditch effort on his part to save... *Wait, what is he trying to save?*

She glanced over at him, and there were storm clouds in his green eyes. His brow was furrowed, and even without reading his mind, she could tell that he was on a mission. In a strange way, it lightened some of the heaviness in her heart. Her life had unraveled into one huge heaping mess, one she couldn't bring another person into out of the knowledge she would never be able to give them everything they deserved, but to know he was trying to help her took some of the pain away.

There was nothing he could do to make it all better, or take back what had happened to Daisy, but he was doing *something*. That said something about him. She had lost count of the people in her life who had made her promises only to find out they were as empty as the hearts of the people who had made them.

He was different, she could give him that. And, if her heart would have been capable, she could have loved him for it—maybe in another life.

Grant put his hand out, palm up, like he wanted her to reach over and take it. Though she wanted to, it would mean things she wasn't sure she wanted to promise. She was hurt, angry and emotionally compromised right now. And hadn't he been the one to tell her that was enough of a reason—being emotionally compromised, that was—not to get involved?

She pretended not to notice his extended hand, like it wasn't some kind of elephant in the pickup. Her fingers twitched like they wanted to come over and take his even without her mind agreeing to the plan. While she held no doubts about wanting him, he was just her type—hot, dominant, strong, and she'd be lying if she didn't say she loved how he protected her.

She liked to think she was tough, as she was more than capable of getting herself out of physically perilous situations, but when it came to the emotional ones, sometimes it was damn hard to be a woman.

"Elle." He said her name like it was a secret on his tongue, and the sound made her skin spark with yearning.

"Hmm," she said, trying to still seem the tiniest bit aloof.

"It's okay for you to hold my hand."

She looked over at him, and warmth rose into her face. Why did she always have that reaction when it came to him? She'd never thought of herself as much of a blusher, but when he talked to her like that and in that tone of voice, she melted.

"I…" she started, but she didn't know exactly how to express to him everything that she was feeling. "I… I don't want to be hurt anymore, Grant."

"No matter what happens, with any of it, I will keep you as safe as I can. I won't promise that you won't get hurt in this life, but I can promise you that I will do everything in my power to make sure that I'm not the one doing the hurting."

He didn't move his hand, and she stared down at his fingers. She wanted to believe him and give herself over to his beautiful words, but there was so much pain in her heart.

She sighed, and her hands trembled in her lap. After a moment, she reached over and slipped her fingers between his. He couldn't take away the pain and guilt she was feeling, but at least she could have one positive thing in her life. And maybe doing this wasn't the smartest thing, getting involved when she wasn't at her best, but if she waited for a *right time*—a time that she was completely ready and at ease—she damned well could have been waiting forever. Her emotions and her life were always in flux. That was what life was, one fight rolling in on the shirttails of the one before.

She deserved something good in her life, and she would figure out how to do this love thing right—that was, if this was going to be a serious thing between them. Did she ask him? Did he ask her for monogamy? She hadn't had a real boyfriend in so long that she couldn't quite remember how things had been made official with her last. In fact, maybe they hadn't been official—he'd been more than happy to step out of their relationship to sate some needs he later told her she hadn't been filling.

Why did she have to think about that right now? When things were starting to turn and go right? She needed to focus on Grant. Only on Grant. And just like earlier, she needed to be here with him. Beautiful, sexy things happened when she gave herself to him.

The thought of him between her legs made her shift in her seat. If she closed her eyes, she could still feel the last place his mouth had been on her. If only she could keep that feeling forever. But maybe that was just the afterglow speaking, all of this…the confusion and the weird feeling that was entirely too close to love. Love was perilous, at best.

But damn it if she didn't think she loved him. There

was just something about being close to him. She loved to watch his mouth form words and the way his green eyes brightened when he spoke about things he enjoyed or memories from his past.

His thumb fluttered over her skin, and she closed her eyes for a moment, just taking in the full sensation that was his touch. Even her hand fit perfectly in his; how was that possible?

They got off the interstate and took a frontage road in the direction of the last ping off the phone. According to the tracking program, the phone was stationary and hadn't moved for the last thirty minutes.

"What are we going to do after this? Do you think we can pull anything else from the flight records? Maybe we should go see Steve again." She tried to swallow back the anxiety that was rising within her.

He squeezed her hand, the simple action more effective to control her anxiety than anything she could have done. "If this doesn't pan out to be anything, don't worry. We will get Lily back. And, I told you…as for your job… you have plenty of options. If you can't stay at the ranch, I will help you find an apartment or whatever. You don't have to leave Montana."

She hadn't even thought about all the ramifications of losing her job with STEALTH yet. Of course, she couldn't stay at the ranch—that was headquarters for a group she no longer worked with. Zoey hadn't mentioned anything, but she had been trying to let her down gently—which was somewhat out of character for her. Zoey was far more the kind to have a spreadsheet and an exit survey to give people upon their firing.

She had been fired.

Her breath stuck in her chest, and her hands started

shaking. She had no job, her dog was possibly going to have long-term damage regardless of what the vet said and now she couldn't breathe.

Grant glanced over at her and frowned as he looked at her complexion. "Babe, take a breath. In. Out. In and out." He breathed a few times like the problem was that she had forgotten how, not that her body was trembling on the precipice of a full anxiety attack.

"Don't freak out." He paused his breathing exercise. "What can I do to help you?" He started to pull the truck over, but she waved him off.

"No," she said, trying to mimic the Lamaze-style breathing. "Don't stop."

He smiled at her like he was deciding whether or not to say what was just on the tip of his tongue.

"What?" She inhaled.

"The last time you said *don't stop* was at your cabin," he said, giggling as he blushed. It was crazy to see him act in a way she had been chastising herself for, and him looking absolutely sexy while doing it.

A giggle escaped her as she exhaled. It felt strange, like with the giggle she was finding her center again.

He laughed harder, but she didn't know if it was at her or the situation or what, and she began laughing harder, too. She laughed until tears started to form at the corners of her eyes. It didn't make sense and maybe this was some kind of mania or magic, but she could feel the craziness that had overwhelmed her seep out with every laugh. Her heart lightened as her tears fell. Maybe this laughter was the catharsis her soul needed, especially since it was brought on by and hand in hand with Grant.

He was changing her life. He was willing to pick her up when she was at her lowest. He hadn't said he cared, but he had to have cared for her. Maybe he couldn't make all of her problems disappear, but he could damned well make things lighter.

The computer flashed, and Grant pulled his hand away so he could navigate the screen while also driving. "The phone is here," he said, looking around like there would be some kind of sign pointing directly to the device.

She let her giggles go dry and ran her hands over her face, wiping away the remnants of stress. Her life would be okay. She had a friend, even more than a friend, in Grant. She could see things lasting for a long time if they would make whatever it was they were doing official, but even if they remained only between-the-sheets friends, then she would have to be satisfied.

Until the future came, all she had to do was help the little girl who needed her the most. She wouldn't give up on her, no matter what.

Grant pulled the pickup onto the side road where the program had dropped the last ping for the phone's location. The road was a fishing access point, and there were several brown-and-white signs marking the spot, one with a drawing of a fish on a line, another with the image of a boat. She'd driven by many of these signs while in Montana, but she couldn't say that she had ever actually driven into one before. They came to a stop at a large roundabout parking area with a boat launch.

The river was flowing, but ice pocked the edges and a white mini-berg floated past them. It was odd to think anything the senator owned would be at a place like this.

Elle picked up her phone. "I need to know if Zoey managed to get the phone records for the number. And check to see if she found anything on Philip." She tapped the message and hit Send, not listening to the voices in her head that told her she had no business reaching out to her ex-boss. Zoey would help them if she could; they were friends.

As she waited for a reply, Elle gazed around the parking area. There were a few trucks parked tailgate into the spot in true Montana man style. What was it about men here that made them all want to prove to the world how good they were at driving a truck? Her smile returned.

In the farthest corner of the lot, away from all the trucks, was a crossover. It was muddy, and its wheel wells were caked in the muddy brown ice brought on after hours of interstate driving in winter conditions.

"There," she said, pointing at the car.

"Good a place to start looking as any," he said, smiling over at her. "Good eye."

He parked next to the red Subaru, and she got out and walked over beside the car. There was no one inside, and from the lack of ice over the engine on the hood, it was clear it had been recently driven. Inside the car was a collection of fast-food wrappers, one from Sonic—a chain that didn't have restaurants anywhere close. Either the driver had been all over the west and had just gotten back, or they were terrible at cleaning up their mess.

She glanced at the car's license plates; it was from Montana and started with a four—the number for Missoula County. Snapping a picture, she texted the plate to Zoey, as well.

Grant turned away and started to type the license plate number into his computer in the truck.

She stepped around the back of the car. In the back seat was a small booster seat. Her heart jumped. Had Lily been in this seat?

She bit back the thought. There was nothing to indicate that this search for the phone actually had anything to do with Lily. If anything, it was just one more possible lead they had to work through only to be left empty-handed. Her hopes were running away with her reality.

"You're not going to believe this," Grant said. "That car is registered to one Philip Rubbick."

Her phone vibrated with a message from Zoey almost at the same time as Grant spoke. Looking at the message, Elle's mouth dropped open. "Zoey says Philip 'Ace' Crenshaw is the owner of NightGens LLC. He hid his ownership under a bunch of other names of businesses, so it was hard to find."

"The company that owned the helicopter?"

"One and the same." She lifted the phone in her hand so he could see the text Zoey had sent them.

He smiled, his eyes filled with hope and excitement. "That means that it's likely Philip 'Ace' Crenshaw and Philip Rubbick are one and the same—Steve's brother."

"Holy crap." Had they finally pieced the puzzle edges together? She put her arms on the windowsill of the truck as she tried to pull together and make sense of everything she and Grant had just learned. "If Steve was working for this other crew, why would he have said he worked with STEALTH?"

"Smart move on his part, really. He sent us on a dead lead. In the meantime, while we were chasing our tails, he got to talk to his brother and tell him that we were getting closer." Grant scratched at the stubble on his chin. "I can't believe I screwed it up. I even noticed the marks on Steve's hands."

"What?" she asked, frowning.

"When someone stabs another person, especially when enraged, they often cut and damage their own hands. And

Steve…well, his hands were mangled. But, to be honest, they matched the rest of him. Like I said, he threw me off my game. I should have paid more attention," he grumbled.

"That's not your fault. Now that we have some answers, we will just get your people to go pick him up."

He wasn't done whipping himself. "I can't believe I never asked Steve if he knew Philip. It didn't even cross my mind that they would be related. I didn't go deep enough. Maybe if I had, we wouldn't have gone on a wild goose chase and Daisy wouldn't have gotten hurt."

"None of that was your doing." She put her hand on his arm, trying to return some of the comfort that he had brought her. "Besides, we did have some *fun* while we were waiting. I have to believe that everything happens for a reason. And we could have looked into a million things deeper and not found answers. Don't be so hard on yourself."

He put his hand on hers and intertwined their fingers. He leaned down and kissed her knuckles ever so gently. "First, I have a feeling that regardless of what would have happened, we would have had some *fun* together. It just wouldn't have been the same."

"Does that mean you still regret it?" She lifted a brow in warning that he should take a minute to think long and hard before answering.

He chuckled. "I regret nothing when it comes to you, and us." He turned her hand over and kissed her open palm. "From the ugliest moments, we can build beautiful futures."

She didn't move. Futures? Did that mean he thought this was going somewhere? They were going to be fly-by-night, or fly-by-the-case, lovers? She loved the thought.

"We..." She pulled her hand back and patted the windowsill. "We probably need to focus."

He looked slightly crestfallen, and she immediately felt guilty for her response.

"I mean, I'm glad you don't regret anything," she said, tilting her head and sending him a gentle smile. "I most certainly don't, because there is something between us. I don't know what it is, but there's something I've never felt before. It's like you and I *fit*."

The look of hurt left his eyes, and his smile returned. "I hope that's not just the kiss talking."

"What kiss?"

"This one," he said. Taking her face in both of his hands, he pulled them together.

She leaned into the cold steel of the dirty truck, not caring about the mud that would be all over her clothes or the way the cold, wet road grime was threatening to pull all the heat from her body. All she cared about was the way his tongue worked over the edge of her lip and flicked at the tip of her own. She pulled his lower lip into her mouth and gently sucked on it. She could never kiss this man enough. His lips were like sugar, addictive in all their sweetness.

He ran his thumbs over her face, gently caressing her skin as their kiss slowed. He leaned back, searching her eyes, and the look in his gaze made her heart shift in her chest—almost as if the entire beast had moved locations in her chest, forward and closer to him.

She took his hands in hers and, removing them from her face, she kissed his open palm. "You are incredible."

"And so are you," he said, his voice husky.

"Let's find this phone. Maybe it has something about Lily on it. Then we can focus on what we are going to do about us," she said, though right now she knew exactly what she wanted to do with him and his body.

"Yes," he said, rolling up the truck's window and turning off the ignition before getting out.

She took the moment to readjust the holster inside the waistband of her pants. She always hated sitting in a car with them, but at least her gun was small and could go unnoticed and unseen.

"You warm enough?" he asked, grabbing a pair of gloves from his door and slipping them on. "You need some gloves?" He motioned to the cubby in the door where another pair of large men's gloves rested.

"No, thanks," she said, aware that her hands would be freezing if they were outside for any long period of time. She stuffed her hands in her coat pockets. "Hopefully we will be moving enough to stay warm and we will make quick work of getting this phone into our custody."

She looked over at the car. "Do you think it's in there?" she asked, pointing at the window.

He shrugged. "If it is, there's nothing we can do without getting a warrant to do a search."

"Did you check the phone's location again? Does it tell you exactly where we can find it?"

He pinched his lips closed. "Unfortunately, it's not pinpoint accurate. That being said, it's going to be close. I'm thinking within five hundred yards of the pin, give or take some."

"Do you think you should call in some more deputies? Maybe they can help us look over the area?"

He took out his phone. "I'll text a couple of them. If they're not busy, they can join us."

She totally understood. "Maybe they're bored and would like to pursue a lead with us."

He laughed. "They might be. There weren't many open calls." He pointed toward his computer inside the pickup. He zipped up his jacket and pulled on his gloves. "On days like these, where there aren't a lot of calls, I used to look for things like this to do. There are times when I miss being on patrol instead of mostly sitting behind a desk and filling out reports, but I don't miss the slow days."

He reached down and took her hand in his.

"Right now, I could use some slower days." Their footfalls crunched in the snow.

"I hear you there, but for what it's worth, I'm glad all this brought me to you."

"I would have preferred different circumstances, maybe meeting you at a bar or something." She leaned into him, touching his arm as they followed the footsteps that led from the car and toward a hiking trail. The snow cover was patchy, with swaths that had thawed and refrozen and areas where the powder had completely receded and patches of cottonwood leaves littered the ground.

The single set of footprints that had led from the mess of footprints around the car soon disappeared and was consumed by the forest. Though they had a lead here, a solid lead to someone who very well could have known what happened to Catherine and Lily, something about the situation still felt strange, *off* in a way that Elle couldn't quite put her finger on.

They walked slowly, searching the edges of the trails for any signs of a discarded cell phone. If Steve had told Philip that they had gotten on their scents, it was more than possible that Philip had discarded the car and the cell phone at this access. It was doubtful that they were actually going to find Philip, but they would do the best they could with the information they had.

The world smelled of biting cold, tall drying sweet grasses, rotting leaf litter, all mixed into the swirling odor of clean river water. Walking around a gentle bend in the trail, they came to the river.

A man was sitting on the bank, his head down and his knees up. His arms were outstretched, palms together. He looked at odds with the world in only a black sweat-shirt and jeans. She couldn't see his face, but there were touches of gray in the brunette hair at his temples. His neck had a long scratch on the back that was still bleed-ing.

"Hey," Grant said, calling out to the man.

The man jerked, and he looked up. His gaze moved from Grant to Elle. His eyes widened as Philip recog-nized her. "What in the hell are you doing here?"

Philip reached behind his back and moved his hand under his sweatshirt to a bulge that Elle knew all too well was a gun. She hoped she was wrong; she hoped she didn't have to do what she had been trained to do in a situation like this, but as he moved the cloth of his sweatshirt back, she saw the exposed black grip and the butt end of a Glock.

Her hand dropped to her own gun, and in one swift movement she cleared her shirt, drew the weapon, aimed and fired. It all happened fast. A single motion. As the round left the gun, she saw the spray of black gunpow-der. She'd never noticed that before with this gun. Was it a dirty round? What kind of ammo had she been using? It was whatever STEALTH had provided. They wouldn't have used dirty rounds.

And then she realized she needed to come back to the

moment. She couldn't stop shooting until the threat was completely neutralized.

When a person was shot, they didn't stop. Inertia and adrenaline could keep a person moving even if they received a fatal wound. Philip was proving to be the kind of target that she had trained for. She let her finger move forward on the trigger, letting it click to reset, and then she pulled slowly again. It was almost a surprise as the second round left the barrel. She wasn't sure where she had hit Philip, but she had been aiming at center mass. In training, she was normally never more than a few centimeters off at this kind of range.

She'd definitely hit him, but Philip pulled his gun. He took aim and she fired again, but as her finger pulled on the trigger, Grant rushed at her from her left and pushed her out of the way, his gun in hand. Shots rang out, but she wasn't entirely sure who had done the shooting.

Her Sig Sauer kicked out the hot brass, and it skittered beside her as her shoulder hit the ground.

Blood. There was so much blood.

Chapter Seventeen

The ground was red around Philip where blood seeped deeper into the snow, melting it and diluting the blood further. The man had dropped the gun in his hand when he had collapsed, his muscles going limp in death. The side of his face was pressed into the ground, and his hands were opened at his sides.

Elle was lying on her back in the snow, and he could make out the sounds of her erratic, amped breathing. He knew that feeling well thanks to the many fights he'd been in while working patrol. That adrenaline hit affected everything.

At her side was a patch of red blood. She'd been hit. He'd been too slow to help her.

It shouldn't have gone anything like this.

"Are you okay?" Grant asked. "Where does it hurt?"

She was running her hands over her body, as though even she wasn't sure where the bullet had torn through her. She had been hit—there was no question about the blood that was pooling around her.

He wished this had all played out differently. If he had been paying attention to what he should have been paying attention to, Elle would have never gotten hurt.

"Is he down?" She pointed in the direction of Philip.

Grant stepped over to him and pressed his fingers against his neck, searching for the pulse. He found nothing. "He's gone."

"That was not at all how I wanted that to go down," she said.

She moved to sit up, but as she did, he could tell the world swam around her and she was forced to lie back down in the snow. "I already called dispatch. The troops should be here soon. But it's a bit of a drive for EMS to get here, so we're going to have to keep you calm and your blood pressure low. I need to take care of that wound. Stop the bleeding." He pointed to her midsection. "Open your coat and lift up your shirt."

She moved to wave him off, but as she did, she grimaced in pain. Her adrenaline must have been starting to decrease and allowing the pain to set in. "I'm fine. Really," she said, though he already knew better.

"Do you have to be stubborn right now?"

"Do you always have to try and get me naked?" she teased, closing her eyes as she laughed.

He squatted down beside her and started to help unzip her jacket. The bullet had pierced through the jacket's shell and the goose down, red with blood, was poking out.

If only he had reacted quicker, he would have been the one to take the hit instead of her. At least she had been able to draw down on the target; she definitely moved faster than both him and the other man.

It was easy to see she had spent thousands of hours training for a moment like that. Hell, from her reaction alone, he doubted that this was her first time in a life-threatening situation. Later, he'd have to ask her about it.

No doubt, somewhere in her contracting past, there were literal skeletons. He didn't judge her for any of it, but he didn't envy her, either. Being in a situation like this, where a life was taken and more lives were still at risk, left long-term scars. And he didn't mean the scars that would be left by any physical wounds.

"I am going to open up your shirt. Is that okay?"

She nodded. "I think I'm okay. It hurts but I'm going to make it."

She was talking to him, which was a good sign, but he had to see the damage for himself. He gently lifted up the hem of her shirt. On the left side of her abdomen was a dime-size hole. "I'm going to roll you slightly. Just tell me if I need to stop. Okay?"

She bit her lip but nodded.

As he moved her, he spotted a larger exit wound on her back where the bullet had passed through her body.

He was surprised, given the velocity in the range of the round, it hadn't hit him, as well. In a single shot, Philip could have had them both.

"The good news is it looks like it went straight through. Hopefully it didn't hit any major organs, but from where it's located, I think it's important that you don't move and we try to keep you as still as possible." He laid her back down, flat. Gently, he lowered her T-shirt and zipped her coat back up, trying to keep her as warm as he could.

"How did the bleeding look?"

"Actually, it looked pretty clean. The bleeding appears to just be oozing, but make sure to hold some pressure on the wound." He stood up.

"What are you doing?" she asked, putting her hands to her abdomen and pressing.

"I'm going to go grab my medical kit. I'll be right back. Don't move." There was a lump in his throat as he jogged back to his pickup and grabbed his red first aid kit. He could at least stop the bleeding and get her stabilized and ready for the EMS teams when they arrived.

Yet he couldn't help the nauseating feeling that he was the one who was responsible for all this happening. It had been his brilliant idea to come out to the middle of the woods, nowhere near emergency care, and then he'd ended up getting her shot.

If he had only reacted faster. Pulled the second he saw Philip's hand moving toward the gun. But he hadn't been completely sure that the man was going for a gun. They hadn't provoked him, but Grant should have known the shape under the man's sweatshirt. He'd seen it a million times before, but his hope had run away with his good sense.

He had promised himself and Elle that he would protect her, and now she was lying out there bleeding into the snow after having taken down a man. And for what? They hadn't found Lily, and Philip had pulled the trigger before they got any answers.

Her shooting had solidly been in self-defense and every jury would side with her, especially with him as her witness, but they would still have to sit through endless rounds of questioning and he would have to sit through IA questions and hearings before being cleared. This was going to take so much out of both of them, and all because he had chosen to go on a wild goose chase.

No. He had just been doing his job to the best of his abilities. He was making choices based on the information they had been able to accumulate up to this point. Sometimes bad things happened, and in this case, inexcusably terrible things, but there was no going back and fixing his mistakes. He couldn't focus on that right now; instead, he needed to focus on helping Elle in the only ways he could.

As he made his way back to Elle, he found she had moved and was now sitting up next to Philip. She was still gripping her side. In her hand was a black phone he didn't recognize. She was tapping away with one finger, and for a moment he wondered if that was in fact the cell phone they had been looking for. But if it was, how had she found it?

"Elle, why are you sitting up?" he asked, looking at her back where the blood had stained her jacket and was oozing freely from the hole.

She shook her head, ignoring his reprimand. "I found his phone."

"Philip's? Where?"

She shrugged as she looked back over her shoulder at him and gave him a guilty smile. "Well, it was ringing from his pocket."

"You and I both know you had no business disturbing the crime scene," he said, walking over to her and opening up his first aid kit.

He hated to admit it, but if he had been in her shoes, he would have probably done the same damned thing—procedure or not.

"Business or not, I think you'd be interested to hear that it was Steve on the other end of the line."

He stopped and stared at her. "Did you answer it?"

She nodded. "The number came up as restricted, and when I answered the guy Steve started talking. He said something about Lily, and then, 'The senator changed his mind. He wants us to keep her safe.' When I didn't say anything, I think he got suspicious and he hung up."

"But you never spoke?" Grant asked, worried now

that if Steve knew they were on the receiving end of that phone call, they could have found themselves in more danger than they were already in.

"No." She shook her head. "He didn't know I was there, I promise."

"But he must know something was up with Philip." His entire body clenched. "And if they were talking about the senator, they must be on his payroll. It's going to be hard to prove in court, if we ever get them there and get Lily back, but I think the senator may have a whole lot more to do with his wife's death than he alluded to."

"No kidding," she said, clicking on the phone screen, but it had locked.

Grant sat down beside her in the snow. "Here, let me get this QuikClot on you. I don't want you losing any more blood. I can't lose you."

She stopped working on the phone and looked over at him with a gaze he hadn't seen her give him before. He could have expected hate, disgust or even disappointment after the situation he had gotten them into and the pain he had caused her, but instead she looked at him with what appeared to be *love*. Those eyes—those beautiful almond-shaped blue eyes—when she gave him that look, he was surprised the snow around them didn't melt.

"Lift your shirt. Let me take care of you."

She put down the phone and pulled up her jacket and her shirt, exposing the exit wound as he slipped on a pair of gloves. He packed the wound and taped down the gauze, then moved around to her front and repeated the treatment. The entire time, he could feel her staring at him, but he wasn't sure why and he wasn't sure he wanted to ask. If he asked and the look in her eyes wasn't love, it would hurt. And he was already hurting because of the mistakes he had made when it came to her.

As he put down the last piece of tape, he finally looked up at her as he took off his nitrile gloves and slipped them into his pocket to throw away later.

"Grant," she said, her voice soft.

"Hmm?" His fingers moved over the tape one more time as if he was checking to make sure that it was firmly adhered, but in truth all he wanted to do was keep touching her. He needed to touch her skin, to know she was okay, to know she was going to make it through this.

"Thank you," she said, touching his face gently with her fingertips.

"No. I'm so, so sorry." His voice cracked with all his feelings, feelings he couldn't make heads or tails of right now. "This happened because of me. If I'd just gotten the drop on him first. Or if we hadn't walked up from behind him… Hell, maybe I should have just tried to take him down before he drew down on us. I screwed up, Elle, and you are hurt because of me."

She shook her head. "I don't care about a stupid bullet wound. I'm telling you now, I've seen things like this happen before—this kind of wound—and I will be all right. If anything, at least I will have a cool story to tell at the bars on a Friday night," she teased. "But really, this wasn't your fault. From day one, actually from the day I put my hand on my first pistol, I knew this could happen. I knew the risks. I made the choices."

"But I put you in front of the round that hit you."

"Technically, you did try to push me out of the way. If you hadn't, I would probably be in an entirely different situation right now. So, really, you saved my life."

She ran her thumb over his cheek as she looked into his eyes. "I owe you my life, Grant."

He was left speechless. All he could do was touch her hand with his and kiss her open palm. He pressed his face into her palm.

"We need to focus, Grant. I can't have you feeling bad. Seriously, we need to focus on Lily. When we get back, we can focus on us."

Though she was making a good point, he didn't want to move out of her hand. He pulled back. "Yeah, Lily." He ran his hands through his hair and down over the back of his neck as he stood up and away from her.

"Do you think Philip did something to her?" She pointed to the scratch on Philip's neck. "Do you think that was why he was sitting here, by the river?" Her gaze moved to Philip's dead body and then out to the icy water.

A little girl couldn't survive water like that even when it wasn't ice cold and whispering of hypothermia. Only a monster would have killed a little girl, but monsters were one thing he was used to dealing with—and though Elle had been strong through this shooting, if Lily was lying out on the riverbank somewhere, that could break anyone.

"I'm sure she's okay." Grant looked around like he would suddenly see the little girl just standing on the riverbank, silently watching them and grateful that they had finally found her. Yeah, right, like they could get that lucky.

He looked over at Philip's body. There had been a car seat in the Subaru. It was possible that Lily could have been around here, but maybe he had dropped her off with someone else—maybe Steve had told him to ditch her and run. There were any number of possible scenarios that could have played out before they came upon this man.

But maybe there was something on the body that could help them find the girl. Something, anything, was better than nothing at all—and though he hated the thought, they needed to have answers even if those answers meant Lily was dead.

Chapter Eighteen

Elle tried not to focus on the pain in her side. She had told Grant she was going to be fine, that she wasn't hurting too bad, but the pain threatened to burn through her like a hot iron. She'd heard it burned when a person had been shot, but she had never expected this kind of intensity. She could only imagine what it must feel like to have a baby; if it was anything like this, she would be adopting.

Parents didn't have to be blood relatives of a child. If Senator Clark had anything to do with his wife's death and his daughter's disappearance like they had come to assume, then it only proved the point that guidance and love determined parentage more than biology. She could provide those things to a kid. She wouldn't even adopt a baby—rather, she would adopt an older kiddo. She wanted to bring a child into her life that had no one, nowhere to go and had felt abandoned by the world.

If Lily was found safe and alive, she silently made a promise to the ether that she would follow through and adopt a kid someday. She would give them more love and guidance than even she had received. If she was hoping and praying to the ether, she added in a prayer for Daisy to be healthy, too.

She also added a plea for Grant to be hers. This time,

thinking about him and their future didn't feel like such an outrageous dream.

Maybe it was too much to ask for it all, but she didn't care.

Picking up the black phone she'd taken from the dead man, she reached over for Philip's thumb so she could open up the device. However, as she moved to touch him, she noticed a tuft of hair. There, under his pointer and middle fingers, was a clump of fine blond hair. It was the same color as Lily's.

Her heart fluttered in her chest. What did that hair mean? "Grant," she said, "look." She pointed at Philip's hand. "That's Lily's hair."

"Are you sure?" Grant asked, moving beside the body and taking his phone out and snapping a picture of the hand holding the wispy blond locks.

The hair was dry. Did that mean she hadn't been in the water or that he had been holding the hair in his hand long enough for it to dry after he had committed murder?

"She has to be around here," Elle said, standing up. "We have to find her."

"Elle, you aren't in any kind of shape to go search for Lily. If she is out here, our team is on their way. We can start our search as soon as they get here."

She put her hand on the cottonwood tree next to her, steadying herself as she got up and on her feet. "And what if she is out there in the water somewhere? Wet and hurt? Do you think she can really wait? It's cold and she is likely alone. She has to be so scared."

He looked down at Philip and then back up at her. "If you promise not to go anywhere—"

"I'm not making any promises to that effect, Grant. So you can either help me look for her or you can get out of my way. We are so close to her. I have to find her. I have to know she is okay."

Grant shook his head. "I'm not going to let you put yourself in more danger. For all we know, you could be bleeding internally. You know I want to find Lily, too. Finding her has been the major driving force behind this entire case. But let's say she is deceased. You risking your life is not only dangerous, but it's downright illogical."

She knew he made sense and that his admonition was coming from a good place, but she wasn't about to sit here and do nothing when the child she loved more than herself was possibly hurt somewhere near. "I'm telling you, Grant, if she is out here and relatively unharmed, she is not going to answer or come near anyone she doesn't know or trust."

Grant ran his hands over his face in frustration, but he had to have known he wasn't going to get anywhere in this fight. There would be no stopping her, not now.

"You know kids. She is probably terrified right now. And they always make everything their fault. That means she likely feels everything that has happened to her up to this point is because of some mistake she made. What if she thinks she is going to get in trouble? Can you even begin to imagine how scared she is right now? She has been through so much." Her voice cracked. "I can't. I can't sit by and do nothing."

Grant sighed like he understood and empathized with what she was saying but still didn't agree.

She loved him for the way he wanted to protect her and keep her safe, but this wasn't about her. This was about someone else she loved, someone she had promised to protect and someone she had let down. This was about an innocent, sweet child.

"I know you want to do the right thing by everyone here. It's what makes you the man you are—the good man, the man I have come to love—but I have to find Lily." She paused. "If only we had Daisy."

"How about I call in the other K-9 teams? We can get them on this." He smiled. "And wait…did you just say you *loved* me?"

She wasn't sure if the faintness she was feeling was because of her admission or because of blood loss, but she found she needed to press her shoulder against the tree so it could support more of her weight. She sent Grant a sexy half smile. "Loving you is easy to do. You are the perfect combination of all the things I have been looking for in a partner. I never thought I'd meet anyone like you, and then you just appeared in my life."

He blushed and looked away.

Shit. She hadn't meant to admit her love for him. Not here. Not yet. And then there he was, not saying it in return. He didn't love her. He was going to run away.

She pushed herself off the tree, not giving him another second to come up with something to say instead of "I love you, too."

As she walked toward the river and away from him, she wasn't sure what hurt worse, the bullet wound or the pain in having her love rebuffed.

"Elle, stop. Wait," he called from behind her.

Yeah, right. The last thing she wanted to do right now was look him in the eyes. She had just made a hard situation impossibly harder. And there was no reeling back in the words she had let fall from her lips. She couldn't believe her own stupidity.

She knew better.

She had always vowed to never tell a man she loved

him before he told her. And there she went breaking her own rules for a man who didn't even feel the same way.

What an idiot.

If she wasn't going to die from her wound, she was certainly going to die from embarrassment. She started walking down the riverbank, downstream.

"Elle, please stop," he said, only steps behind her.

She shook her head, afraid that if she opened her mouth to speak, all the pain she was feeling would come spilling out and she would say more things that she would regret.

"Don't be like that, Elle. You just caught me off guard. I didn't expect you to—"

"Lily!" she yelled, cutting him off. She didn't want to hear his excuses. There was only one acceptable response to someone telling a person they loved another. He started to make a sound. "Lily!" she called again.

If Elle could have run away, she would have, but her feet slipped on the icy river rocks and every step she made was deliberate to keep from sliding and falling. She didn't need Grant having to rescue her again.

Thankfully, the third time he tried to talk to her and she called out Lily's name, her adolescent stonewalling took effect and he stopped trying. She felt stupid for treating this situation—a situation she had caused—like this, but she couldn't think of another way to make things less awkward. It just was what it was at this point, and she had no one else to blame than herself. She had read the feelings between her and Grant incorrectly.

As they walked, the only sound became the gurgle and rushing sounds of the river, their footsteps clattering on the cobbles, and the occasional call of magpies and ravens in the distance. Her ego was definitely feeling more pain than her side, and it threatened to bring her to her knees.

It was fine, though. After they got through this investigation, she could go back to being by herself. She could find another job, and if nothing else she could train dogs at some chain store or something. The last thing she wanted to do was go back into contracting work, going overseas and watching as hellish crimes happened to the most innocent people. Though, admittedly, she didn't have to go overseas to find those kinds of monsters.

To her right, she heard the sounds of whimpering. The sound was soft and mewing, and Elle stopped walking in hopes it wasn't just in her imagination.

"Ms. Elle?" Lily's voice broke through the pain filling Elle's soul.

"Lily? Lily, is that you?" she called, her voice taking on a manic, relieved tone.

Tucked into the hollowed-out center of a cottonwood, barely visible in the distance, was Lily. She was wearing a dark blue coat and white boots, and she waved a dirt-covered gloved hand.

Tears sprang from Elle's eyes and poured down her cheeks as she forgot about her own pain and rushed toward the little girl. She stepped over downed trees and pushed through the brush, and as she grew closer Lily stood up and started to run toward her. Lily extended her arms, throwing them around Elle's legs as they found one another.

As she pulled her up and into her embrace, Elle wasn't sure who was crying harder or was more relieved.

Chapter Nineteen

The hospital staff had been incredibly kind in allowing Lily and Elle to stay together in the emergency room. In all reality, even if they had tried to pull them apart, Grant was sure that neither would have allowed it. Even during the ride in the ambulance, the two ladies had been inseparable, according to the EMS workers.

After Elle had told him she loved him, all he could think about was her, and if Lily hadn't called out to them, he was sure that he wouldn't have seen her hiding away in the tree. Elle had been right, and as much as he had hated the idea of her striking out into the woods to find the girl, it was because of her that Lily had been found.

He made his way toward their room and knocked on the door frame. Elle was lying down in the hospital bed, Lily's head on her chest. Lily's eyes were closed, and from the steady rise and fall of the little girl's back, he could tell she was fast asleep.

Elle looked up at him as he made his way inside. There was hurt in her eyes, but he doubted it had anything to do with her side. Whatever she had been feeling from that had likely been fixed with some kind of meds by now, which meant the pain in her eyes was one he had put there.

"How are you two doing?" he asked.

She nodded. "Lily is all good. They checked her out, and aside from a few bruises and a missing patch of hair, she seems to be not too worse for the wear. The only thing they want me to watch are her feet. Her little toes were pretty cut up after walking barefoot in the snow when Steve took her from the house."

"Is that what she said had happened?"

Elle nodded. "She won't tell me what happened with her mother, but I'm hoping it is because she didn't see her mother's death. I didn't press her too hard about details. I'm sure when she is feeling a little better, we can talk more, and I'm sure she'll be assigned a counselor. I just wanted her to feel safe and secure for now." Elle paused. "The hospital asked if they should contact the senator."

"What did you tell them?"

"She is a minor, and he is her parent. They were put into a tough situation." She paused. "I told them we needed to wait to hear from you. You are in charge of this investigation."

"I appreciate that." He smiled, stepping closer to her and putting his hands on the rail of her bed. "I think we can make that work. I'll call my teams in and we can arrest the senator in the parking lot—away from Lily. They have already taken Steve into custody. He didn't put up a fight, and he has been happy to talk."

"That's surprising." She chuckled gently, as though she wanted to keep her movement to a minimum in order to not disturb the sleeping child.

"Yeah," Grant said, smiling. "The only thing he was worried about was the stupid goat. He made sure that it was taken to the neighbor's house before he left. Sounds like he is going to give up everything—including the senator. He already told my team all about the senator hiring him and his brother—and how the senator was going to try and pin everything on them thanks to the falsified death threats."

"No doubt the senator has lawyered up by now," Elle said, rolling her eyes.

He felt exactly the same way. "I'm sure he has."

"Did Steve tell your team why the senator hired them? Was it his intention to kill the girls?" Elle whispered.

"I think he wanted his wife out of the way—they were having problems, she had even contacted a divorce attorney—but I don't know about Lily. From what Steve said, with the election coming up, Dean Clark was hoping to pull sympathy votes thanks to his wife's death. He'd already hired a publicist to handle the press and manipulate the public's opinion of him."

"So, he was planning on killing two birds? Using his wife's death to avoid public scrutiny and also to gain votes? He was pandering to the public's sympathies to win?"

"Are you really surprised? What won't a seasoned politician do to make people bend to their whims?"

"You have a point." Elle nodded. "If it turns out that he was planning on having Lily murdered, too, what do you think will happen to the senator?"

"Regardless of what he had intended, we will arrest him for a murder-for-hire plot, but what else the district attorney will go for is up to her—I'm hoping homicide gets added to his charges. The good news is that, no matter how good a lawyer he has, he will be going to prison. And if they prove that he was also planning on killing his daughter, then I'm sure he will likely never leave that prison."

"And what will happen to Lily? Where does she go from here?" She hugged Lily tighter.

He sighed, knowing it was unlikely she was going to like the answer. "She will go into the care of CPS for now while they try to contact the next of kin. If they agree to take her, then they will be her legal acting guardians."

She nibbled on her lip. "I would ask that they go to Catherine's side."

He nodded. "I'll make sure to recommend that to protective services."

"I know that they have a large, distinguished family, so I'm sure they will take her, but I would love it if I could come and see her once in a while."

He reached over and brushed a strand of her brunette hair out of her face and pushed it gently behind her ear. "You saved this little girl's life. She is alive because of your quick actions and unwavering efforts to find her. I'm sure that no one would have a problem with you seeing her. You are her hero."

She smiled and tears welled in her eyes.

"Elle, you're *my* hero." He smiled. "And I hope you know I love you."

She reached over and took his hand in hers. "You don't have to say that if you don't really mean it. It's okay. You don't owe me that."

"Elle, you know I say what I mean. And I may be slow to know my own feelings, but there is no question in my heart about how I feel about you. I *love* you. I know we haven't been together for all that long, but I can't wait to see where things go. And, as cheesy as this might sound, I can see being with you forever."

"I love you, too, Grant." She smiled, and a tear trembled at the corner of her eye. "And I can see loving you always. You are the man I've been searching for."

He leaned in and gently kissed her lips. "And you are the woman I can't imagine spending a moment without."

There was the sound of clicking, like toenails on tile, and then there was a knock on the door. Grant stood up.

Standing in the doorway looking at them, wiggling manically, was Daisy. She wore an inflatable tube-shaped blue collar, and the effect made him chuckle. The dog didn't seem to notice; she only had eyes for Elle. If anything, he could understand the dog's need to be near her.

"I hope we're not interrupting," Zoey said, smiling. "But someone needed her mom. She's been whining ever since we left the vet's office."

Elle smiled widely. "Oh, Zoey, thank you so much. Is she doing okay?"

Zoey nodded. "She has a few stitches and will have to wear the inflatable collar for a while to make sure she doesn't get at her stitches, but she will be fine."

"What about the other dog?" Grant asked. "If she doesn't have anyone, I have a buddy who has been looking. We can get her a home."

"That would be perfect." Zoey smiled. "And speaking of home, Elle, you are welcome to come back to our team whenever you and Daisy are ready." Zoey let go of the dog's lead.

Daisy was a black dart as she charged past him and jumped into the bed beside Elle. She lay down and started licking Elle's face wildly, nudging Lily awake.

Lily opened her eyes and smiled at Daisy. Just when Grant had thought there was no sweeter sound than hearing Elle say, "I love you," Lily started to giggle. He had never experienced a moment more pure or entirely perfect, and in the sound, he knew he had found his future.

* * * * *

FOR THE DEFENCE

MAGGIE WELLS

For Bill, my sweet-talking Southern man.
We're two decades into this fling and you
still make my heart sing.

Chapter One

"Interview with Deputy Lourdes Cabrera, Masters County Sheriff's Department. Deputy Cabrera, would you please tell us what you witnessed in the early-morning hours of September 28?"

Lori had to refrain from rolling her eyes while Danielle Anderson spoke into her cell like it was a microphone. She understood the need for an official statement, but the assistant district attorney sounded like she was reading from a television script. They may not have been besties, but they worked in separate wings of the same building. Heck, they'd been at the same Chic Chef housewares party the previous weekend. But for the sake of the teenage girl she'd picked up walking Highway 19 alone at two in the morning, Lori tamped down the urge to snark and spoke directly into the microphone on the proffered device.

"I was returning from a call when I saw a young girl—uh, a female who appeared to be underage—walking along the side of the road."

"You'd had a call so late?" Danielle interrupted.

This time, Lori did smirk, and she shot a look at the sheriff seated at his desk at the back of the room. Sheriff Ben Kinsella wore a bemused half smile. They complained all the time about how civilians didn't actually understand their jobs, and their own assistant district attorney had proved them right. Calls in the wee hours were not at all out of the ordinary in their line of work, even in small rural communities.

"Yes. There'd been a report of a domestic disturbance at a home on Highway 19 west of the county line. I took the call through direct dispatch. I was already out on patrol and requested backup from Prescott County since many of the lots in the area straddle the county line. We often provide backup for one another in those situations," she explained.

"You were heading back toward Pine Bluff when you noticed the young woman walking alone so late?"

"Yes." Lori shifted closer to the edge of the chair.

"Can you tell me what made you stop?"

Lori blinked. Sometimes she forgot not everyone would have pulled over for a stranger walking along the road at such a dangerous hour. Cop or not. "I stopped because it's dangerous for people to walk along unlit county roads in the dark of night," she replied evenly.

"The person you picked up, was she known to you?"

Lori had to force herself to remember they were having this pedantic discussion for a reason. Leaning closer to the phone, she looked up at the ADA and spoke directly into the phone. "No, ma'am. I had never met her." She moved back, carefully maintaining eye contact with the lawyer. "I pulled to the side of the road and approached her from behind, identifying myself as a sheriff's deputy."

"Did she try to run?"

The question made Lori frown. "No." She paused, trying to figure out the attorney's angle. "Well, I guess technically she did, but she ran toward me," she said, enunciating each word for the sake of eventual transcription.

"She ran toward you and said what?" Danielle prompted.

"She said, 'Thank God. Can you help me? I want to go home.'" A shiver raced down Lori's spine when she recalled the edgy desperation in the girl's voice.

"What happened then?"

"I took her name and address. Bella Nunes. She gave me a street address in Jennings, Florida. When I found her, she was dressed in a pair of bathing suit bottoms, a tank top and a pair of cheap rubber flip-flops. No purse, no ID."

She stopped there, thinking back over the information she'd been able to glean from the trembling girl between sobs.

"She told me she was fifteen. She said she'd been staying with a friend who moved up here, but that she wanted to go home. When I pressed her about the friend's identity, she clammed up."

"Ms. Nunes offered no other information? Where this friend lived? A name?"

Lori shook her head. "No. She refused to tell me where she was coming from or who she'd been with."

"Did you have some suspicions based on where she'd been walking and knowledge of the residents in the area?" Danielle probed.

Lori glanced over at her boss, needing the reassurance she hadn't gone off half cocked when drawing her conclusions. The sheriff inclined his head, urging her to continue.

"There are only three residences within a two-mile radius of where I found Ms. Nunes. I didn't see her on my way out there, and when I found her, she wasn't walking at a brisk pace. One of the straps on her sandals had broken. The edges of the road are crumbling. She told me she was scared to walk in the grass because of snakes."

"Snakes?"

"Said she'd seen enough snakes to last a lifetime," Lori answered flatly.

"And she wouldn't say where she was coming from?" Danielle repeated.

"No." Lori leaned forward, her gaze locked on the other woman as she spoke. "There are only three residences in the radius. One was the residence I was called to for the domestic disturbance. One is owned by a widow named Hazel Johnson and is located closer to town. When we passed, I checked, and all of the lights at Mrs. Johnson's place were out."

"And the property belonging to Samuel Coulter was the only one left?" Danielle asked.

"Yes."

"What type of business does Mr. Coulter run on his property?"

Lori was about to answer when the door to the sheriff's department swung open and the district attorney, Harrison Hayes, strode in. "Hold up," he said, lifting a hand to back up his order.

Danielle jabbed at the screen to stop the recording. The familiar squeak and roll of Ben's desk chair told her the sheriff had come to his feet. The grim resignation on the DA's face made a knot of ice form in her stomach. Obviously, the DA's meeting with Samuel Coulter and his attorney hadn't gone as expected.

Rising to her feet, Lori peered through the floor-to-ceiling glass walls into the reception area separating the county's legal offices from the law enforcement branch. She spotted them by the empty mosaic-tiled fountain. Two men, one nearly as handsome as the other, but both equally repugnant to her.

Coulter and his attorney, Simon Wingate, stood with

their heads bent close to one another. Lori's lip curled. There'd been few sightings of the eccentric millionaire since he'd bought the massive acreage out on Highway 19. She'd heard rumors about the man being good-looking, but... Lori narrowed her eyes. He wasn't just handsome; he was gorgeous.

Disgusted with the thought, she shifted her attention to the man's clothes. What did a man suspected of endangering young women wear to be questioned by the local prosecutors? Loose linen pants and a finely woven white shirt. And flip-flops. Not the cheap dollar-store shower shoes Bella'd been wearing. No, his had wide straps fashioned from supple leather. He looked like a guy on vacation.

The sandals were a sharp contrast to the impeccably shined wing tips the man standing next to him wore.

Simon Wingate looked every inch the prep-school-educated politician's son.

Lori clenched her back teeth and focused on the man in the expertly tailored suit. He was the light to his client's dark. The perfect foil. All warm, gold-tipped curls, crinkly blue eyes and sun-kissed skin. Lori was woman enough to admit her mouth sometimes watered when she saw Simon Wingate. Not today, though.

Masters County's newest resident had lawyered up and come to head them off at the pass. No doubt Coulter waved a wad of cash, and city slicker Simon had come a-runnin'. Judging by Coulter's unperturbed expression and the district attorney's abrupt halt to Lori's statement, whatever they said had worked. He was about to slither out the doors of Masters County Municipal Center a free man.

"Snakes," Lori said, her gaze following the two men exiting the building. The outer door closed behind them, and she refocused her indignation on the DA. "The man buys, sells and breeds exotic snakes."

"Which is not illegal," Hayes replied calmly.

"Bella Nunes said he threatened her with his damn snakes," Lori blurted, losing her cool at last.

Hayes held up a placating hand. "I am aware of Ms. Nunes's accusations. I am also aware she is not fifteen. She is actually eighteen years old, a three-time runaway prior to her eighteenth birthday, and has a history of embellishing stories when she gets caught in a difficult spot. Or so her parents say."

Sheriff Kinsella approached. "You're not pressing charges?"

Hayes shrugged. "Would if I thought I could get something to stick. All I have is a complaint filed by a young woman who claimed to be fifteen, when in fact she is eighteen. She is an adult who admits she came here of her own free will, whether she regrets that decision now or not. She said herself no one was around when Coulter allegedly—"

Offended on Bella's behalf, Lori bristled. "He locked her in a cage with a boa constrictor!"

"So she says," the district attorney retorted, his expression grave. "He says he didn't and has offered to provide witnesses to refute Ms. Nunes's claims. She has no witnesses to say she was mistreated. Our hands are tied."

The man's mouth flattened into a grim line, and Lori could see he didn't care for the outcome of his interview with Coulter any more than she did. Exhaling with a whoosh, she dropped back into her chair and made a concerted effort not to appear sulky.

"Right. I get you," she conceded.

The prosecutor inclined his head, the corners of his

mouth pulled tight. "Mr. Coulter has generously offered to pay for her bus ticket back to Florida."

"What a guy." Danielle pocketed her phone and headed for the door.

The rhetorical statement caused the sheriff to snort. Harrison Hayes's expression, on the other hand, remained somber while he watched his associate approach.

At last, the DA cracked. A smirk twisting his lips, he held the lobby door open for Danielle. After making sure the door was closed again, he pivoted, a hand raised in helpless surrender. "For what it's worth, I don't disagree with your instincts, Deputy. There is something off about the guy, and I'm not only talking about the snake eyes."

"Snake eyes?" Ben asked.

"So he does have creepy eyes?" Lori asked, swiping Bella Nunes's choice of descriptors.

Hayes gestured to his own left eye. "Elongated pupil," he explained. "I'm man enough to admit it's disconcerting, given the guy's obsession with reptiles."

Lori nodded, her lips quirking at Hayes's barely concealed shudder. "You think he's some sort of cult leader?"

"He may be, but I can tell you this," the DA said, opening the office door again. "I wouldn't follow the guy across the street."

When they were gone, Lori swiveled her chair to face her boss. "Well, damn."

Ben nodded and moved back to his own desk. "She's spent the morning at Reverend Mitchell's house. I'll go by and let them know what's happening. I'm sure I can work something out with him on the bus ticket. Maybe there's some kind of charity fund. If not, I'll talk to Marlee. I don't want Ms. Nunes to feel beholden to Coulter in any way."

Lori hid her smile. When Ben's girlfriend, Marlee

Masters, had come home to Pine Bluff, most of the townspeople had been poised to write her off as nothing more than the small-town princess she'd been once upon a time—pretty and petted and cooed over by everyone. Marlee had changed since the loss of her only brother. Her father had suffered a debilitating stroke a few months prior, and Marlee had not only taken over the reins of the family business, but she'd also stepped straight into the role of civic leader.

Marlee was a Masters of Masters County, Georgia. If she wanted there to be a charity doling out bus tickets home to wayward young women with questionable taste in men, by God, there'd be one set up by morning.

"Thank you." Lori sighed and closed the spiral notebook she had open on the desk. She'd had her notes all ready in case she needed to refer to them while making her statement, but she might as well ball them up and toss them in the trash.

"We'll maintain a closer watch on things happening out along Highway 19," Ben said, keeping the order casual and open. "Tourists have started coming to visit Cottonmouth Coulter's Reptile Rendezvous. From what I hear, it's all the kids in town can talk about. We should be on guard for an uptick in activity."

Lori bit her lip. She knew she was too personally invested in Bella Nunes's drama. She used to be better at compartmentalizing stuff like this, but lately... Lately Lori was having a harder time keeping a tight lid on her emotions. She sensed Ben was aware of her struggle, was throwing her a bone. Lori appreciated his concern but at the same time wished she could just suck it up.

Thankfully, Ben believed in her hunch about Coulter. They were experienced, intuitive cops who put stock in niggling suspicion. Suspicion often turned into hard evidence. They were both the sorts who weren't afraid to pick and pull at the flimsiest of threads to see what unraveled and what they could learn from the results.

"I'll talk to Mike about it when he comes on shift. Give him some pointers on what to look out for." She dropped her notes on the Nunes incident into the shredder near the desk she shared with Deputy Mike Schaeffer.

Mike's seniority irked her. He'd only been at the sheriff's department two weeks longer than her and had less experience. She'd finished her initial entry training at Fort Leonard Wood and stayed on for military police school. She finished her stint in the corrections brigade at Fort Leavenworth, Kansas. Mike, a homegrown boy who'd graduated a year behind her, had partied at the University of Georgia for a couple of semesters. After he failed to make the grade there, he landed at Georgia Piedmont Tech's law enforcement academy, and he was hired two weeks after his twenty-first birthday.

Loyal and almost too eager to please, Mike was a nice guy. Which made it even harder for her to resent him. Most of the time. Though it irked her that she seemed destined to train men who outranked her.

"How about a milkshake?" Ben asked, jolting her from her thoughts. "I sure could use something cold and sweet to wash this sour taste out of my mouth."

Lori saw him wriggling his wallet from his back pocket. "You buying?"

"I'll buy if you fly," he offered.

"Done." She pushed back from the desk, thankful to have an excuse to go for a walk. The Daisy Drive-In was only a few blocks away. Maybe a short walk and a tall shake were exactly what she needed.

Outside the stagnant office, the day was warm, though the calendar claimed it was still September. In South Georgia, autumn didn't come around until late October. Tipping her chin up, she tugged at the front of her uniform shirt in hopes of wafting cool air over her superheated skin. She took two deep breaths and reminded herself it was okay to feel shaken, as long as she didn't let setbacks knock her down. Or so a therapist had once told her.

Unclenching her fists, she set off for the drive-in, but no matter how fast she walked, she couldn't outpace her frustration. She couldn't believe they would let Coulter go without a reprimand. It galled her to think of the slime bag luring young women to his "refuge," tormenting them into thinking he was doing them a favor by letting them stay there.

As if she'd summoned the devil by thinking of him, an engine roared and a sports car shot past her. She caught sight of Coulter's tanned skin and dark, wind-tousled hair. *Of course he drives a Viper*, she thought with a sneer. What a cliché. Reflective sunglasses glinted in the sunlight, and her stomach flipped when he lifted a hand in a mocking wave and punched the gas.

He sped out of town at about thirty over the posted speed limit.

She pressed the button on the mic she wore clipped to her shoulder and tipped her head to the side, watching the car shrink into a pinprick in the distance. "Mike? What's your twenty?"

There was a crackle of static. Then the deputy on patrol answered. "I'm on Sawtooth Lake Road near the county line. Over."

Scowling, she peered at the strip of highway leading from the center of Pine Bluff toward the eastern half of

Masters County. Mike was somewhere in the northwest quadrant. There'd be no catching Coulter today.

"Didja need me?" Mike asked, breaking into her thoughts.

She shook her head and keyed the mic. "Nope. False alarm. Carry on."

"Ten-four," Mike responded. "See you back at base."

They'd catch up to Coulter one day. They'd figure out exactly what he had going on and they'd stop it. They had to. Something bad was happening out there. She felt it in her bones.

Lori straightened her shoulders and refocused on the sight of the Daisy Drive-In in the distance. Today might not have been the day, but it was coming. Soon. She only hoped it would be soon enough to help the next young woman they found wandering the side of a rural highway in the dead of night.

Chapter Two

Simon Wingate kept the smile he wore plastered to his face until the client he'd waved off was nothing but a distant roar heading down the highway leading out of town. As he spun toward the converted Victorian that housed his grandfather's—now his—law offices, a shudder ran through him. If his grandfather were here, he'd have been able to get the old man's opinion on his new client. But his grandfather spent most of his time in Valdosta these days, having decided to run for a seat on the circuit court bench.

And Simon was here in Pine Bluff—also known as purgatory.

He missed Atlanta. What he wouldn't give for an evening spent talking strategy with his clients in restaurants with cloth napkins or sampling single malts with his fellow lobbyists at a whiskey bar. He never thought he'd come to appreciate what he'd once considered froufrou food, but when the only dining options in town were a bakery, a diner and a drive-in specializing in burgers and onion rings, even a man's man started dreaming of non-deep-fried food.

His stomach growled as he stared at the front door of the stately old home his grandfather had converted into law offices. He wasn't ready to go back in there. He wasn't in the mood to answer his secretary's questions or entertain her commentary on how his grandfather would have handled things. He was all too aware this was his grandfather's town. And Simon couldn't shake the niggling suspicion he'd never be able to fill Wendell Wingate's shoes.

Pivoting on the heel of his cap-toe oxford, he walked away from the office. He'd go to the drive-in and get something to eat. Then he'd come back and listen to Dora's litany of all he'd done wrong that morning.

He hadn't gone more than a half block before he felt his shirt adhere to his back. An hour earlier, the charcoal suit with the windowpane pattern seemed the perfect choice to represent a client at the DA's office. Now he was sorry he'd wasted the fine tailoring on a man who believed flip-flops were acceptable footwear anywhere not covered in sand.

He paused at the corner of Red Pine and Loblolly and looked back. The old courthouse planted in the center of the town square gleamed white in the late-morning sun. It had long ago been converted into a museum and home to the historical society, but a part of him wished they heard cases in the gracious old building rather than in the bland municipal complex.

He hooked a right on Pond Street, and the canopies of the Daisy Drive-In came into view. His steps faltered, but his stomach growled again. He pressed a hand to his abdomen to quell the uprising. He'd eaten at the dairy bar far too many times since he'd come back to town. So many times, in fact, that he'd started jogging. Outdoors. In the South Georgia heat. Because there were no gyms in this godforsaken—

"Morning, Simon," a cheerful voice called.

Jolted from his snit-fit, he whipped his head around

to see Reverend Mitchell coming down the walkway in front of a small brick home. "Good morning, Reverend," he said, mustering his smile once more. Thankfully, he didn't feel the need to woo the clergyman the way he would a client, so he didn't amp up the wattage. Nodding toward the brick house, he asked, "Is this your place?"

The older man chuckled. "My lawn is not particularly well-kept. This is Maisy Tillenger's house. She's been under the weather, so Luellen and I have been checking in on her. Since we had company this morning, Luellen sent me."

Simon was aware the sheriff's department had taken the young woman who accused Coulter of mistreating her to the pastor's house. He let the comment about company slide by without remark. "Kind of you."

Good thing the reverend was a discreet man himself. "All part of the service," he replied jovially. He pointed to a shiny Buick parked at the curb. "You headin' for the Daisy? I could give you a lift."

Simon hesitated. Though he enjoyed the same easy country manners employed by his grandfather, he couldn't help being suspicious of the small-town bonhomie exhibited by so many of Pine Bluff's residents. He was a city guy. The son of a politician to boot. He firmly believed the world was fueled by quid pro quo. Perhaps the preacher wanted to score some free legal advice? Man of the cloth or not, he'd hardly be the first person who tried to wriggle around paying billable hours by engaging in some friendly conversation.

"I appreciate the offer, but if it's all the same to you, I think I'll walk. I've got some stuff I'm thinking through."

Reverend Mitchell didn't seem fazed by the refusal. "I understand." Rather than moving toward his car, the man stepped directly into Simon's path. "If you need a sounding board for anything you're noodling, you can always come to me. Again, all part of the service."

He smiled, and Simon was struck by the other man's innate ease and warmth. Regret twisted in his chest. He hated being so jaded. He didn't want to believe he was the kind of man who read something into everything. Then again, he'd learned at the foot of the master. A lifelong politician, his own father was the king of wheeling and dealing. From birth, Simon had been groomed to enter the arena.

"Thank you, sir," Simon said evenly. "Enjoy your day."

"You too, son," the reverend replied, clapping him on the shoulder. "Might I suggest you ask Miss Darlene to add extra cherries to your co-cola? There's no better pick-me-up for a bad day."

Simon's jaw slackened when the older man slid behind the wheel, slick as an eel. "How do you—"

The *ka-thunk* of the car door cut off the question. Reverend Mitchell cranked the engine and lifted two fingers from the wheel in farewell and pulled away from the curb.

"Friggin' fishbowl," he muttered. Stepping over a hump where a tree root had broken through the sidewalk, he resisted the urge to kick the loose pebbles skidding beneath the soles of his shoes because rocks and fine Italian leather rarely mixed well.

In a concession to the warmth of the day, he unbuttoned his suit jacket and loosened the silk tie enough to open his collar button. A fine coating of perspiration slicked his forehead and made the thin white cotton of his undershirt cling. Undaunted, he pressed on.

The grumble and pop of a souped-up engine brought him up short when he reached the cracked asphalt of the Daisy Drive-In's parking lot. A dinged-up subcompact with a ridiculous-looking spoiler rolled right past him, not bothering to yield to his right of way. Simon glared at the driver. The kid's arms were covered in mixture of amateur and professional tattoos. He was wearing a dirty ribbed undershirt and a trucker's cap with the bill turned to the side. Like he was some kind of backwoods hip-hop star. The worst of it was he had the gall to sneer when he gave Simon the once-over as he crept past.

The engine popped and roared, drawing the attention of nearly everyone waiting in line. The rear end fishtailed when the kid punched the accelerator and zipped toward the highway. Customers shook their heads as they stood in line at the order window. Simon approached, winding his way through the clumps of people chatting as they waited for their orders. No one greeted him, though he was sure they knew who he was. Or rather, who his grandfather was.

He nodded to a couple of men about his age. He hadn't been back in town long enough to renew the few acquaintances he'd made when his parents used to insist he spend his summers at his grandparents' house. Of course, he'd revisited here and there. Mainly quick swings through town when his father, a state assemblyman, was up for reelection.

He'd been studying abroad when his grandmother passed nearly ten years earlier. Both his father and grandfather insisted the trip home from Tokyo would require too much time off from his program. The people of Grandpa Wendell's beloved town hadn't understood or cared about their reasoning. Unlike the shameless flirts and meddling matchmakers he ran into in Atlanta, the over-sixty set in Pine Bluff had little use for him. He could swear he'd seen one or two of them steer their precious granddaughters away from him if they happened to pass in the Piggly Wiggly. Most settled for giving him the hairy eyeball.

Simon jerked to a stop two feet behind the last person in line. A woman turned to glare at him, but he tried not to take it personally. Brushing the sides of his suit coat back to allow some air to flow around his heated body, he lifted his gaze to meet hers and she quickly looked away. The woman turned away and he realized there was something familiar about her. She was young. And obviously not a fan.

Simon searched his memory, sure he'd have remembered her if they'd been introduced. Shifting from one foot to the other, he tried to get a better look. She wore her rich, dark hair pulled ruthlessly back from her face and coiled into a massive bun at the nape of her neck. The effect should have been severe, but for some reason, it intrigued him. He wanted to pull the pins from the knot and let the heavy locks down. He wanted to see how far down her back they flowed.

The line moved forward, and when they settled into their new formation, he saw the woman stepping up to the window. She wore a tan-and-brown uniform with a patch sewed onto the shirtsleeve that declared the wearer to be a member of the Masters County Sheriff's Department. Simon grimaced when he realized this was probably the deputy who'd taken the statement given against his client. Simon wasn't dumb enough to think he'd be high on the sheriff's office's list of favorite people after helping Samuel Coulter wriggle off the hook. Judging by the scornful look in her eyes, he wasn't wrong.

Simon stood frozen in place, watching her bend low to speak through the screen window. She must have a standing order, because with a minimum of words exchanged, the woman walked away clutching the tiny white slip with her order number printed on it.

Simon wanted to step out of line and directly into her path as she moved to join the people milling and lounging near the pickup window. Explain that he'd only been doing the job he'd been hired to do, and that truthfully, Coulter gave him the creeps too. She wouldn't believe him even if he told her. Her glare made her disdain clear.

When his grandfather had droned on and on about how providing defense from the law was truly one of the most honorable things a man could do, Simon had only listened with half an ear. He'd been surrounded by and immersed in politics for too long to truly believe most people were innocent until proved guilty. In his experience, most people were guilty as sin when it came to being self-serving. Including himself. Look where that had landed him...in Pine Bluff.

Coulter certainly had his own best interests at heart. When Dora Houseman, the secretary he'd inherited along with his grandfather's firm, informed him the man's nickname was Cottonmouth, Simon had assumed it was because he was in the business of importing, breeding and selling exotic snakes at the multiacre refuge he'd set up on the other side of the county. In meeting him, Simon had to admit Coulter had likely earned his nickname based on his slithery personality. And his weird eyes.

The man's left pupil bled down to the bottom of his iris. The anomaly alone wasn't what made his stare so disturbing. A flat ruthlessness shone from his gold-green gaze. Simon himself had avoided looking directly at Coulter for any protracted amount of time.

Shaking off his discomfiture, Simon stepped to the order window when the woman ahead of him moved aside.

"Heya, Mr. Simon," the gum-smacking older woman

called Darlene greeted him, her grin bordering on a leer. "Cherry Coke?"

Her presumptive friendliness rankled, but he refused to let it show. Any misstep he made in this town would be reported to his grandfather within hours, no doubt. "Yes, please," he confirmed with the distant smile he'd perfected when he was a child trotted out at campaign events. "And today I'll try the club sandwich."

Darlene whooped and scrawled the order on her pad. "Mr. Simon Wingate is finally ready to join the mile-high club," she crowed. She ripped the claim check from the bottom of the order slip and slid it across the counter. She tapped it twice with the pointed tip of one blood-red acrylic nail. "I'm the woman to make it happen for ya, sugar."

The woman working the grill cackled. The young lady working the milkshake station ducked her head and murmured a mortified "Mama!"

Darlene smiled up at him, unrepentant. "I'll give a shout when it's ready, darlin'."

Simon could feel the heat in his cheeks and ears, and hoped anyone looking might attribute his blush to the temperature and layers of clothing. He moved from the window, hoping to find a shady spot along the side of the building far away from Darlene to wait, but found himself face-to-face with the woman with the tightly coiled hair. Lourdes Cabrera. She of the soulful eyes and Masters County Sheriff's Department uniform. He didn't have to check her name tag to be sure. The hostility in her stance said it all.

"Deputy," he said, giving her a polite nod.

"Snake handler," she replied, keeping her voice even, though her eyes glowed with banked fury.

He chuckled, mentally tallying up a point in her favor.

"Just doin' my job, ma'am," he answered, giving her a tip of an invisible hat.

Peeking around the corner of the building, he spotted a sliver of shade he might claim for himself. He was about to wind his way through the waiting customers when he heard her mutter, "Whatever helps you sleep at night."

"I sleep the sleep of the innocent, Deputy Cabrera," he said, meeting her gaze. "Every night I indulge in the peaceful, unfettered rest of a man with a clear conscience."

"You're certainly no Wendell Wingate," she retorted, not backing down an inch.

He shook his head. "Ah, I hate to tell you this, but you're wrong."

"Oh?" she asked archly.

"Since we have yet to be formally introduced, you can't be expected to know my full name." He extended a hand to shake. "I'm Wendell Simon Wingate III."

"Are you serious?" She snorted a laugh, a sound he usually found distasteful. For some reason, when this woman did it, he wanted to crack a smile. Her hand flew up to cover her nose and mouth, and two spots of bright red appeared on her high cheekbones.

"I am always serious about meeting a pretty woman." He hit her with his best smile. "I'm new to town, and I appreciate you making me feel so welcome."

When she lowered her hand, a sheepish smile curved lush, full lips. Simon's gaze dropped to them, and he found he had a hard time tearing it away. "You are welcome here," she relented. "And I'm sorry. I'm—"

"Miffed?" he supplied.

She laughed again, and this time it rang clear and true. "Not the word I would have chosen."

"It was nothing personal, Deputy," he assured her in a

low voice. "He retained me to be his counsel. You didn't have much of a case."

She opened her mouth to say something, but Darlene called for her. "Lori, honey? Your shakes are ready."

She stood her ground, her defiant glare locked on him. Simon found he didn't mind this particular woman's boldness. "You didn't have to take him on."

"You may not have noticed, but lawyers aren't thick on the ground here. At least, not defense attorneys."

She tipped her pointed chin up a notch. "He could have gone elsewhere for representation."

He leaned in and dropped his voice to a conspiratorial whisper. "Big-money clients are few and far between in these parts. I promised my granddad I wouldn't run the place into the ground in the first six months," he added with a wink. Simon winced inside. His mother would have tanned him for making such a tawdry move. "He's already handed all the Timber Masters business over to their new in-house counsel, so I've been tasked with keeping the place afloat."

Until a few months ago, the majority of the firm's business had come from the Masters family and their family-owned forestry and lumber business, Timber Masters. Marlee Masters had come home to roost after earning her law degree, and his grandfather got the notion to make a run at one of the elected posts on the circuit court. The timing of it all seemed…inevitable, if not exactly fortuitous.

The problem was, Simon wasn't sure he could keep his promise to his grandfather. Other than writing a new will for Eleanor Young, a timid divorcée who'd lost her only son earlier in the year, he hadn't done a single lawyerly thing since he'd moved to Pine Bluff. The call from Samuel Coulter needing someone local to represent his "various business and personal interests" had broken weeks of Dora reminding him his calendar was distressingly open.

"So, naturally, you scraped the bottom of the nearest barrel to find a client. Congratulations," she added as she shouldered past him to get to the pickup window. "You've got yourself a real winner there, Wingate."

Chapter Three

"Hi, Mama, I'm home," she called out as she walked through the back door of her childhood home.

Her mother shot her a bland look over her shoulder. "Hello, Lourdes."

Lori cringed at the formality of the greeting. Not long ago, she would have been *mija*. But everything had gone sideways when she moved out.

Sophia Castillo-Cabrera was not a woman who thawed quickly. Her mother added another unlabeled jar to the collection in the crook of her arm and straightened, letting the door swing shut without looking directly at Lori. "What brings you by?"

Lori quickly squashed the flash of hurt. Moving out of her girlhood home had started out as a bone of contention and had finally simmered down to a touchy subject. The family was still reeling from the death of her father and aunt in a car accident when they'd discovered Anita Cabrera had left her house to Lori in her will.

Her mother had expected Lori to sell the property and use the proceeds to help fund her younger siblings' education. Instead, she'd packed up her clothes and what few worldly possessions she'd accumulated since leaving the army and moved into the cozy bungalow.

Why couldn't her mother understand that Lori needed

the freedom of living on her own for the first time in her life?

Her mother believed Lori was thumbing her nose at the family by moving out. Females were to stay in the family fold, living in the house of their father until they moved in with their spouse. Somehow, Sophia managed to skim over the years Lori had spent sleeping in military barracks. As far as she was concerned, her first-born child was besmirching the family name with her father and aunt barely gone a year.

Lori should have felt guilty, but she didn't. Which caused her even greater remorse.

Forcing a smile, she held up a plastic grocery bag. "I came by to drop off a couple of T-shirts for Lena." She made a face when her mother stared back at her, unreadable. "She said something about the military look being back in style."

"That's nice of you," her mother answered distractedly.

The gulf between them was widening, and Lori had no idea how to stop it. "Mama, I love you."

Her mother moved to the stove and stirred the sauce simmering there. "You love me so much you don't want to live under my roof."

"I was gone for four years and you never gave me a hard time," she pressed.

"Totally different."

"Not different. I am literally less than a mile away," she argued.

"I am aware," Sophia replied.

Lori sighed and repeated the same mantra she'd been using since the day Wendell Wingate almost apologetically informed them her aunt Anita had drawn up a will. "Mama, I'm a grown woman. I need space of my own."

Her mother's shoulders stiffened. "You don't think I was a grown woman when I married your father and moved into his house?"

This was a worn, old circular argument. She understood why her mother wanted her to sell the property. Sophia was worried about paying for school for the younger kids and expected Lori to dump the proceeds from the sale into the family coffers. But there was life insurance money, and Lori would help however she could. Sure, sometimes she felt selfish for hanging on to the place, but she couldn't help thinking Anita had known she needed her own space.

"I'll go find Lena," she said, gesturing to the narrow hallway.

She followed the thump-thump-snare roll of a pop song to the door decorated with a satin-and-ribbon memory board with *Marialena* spelled out in paste rhinestones and pearls. Casting her memory back, Lori tried to recall whether she'd ever had anything half as sparkly. She didn't think so. The most elaborate article of clothing she'd ever owned or worn was the sherbet-peach ball gown each of the Cabrera girls had worn for their quinceañera celebrations. Lori had complained to her mother about the flounces and lace. The previous year, Lena had moaned about not having a gown of her own. Lori had offered to pay for a new one, but neither her mother nor her sulking younger sister would hear of it, so she'd backed off.

A week after the party, her father and his sister had been driving home from a restaurant supply store in Albany when they were killed by a farmer from Prescott County who'd fallen asleep at the wheel and crossed the centerline.

The memory board jumped when she rapped twice,

then called through the hollow-core door. "Hey, Lena-da-queena. I brought you some cool soldier-girl clothes."

The volume decreased and Lena called out a desultory "Come in."

Lori opened the door to find her sister stretched sideways across the twin beds Lena'd shoved together. She tried to stifle the pang of grief when she saw her sister had removed Lori's pictures and mementos from the walls and the frame of the old-fashioned vanity mirror. Although Lori had hardly given them a second thought in years, she couldn't help feeling stung when she saw the bare spots.

"Wow. You've rearranged."

Lena pressed the button on the side of her phone to lock the screen. She barely spared Lori a glance. "I figured you wouldn't care."

Lori couldn't help but be impressed by her sister's nonchalance. Everyone else in the family—her brothers included—had been insulted by her defection and been vocal in their opinions. But her sister held her cards close to her chest. Lena had always been quiet, far more reserved than the rest of them, which sometimes made Lori uncomfortable.

Her gaze traveled to the phone her sister had oh-so-casually locked and placed facedown on the bedspread, and Lori decided *reserved* wasn't exactly the right word for her baby sister. Lena was secretive. An island unto herself amid the noise and chaos of their family.

Without waiting for the invitation she was fairly sure wouldn't come, Lori strode into the room and dropped heavily onto the edge of the bed. "Did you have a bonfire or something?"

Lena shook her head, pointing to the closet. "Nah, I put it all in a box. It's there if you want it."

It hurt to have been erased from the room, but Lori was pleased her sister hadn't simply tossed her mementos in the trash. Pressing her hand to her throat, she massaged away the unexpected tightness she felt there. "Thanks. I'll take it with me," she said, striving to keep her voice light. "I brought you some shirts. One has the crossed-flintlock-pistols logo. Pretty cool," she said, dropping the grocery bag containing the army T-shirts onto the bed.

Lena frowned in puzzlement, and Lori wondered if she'd imagined their previous conversation. The one where her sister was waxing poetic about how cool it was that Lori'd been in the army, and how Lena could rock her new pair of khaki cargo pants if she just had the right shirt to go with them. The pucker between the younger girl's untweezed eyebrows deepened, and Lori felt the urge to rush to the kitchen and thank her mother for making her baby sister adhere to the same strict edicts she'd had to endure.

"You brought me some old shirts?" Lena said, enunciating with such a deep drawl the words almost sounded foreign and exotic.

Lori pursed her lips, willing herself not to snap. Lena might be quiet, but she was still capable of serving up heaping helpings of teenage snark. Only their father, who thought the sun rose and set on his precious baby girl, had been exempt from her contempt. If Sophia hadn't been giving her elder daughter such a hard time for wanting to live her life on her own terms, Lori was sorely tempted to actually jump up and run to the kitchen to give her mother a hug. Coming home to her family after years in the military helped her realize parenting was very much like engaging in hand-to-hand combat on a daily basis.

"You said you needed something to go with your cargo pants."

"So you brought me some hand-me-downs you probably sweated through, like, a hundred times?"

Tired from the bad start to the day and a shift filled
with particularly annoying calls, Lori decided to disen-
gage. She didn't want to snap at her sister and become
more of an outlaw within her own family. Lori pushed
off the bed, irked by the sneaking suspicion the teen was
baiting her, and went to the closet to retrieve the shoebox
of old photos, certificates and ribbons Lena had removed
from the walls. "You know what...? Never mind."

With the box wedged under her arm, she was about to
leave when she caught her sister peeking at her phone.
Lena frowned at the screen, her bottom lip caught between her teeth. Suddenly, Lori saw a flash of the girl
who used to crawl into her bed on Christmas Eves, worried Santa never got her letter.

"What's wrong, Le-Le?"

Her sister's face hardened for a millisecond, but she
quickly crumbled. "It's Jasmine," she whispered.

The quaver in Lena's voice nearly broke Lori. She
moved back to the bed and reclaimed her spot, setting
the box at her feet. Reaching out, she placed a comforting
hand on the younger girl's back. Lena and Jasmine had
been inseparable since their preschool days. If her sister's
bestie was in trouble, Lena would feel it too. "What's Jas
up to these days?"

"She's, um..." Lena's gaze shifted to her phone as she
weighed how much to divulge. "She's been, uh, blowing me off."

"No way."

"She is."

Crossing her legs at her ankles, Lori tried for disinter-
ested nonchalance as she gently pressed. "Any idea why?"

Lena's lips tightened then trembled as she said, "She met some boy."

"I see. And she doesn't have time for you?" Lori asked, sympathetic. She recalled all too well how much it hurt when her own childhood friends started to drift away.

"She's all into this Rick guy. He's so smarmy. All muscly and tattooed." She wrinkled her nose in disapproval.

"Tattooed?"

Lori reared back. Pine Bluff may be the biggest town in Masters County, but it was hardly a booming metropolis. He must have lived outside of town. People around here tended to be conservative. Clean-cut. At least on the surface.

Lori didn't have anything against tattoos. She herself had one of the crossed flintlock pistols of the military police emblem done the evening after their graduation. Her classmates had teased her for making the artist do hers about one-fifth the size of the sample. And on her hip. Sophia had walked into the bathroom as Lori was climbing from the shower one day and nearly fainted. Or so she claimed. She'd been an adult, but her mother had been horrified to discover her daughter had "ruined" her "beautiful" body.

But who would let their kid get all inked up at fifteen? "Isn't he young to be getting tattoos?"

Lena shot her a scornful side-eye. "He's not our age."

"No?" Lori squawked.

"God, no. Boys our age are so…disgusting."

Lori couldn't argue with Lena's logic. Having grown up with younger brothers, Lori was all too aware of how unattractive fifteen-year-old boys could be. "I'm assuming he's older?"

Lena shrugged. "Eighteen or nineteen, maybe? Out of high school."

"Ah…wow," Lori murmured, her mind racing as she scrambled for a way to get back to the place where Lena felt comfortable confiding in her. "I guess I had no idea Jas was into older guys."

Lena stared hard at the phone but her face crumpled. "Me either. But she turned sixteen and she has her provisional license and can drive now, and I'm not good enough…" Her sister trailed off into a hiccuping sob.

"Oh, Le-Le." Twisting around, Lori pulled her sister into an awkward hug when the girl started to cry in earnest. She wanted to ask if Jasmine's parents knew she was flirting with some strange guy, but instinct told her she'd lose cool points for the question, and right now she wanted to keep Lena talking to her. "I'm sorry. I know it hurts."

Sixteen. Lori knew from experience it was a dangerous age. It marked the tipping point where parental approval started coming second to what your friends thought. When a girl's body started telling her she was a woman, and she was all too willing to believe the hype. Sixteen. It was the age of consent in Georgia, though Lori was fairly certain her sister and her friends couldn't even tell her what consent really meant. Her blood boiled and her heart raced as she squeezed Lena tighter, holding out hope that her sister would choose to remain on the "girl" side of that dividing line a little longer.

"I don't get why we can't be fr-friends anymore," Lena sobbed. "I'm cool," she added with a small hiccup.

"You are," Lori cooed, stroking the younger girl's silky hair. "You're the coolest."

Lena gave a watery laugh and tried to pull away, but Lori wouldn't let her go. Thankfully, Lena relaxed into the embrace, resting her cheek on her big sister's shoulder. "And the stupid thing is, she told him she's seventeen. Like that makes a big difference. She doesn't even look seventeen."

Lori swallowed the lump in her throat. "No, she doesn't."

And it made no difference in the eyes of the law. But in the life of a young woman, those tender years mattered. Lori remembered them all too well. The confusion. The heady power that came from being noticed by boys for the first time. The constant roller-coaster ride of emotion. The tug-of-war between what her friends were doing and what her parents expected of her. Oh, the drama. And most of all, the aching desire to get adolescence over with so she could get on with what she once thought of as "real life."

"She's too young to be fooling around with guys of any age."

"It's gross," Lena retorted.

Lori couldn't help but smile a little as she smoothed her sister's hair. "That too."

"And I don't think they're even really going out. I mean, they text and she sends him messages on Pictur-Spam and stuff, but she's—" Lena drew a shuddering breath "—she's blowing me off, and I miss her. We've been friends forever, and now she doesn't have time to text me back."

"I get it," Lori assured her. "Stinks."

"And he's so…gross."

Lori chuckled softly at her sister's choice of adjective. "It sucks when you see your friend hanging out with a guy who's…gross."

Her baby sister's giggle was a balm. "It's the perfect word," Lena insisted. "Get this. He has this job where he takes snakes around to these weird churches and stuff. Can you think of a nastier job? Jasmine went to a tent revival with her mee-maw and now she's all into him."

Lena shuddered and Lori froze. "I guess they must pay okay and all, but ew. He works for the millionaire guy who owns the snake place they advertise on the highway. The Reptile Rendezvous?"

Lori held her sister tighter. "Oh, yeah?" she replied, her voice weak.

She wrinkled her nose. "Yeah. All the kids are talking about that place. That's why they're all dressing in camo and safari stuff. Like they think it's so cool."

"They do?"

"Yeah. I think it's mostly because the guy is so rich and all," she said with a shrug. "I really don't get it, but Jasmine's all worked up about him."

This time, Lori pulled back, needing to read her sister's face. "The snake guy? Coulter?"

Lena scowled. "No. Yeah. I mean, his name is Rick. Weren't you listening?"

"Right, yeah, Rick. The tatted-up snake guy," Lori confirmed, relief washing through her at the realization her sister's friend was at least one step removed from Coulter's clutches.

"If you do get Jas to text you back, tell her Lori said to ditch the snake guy—he's too old for her. And to stay away from Reptile Rendezvous."

Lena snorted. "Yeah, right. I'm her best friend. If she won't listen to me, she's sure not gonna listen to you."

"Yeah, well, I'm her BFF's big sister, which makes me kind of hers too." She gave Lena another squeeze, then grabbed the shoebox as she rose. "Just keep trying with her, Le-Le. That's all you can do."

"I will."

Lori backed out of the room with a smile and a wave, determined to give Jasmine's parents a heads-up. Jas was playing a dangerous game, and even if she was considered old enough in the eyes of the law, she wasn't in reality. Someone needed to try to help Jasmine make better, smarter choices.

If Lori couldn't help with that, she could always go in another direction. She would bet this Rick guy didn't know or care about the legalities. She might be able to scare him off, if Jasmine's parents didn't beat her to it.

Passing through the kitchen, she asked, "Mama? Do you have Keely Jones's phone number? I think Jasmine might want some of my shirts too," she fibbed.

"In my phone," Sophia replied, waving a spoon toward the kitchen table without looking up.

Lori used her parents' wedding anniversary date to unlock her mother's phone and quickly forwarded Jasmine's mother's contact information to her own phone. The moment she set the mobile back on the table, her mother appeared at her side with a plastic container.

"Here. You can have these for supper."

Lori smiled, kissed her mother on the cheek and graciously accepted the warm-from-the-oven enchiladas. "Thank you." As she headed out the back door, she called back another "I love you, Mama" just for good measure, then headed for her car.

She left the house wondering if her stomach would ever stop roiling enough for her to eat a bite of those delicious-smelling enchiladas. Climbing into her car, she placed the box of mementos and food container on the passenger seat. Gripping the steering wheel tight, she counted to four as she drew a breath in, held it for four, then let it go slowly.

She drove to the end of the block, hooked a right, then pulled to the curb. Out of sight of her childhood home, Lori took her phone from her pocket and pulled up the contact information. As she waited for Jasmine's mother to answer, she gnawed her lip. Her intervention in the teenager's life would most definitely be unwelcome, but she had a duty. When the other woman answered, cheerful in her oblivion, Lori knew in her gut she was doing the right thing. The last thing she wanted was to find her sister's best friend walking down the side of Highway 19, scared and crying. Or worse.

Chapter Four

The following morning, Simon was heading for the district attorney's office when he ran into Deputy Cabrera in the atrium. Well, he didn't run into her so much as she stopped dead in front of him and directed her death-ray stare at him. "Good morning," he said politely.

The deputy narrowed her eyes warily and he fought back the urge to smirk. Her expression said any smiling or smirking would be completely unwelcome. And, well, for some reason, he wanted her to welcome seeing him.

"Good morning."

They stood staring at one another awkwardly. At last, Simon gestured to the door behind him. "I was heading to a meeting with District Attorney Hayes."

"Good for you."

He ignored her smart remark and switched to a different tactic. "When I was talking to him the other day, he told me about the methamphetamine problems you all have been sorting out these past few years."

She pursed her lips. "I'm surprised you didn't hear about those cases from your grandfather. Wendell handled the defense for most of the accused. At least, those who were locals. Maybe he figured you wouldn't be interested in Pine Bluff news."

Simon swallowed a wince. People around here had

a way of making it clear they disapproved of his absence from his grandparents' lives without coming out and saying so.

"I suppose it was sort of abstract for me," he answered honestly.

She crossed her arms over her chest and widened her stance. The combative move should have made her more intimidating, but perversely enough, Simon found it attractive. He had always been attracted to women who weren't afraid to stand their ground.

His mother might look the ultimate politician's wife on the outside, but there was no question who ruled the roost. Simon had been raised to respect women. In a weird way, Deputy Cabrera reminded him of his mother, though the two of them couldn't have been more opposite in appearance and demeanor. Bettina Wingate was petite, blonde and perfectly put together.

Lourdes Cabrera was also petite, but the similarities ended there. She was curvy. Shapely. She reminded him of those World War Two–era pinups guys painted on the fuselage of their planes. He'd only seen her in uniform, but her figure was impossible to hide.

And she made those curves look dangerous. Powerful. This woman couldn't play the delicate Southern flower if she tried. She was commanding, with her intense dark stare and the utility belt stuffed with weaponry. Don't think he hadn't noted how the nylon belt hugged her rounded hips.

Hooking a thumb over his shoulder, he said, "Well, either way, I got my first taste of how seriously people feel about drug trafficking in these parts early this morning."

She nodded, her expression sober. "The Showalters called you, I'll bet. I heard Mike busted Timmy Showalter for possession with the intent to distribute last night."

The corner of Simon's mouth kicked up. Though he'd spoken with his client for only five minutes, there was absolutely no doubt in Simon's mind that the story the kid was feeding him was complete BS. Good thing it wasn't Simon's job to believe him or not. It was Simon's job to make sure he had an adequate defense. "My client has absolutely no idea how those pills ended up in his backpack. This was his first offense, and he's a minor."

Her frown deepened. "He's seventeen. Timmy and my brother Lorenzo are in the same class. They were in Cub Scouts together."

Simon wanted to kick himself for sounding so cavalier about the kid's arrest and the seriousness of the charges. It was easy to be flippant when one didn't have a relationship with the people one was representing. He had to remember he wasn't in Atlanta anymore. With the metropolis's booming population, it seemed hardly anyone was a local. Almost everyone he came across in this town was someone to somebody else.

He felt a brief longing for his old boring job of cajoling senators and representatives on behalf of special-interest groups. In politics, the lives hanging in the balance were far more removed than those in his present situation. In politics, you had to watch your every step. Even if you were playing within bounds, there was always someone who would spin the angle to suit them. He'd learned that the hard way.

"I'm sorry. It must be tough seeing a kid you watched grow up get into trouble. I'll do my best for him."

"Please do."

Simon took a deep, steadying breath. In any other jurisdiction, a cop would be hoping Simon's client got the book thrown at him. Hard. Here, she wanted him to do a good job defending the kid. The fact of the matter was, he wasn't entirely sure he was going to be any good at providing adequate defense to people he felt were absolutely guilty.

He'd lain awake for hours the previous night thinking about Coulter's cold eyes, and the smug, reflexive smile the man wore like a mask. Perhaps it was simply because Coulter had money and was used to getting his way, or perhaps he was born a supercilious ass. Either way, the man's attitude didn't settle well with Simon.

She unfurled her arms and let them fall to rest on her belt. "To be honest, I don't get how you defense attorneys do it," she said, shaking her head in slow wonder. "I spent a lot of time trying to lure your grandfather away from the dark side."

Surprised, Simon gazed at the woman. "We have all the cookies," he replied, falling back on flirtation.

Wendell had never mentioned anything about the sheriff's officers other than to commend the work Ben Kinsella and his crew did in picking up the pieces after the Drug Enforcement Administration left the county in tatters.

"You and Wendell were friends?" he asked, hating the suspicious roil of his stomach.

Her narrow gaze became distinctly disdainful. "Yes, Wendell and I are friends," she replied, correcting his tense. She spun on her heel and headed for the sheriff's office. She'd about reached the door when she paused and looked back at him.

Simon froze, arrested by the intensity in her eyes. "Was there something else, Deputy?"

"Yes." She let her hand fall away from the door handle and took two steps back in his direction. Simon silently willed her to take more, but she stopped. The rubber soles of her utility boots squeaked on the tile floor when she drew to a halt. "How well acquainted are you with the people who work for your client?"

Simon was not at all surprised by the derisive tone she used when she spoke the word *client*. He got her meaning, but he needed her to be more direct.

"I'm not sure I'm following the question," he replied cautiously.

"The people who work for Coulter. Have you, uh, met any of them?" she asked, hitting him with her impenetrable dark gaze.

He shook his head. "I have not. I am not well enough acquainted with people around here to identify who works where and for whom. Why do you ask?"

Deputy Cabrera hesitated. For the first time since he'd laid eyes on her, he saw her fidget.

Granted, it was a small tell. Her fingers toyed with the Velcro closure on one of the compartments on her belt. A nervous twitch of her hand he might not have noticed if it weren't for the ripping of Velcro hooks tearing through the silence between them. Over and over again, she opened the flap, then smoothed it down again. He hoped it wasn't the pocket with a Taser or similar weapon.

"I'm worried about my younger sister," she began abruptly, jolting him from his study of her nervous movements.

"You are?"

She wagged her head, stunned to find herself confiding in him.

"Well, not her... One of her friends."

Sensing she was struggling, he fell back on doing what lawyers do best—ask questions until the person unwittingly tells everything.

"How many siblings do you have?" he asked, keeping his question light and friendly.

"Five. Four brothers and one sister."

The rigidity in her stance and the succinct answer told him she hadn't wanted to disclose any more information. His breath caught when he saw the pretty pink wash of a blush flare high on her cheeks. Obliged by his upbringing, he did the gentlemanly thing and helped her out of the corner she'd talked herself into. "Your sister is how old?"

"Fifteen. She's a sophomore. Her name is Lena."

"Pretty name." He made a motion for her to go on.

"Lena has a friend. They've been friends since they were in preschool. Her name is Jasmine."

She stopped there, and Simon waited patiently. He got the feeling Deputy Cabrera wasn't accustomed to confiding secrets. He was certain it was costing her more than she let on to share information with him, of all people. He was fairly sure she'd pegged him as public enemy number one.

"Jasmine. Got it."

She wanted something from him. Needed his assistance in some way. And when a woman as competent as Deputy Cabrera asked for help, a smart man sat up and took notice, because something big had to be weighing on her.

"Her friend is…kind of hanging around a guy who works for your client."

The way she spit the words *your client* at him made him flinch.

"I see." He scowled. "She's fifteen, you say?"

"Jasmine is sixteen, but this guy… From what Lena tells me, he's older."

"And you want me to poke around and see if any of the guys who work for Coulter have been in trouble?"

No sooner had the words left his mouth than she threw

up her hands and backed off again. "You know what? Never mind."

He took a step closer, and when she didn't back away, he pressed. "I'm not your enemy. You asked for help. I'm willing to help."

"You know what? I don't need your help," she snapped.

"Deputy, I'm doing the exact same job Wendell would have done. I'm not the bad guy here."

"I don't think you are," she answered a shade too quickly.

This time he couldn't repress his smile. "You do, but I'm going to do my best to convince you you've got me all wrong."

"Why do you care?" she asked, bristling.

"Because I want us to be friends," he answered.

"Why?" she asked again. This time, the single word sounded bewildered. Simon saw his opening and was careful to tread lightly.

"I don't have any friends here," he said, opting for the blunt approach. "Being new in town and all, I would prefer to have more friends than enemies." He made sure he was looking straight into her eyes. "And we are on the same side, Lourdes."

"Lori."

Simon fought the urge to grin because her expression was so expressively solemn. She'd offered him the diminutive, and damn it, he was going to take it. "Lori," he corrected.

She blinked, breaking the connection between them. "I don't understand how you figure we're on the same side. Hayes and I, we're on the same side. But you…" She shook her head. "I can't understand how defense attorneys can defend people they know are up to no good."

"We can do it because everybody has a right to an

advocate," he said, repeating the party line his law professors hammered home about the topic. "It's all about checks and balances. It doesn't mean I'm on their side or condoning heinous and criminal behavior."

She chuckled and gave her head a shake. "You contradict yourself, Counselor."

"Simon," he interjected.

"Simon," she amended with a jut of her pointed chin.

He wanted to ask her to say his name again, but based on the conversation they were having, he didn't think she'd be inclined to indulge him. So, he fell back on another of his grandfather's favorite sayings.

"There are some who say the defense attorney is the only person without an agenda in the courtroom."

"Yeah, Wendell used to use the same con. He didn't have any better luck getting me to swallow the line than you will."

She backed off a step and reached for the door again. Rather than fleeing into the offices of the sheriff's department, she glanced back again. Simon mentally snapped a picture of her. With her expressive dark eyes and the heavy knot of hair pinned tightly to her nape, she was utterly arresting.

"I understand what you're saying, and I'm aware this isn't an easy town to live in when you're an outsider."

The phrasing of her statement was almost as compelling as the husky rasp in her voice. He cocked his head and waited for more. Prayed there'd be more.

She gave the door handle a yank. "We won't be enemies, but I'm not so sure about the friends thing."

He nodded and shoved his hands into the pockets of his suit pants, not caring if he ruined the line of the tailoring. "I'll take not-enemies for now."

She ducked into the office, and the door swished shut

behind her on its hydraulic hinge. He withdrew his hands from his pockets and looked around at the municipal building's dormant atrium, wondering if the budget was so tight they couldn't afford to at least run the fountain.

They weren't going to be enemies, he repeated to himself as he studied the pattern in the mosaic tiles. He would work on the friends part. He would, because something told him Lori would be a good friend to have. She had already shown herself to be fierce and protective. She was asking after some guy who was messing with a friend of her sister. She was obviously the type to be loyal and unwavering in her companionship. It sure couldn't hurt to have a friend in this insular town.

Christ. He scrubbed a hand over his face. He didn't want her to see how conflicted he truly was. Simon didn't want to go poking around in his client's personnel records. He hadn't expected to find all this…unsavory stuff here in Pine Bluff. Had his grandfather spent his entire life defending drug dealers and perverts? How did the old man sleep at night?

The outer door opened and Simon physically shook himself out of that line of thinking as the district attorney walked in. Simon gave Harrison Hayes a closer inspection this time. He'd been too blinded by Coulter and the potentially hefty billable hours to pay much attention to the man he'd be facing in court on a fairly regular basis. To his relief, Hayes looked much like the guys Simon had come through undergrad and law school with. In other words, he wore a decent suit, kept his shoes polished, leaned conservative in the barber's chair, and his sharply intelligent eyes caught everything.

The prosecutor drew up short when he saw Simon standing there. "Did we have a meeting?"

Simon gave the other man a wan smile. "I'm here to represent Timothy Showalter," he announced.

Hayes headed toward the door opposite the sheriff's department, what Simon had earmarked the justice side of the county's law and justice headquarters. The second floor of the municipal building held the county clerk, emergency management, economic development and finance offices. Fire and rescue were housed in a prefabricated building on the edge of town.

Holding back, he watched as the DA pulled a key ring from his pocket and juggled his briefcase from one hand to the other. "Come in. We'll talk."

What Lori had said about the guy messing with the high school girl niggled at Simon. "Have you guys had a lot of trouble coming out of Coulter's place?" he asked when the other man swung the door open wide.

"I wouldn't say a lot," Hayes equivocated. With a practiced swipe of his hand, he switched on the fluorescent lights. "There was the girl Lori picked up the other night. A few of the local teenagers have scored weekend jobs out there, so that's made it something of a hot spot. Some have tried to sneak in."

Simon blinked, giving his pupils time to adjust to the sudden brightness after standing in the dim atrium. Glancing back, he realized not only was the fountain drained dry, but also the two-story lobby itself was lit only by skylights and the glow spilling from the glass-walled offices surrounding it. "The refuge is open to the public."

"Only on weekends and for the price of admission," Hayes answered. "Some people don't care to pay admission. Mostly it's been kids daring each other to sneak in and that sort of thing. Up until recently, Coulter's been cool with letting Ben put the fear of the law into them, but now that he's retained you, who knows. We may be seeing more trespassing charges pop up." He motioned for Simon to follow. "Come on back."

With a jerk, Simon dragged himself from the doorway and followed the other man into his office. He wanted to press harder, find out exactly what Masters County's law and justice departments had run into with Coulter before he'd been retained, but frankly, he was more than ready to deal with a case that didn't involve his biggest client.

Hayes pulled a file from his briefcase and flipped it open.

"Timothy Showalter. Seventeen years old, first offense. Charged with possession with intent to distribute," Hayes recited without looking down at the page once. "Deputy Schaeffer says he was holding the bag in his hand and showing it to some friends when he approached. When he spotted Mike coming, Timmy shoved it back into his backpack. He tried to tell the deputy he'd need a search warrant to look in there."

The two men shared a chuckle. Simon made a mental note to tell Timothy Showalter not to take TV legal dramas too seriously. He needed a civics lesson on the basics of search and seizure.

"He says he has no idea how it got into his backpack, and he was showing it to his friends to ask if they put it there."

"Mmm-hmm," the DA hummed. At last, he dropped his gaze to the file and skimmed the police report. "If your client agrees, I'm willing to go with a plea of nolo contendere under the First Time Offender Act."

"We'd ask the judge for a conditional discharge of probation plus community service in lieu of jail time," Simon countered.

Hayes nodded and closed the file. "I can agree to those

terms." Sighing, he dropped heavily into his chair. "I hate sending kids to jail for being stupid." He looked up at Simon, his expression hard. "You tell him this is his one get-out-of-jail-free card. People around these parts are pretty edgy when it comes to any kind of drug dealing. They may look the other way if I let one of their own slide on some weed, but if he's busted again, I will come after him before the townsfolk can come after me with pitchforks. We clear?"

"Crystal."

Hayes nodded, then reached up to shake Simon's hand. "I hate starting the day this way. Timmy Showalter lives down the street from me. His mama called my house at least three times last night begging me not to send her baby to prison. Apparently, Timmy sleeps with a scrap of his old security blanket."

Simon nodded, keeping his expression carefully neutral. "I will make sure he is aware that if there is a next time, he will feel the full weight of the law *and* his mama. I'll also threaten to leak the information about his blankie."

The two men exchanged wary smiles.

"I'll talk to my client, speak to his parents and get back to you by the end of the day," Simon promised.

"I'm surprised Barb Showalter isn't blowing up your phone already. She says he's been giving her nothing but trouble ever since he went to work at the Reptile Rendezvous, and everyone knows you're Coulter's guy."

"I am not 'Coulter's guy,' and I keep my phone on silent mode," Simon said gruffly.

"Probably wise."

Unease crept up Simon's spine as he made a mental note to ask Mrs. Showalter exactly what kind of trouble young Timmy had become since taking the job at the refuge. "I'll, uh, I'll speak with her about her concerns when I call to talk about the plea."

"Good."

There was a note of finality in Hayes's response, and it jerked Simon from his thoughts. He eyed the DA warily, but found he was in no hurry to leave. Frankly, he was tired of talking to himself…and Dora. He wanted to make some friends in this town, and what better place to start than with the man across the desk. After all, there was nothing wrong with being friendly adversaries. If he won the district attorney over to his side, maybe he could get beautiful Lori Cabrera to stop giving him the stink eye each time their paths crossed.

Rubbing his cheek, he ventured out onto the limb. "I was thinking of inviting some people over to watch the game Saturday. I'll fire up Wendell's old Weber grill and all." He made a vague, all-encompassing gesture. "I'd like you to come, if you're free." Hayes looked up, his surprise evident. Simon tossed off a nonchalant shrug. "I was going to invite Sheriff Kinsella and Marlee Masters, whoever's not on duty across the hall…"

He prayed Mike Schaeffer would be on shift at kickoff time. Not because he had anything against the guy, but he was more anxious to see Lori again. It occurred to him she might not be available. He hadn't spotted a wedding ring. A lack of jewelry didn't mean anything. For all he knew, she could be involved with Hayes.

"Hey, I didn't even ask," he blurted. "Are you married? Seeing someone? Either way, you're welcome to bring a plus-one or something."

Hayes looked taken aback by the question. "Yeah, uh, no. I'm not married. Sure, I'll come over to watch the game. Need me to bring anything?"

Simon's mind raced and he started to panic at the

thought of throwing an impromptu party together. Then he remembered Dora. For the first time since he'd arrived in Pine Bluff, he blessed his grandfather's longtime secretary's almost compulsive need to assist him. She could help him pull this together. And Miss Delia, Wendell's mostly retired housekeeper.

"Uh, no. I don't think so. I was going to keep it simple—burgers, dogs and stuff."

Hayes nodded. "Cool. I'll bring some soft drinks and beer. Maybe some chips."

"That would be great." Simon began to back out of the room. "I need to double-check the schedule. I think we have a six-o'clock kickoff."

"It is."

Simon stifled the urge to chuckle. This was Southeastern Conference football country. He wouldn't be surprised if everyone in town had the Georgia Bulldogs football schedule memorized whether they were fans or not.

"I'll have the charcoal ready."

"Sounds good."

"Great." Simon nodded enthusiastically. "See you Saturday."

"Yep." Hayes smirked and fired up his laptop. "The sooner you talk to your client about the deal, the better. I don't keep my phone on Silent, and I get annoyed when helicopter parents try to land on my head."

"Gotcha." Simon beat a path out of the man's office. He had a party to plan.

Chapter Five

Deputy Steve Wasson of Prescott County called to give
her a heads-up. An Amber Alert was being issued. Fourteen-year-old Kaylin Bowers had been reported missing
by her parents when they woke up to find their daughter's
rumpled bed empty. Lori stared at the computer screen,
studying the photos the girl's parents had collected. Most
were the usual posed shots taken at school, but the one
Steve sent through was different from the others. This
was a selfie pulled from a PicturSpam account Kaylin's
parents had no clue she'd opened.

One in which fourteen-year-old Kaylin claimed to be
an eighteen-year-old model and actress. In the photo un-
earthed by the techy deputy at the Prescott County Sheriff's Department, she looked every day of eighteen.

"Like waving a red cloth to a predator," Lori murmured to herself. "Was I that trusting at that age?"

Lori didn't ponder the question long. Her parents had
been strict with her—something she remembered chafing
against, but was now thankful for in retrospect. Teenagers in general were given to poor impulse control, something she'd had to bite her tongue to keep from pointing
out when Steve told her Kaylin's parents didn't monitor
her social media accounts closely because they didn't

want to "invade" their daughter's privacy. Lori would bet her badge they were regretting not being nosier now.

She was pulling up her own PicturSpam account to do some stalking when the door to the sheriff's office opened and Simon Wingate walked in. Minimizing the window, Lori watched in amazement as Julianne, their normally unflappable dispatcher, flittered and fluttered, practically cooing her hellos to the man. Their determined flirtation was so painful to watch, Lori felt the need to put one or both—or all of them—out of their misery.

"Don't you have any work to do?" she demanded, glaring at Wingate. "I can call fire and rescue. Maybe they'll let you chase an ambulance around for a while so you can stay in business."

Her snark cut through Julianne's excitement like a hot knife.

Simon didn't fluster easily. He simply smiled and said, "Great idea! I've been looking for a good gym around here. I guess y'all make your own CrossFit, huh?"

Lori was still coming up with a retort when he raised a hand in greeting to Ben, who was lounging in his chair, watching them go at each other. "Hey, Sheriff, how's it going?"

"It's going well as can be expected," Ben answered laconically. "What brings you in, Counselor?"

Simon smiled so wide a boyish dimple appeared in his left cheek. "Call me Simon."

Lori wanted to sneer at him and his stupid dimple, but she couldn't. She wanted to touch it, which might explain why the mere sight of the flirty dent made her agitated.

"I come in peace." He raised both hands high in surrender. "I was across the hall talking to the DA, and I realized I hadn't socialized with anyone since I moved here."

Lori scoffed. "I'm sure you think we were all feeling the loss keenly."

He aimed the full wattage of his charming smile on her, and she almost fell back in her seat. "Well, the thought had crossed my mind, so I thought I'd put you all out of your misery and let you get to know me."

Julianne laughed out loud. "You're every bit the rascal you were when you were twelve years old," she cooed. "You remember the time your grandmama paid me to keep an eye on you for a couple of hours so she and your granddad could go to the spaghetti supper at the church? Your granddad was a deacon, and you were the devil incarnate."

"Remember?" Simon dropped a wink at the dispatcher. "I had the biggest crush on you, Miss Julianne."

"Liar," she purred.

"No." Simon shook his head vehemently. "No lie. I was twelve and you were seventeen, and I thought you were the prettiest thing I'd ever seen in my whole life."

Julianne went back to her keyboard, a primly pleased smile twitching the corners of her mouth. "I'll let you go on thinking I was only seventeen to your twelve."

Simon guffawed. "There is no way on earth I'm going to believe there's a bigger gap between us."

Lori almost growled. Julianne was at least ten years older than Simon Wingate. She was twelve years older than Lori herself, and Lori was fully capable of doing the math.

"Anyway," Simon said, interrupting her thoughts, "I came by to invite you all over to watch the football game on Saturday night. Granddad left his grill on the patio, and I'm capable of scorching some hamburgers." He added a winsome smile to the assault. "If y'all would come by, I'd be much obliged. It gets pretty quiet in the old house on the weekends."

Lori felt a pang of pity for the man, and it irked her. Pity was exactly what he'd been counting on. He was new in town, and he probably was lonely. She wasn't a fan of being cajoled into anything, and this whole barbecue setup reeked of manipulation.

"I'll speak to Marlee and see if she has any plans for Saturday night," Ben answered.

"Do that," Simon implored. "I ran into her at the Piggly Wiggly the other day. She was in a rush, so we didn't do much more than exchange hellos. I'm sure she has her hands full with Timber Masters now that her daddy is semiretired."

Semiretired. Lori noted the terminology. Henry Masters, Marlee's father and the man who practically ran the whole town, had had a debilitating stroke in the spring. Marlee had stepped in to take over the reins at the lumber company that kept many residents of the county employed.

"She does, but I'm making sure she takes time off. A cookout sounds great," Ben said agreeably.

"Great!" Simon's expression sobered, and the shine in his blue eyes seemed to dim a shade. "Marlee, Jeff and I used to run around together when we were kids, see what trouble we could find. Hard to believe Jeff is gone."

Lori ducked her head. In the past year, Pine Bluff had lost some of their best and brightest to a wannabe drug kingpin's power play. One of those men had been Marlee's brother, Jeff. The man Lori had been falling for. The one who had died in a tragic tangle of unsavory circumstances. She could feel Ben staring at the back of her neck and held herself still. She refused to let her discomfiture show.

Oblivious to the undercurrents, Simon blathered on. "I look forward to getting reacquainted with Marlee. And yourself, of course."

Lori wanted to chuckle at the man's attempt at a save, but the mere mention of Jeff Masters dampened her ability to laugh. Instead, she drew a deep breath when she lifted her head again. Big mistake. Simon Wingate was staring at her.

"I realize some people see us as being on opposite sides…" Only a fool would miss the tiny smirk that twitched his lips. "I don't believe we are. Sure, we have different functions within the judicial system, but at the end of the day, we're all after justice."

Lori opened her mouth to make a scathing comment, but Ben cut her off.

"You're absolutely right. I've been on the other side of the table, and all too aware of exactly how important it is to have someone sitting by your side when people are coming after you."

Lips thinning into a line, Lori studied her boss. Ben's expression remained open and inviting. She couldn't help but marvel at his perspective. Ben had once been an undercover agent for the Drug Enforcement Administration, but his cover had been blown in a bust gone horribly wrong. He'd been doubted, questioned and practically tossed away by the agency he'd given years of his life to serving. If such a thing were to happen to her, Lori doubted she'd be philosophical about it.

"I'll speak to Marlee, and give Dora a call to let you know if we can make it," Ben said evenly. "Can we bring anything?"

Simon inclined his head. "Cool. Uh—" he pointed toward the office across the lobby "—Hayes is bringing drinks. I'm not sure…" He trailed off with a shrug. "Whatever else you think we might want."

"We'll swing by the bakery and bring some dessert. Marlee's always up for something sweet," Ben offered.

"Awesome. Great." Simon clapped once and pivoted toward Julianne. "You in?"

She shook her head sadly. "I'm afraid we can't. My mother-in-law is doing poorly and we're going up to Macon to check in and spell Dylan's sister off for a couple of days."

"I'm sorry. You'll be missed," Simon replied, and oddly enough, he sounded sincere.

Lori clenched her teeth and closed her eyes, physically willing herself to stop thinking the worst of this man. He was right; he wasn't doing anything wrong. If his clients were the scum of the earth, that didn't mean he was. Did it?

She opened her eyes to find Simon staring at her. "Deputy Lori?"

The way he drawled her name both excited and annoyed her. She opened her mouth to say something smart, but all she said was "Saturday is my day off."

To her horror, she realized that rather than coming across as an excuse, it sounded like she had unlimited availability. She hastened to correct the impression.

"I plan to spend the day with my younger sister." It wasn't exactly a lie. The thought had crossed her mind that she needed to spend some quality time with Lena, and when she saw the photographs of Kaylin Bowers, she'd vowed to make it happen.

"The game doesn't start till six, and you're welcome to bring anyone along. I assure you we will keep things family friendly. My first soirée back in Pine Bluff can't be some kind of Roman orgy."

Lori's cheeks heated with a fiery flush. Julianne hooted and Ben let out a snort of laughter. A part of her couldn't believe he'd actually uttered the word *orgy* out loud. The devil on her shoulder told her it was completely on brand for Simon and the people he chose to defend.

"I'll keep the invitation in mind," she replied, enunciating each word carefully. Then she tacked a belated "Thank you" on, but it tasted grudging on her tongue.

Ben shot her a look, but she couldn't be bothered wasting the niceties on Simon Wingate. Not when the man made her feel so knotted up inside.

"Great, well, I'll see whoever can make it." He backed away. "Oh, and I assume Deputy Schaeffer will be on duty, but would you make sure to tell him to swing by to check on the score? We'll load him up with something to eat."

"Will do," Ben answered with a nod.

Simon lifted his hand in farewell. "Y'all have a nice day."

The door shut behind him and Julianne whirled on her. "Girl, are you blind? What the devil is wrong with you?"

Bristling, Lori glared back at her. "I'm not blind, and there's nothing wrong with me."

"There must be, because a gorgeous man walked in here specifically to ask you to come over to his house for a get-together and you... Ugh! What am I going to do with you?" Julianne cried.

"You do not have to do anything with me, and he did not come in here specifically for me. He invited everyone," Lori shot back. Behind her, Ben chuckled. Swiveling in her seat, she glared at her boss. "What?"

"I'm gonna have to side with Julianne on this one. I'm pretty sure she and I were not his target audience."

Lori splayed her hands. "He said he invited Hayes."

"Okay, so maybe it's a toss-up between you and Harry," Julianne said tartly. "Get in there and fight, girl. You think handsome single guys plop themselves down in friggin' Pine Bluff, Georgia, every day?"

"It's not a toss-up," Ben said. "Harry is an excuse, and Marlee and I are cover. Though, now that I think about it, he may have been counting on you for a covered dish or something, Julianne." Ben zoomed in on Lori. "How are your baked beans?" he teased.

The question earned him a wadded-up piece of paper tossed directly at his head. "They're delicious, but I may not want to share them."

Ben was not deterred. "The point is, he specifically asked you."

"He said I could bring anybody I wanted. I could bring a date."

Ben shook his head. "Oh, no. Not cool. Go or don't go, but don't bring a date," he advised.

Lori gaped, looking from Julianne to Ben and back again. "I don't get it. What are you two picking up on that I'm not? What makes you think he's concerned about whether I come or not?"

"I can't speak for Ben and his masculine intuition…" Julianne paused and her smile softened. "But I'd say it's because he looks at you the same way he used to look at me when he was seven—I mean, twelve."

Lori was surprised by how receptive Lena was to spending the day with her on Saturday, but when the teenager slid into her car, Lori suspected there'd been an ulterior motive behind Lena's eagerness. Eyeballing her sister as she settled into the passenger seat, she asked, "What has you all perky?"

Lena shook her head a tad too vigorously. "Nothing. I'm excited to spend the day with you."

The bright, cheerful greeting was so out of character with everything Lori had heard come out of her sister's mouth for the past six months, it set her antennae vibrating. "Uh-huh."

She put the car in gear and checked over her shoulder as she pulled away from the curb and her mother's house. "Okay. Hey, do you want me to take you somewhere to practice driving? Or maybe up and down some back roads? You have your permit on you, don't you?"

"Yes, but the permit says I can only drive with a parent or guardian."

Lori cut her sister a sidelong glance. "You might have heard—I have an in with the cops in this town," she said dryly.

Lena gasped in mock horror. "You're suggesting we break the law?"

"Never mind. It was only an idea." She drummed her fingers on the steering wheel. "So, what do you want to do today?"

Her sister clapped her hands together and whispered in an excited rush, "I think we should go to the Reptile Rendezvous."

Lori reared back, wrinkling her nose at the thought of going anywhere near Samuel Coulter's place. "What? Why?"

"Because I want to get a look at it," Lena insisted. "It's all anyone at school is talking about, plus the whole deal with Jasmine."

"Right," Lori said slowly, hating herself for warming to the idea.

"I want to go and see what the big whoop is," Lena

said, a note of wheedling undercutting her overenthusi-
astic response.

"Honey, going there is not a great idea."

"You asked what I wanted to do today. This is what
I want to do." In a blink, the chipper girl who'd greeted
her was gone.

She slowed the car to a roll, but Lena seemed oblivious. She jolted them to a stop at the corner, garnering her
sister's full, if sullen, attention. "You want to do this?"
she asked, pinning Lena with a pointed stare. "It could
be supercreepy there."

Her younger sister rolled her eyes. "Of course it's
going to be creepy—it's full of snakes."

In a half-hearted attempt to steer their day toward
something brighter, Lori offered a tempting alternative.
"I could drive you up to the mall," she said enticingly.

Lena chewed her lip, clearly weighing the pros and
cons of wheedling a new top or two out of Lori's last pay-
check versus getting an eyeful of the guy her best friend
was ditching her for.

Finally, Lena heaved a sigh and said, "They're only
open to the public on Saturdays and Sundays. It might
sound stupid, but I need to see this guy." When Lori
started to answer, Lena held up a hand. "I know, I've
seen his pictures online, but I want to see him live and
in person. I have to see if he's all that." Her dark eyes
were bright with unshed tears. "Why is he so special he's
worth ditching twelve years of friendship?"

"Oh, honey." Lori reached across and gave her sister's
hand a squeeze. "I wish I had the right things to say."

Her sister gave a watery laugh. "There's nothing to
say. And I need to see why everyone is making such a big
deal about this place. Half the kids at school are trying

to get jobs there. It's all anyone talks about. It has to be because it's so creepy, right? With the snakes?"

Lori could hear the tears clogging Lena's throat, so she swallowed her own apprehension and hooked a left, heading for the highway. "You're probably right. If you think it will make you feel better, we'll go get creeped out together."

Twenty minutes later, she approached the sign directing them to the parking area for the Reptile Rendezvous, wondering for the hundredth time whose palm Coulter had greased to get the permits for this place. Did he have Simon's dad in his back pocket? Lori shuddered at the thought.

Though Dell Wingate was in Atlanta far more than in his native Pine Bluff, Lori had always respected their assemblyman. The Wingates were a case study in superior genetics. Dell was open, affable and handsome. She also believed he held their district's best interests at heart. Would he have helped a scumbag like Coulter set up shop in their own backyard?

She followed the waving hands of a pimply-faced teenager in a yellow safety vest. She and Lena didn't speak as they bumped across a field mowed down to be the parking area. He waved her into a spot beside a pickup truck so dented and rusted Lori feared for her car's doors and quarter panels. Reaching across, she held on to her sister's arm to keep her in place until another car slid into the spot on the driver's side. "Hold up. Let's let them all get out first."

Lena huffed, but waited. When the coast was clear, they opened their doors cautiously, careful not to touch the vehicles wedged in tight. Lori didn't exactly drag her feet as they headed toward the entry, but she did hang back. Years of training had her on high alert, scanning the crowd, the single points of entrance and egress, and eyeballing the uniformed staff manning the gate.

Lena raced ahead toward the plywood outbuilding marked Ticket Office, but Lori walked slowly, checking out the patrons who'd chosen to spend their Saturday afternoon and a chunk of their paychecks on this, of all things.

Lori purchased their tickets, all the while resenting the thought of her hard-earned money going to line the pockets of a guy who was reportedly already a millionaire. She followed her sister to the turnstile inside where arrows pointed them in about four different directions. None of the offerings remotely appealed to Lori.

"I don't suppose we can start with the turtles?" she asked Lena, indicating one of the arrows.

The younger girl smiled but nodded to another arrow. "I'm pretty sure Jas said something about boa constrictors being the least gross of all the snakes."

Lori hiked her purse high on her shoulder and followed when Lena set off in the indicated direction. "How do you think she figures they are the least gross?"

Lena didn't glance back when she shrugged. "They swallow things whole, right? No biting?"

"I have no earthly idea," Lori replied honestly. "I think maybe they bite, but they aren't venomous. They paralyze their prey and just…squeeze." She blew out a breath when the path widened to what appeared to be some kind of viewing area. "I don't think I want to know."

Lena giggled when an enclosure covered in fine wire mesh came into view. "I don't either."

"Maybe no one will notice if we look away," Lori whispered. They moved to the back of the group of people knotted at the rail and peering into the massive cage.

Lori's heart rate kicked up a few notches when she saw

the slow slide of a thick, scaly creature moving along the base of the enclosure. "This can't be safe," she muttered.

Lena snorted a laugh but took a step back, nearly crushing Lori's big toe in the process. "He can't unlatch the gate thingy," she answered. "No thumbs, remember?"

A few more people came up behind them, and the two of them sank deeper into the back of the crowd, eyeing the enclosure warily. Nearby, Lori heard a woman say something to her companion about it being nearly feeding time, and she shuddered when her own ghoulish stomach gave a loud rumble.

Then a young man wearing khaki pants and a safari-style shirt with an interlocking-*R* logo on the patch pocket stepped out of a hidden doorway at the back of the enclosure. The short sleeves of his uniform shirt did nothing to hide the artwork on his arms. Tattoos of serpents slithered out from under the cotton to wind around his forearms. When he lifted a five-gallon pail by the handle, Lori caught a glimpse of a flat-eyed snake head inked into the back of his hand.

She tore her gaze away from those mesmerizing tats to look up at the guy's face. He was young—nineteen, tops. The scruffy beard he was cultivating did him no favors in the looks department, but the even white smile he flashed at the crowd more than made up for his appearance.

"Oh, my God," the sisters said in unison.

"That's him, isn't it?" When Lena didn't answer, Lori glanced over and saw her sister staring at someone in the front row of spectators. "What? What's wrong?"

Lena nodded to the rail, and Lori saw a petite dark-haired girl grinning and waving to the young man inside the cage. "Is that Jasmine?"

Lena swallowed hard and nodded emphatically.

Lori tracked the guy she presumed to be Rick. He made his way around the enclosure with practiced ease. When he launched into a fairly generic-sounding spiel about boa constrictors, their natural habitats and the characteristics unique to the species, she tuned out. Lifting her gaze, she caught sight of another, smaller snake wound around the branch of one of the enclosure's trees and wondered if this was the cage Bella Nunes had been locked in, or if Coulter chose to use more-venomous creatures to terrorize his guests.

Forcing herself to focus on the task at hand, she leaned closer to her sister and whispered, "Did she say she was going to be here today? Is that why we came?"

Lena's narrow shoulders jerked up and down, but she shook her head. "She said she was doing something with her mom."

Lori was about to launch into a round of reassuring comments when her sister whirled to face her. "Can we go now?"

It was on the tip of her tongue to remind Lena she'd paid fifteen dollars a ticket to get them through the gate merely five minutes ago, but the desperation written all over her sister's face was enough to discount the price of admission.

"Yep." Wrapping her arm around Lena's shoulders, she nodded to the path leading back to the front gate. "Come on. Let's get out of here."

They'd almost made it back to the entrance when Lena said sullenly, "He's not even cute in person."

Lori could see why the guy would appeal to a young woman looking for a walk on the wild side. She wouldn't defend Jasmine's questionable taste in guys, so she said the only thing a real sister could say. "No, definitely not."

Lena veered toward the small building marked Restrooms. "I'll only be a minute," she promised, darting toward the ladies' room. Lori could have used a pit stop herself, but something in the way Lena moved said her sister needed a minute alone, so she held back.

Leaning against a block wall, Lori watched a steady trickle of people come and go. It was by no means a Six Flags crowd, but for a patch of nothing in the middle of nowhere, she had to admit old Sammy was doing a steady business on a sunny Saturday afternoon.

Her gaze strayed to the small thatched roof of a kiosk where a young girl stood selling souvenirs. There was something familiar about the girl, but the niggling sensation wasn't unusual. Most of the families in rural Masters County came to Pine Bluff to do their banking and shopping. It was possible she'd been seeing the girl around town for years without truly noticing her.

Lori's gaze drifted away, but she jerked her attention back when she realized exactly where she'd seen the girl. She pulled out her phone and checked the notification she'd saved. Straightening away from the building, she locked in on the girl and whispered, "Kaylin Bowers."

Instinctively, she reached for her belt, forgetting she was off duty. Her trusty Glock was in her purse, but drawing a weapon in a crowded place was not a good idea. She needed to get a better look at the girl. Lori took two steps toward the small souvenir stand. Kaylin didn't seem to be there under duress. As a matter of fact, she was smiling. She was about to approach the girl when her sister came out of nowhere to grab her arm and spin her toward the exit.

"Come on. I want to go," Lena insisted.

"Okay, but, honey—" Lori twisted to look back over her shoulder to be sure her eyes weren't deceiving her.

"Now, Lori, please?" Lena wheedled.

Lori planted her feet and looked back at the souvenir stand. Kaylin smiled wide as she was relieved from souvenir duty by another young man with a crisp khaki shirt.

"Well, damn," Lori muttered to herself. "Everyone does want to work here."

"Can we go?" Lena repeated. "I want to get out of here."

Judging by the girl's happy demeanor, Kaylin had obviously left home of her own free will. If she approached, she might scare her off. Aware that her own teenage sister was watching, Lori backed away a step. Lena would not appreciate Lori drawing too much attention to them, particularly when she was so desperate to leave without Jasmine knowing they'd seen her. The best thing she could do was to call in the sighting and let the officer on duty handle things.

"Okay, but I need to make a call."

They pushed their way through the exit, and Lena took off across the rutted field. Lori pulled her phone from her purse and speed-dialed the office. "Mike? Listen, I'm out of uniform and with my sister, but can you saddle up and make your way over to the Reptile Rendezvous?" She paused when they reached her car, and she looked back at the entrance. "Yeah. Reptile Rendezvous. Alert the fellas over at Prescott County. I've spotted Kaylin Bowers selling souvenirs on Samuel Coulter's property."

Chapter Six

Simon's Saturday started going downhill late Friday afternoon, which had to be some kind of record. He'd received a call from Samuel Coulter as he was packing up his briefcase.

"I've shipped a package to your office overnight express. It's valuable. I need you to be there to sign for it," Coulter announced without preamble.

Taken aback by the man's audacity, Simon answered with only a murmured "Tomorrow is Saturday."

"I am aware, but I'm in Florida to do some, uh, fishing." Coulter paused. "I was informed the merchandise I ordered was available for immediate shipment, so I asked them to direct it your way."

"I'm not in the habit of receiving packages of unknown origin or packages addressed to persons other than myself," Simon informed him.

"A good policy in general, but I am your client. I recall a rather hefty retainer tacked onto our agreement for billable hours." The other man chuckled, and Simon stiffened. "I'm sure the retainer must cover signatory services."

"Why not send it to your own business?"

"I can't trust some hourly knucklehead with anything

truly important. I only pay them a dollar over minimum wage. This box is valuable. I'd hate for it to go astray."

"I can't accept delivery of anything illegal."

"Then I suggest, for your own comfort, you stop asking questions and don't try to open my box."

With that, his client had hung up. Simon could only assume the man had silenced his phone, since repeated attempts to call him back went unanswered.

And so, he'd gone into the office on Saturday morning. While he was waiting, he called his grandfather. "Hey, do I have the pleasure of speaking to the almost honorable Wendell Wingate?" he asked when the older man answered.

"There are some who'd argue the 'almost' should apply even if I am elected," Wendell answered with a chortle.

"*When* you are elected," Simon corrected. "I think most of us would be okay with being called almost honorable. Beats being called a slimy snake handler."

The old man guffawed. "I take it your new client isn't winning any popularity contests?"

"Not with the local law enforcement," Simon answered, a wry smile twisting his lips when he pictured Lori Cabrera squaring off with him at the Daisy Drive-In. "I have to admit, I'm not particularly a fan either."

"Well, you don't have to befriend the man. You only have to be his lawyer," his grandfather reminded him.

"Right." Simon rocked back in the enormous leather chair the old man had sat in and studied the shelves of leather-bound volumes behind the desk. "Which is why I'm at the office on a Saturday morning. Coulter had a package shipped to our offices. Says it's valuable and will require a signature."

In an instant, his grandfather's jovial bonhomie disappeared. Wendell was all business when he asked, "Did he say what the package contained?"

"He did not give specifics, and I did not ask for them," Simon replied, skimming over the gilt-lettered spines of decades-old law books.

When he was a kid, he'd often wondered if they were for show. If maybe those expensive cordovan covers were simply a shell for blank pages, or perhaps they were hollowed-out hidey-holes. His first foray into a law library left him feeling overwhelmed and vaguely disappointed. Though he'd slogged through all three years of law school, he graduated with a new understanding of why his father had chosen politics over the practice of law.

"Good," Wendell grunted, interrupting his wandering thoughts. "Now, here's what I want you to do. Call Dora and bribe her to come in and witness you signing for this package. Take photos of the box from all different angles to show no one has tampered with it in any way. Have Dora email the photos to you and copy the client. The delivery driver will have a time stamp, and you'll have one too. When Coulter comes to collect the package, I want you to take pictures of your own to show the package was intact when he took receipt."

Simon sat up straight, the back of the leather chair snapping back into place with a thunk. "Isn't that overkill?"

"Better too much caution than too little," his grandfather admonished. "What's the first thing you learn in law school? Either bury the facts, or bury them *in* facts. Depends which side you're on."

"I'm starting to wonder myself," Simon muttered.

"You're on your side," Wendell replied stubbornly. "Now, you listen to me. I worked those backwoods my

entire life. There are people there who are fine, upstanding citizens. Then there are those who should live under
a fallen log." Simon snorted, but Wendell plowed ahead,
his tenor becoming more strident with each word. "You
think you're dealing with a bunch of banjo-playing hill-
billies out there. You think you're smarter than they are
with your diplomas and tailored suits, but the biggest mistake you can make is thinking they can't outmaneuver
you. There are no shadows deeper than those cast in the
woods, and Coulter's kind have been creeping through
them their whole lives."

"Or slithering," Simon countered, unable to resist putting up at least a token resistance to the truths his grandfather was doling out.

"As the case may be. Make no mistake—his type of
man doesn't flourish in sunlight."

"How did you do this? How could you spend your
whole life defending people who are up to no good?"

Wendell paused long enough for regret to pool in Simon's gut. An apology poised on the tip of his tongue,
he rested his forehead on the heel of his palm. "Granddad—"

"Believe it or not, it wasn't always this bad," Wendell said, a wistful note entering his tone. "Sure, I had
moonshiners and the usual run-of-the-mill ruffians to
deal with. The worst were actually the men who thought
it was okay to knock their wives around. I didn't have
much stomach for defending them."

"I don't blame you."

"Of course, there were some ugly incidents between
the whites and the blacks. Most of the time it came down
to some white boys inciting trouble, then twisting things
around until they could press charges against the peo-

ple of color, so I actually got to defend a passel of those cases. Won a few of them too, though not as many as I should have. Depended on the judge and jury."

Simon rubbed his eyes with his thumb and forefinger. He'd hardly slept the previous night, and listening to his grandfather talk about all the tough choices he'd had to make over the years made him feel whiny for complaining about this one guy.

"Granddad, I'm—"

Wendell cut him off. "It's not an easy job, Simon, but it's a necessary one." His voice warmed and gentled. "Focus on the good you'll do."

"Hard to do when I haven't done much more than get people out of speeding tickets. And defend scumbags so I can keep the lights on," he added.

"It's enough for now. You're not building your life's work there," Wendell reminded him.

"I could ruin yours," Simon answered gloomily.

"Nah. Anyone can draw up a will on a computer these days. We're mainly there to read things through and provide reassurance. You need this time to figure out what your path is going to be." He paused, and Simon braced himself for further discussion about the stumbles he'd already made on that path, but his grandfather surprised him by reverting back to Coulter.

"I assume you did some research on this guy before you took him on?"

"Of course I did." Simon tried to squelch the defensiveness in his tone, but wasn't entirely successful.

"Give me a rough sketch."

"Born in Miami. Solidly middle-class upbringing. Went to Florida State for a couple of years, but dropped out when he discovered the stock market," Simon reported dutifully. "Made a pile of money trading online. I think he was a millionaire before he turned twenty-five."

His grandfather let loose with a low whistle. "Impressive."

Simon scowled. Something in him didn't want Wendell to be impressed by the likes of Samuel Coulter. "Anyway, started running with a bunch of South Florida high rollers. Some fairly sketchy, others legit. Soon, the company he was keeping and the money he was making drew the attention of the Feds."

"Charges?"

Simon shook his head, though he knew his grandfather couldn't see him. "Investigations, insinuations, but nothing concrete. Coulter scaled back on his trading and turned to his other hobby."

"The snake thing," Wendell concluded.

"Started as a collector, but likes to refer to himself as a naturalist, or a conservationist," Simon reported dryly.

"And the move from Florida to Georgia? That's a hell of a change in social scenery."

"I'm not entirely clear on the ins and outs of it all, but he claims he was feeling hemmed in by the city. I think he got sideways with the Florida Fish and Wildlife Conservation Commission on something and wanted to be somewhere where people might not be paying close attention."

"If he moved to a small town for anonymity, he made a grave miscalculation," Wendell said with a chuckle.

Simon forced a laugh himself. "No kidding."

Tired of talking about Coulter, and hoping to avoid any rehashing of the mistakes that had landed him in Pine Bluff, he switched the subject to his attempt at making life in town more palatable.

"I'm hosting a cookout at your place, and Marlee Masters is supposed to come," he said gruffly. "I'm going to offer to take some of the Timber Masters business back from her, since she has her plate full."

Wendell chuckled. "That's my boy. Generous to a fault."

"I've also been trying to make nice with the folks over at the municipal building. I invited Harrison Hayes, Sheriff Kinsella and the deputies."

"Smart move. They're good people."

"Hayes and Kinsella seem to be okay with me, but Deputy Cabrera hates my guts."

"Lori?" Wendell sounded genuinely surprised. "I doubt she does."

"She thinks I should go crawl under a log with my client."

Wendell chuckled. "Yeah, well, she always has had a strictly defined line between right and wrong. If she thinks you've crossed it, she'll make you work to get back on her good side."

"You're speaking from experience," he observed.

"I got a few of her perps off the hook, so I wasn't on her list of favorite people for a while there."

Unable to resist, Simon asked, "How'd you get back on there? She speaks pretty highly of you now."

"I helped her aunt once. Miss Anita's husband died of cancer a few years after they signed a pickle of a rent to own agreement on a house. The whole setup was illegal, but the owner never figured on an immigrant being brave enough to call him out. I got the judge to order a settlement and rendered the property paid in full."

"Oh, so all I have to do is pull a rabbit out of my hat," Simon said wryly.

"She's a tough cookie. And a smart one. Anita left her house to Lori in her will."

"Her will?"

"Car accident. Both Anita and Lori's father, Mateo, were killed. Been over a year, but the family is still reeling. They had a restaurant in town, but it was all too much for Sophia, Lori's mother, to keep going. There was some life insurance money, so she closed the business and has been focused on her children."

"I'm sorry to hear that," Simon replied, ingrained manners kicking in.

"It's been a rough couple of years for Lori. Losing Jeff Masters, then her father and aunt. The house was a nice gesture on Anita's part, but I don't believe Lori's mother has taken kindly to her moving out of the family home."

Simon's curiosity was piqued on several levels, but he went for the easiest question first. "Why not?"

"I'm told it's a cultural thing," Wendell explained. "Young women are expected to live at home with their parents until they marry."

"She served in the army," Simon said with a perplexed laugh.

"Doesn't count," Wendell replied.

"Huh. Well, okay," he said, giving up on that line of questioning for one he found more intriguing. "You said something about Jeff Masters?"

"Well, I wasn't aware of it at the time, but it turns out that Lori and Jeff were…involved at the time of his death. Naturally, she was quite upset when we believed he committed suicide, but when it became apparent it was murder… Well, I think the events of the past couple of years have shaken her confidence."

Simon couldn't contain the short laugh that escaped him. If this was Lori feeling shaky, she must have been formidable in the days before life threw all that grief at her.

"Are you hopin' to impress our lovely young deputy at this cookout?"

He should have seen the sneak attack coming, but he never did. He laughed, the sound bursting out of him so abruptly, he realized he couldn't remember the last time he'd done it. Recovering quickly, he took a mental step back and parried the question.

"I'm simply hoping to get off one list and onto the other."

The evasion came so naturally to him, Simon wondered if he might have spent too much time in rooms filled with politicians. Either way, he needed to end this call and get his plea in with Dora if he wanted to have someone witness the delivery of Samuel Coulter's mystery package.

"I'd better go, Granddad. I need to catch Dora and see what her price will be."

"Oh, she's an easy one. Cash money. Tell her you'll pay her triple time, and she'll hightail it right on over. She lives to spoil those grandbabies of hers, and the eldest has his heart set on a trip down to Disney."

"Money it is," Simon agreed.

"And don't make Lori mad. The woman carries and she's a crack shot."

"Talk to you again soon, Granddad."

"Okay, and be sure to cover your flank." His grandfather's affectionate laugh was a balm. Unfortunately, the comfort the call provided didn't last long.

HE'D STARTED THE day by paying a small fortune to secure a witness to his taking possession of a box full of what he suspected may be contraband snakes. Once the job was done, all he wanted to do was go home and take the second shower. Unfortunately, he received an irate phone call from his client telling him the deputy Simon hadn't been able to get out of his mind had staged a one-woman raid on his client's property.

Simon's nostrils flared. He tried to control the irritation bubbling inside him. One Saturday. All he wanted was one Saturday to hang out with some people and possibly lay the groundwork for friendlier relations between himself and some of his new colleagues and neighbors.

But no. He'd spent hours chasing down enough information to satisfy his client. Thankfully, Coulter wasn't in any real trouble this time. He might get some flak for his manager's suspect hiring practices, but the fourteen-year-old runaway they'd picked up at the Reptile Rendezvous admitted to having used a fake ID to get the job.

Her "boyfriend," one of the half-dozen scruffy young guys Coulter had hired to work the exhibitions, claimed he had no idea Kaylin Bowers was underage. Fortunately for young Justin, he was only seventeen. The combination of his age and the evidence of Kaylin misrepresenting her age on social media had kept the boy out of any further legal trouble, but the unwelcome spotlight the girl's recovery had shone on Coulter had likely cost the kid his job.

His client was somehow involved in yet another girl-in-peril situation, and it didn't sit well with Simon. Neither did the discovery that Lori Cabrera had been the one who'd spotted the missing girl working at the Reptile Rendezvous. What business did she have hanging around his client's property? She'd said she was spending the day with her sister. Had she gone there to check on the guy she said her sister's friend was into? Or had she been fishing for something bigger to hook his client?

Simon vented his frustration by scooping the contents of pint containers of deli-prepared potato salad out with

a spoon and thwacking the globs into the festively pat-
terned melamine serving bowls his grandfather's supposedly retired housekeeper insisted he use for cookouts
with "company."

He'd made the mistake of asking Miss Delia where she
stashed his grandfather's grilling supplies. She'd shown
up at his door an hour earlier and marched through the
kitchen pulling plates, platters, bowls and utensils from
cabinets and drawers, all the while spewing a stream
of instructions Simon hadn't had a chance in hell of remembering.

She'd smirked when she saw he'd bought both mustard
and mayonnaise varieties of potato salad, but said nothing. He'd bought both because he had no idea what people
around here preferred, but Simon had no doubt what-
soever there'd be strong opinions on the matter. There
seemed to be strong opinions on about everything in
Pine Bluff, large and small. Delia had offered no clues.
She'd simply laid everything out on the kitchen counter,
told him she and her husband would be back in time for
kickoff, then left with a pat on the cheek.

Now he stood seething in the kitchen, half-afraid he
might cross-examine Lourdes Cabrera about her motives
if she dared to show up. He was trying to make the best
of his time here in Purgatory Bluff, damn it. The woman
seemed determined to take his client down, and here he
was, torn between forcing her to take a step back and
wanting to make a move on her. He needed to get a grip.

The doorbell rang and he checked his watch. It was
only five o'clock. His first guest was thirty minutes early,
and he hadn't even had time to change. Hurrying to the
front door, he wiped his sticky hands on his gym shorts
and hoped whoever it was had come prepared to help.

When he sneaked a peek through the sidelight window, he drew up short. Lori stood on his porch wearing oven mitts and carrying a large cast-iron pot.

She must have caught him peeking, because she called through the closed door. "Hurry. This thing weighs a ton."

He pulled open the door. The percolating bubbles of anger had carried him through the afternoon, but fizzled out the second he saw her. Her thick coffee-colored hair was caught up in a big messy bun on top of her head. Tendrils escaped at her temples. He itched to touch one, but curled his fingers into his palm to keep from acting on the impulse. Staring into her wide brown eyes, he could barely contain his pleasure at seeing her. "You made it."

"Hi. Yes. I'm early, but I brought baked beans, and I wanted the chance to talk to you alone."

He swung the door open wide and gestured for her to enter. "I'm not quite set up yet, but come on in."

He caught the scent of a light floral perfume as she passed him. She wore olive green cargo shorts. They probably wouldn't have been as sexy on anybody else but appeared to have been made with Lori in mind. Her lush curves stretched the fabric taut, but not too tight. A formfitting gray T-shirt with a deep V-neck and the University of Georgia's trademark *G* completed the look.

Afraid he'd been caught ogling the lucky consonant, he waved a hand toward the back of the house. "Come on back to the kitchen." Extending his hands, he nodded to the heavy-looking pot she held. "Here. Let me take that."

She pulled the pot closer to her. "I better hang on to it. It's hot from the oven."

He led the way to the kitchen. She marched directly to Delia's six-burner stove and plunked the cast-iron pot down on the grate. "Beautiful kitchen," she said, her face aglow with admiration.

"It was a bribe."

She glanced at him in surprise. "A bribe?"

Simon simply shrugged. "Miss Delia wanted to retire about a year after my grandma passed, but Wendell
wasn't quite ready to take on the bachelor life. She said
she couldn't go on working in such an outdated kitchen,
so he had this built for her."

Lori turned in a slow, appraising circle. "It's gorgeous.
I love the way it opens out onto the patio."

"I think Delia only sticks around because her kitchen
at home isn't up to snuff now."

"Does she cook for you?"

He shook his head. "No. Once Wendell left, she abdi-
cated. She comes by every now and again to make sure
I'm putting the forks in the right slot." Simon watched
with keen interest when Lori bent to adjust the gas flame
to burn low and steady underneath the pot.

"Wow." She ran a hand over one of the heavy grates.
"My mother would kill to have this stove."

Simon felt a pang of sadness when he recalled Wendell's story about the family restaurant, but didn't want
to let on they'd been talking about her, so he stuck to the
facts. "Miss Delia has good taste in almost everything."

Lori stepped away from the range and slid the other
oven mitt from her hand. She placed the cartoon two-
some on the counter and stepped back to have a better
look around. "Almost everything?"

"Well, we've always found her loyalty to my grandfather suspect."

Lori laughed, and the sound punched him right in the
gut. He braced himself for impact, but realized there was
no way on earth a man could be prepared for her un-
guarded smile. His wits scattered, he switched straight
into babble mode. "I didn't think you were coming."

"I wasn't sure if I would," she replied with her usual candor. Crossing her arms over the *G* emblem, she leaned back against the counter and studied him through narrowed eyes. "I assume you spoke to your client today," she said, her demeanor a shade shy of confrontational.

"I have several clients, but if you are referring to Mr. Coulter, yes, I have," he retorted.

She rolled her eyes. "Let's shoot straight, okay?"

The agitation Simon tamped down came roaring back to life. "I always do, whether you choose to believe me or not." Needing to keep busy, he moved back to the counter lined with platters and bowls and continued transferring potato salad from the deli container to the approved serving bowl. He then peeled the lid off a container of mustard potato salad. "Why were you there?" he asked as he started whacking spoonfuls into another bowl.

"I went because my sister asked me to take her to the refuge." She moved to stand beside him and began checking the labels on the containers stacked there. "How many people are you expecting?" she asked, clearly amused by his propensity to overshop.

"I wasn't sure what to get, so I bought a little of everything. Plus, I think word has spread."

Lori reached for one of the serving bowls. "It always does around here."

He watched out of the corner of his eye as she pried the lid off a container of three-bean salad and dumped it into the bowl.

"One of Lena's friends is into a guy who works at Coulter's place."

"You mentioned something about that when we talked the other day."

"She was curious. Lena was, I mean. She wanted to get

a look at the guy her best friend has essentially dumped her for."

He turned to look at her, concern furrowing his brow. "You said she was only sixteen. Is she dating the guy?"

Lori shrugged. "It sounds more like chasing than dating, but who knows. Kids can be so secretive at that age."

His mouth drew into a tight line. She wasn't wrong in that assessment. Few kids were immune to teenage rebellion. He himself had had some exploits that would have made Dell tear his expertly barbered hair out if he'd caught wind of them. "Yes. They can."

She went to work on the macaroni salad next, her head bent in concentration. "I didn't go there looking for Kaylin Bowers, and I want you to hear me when I say I wasn't looking for a reason to harass your client."

"I hear you, but I got a call all the same." He grabbed two of the bowls he'd filled and made his way to the refrigerator.

Lori took hold of hers and followed. "I'm sorry if I caused you trouble, but I was only doing my job. If I'd seen her at the Daisy or in the Piggly Wiggly, I would've done the exact same thing."

"Understood. I hope the young lady is okay," he said tersely.

When their gazes met, he let his shoulders sag as he breathed out some of the frustration that seemed to be part and parcel of doing business with Samuel Coulter. Then he shook himself. He definitely didn't want to think about parcels. God, Lori's head would probably explode if she found out he'd signed for a mystery box for Coulter.

Shaking it off, he gave her a wan smile. "Can we… change the subject?"

"Okay," she agreed readily. "What's the saying about the evils of the day being enough?"

Simon smiled. "'Sufficient unto the day is the evil thereof.'"

"Exactly."

They shared a smile, and for the first time since she'd crossed his threshold, Simon wished he'd had the time to change out of his gym shorts. "I, uh… Do you mind entertaining yourself while I change?"

Lori's smile widened and her cheeks colored when she gave him a quick once-over. "Oh, sure, but you look fine." The color staining her cheeks deepened. "I mean, it's a football game."

He plucked at the front of the plain charcoal T-shirt he wore. "Thanks, but I need to support the home team. Wouldn't want people thinking I'm pulling for the other guys."

She laughed and moved to the counter. "The other team is gonna need all the help it can get," she said, gathering the discarded deli containers. Walking them over to the stainless-steel trash can, she made a show of stepping on the pedal to lift the lid. "And this one time, I'll even help you bury evidence, Counselor."

Chapter Seven

Something about being left alone inside Simon Wingate's personal space felt decadent. Lori stood in the kitchen letting her gaze travel along the veins in the marble countertops. She caught a glimpse of her reflection in a glass-front cabinet and lifted a hand to her hair. She felt slightly undone by her surroundings. She could only dream of having a house this big and comfortable. She was both enraptured and discomfited.

The stylish surroundings weren't what was making her feel antsy now. Or the feeling she didn't belong there. She was used to not quite belonging. It was Simon. She was more susceptible to the man than she wanted to be. Which meant she needed to tread carefully around him.

She wandered down the hall to the large family room she'd spotted on her way in. An enormous, comfortable-looking sectional dominated the space. A flat-screen television that appeared to have been selected for its ability to match the size of the couch hung on the wall above a gas log fireplace. The room was filled with books, knick-knacks and family photos.

They couldn't be Simon's. If he had been the one to decorate this room, she would lay odds that the studio shot of the freckle-faced, mildly gap-toothed Cub Scout sitting front and center on the middle shelf would have been stashed in the deepest drawer he could find.

She was drawn to it like a beacon.

How could a boy who'd sworn the Scout's oath grow up to be a man who defended a suspected man like Samuel Coulter?

Swallowing her distaste, she studied the photo for hints of what this innocent, winsome Simon would become. His hair had darkened only a shade or two. His eyes sparkled with the same mischievous gleam he'd inherited from his grandfather.

Annoyed, she placed the photo carefully back on the shelf and walked away. She spotted multiple shots of Simon's father, Dell. The second Wendell Wingate, she thought to herself, was a man made for public life. He was a handsome man, but his looks skewed more toward Wendell's affable country gentleman than Simon's cool, urbane facade. He was clean-cut, where his son leaned toward polished.

Lori could only conclude Simon inherited his sheen from his mother. She reached for one of the posed family photographs that showed Bettina Wingate to be the epitome of all-American blonde beauty. She had a sort of old Hollywood glamour. Like Grace Kelly dressed up as a sweet Georgia peach of a girl next door. Her smile was wide and winning, like her son's, but she gleamed with a fine coat of gloss.

She was startled from her reverie by the sound of Simon clearing his throat. Lori quickly set the photograph back in its spot and flashed him a sheepish smile. "Sorry. I was snooping."

His amused smile grew into an unabashed grin. "You're a cop—you could probably classify your snooping as detective work, and no one would argue any different."

"Should I be investigating your family?" she asked, raising a challenging eyebrow.

Simon laughed and pulled his hands from the pockets of his jeans. "Snoop away. My dad has held some form of elected office nearly my whole life. If the press hasn't managed to unearth any dirt vile enough to damage the family reputation, I'm feeling pretty confident there isn't any to be had."

"What you see is what you get?"

She tried to make the question sound casual, but the way her heart beat a staccato when she noticed the way his damp hair curled where it brushed the collar of his red-and-black-striped polo made her feel the opposite of cool. The Georgia Bulldog embroidered over one nicely outlined pec gave her an I-see-what-you're-doing stare, but she refused to be intimidated by a mascot.

Lori studied him closely. "How about you? Is politics your plan too?"

Without hesitating, he nodded. "My dad plans to run for the Senate when Senator Riley's term is up. I may throw my hat in the ring for his seat in the Georgia General Assembly."

Despite herself, Lori was surprised by the bomb he'd dropped into the conversation oh so casually. "Wait— Senator Blake Riley?"

He nodded and her heart kicked up at the thought of it. Blake Riley had served in the Senate for longer than anyone cared to remember. He was a jerk. A camera-hamming bigot. Lori found it odd for someone who lived to draw attention to himself to head quietly into retirement, but she wasn't about to complain.

"Your dad is running for the US Senate?"

Simon's mouth curved up on one side. He held a finger

to his lips. "That's a state secret. And no one is beating down the door asking me to run for anything."

She noticed Simon's self-deprecating drawl deepened when he was doling out glib bits of unvarnished truth. The knowledge did something to Lori's insides. Something she wasn't sure she liked. With every slow, soft-spoken syllable, her resolve to keep her distance from this man softened and stretched like taffy pulled on a hot summer day.

"What can I get you to drink?" he asked, jerking her out of her thoughts.

"Anything's fine," she replied.

"I can offer you water or, uh, water," he said with a shrug. "Hayes said he'd be bringing the beverages."

"How about water?"

"Be right back."

She didn't want to have sticky-taffy feelings for Simon Wingate. Liking him would only complicate things. He had plans for moving up and out of Pine Bluff. She had a family who needed her to stay grounded. Or get re-grounded. More than anything, Lori wished she could be the woman she was two years ago. Someone strong, confident that she could hurdle any obstacle thrown at her. And she had. She'd steered her family through the loss of her father and aunt. She'd helped her mother re-calibrate her life as a widow and stepped into the void her father had left as best she could.

But then Jeff Masters killed himself, and her belief in her ability to be the person her loved ones needed was shaken to the core. He'd left no note. There'd been no hint of dissatisfaction. She'd been as shocked as the Masters family. But she wasn't a part of the family. Most people hadn't even known they were dating, so how could she explain how deeply she grieved his loss? The discovery that Jeff had been coerced into pulling that trigger was just one more blow to her already shaky self-assurance.

Lori stared at the Wingate family portrait. Simon would marry a woman like his mother, composed and serene. A woman with a heaping helping of confidence and free of messy complications. If Ben Kinsella hadn't snatched up Marlee Masters the minute she sauntered back into town, Lori would've laid odds that Marlee and Simon would be planning a trip down the aisle by now. Surely the thought had crossed Henry Masters's and Wendell Wingate's minds.

Simon returned with two bottles of water, a bag of chips and a bowl filled with bright red salsa. "Dig in." He paused, frowning at his offering. "I didn't make it. They have containers of it in the refrigerated case. The cashier, Tina? She said it was locally made."

Lori's smile started to unfurl. "Was it called Bonita Anita?"

Simon set the bowl on the table in front of her. "Yes. Have you tried it? It's so good."

The smile widened to a grin. "Yes, I have. My mother makes it."

"Are you kidding me? I'm totally hooked on the stuff."

Lori's limbs loosened. She beamed with familial pride. "I'll be sure to pass your compliments along." She inclined her head. "And thank you for your patronage."

He shook his head in wonder. "Your mother makes it? I've been eating it nonstop since I moved here. It's the best thing about this whole town."

Torn between flattery and insult, Lori stared at him. "Wow. Thanks for the rousing endorsement."

He opened his mouth to correct himself, then gave up with a shrug. "Foodwise, I mean."

Tickled by his stubborn refusal to show the town any

love, she unleashed the laugh she'd been holding back. "Poor city mouse, stuck out here with us country bumpkins. My aunt used to have a restaurant. This was a family recipe."

Rather than the smart reply she'd expected, Simon stared at her. This time, there was no derision in his gaze, only compassion. Which meant he knew about her father and her aunt. Talk about a conversation killer. She could feel the blush creeping up from her chest. Lord, if she kept blushing beet red every time he looked at her, he would think she was an actual redneck.

"No one here but us rubes," she whispered.

"Wendell told me not to make you mad. He says you carry."

"I do."

"I heard you're quite the shot."

"I am, but they don't let me fire at live targets," she replied, unable to keep her pride hidden away like the compact Glock she carried when off duty.

"I'm torn between being impressed and terrified."

"Both will do." She narrowed her eyes. "Did you want a demonstration or something?"

A knock made them both jump, and the front door hinges squeaked a warning.

"Hello? Simon?" Dora called out, letting herself in. "I made Rotel dip," she announced, carrying in a slow cooker with its cord dangling right past the doorway to the foyer. "I chopped up some of those canned tamales and tossed them in. I figured if your granddad liked—" She backpedaled, craning her neck when she spotted them in the family room. "Hey, Lori." Dora's smile was friendly, but something sharp and speculative gleamed in her eyes. "You made it after all."

Simon rushed across the room to relieve Dora of her

burden. "I told you I invited everyone." He divided a look between Dora and Lori, then ducked his head. "I'll just take this to the kitchen."

Dora watched him hurry down the hall, then took a giant, showy side step into the family room, where Lori sat frozen. "I'm so glad you're here. I swear, Simon's been living like a seventy-year-old bachelor since he came to town."

For some reason, Lori felt compelled to set the record straight. "Oh, no, I, uh—"

"Hush. He needs something more pleasant than work to think about. Particularly with old Cottonmouth Coulter treating him like he's some kind of errand boy."

"Errand boy?" Lori started to rise.

"Not important," Dora said with a dismissive wave. "I'll go get my dip set up so it stays warm and send Simon back in here. You stay put."

The woman click-clacked down the hall in a pair of red leather mules with giant *G*s emblazoned across the insteps.

Rather than staying out as ordered, Lori paced. The gleam in Dora's eye, combined with the heat in Simon's, made her feel antsy. Like her skin was too tight. Shaking out her hands, she prowled the space while her lizard brain debated between fight or flight.

A clatter arose from the kitchen, followed by Dora's raised voice ordering Simon from the room. Then it struck her. She didn't trust herself to be alone with him. If they were left alone, God only knew what she might ask him.

Are you Coulter's errand boy?
What kind of errands?
Do you like me?
Are you planning to stay here in Pine Bluff?

Do you want to kiss me?

Why couldn't I want to kiss Hayes instead of you?

The thoughts ping-ponged around in her head. Scared she'd open her mouth and one might pop out, she decided to take the coward's way out. Abandoning her water, she skirted the end of the sectional and headed for the hall, her sights set on the front door.

She almost made it.

One step into the hall and she collided with Simon so hard her bun wobbled. He grasped both of her arms to steady her.

"Whoa, there." He exhaled and planted his feet wide, absorbing the impact with a chuckle. "Where are you headed in such a hurry?"

Mortified, Lori tried to pretend her mouth had not almost come in contact with the Georgia Bulldog appliquéd to his shirt. A flash fire of a blush overheated her face. She tipped her head back, and the weight of her hair pulled at her scalp. She wished she could say the sensation was unpleasant, but when a girl found herself wrapped up in Simon Wingate's arms…

Her lips parted and she scrambled for an excuse to leave. Any excuse. Then his gaze dropped to her mouth and any words she might have conjured dried to dust. He tilted his head to the side and she automatically did the same. She couldn't help it. He was going to kiss her. And she was going to let him, because how could she not?

He dipped his head and—

The doorbell rang.

The courtesy had been perfunctory at best. She'd barely had time to register the sound when the door swung wide and Marlee Masters hollered, "Go, Dawgs…"

"Doesn't anyone wait to come in around here?" Simon muttered.

Lori stepped back, her gaze locked on Marlee. To her credit, her friend swapped her stunned expression with a blazing smile in the blink of an eye. "I have a peach cobbler!" she said in lieu of a response.

Bless her heart, Marlee stood there in the doorway, trying to take up all the room a lanky blonde holding a casserole dish possibly could. Lori could see Ben coming up behind her. Thankfully, he looked to be absorbed in helping Henry Masters navigate the shallow front steps with his walker.

Lori took another step back, plunging her hands into the pockets of her shorts. She fingered her car keys like a talisman capable of warding off hot attorneys of questionable morals.

"I have to go," she announced abruptly.

"What?" Simon's eyebrows drew together, and a deep but not unattractive furrow appeared.

Lori sidled past him as if he were radioactive, then came face-to-face with Marlee. The other woman's smile had frozen into place, but her eyes were sharp. "Go? The game hasn't even started yet."

"I'm sorry," she said, hoping a blanket apology would suffice. "My, uh, sister called. She's upset," she stammered. "About today." She stood to the side of the foyer, nodding greetings to Marlee's parents and Ben when she slipped past them. "Don't worry about the pot with the baked beans. Send it with Ben or I'll get it whenever," she told Simon, hoping she sounded far more casual than she felt.

The second Ben cleared the entry, Lori ducked out. "Have a good time tonight," she rambled. She waved when she saw Miss Delia, who was making her way up the walk with a covered plate in hand, and skittered across the lawn to where her car was parked at the curb.

When she glanced back, she spotted Simon glaring at her from the center of the knot of people crowding his foyer. Reaching for the door handle, she called back an exuberant "Go, Dawgs!" before making her escape.

Chapter Eight

The day was going to be a total Monday and the sun was barely above the horizon. Lori didn't simply hate sleepless nights; she resented them. She was living a righteous life, and yet she spent hours tossing and turning. For two nights in a row. And losing not one but two nights of sleep fretting over a man who may or may not have a moral compass irked her.

She felt a twinge of guilt for letting the thought creep in. It wasn't true. She might want to vilify him, but Simon did have standards. The problem was, his standards stood in direct opposition to hers.

He had almost kissed her.

After reliving the almost kiss over and over again in her mind for thirty-six straight hours, she wasn't entirely sure if she wanted him to or not.

Dragging her feet, she trudged from the small lot beside the municipal complex to the front of the building. The moment she stepped onto the sidewalk, she was nearly mowed down by a couple jogging past. Stumbling back in her thick-soled utility boots, she let out a startled "Whoa!"

"Sorry!" Marlee Masters called without breaking stride, her golden ponytail gleaming in the early-morning light. Marlee smiled over her shoulder and gave Lori a wave. "Morning, Lori!"

"Morning, Lori," a second, much deeper voice echoed. She blinked and spotted the man who'd caused her sleepless nights striding easily alongside Marlee. Simon Wingate was out jogging like nothing had ever almost happened between them. The jerk.

A tad more incensed than she probably should have been, Lori hustled around the corner and made a beeline for the main entrance. She barreled into the office with a full head of steam. The second her gaze fell on Ben Kinsella, she blurted, "Are you aware your girlfriend is running around town with Simon Wingate?"

Ben, who'd pulled an overnight shift on their current rotation, looked up and said, "Good morning to you too."

"They're jogging together," Lori said, indignant he wasn't sharing her irritation.

He rolled his neck to stretch it, then launched from his seat and thrust his hands into the air, yawning widely. "Better him than me," Ben said with a tired smile.

"It doesn't bother you?"

Both Ben and Julianne froze for a second, and Lori realized the question had come out with a touch too much vehemence. "Should it?" he asked calmly.

Heat crept up her neck. She stalked to the desk she shared with Mike and dropped her bag into the empty bottom drawer, all too aware she was making a fool of herself over nothing. Her ears burned and she grimaced. "No."

Ben gathered his keys and wallet from his desk drawer. "You must not think much of me if you think I'm going to be intimidated by a guy they used to call Windbag."

Julianne laughed, but Lori's interest was immediately piqued. "Who called him Windbag?"

"Apparently, he was ahead of Marlee at Emory law. She says it took him a couple of months to realize most every kid there had a big-shot parent or two, but he became a cautionary tale. Simon Windbag."

"I see," Lori murmured.

And she did see. All too well. Rather than making her feel superior to Simon and his pompous past, she found herself thrust back to those early days of basic training when every soldier in her company ran their mouths too much.

"Yeah, so let's hope your pal Simon has enough oxygen left in his lungs to keep up, because if there's anyone who won't let him live down a failure to keep up, it's my Marlee."

The pride in Ben's commentary reminded Lori of the way her father used to brag about her shooting skills. An avid outdoorsman, Mateo Cabrera had taught his children everything about firearm safety, precision shooting and the responsibility of hunting only what the family could consume. She'd loved every minute spent under his tutelage. And by the time she was sixteen, she'd won every shooting competition in a three-county radius.

She hadn't been shy about bragging either. When she entered basic training, she drove the other members of her company crazy with her boasting. When she dared to back her words with skill, their drill sergeant had dubbed her Annie Oakley. A nickname she later realized was sort of a backhanded honor. She was labeled a show-off. A fluke. A sideshow sharpshooter.

"Yeah, let's hope he can keep up," she said. "I'd hate to be the one to tell Wendell we broke his grandson."

"Simon will hold up," Ben said gruffly. "Okay, well, I'm out," he announced. "You ladies have a good day. Call if you need me for anything."

Lori waved, then pulled a random file from the drawer and spun back to her desk. When she looked up, she found Julianne's bright green eyes fastened on her. "What?"

"Nothing," the older woman answered, making it clear there was something.

"Out with it," Lori demanded.

Julianne shrugged. "It sounded to me like Ben wasn't the one who was jealous this morning."

"What do you mean?"

"You weren't concerned Marlee was running with Simon. You didn't like that Simon was running with Marlee."

Lori fixed her with a challenging look. "You make no sense."

"It makes perfect sense."

Lori cringed and her cheeks heated. "Why do you think?"

"Because you've never been too terribly interested in Ben and Marlee's relationship up until this point," Julianne replied tartly. "She's not the one you're worried about."

Lori flipped open the file folder she'd pulled from the drawer. "You should take the detective's test, Julianne. You seem to find clues everywhere."

Julianne chuckled. "Say what you want, but I have two eyes. You may think you're inscrutable, but you're not. In fact, you wear your feelings on your face more often than you think."

Insulted, Lori gaped at the woman. "I do not."

Julianne pointed at her. "Outraged," she commented mildly.

"Am not."

"Defensive."

"Okay, stop it." Lori spun away again.

Julianne chuckled. "I'm not nearly caffeinated enough to face this day, and I don't think yogurt is going to cut it this morning. I'm going to run over to see if they have any of those egg-white wraps at the bakery. Do you want anything?"

Lori closed her eyes and envisioned the bakery case at Brewster's. Her mouth watered, but her stomach was twisted in a knot. "Coffee would be great. Something flavored. Caramel macchiato?"

Julianne nodded. "Done." She picked up her purse and strolled to the door. "You'll listen for the phone?"

This was part of the routine. Lori smiled. "And an eye on the door."

Julianne waved. "I'll try not to let Camille hold me up for too long, but if anything juicy happened over the weekend, I'm going to have to get the details," she warned.

Lori spun back and gave her a salute. "Understood."

The door swung shut behind Julianne, and Lori clicked open the file containing the report she'd taken from Bella Nunes the night Lori had picked her up on Highway 19.

The girl looked so bedraggled and terrified—and young. She seemed so vulnerable—dumped out there without any money or ID. And maybe Lori had jumped in without getting all the facts first—something so unlike her. She was usually the slow, methodical one. But no. Something about Bella Nunes's story lit a fire inside her. She wanted Coulter brought in, and she acted without making sure she had him sewn up. It was the kind of mistake rookies made, and it galled her to know she'd fallen victim to her own emotions.

She was stewing on all of this when the outer door opened. Lori closed the file. "Must not have been any juicy news this morning," she commented, without looking up.

"Exactly what kind of juicy news were you hoping for, Detective Cabrera?" a smooth, deep voice asked in reply.

Lori's head jerked up and she whirled, rising from her chair in one fluid motion. Then she found herself looking directly into the amber eyes of Samuel Coulter.

"What are you—" She caught herself, suddenly remembering this man was one of the residents of the county she was hired to protect and serve. Plus, she hated to admit he'd managed to burrow under her skin. After all, they hadn't even met. Not officially. "May I help you?" she asked, striving for cool, professional detachment.

He stepped farther into the room, and it was all Lori could do to stand her ground. "I realize we haven't been formally introduced, but I'm guessing I don't need to tell you my name either."

"No. What can I do for you, Mr. Coulter?"

Lori held her breath as he took a long, leisurely look around. Logically, she knew she had no cause to be concerned. She was armed. Skilled in about a dozen different ways to take a man down. Still, she caught herself reaching for the flap on her belt. Ben often teased her about fiddling with it when she felt uneasy or antsy. She curled her hand into a fist and lowered it to her side. The last thing she wanted to do was let Coulter know he had gotten the drop on her.

His quick glance at her hand told her he'd noted the movement. His lips twisted into a tight smile. "I wanted to stop by and speak to you in person."

"Okay," she said, lowering herself into her chair again.

He moved toward her with the loose-limbed grace befitting an invertebrate. Thankfully, Mike had left a bag of clutter he'd cleaned out of his patrol car on the guest chair positioned directly in front of her desk, so she gestured for him to take Julianne's abandoned seat.

He settled himself onto the desk chair, planting the heels of his shoes on the waxed tile floor to keep the chair from rolling. They were expensive-looking leather moccasins. The kind meant to be worn with no socks. Lori hated herself for looking, but she caught a glimpse of tanned ankles sticking out from the hems of his artfully distressed designer jeans.

"What can I do for you, Mr. Coulter?"

"I wanted to come in and tell you directly I had no idea the girl you found working at my refuge was underage or reported missing."

Lori found herself transfixed by the gold flecks in his amber eyes. How could a color so warm appear so…hard?

"Apparently, she's been involved with one of my employees and led him to believe she was older than she is."

He spoke in the soft, honeyed tones of a man born in the Deep South. His diction was cultured. Careful.

"I will, of course, speak to my employee when I am on the premises today—"

She watched him talk. The man was no doubt breathtakingly gorgeous. Lori wondered if he was indeed some kind of demon from hell dallying around with the mere mortals.

"But, since I had to come into town to pick up a package, I wanted to stop in and speak to you in person."

"I appreciate that," she said evenly. "But there was no need. There was an Amber Alert issued, and I was simply doing my job by reporting the sighting. I told your attorney I would have done the same if I spotted her at the Piggly Wiggly."

She focused on a sticky note affixed to Julianne's computer monitor and hoped it appeared she was looking at him. Lori didn't want to appear intimidated, but she really wanted this conversation to be over as quickly as possible.

"Good. Right. As you should." He slapped his hands to his denim-encased thighs and rose gracefully from the wobbly seat.

Coulter paused, a tiny frown line marring the perfection of his high, smooth brow. He peered down at her intently. "Somehow you and I managed to get off on the wrong foot," he said, pairing the sentiment with a smile so tempting she totally identified with old Eve. "I seem to have offended you and I—"

Drawing on the same stubborn streak she'd used to plow through her stint in the army and her mother's disapproval, Lori held up a hand to stop him. In doing so, she also partially obscured his ridiculously attractive face, which helped.

"It's nothing personal, Mr. Coulter."

His smile didn't falter, but it shifted ever so slightly. The wattage had somehow switched from full power to a backup generator. His eyes, though. Those disturbing golden-brown eyes cooled a few degrees. "It feels personal, Deputy."

Such a blunt admission from a man who wielded so much money and power might have thrown her off balance, but she'd handled all manner of manipulation over the years. Coulter was offering up his so-called feelings as bait. But she wasn't biting.

"I'm sorry you feel that way." She tried to keep the smile cordial. "I assure you, in both instances, I was merely following up on information brought to my attention. If either Sheriff Kinsella or Deputy Schaeffer had been the officer Ms. Nunes confided in, they would have done exactly the same thing."

"The sheriff and your fellow deputy didn't feel the need to visit my park," he said, drawling the observation and somehow twisting it into an accusation.

"I wanted to see the place." She didn't offer him any reason why. She didn't believe he deserved one. "I paid the admission."

He lifted a hand, his long, graceful fingers curled slightly, as if he couldn't be bothered to dig down and find the energy to straighten them all the way. He stared directly into her eyes, and though she cringed inside, she didn't look away. "I have security cameras mounted all over the park."

A ripple of foreboding scurried down her spine, but she didn't dare break eye contact, half-afraid he would strike the second she did. "Good to know," she managed to say, her voice surprisingly even. She somehow injected another millimeter into her smile.

His expression was sardonic. "Did you enjoy yourself?"

Lori gripped the edge of her chair, her fingernails digging into the fabric of the cushion. She refused to cede their staring contest. "My sister discovered she didn't have much of a stomach for snakes."

He nodded slowly, but she'd swear the man didn't blink. "Not everyone does. How about you? What did you think?"

Her chin came up a notch. "I'm not afraid of them, but I can't say I'm a fan."

"Fair enough," he said, stretching the words out. He ducked his head, breaking eye contact.

She met him platitude for platitude. "To each his or her own."

He'd made a move for the door when it swung open wide and Julianne appeared with a tray holding to-go cups gripped in one hand, a white pastry bag dangling from her fingers. "You'll never guess who I ran into—" She stopped when she spotted Samuel Coulter standing in front of her desk chair. "Oh, hello."

"Hello." He flashed his powerful smile at poor Julianne, and Lori would swear she saw the woman stagger back a step.

Julianne's gaze shifted from Coulter to Lori, obviously trying to read the mood of the room. Lori wasn't exactly sure what her face showed, but whatever Julianne saw there had the other woman straightening her shoulders and standing her ground. "Am I interrupting or is there something I can help you with?"

"No. Nothing," he assured her with another of those devilish grins. "I was having a quick word with the deputy while I'm in town to pick up a package."

Julianne slid the tray onto her desk and plopped the bag on top. She made a show of glancing at the slim watch on her wrist. "Pick up a package? You're way too early for deliveries." She gazed up at him with wide, innocent eyes, but there was a pinch to Julianne's lips. "The post office doesn't open until ten, and the express delivery trucks don't usually make it to Chet Rinker's store until well after noon."

Coulter's friendly expression faltered. He must have realized Julianne was giving him the bless-your-heart treatment and didn't appreciate it. "Well," he murmured, tucking his hands into his jeans pockets and rocking back on the heels of those spendy leather shoes. "It's a good thing I had my attorney sign for it on Saturday. Thankfully, I won't have to do any sittin' around waiting for the pony express to amble on through."

To her credit, Julianne's smile only dimmed slightly. "Smart thinkin'," she agreed. Sliding past him to reclaim her territory, she busied herself with their coffee and pastries. "Now, I love young Simon, but I don't mind admitting I miss seeing Wendell around town."

"Me too," Lori murmured.

One corner of Coulter's luscious mouth jerked upward, but he stepped away. "Yes, well, if you ladies will excuse me, I'll head on over to see 'young Simon' now." He sauntered to the door. "You have a wonderful day."

Lori caught her bottom lip between her teeth, not daring to even exhale until the door closed behind him.

"My word—" Julianne began, but Lori held up a hand to shush her.

"Wait. The man probably has the hearing of a vampire." She half rose from her chair so she could watch until Coulter had exited the building entirely. Certain he was gone, she dropped back into her seat with a loud whoosh of air. "God, he gives me the heebie-jeebies," she said in a rush.

"Does he?" Julianne eyed her curiously. "I was gonna say he's handsome as Lucifer himself." She rocked back in her chair and fanned herself with her hand.

"I had the exact same thought," Lori admitted.

"Men like him are like catnip to some women," she said, pointing to the windows.

Lori shuddered and shook her head. "Not this woman."

Julianne pried their coffee cups from the carrier. "Not you. But there are plenty of women who would consider trading in the afterlife for some hot times with a dangerous man," she said matter-of-factly. Lori opened her mouth to justify her bias, but Julianne thrust a cup at her.

Lori accepted the cup and sat back with a laugh. "From what I can tell, he is the devil himself."

"Bet you can think about gettin' up to a little naughtiness with Simon Wingate," Julianne teased.

Lori's eyes widened when she took her first sip of the delicious caramel macchiato. "Simon isn't evil."

"Of course he's not. I'm glad you're coming around."

"Coming around on what?" Lori asked, exasperated.

"Rumor has it Simon was mighty happy to see you at his cookout the other night." Julianne gave her a smug smile.

Lori set her cup down on the desk so hard coffee sloshed out of the tiny opening on the lid. "Whose rumor has what? I was barely there thirty minutes."

"Really? Darn." Julianne's hopeful expression slid from her face. "I told Camille Brewster she had it wrong. It's too bad, though. Simon...he's the whole package."

Lori wasn't prepared to talk about Simon or the kind of package he might be, so she pivoted. "Speaking of packages..." Lori frowned. "What kind of package do you think Coulter had shipped to Simon's office?"

"No idea," Julianne said, extracting her breakfast wrap.

Lori scowled at her coffee cup, feeling put out. The better question was, how come Simon hadn't mentioned anything about this delivery? Of course, what he did for his clients was his business and none of hers. But something had happened between them at his house on Saturday. Maybe that was why the thought of his keeping Coulter's secrets bothered her so darn much.

Chapter Nine

Simon stared at the back of Samuel Coulter's head when the man placed the heavily taped parcel on the Wingate Law Firm's conference table. He slid a hand into his pocket and extracted a small multifunction tool dangling from his key ring. Panic flooded Simon's chest. There was no way he was letting a box marked Perishable and Live Animals be opened in his office. Not by this man.

"Whoa, wait. Are there snakes in there?"

Coulter glanced back at him, his expression amused. "Of course."

"I have no desire to see what is inside."

Coulter fixed his dead-eyed gaze on him. Simon felt about as small as he had the day his professor insinuated his father's involvement in politics made it difficult for Simon to identify with the concept of ethical behavior. "Scared?"

"More like terrified," Simon retorted.

Flipping open the pocketknife, he slit the tape securing the box. "These are hatchlings."

He opened the flaps, then paused to point out the writing on one of them. It indicated the box contained four nonvenomous ball pythons and gave what Simon assumed was a Latin name for the species. When Dora had seen the labeling, she immediately almost doubled what was already her triple-overtime rate. She also insisted Simon place them in the storeroom, far away from her desk.

There wasn't anything technically illegal regarding the shipment of the snakes, but Simon's gut told him there was something more going on here. Something he couldn't be a part of if he wished to remain within the bounds of legal and social ethics.

"As your attorney, I advise you to wait and open the box when you get home."

"What's the big deal?" Coulter insisted. He lifted a piece of packing material from the top of the box and peered into the cavity. "Normally, I would unbox them immediately upon arrival, but this time I didn't have the timing right." He removed what looked to be a linen bag from the box and began to unwrap the tightly wound drawstring. "These should all be albino morphs," he murmured, opening the bag to reveal a clear plastic container. "I hope they're okay."

Simon swallowed hard, noting the lidded bowl looked disconcertingly similar to the containers in which he'd brought home deli salads for his party. His spine stiffened when he recalled Lori pushing those deli bowls deep into his trash can and making a joke about burying evidence.

Holy hell, he hated this whole thing. Hated his creepy client with his Saturday shipments and sleazy backwoods operation. Hated having to accept delivery of a box that made him so uncomfortable he'd had to document every aspect of his involvement in its custody. Hated having to keep this man's secrets, whether his dealings were aboveboard or not. Hated having to deny himself the pleasure of kissing Lori Cabrera because she'd loathe him if she discovered he'd signed his name on this man's behalf.

"She seems no worse for wear," Coulter said, jolting Simon from his ruminations.

For a minute, he thought Coulter was commenting on Simon's forgoing his natural instincts where Deputy Cabrera was concerned, but the other man slipped the plastic container back into its drawstring bag and wrapped it tight again. To his relief, Coulter returned the tiny snake to her brethren, placed the packing material back on top and loosely secured the flaps.

"I'll check the rest of them when I get home." He hefted the box in his left arm, offering his right to Simon to shake. "I'm sorry to have disrupted your Saturday." He headed toward the office door. "Thanks, Wingate," he called over his shoulder. "Don't forget to bill me for any extra expenses."

Simon held his tongue until he was certain the man was gone. "Yeah, like I'm gonna forget," he muttered.

He strode down the hall to his office. Dora's chair squeaked when she swiveled to glare at him, her animal-print reading glasses perched at the tip of her nose.

"Tell me he didn't open it in here."

"I wish I could," Simon answered dully.

"Wendell Simon Wingate, I told you I didn't want him opening that box on these premises," she scolded.

"The man's billables are what makes it possible for me to pay you quintuple overtime to snap a few pictures."

"Haven't you seen *Snakes on a Plane*?" she asked, incredulous. Dora swiveled away from him. "And...you wouldn't need to pay anyone quintuple overtime if you didn't have men like him for clients."

"This is a vicious circle."

"Don't tell me it's a chicken-and-egg thing. This is a choice," she insisted. "You don't need to sell your soul to make a living here. There are plenty of people who need wills or land transfers done. I spoke to Marlee at the party, and I truly believe she would be happy to let you take some of the Masters family business back. The poor girl is overwhelmed."

"I planned to talk to Marlee myself," he shot back. "I don't need you drumming up business for me."

"Despite all evidence to the contrary." Dora softened. "It was nice of you to tell Marlee to bring her mama and daddy along. I doubt Marlee would have been able to relax otherwise. It's been a tough row to hoe for all of them, what with having to deal with Henry's health issues on top of dealing with the loss of Jeff all over again." She shook her head sadly. "I honestly can't imagine which would be worse—believing your child committed suicide or discovering he'd been murdered."

"Yeah, no idea," Simon agreed. Sighing, he perched his hip on the edge of Dora's desk. "Listen, I'm not a Coulter fan either, but a part of me thinks it's better this way." When she opened her mouth to argue with him, he held up a hand. "Keep-your-enemies-closer sort of thing. Sometimes, it's better to have the inside scoop on someone you don't trust entirely."

"Yes, but it does no one any good when insider information is protected under attorney-client privilege," she retorted tartly.

Pressing his lips together, he exhaled long and loud from his nose. "You let me worry about what I need to keep quiet."

Dora pushed back from her keyboard and looked him straight in the eye. "I'll tell you the same thing I told Wendell. I have only three years until I can retire with full medical and pull from Dewayne's railroad retirement. I need this firm to stay open and operating until such time. I've given your grandfather almost thirty years of my life. Longer than I had with my husband, God rest his soul."

"Dora—" he assured her.

"I cannot be out looking for a job at my age. I have no desire to relocate."

Simon nodded solemnly, all too aware of all the ways Wendell and Dora were counting on him. "I understand."

"I cannot be your secretary if you get yourself disbarred," she added. "And I cannot buy a place in Kissimmee if I don't have a job."

Placing his hand over his heart, he held her gaze. "Neither Granddad nor I will do anything to mess up your plans."

"You need to find a way to get free of Coulter," she said, nodding to the door.

"Your concerns have been heard and noted." Heaving a sigh, he slid from the desk and made his way to his office. "When you note the billable hours for Saturday, add in about half of your quintuple overtime into the incidental expenses. If I have to pay your extortionist rates, he's gonna split them with me."

Chapter Ten

Lori was surprised to see Ben's door closed when she came in that afternoon. Julianne looked up from the salad she was stabbing with a plastic fork, but her expression was hard to read.

"What's going on?" Lori asked, moving to her desk.

"There's someone from the DEA in there. Ben said they used to work together."

Lori frowned. It was common knowledge that Ben's forced exit from federal duty had left a trail of hard feelings on both sides. Julianne wasn't the only one surprised a DEA agent had ventured all the way to Pine Bluff. Then again, the town had garnered its share of attention from the agency. Lori's stomach rolled when she cast a glance at the closed door.

"How did he act? Do things seem to be going okay in there?"

Three lines appeared on Julianne's forehead. "Well, there's been no yelling," she said cautiously. "Special Agent Simmons is a woman."

"So?" Lori wasn't as surprised by the agent's gender as she was by the accusation embedded in Julianne's statement. "Does that matter?"

Julianne shot another look at the closed door. "I suppose not, but... He said they were coworkers, but he didn't greet her the way he would greet you or me," Julianne said, slanting a pointed look at Lori. "There was hugging and a kiss on the cheek."

Lori fought the impulse to laugh at the condemnation in Julianne's sober assessment. "Dear God, hugging?" she said, playing up her effrontery.

Julianne wadded up a paper napkin and tossed it at Lori. "Don't mock," she snapped.

Lori snagged the napkin from her desk and redeposited it into the trash. "Okay, I won't. I don't think Marlee has anything to worry about. Ben's not about to do anything to jeopardize what he's got going on with her."

Holding her Tupperware container, Julianne swiveled her chair toward Lori. "You don't think he'd ditch the job of backwoods sheriff for another go at being a hotshot federal agent?"

Lori matched Julianne's scowl with one of her own. "You think they're here to lure him back?"

Julianne shrugged. "They've been in there with the door closed ever since she got here."

The door in question opened and both women gave a guilty start. Ben loomed large in the opening. "I thought I heard voices out here. Hey, Lori, would you come in here? I want you to meet Alicia Simmons."

Lori nodded. Shooting a glance in Julianne's direction, she rose from her desk. "Marlee said to tell you she'd call you later this afternoon." She spoke in a voice loud enough to carry well beyond Ben's ears. Behind her, Julianne let out a small hiss of approval.

Ben ducked his head and he stepped aside to let Lori pass into his office. "Uh, okay…"

Lori willed her cheeks not to burn with a telltale flush at the embellishment. "Yeah, sorry. Julianne and I were just—"

Ben closed the door behind them.

A tall, dark-haired woman rose from the chair opposite Ben's desk. She wore gray slacks and a white blouse. Lori figured the pieces would look completely nondescript on any mere mortal, but on this woman they had a certain I-mean-business flair. The woman's smile was cordial but not quite warm. She extended a hand and Lori grasped it.

"You must be Deputy Cabrera," she said in one of those husky Hollywood-siren voices. "I'm Alicia Simmons. Ben and I go way back." She nodded in his direction as he reclaimed his seat behind the desk. "He speaks highly of you," the agent continued as she and Lori sat in the chairs in front of the desk.

Lori inclined her head. "Gratifying to hear. I think highly of him."

Ben cleared his throat. "Okay, lovefest over," he announced, clearly discomfited by their vocal admiration. "Lori, Alicia has some information I think you might find interesting."

Lori fixed a polite gaze on the other woman. "What kind of information?"

"I hear you've been taking a particular interest in the activities undertaken by a Samuel Coulter," Special Agent Simmons said, pursing her lips. She'd played her trump card.

"What about him?"

Simmons sank back in the chair, practically lounging in the hard wooden seat. She stretched her long legs out and crossed them. "Ben thinks you would be interested to learn we've been watching Coulter for quite some time."

"Watching him for what reason? And for how long is quite some time?" Lori asked, firing off the questions in rapid succession.

Simmons threaded her fingers and let them rest on her flat stomach. "Five years. We picked up on him when he was living in Miami, started to take a closer look when he moved up Jacksonville way. We got even more interested when he moved up here into the middle of nowhere."

"It's not the middle of nowhere," Lori responded, instantly defensive. When she caught Ben's amused glance, she blew out a breath. "Sorry. I hate to break it to you big-city folk, but anywhere outside of Atlanta is not the middle of nowhere."

"My apologies," Special Agent Simmons said with a regal nod. "He moved here to the most rural corner of southern Georgia."

The correction didn't do much to assuage Lori's ire, but the DEA agent went on.

"Coulter isn't exactly a country boy. As I'm sure you know, he was born in Miami and lived there and made an excellent living there. Enough to indulge his…eccentricities," she said, letting her distaste twist her lips. "The Securities and Exchange people took a shot at him, but couldn't make anything stick. But then old Samuel fell in with a new crowd of highfliers. And I do mean high," she said with a pointed look at Ben.

"You think he was dealing?" the sheriff concluded.

"We think he was…is moving inventory," she corrected. "We were pretty close in South Florida, but he had someone inside who tipped him off. He migrated north to Jacksonville to let things cool off, but he wasn't particularly great at keeping a low profile."

"Probably not one of his strong suits," Lori concurred grudgingly.

"From what we've seen, and what Ben's been telling me, he hasn't exactly managed to blend in here either."

"No, he hasn't." In the blink of an eye, the agent sat up and leaned forward, bracing her elbows on her knees. She gazed at Lori intently. Startled by the sudden movement, Lori pushed back deeper into her own seat. Special Agent Simmons gave the impression of an animal about to pounce.

"Samuel Coulter is a dangerous man. Volatile. Demanding. He surrounds himself mainly with young, impressionable people who are more than willing to do his bidding." She pursed her lips. "Mostly runaways or petty troublemakers. The kind of people few will make a fuss over missing when he's done using them."

"Young people," Lori repeated, horror rippling through her like a shock wave.

Simmons leaned forward in her seat. "Tell me about the girl you found walking along the highway."

It was an order, but the underlying softness in the other woman's request compelled Lori to speak.

"Bella Nunes," Lori said, enunciating the girl's name. Speaking it out loud because, whether they could prove it or not, Lori was convinced she was a victim. "She claimed she was held captive at Coulter's compound. Locked up inside one of the cages with a snake. She was young. A runaway," she said, glancing at Ben as they connected the dots.

Simmons wet her lips and nodded, sliding back in the seat once more. "Would it make you feel better or worse to discover she's not the first young woman to claim such a thing?"

Lori paused to reflect on the question. The truth was, there was no good answer. Nothing was going to make her feel better, and hardly anything could make her feel worse for not being able to do more for the frightened young woman she'd found walking along the side of the highway.

"Neither," she answered at last.

Special Agent Simmons stared at her appraisingly. "Exactly."

Lori's brow furrowed. "Why is the DEA involved? Are you all dabbling in human trafficking these days?"

Simmons chuckled and resumed her slouch, the picture of relaxed repose. "Not exactly," she said in a drawl so soft it sounded dangerous. "We have plenty on our plate with the drugs, but when you add allegations that he's collecting and detaining young women, it becomes even more sinister."

Lori sat straighter. "It certainly does. Do you think he's having them move drugs for him?"

"It's possible. Or they could be another revenue stream for him in addition to whatever product he's funneling through his contacts in South Florida."

Lori stared at her. "Product?"

"Heroin," Simmons supplied.

"Heroin?" Lori shot a look at Ben, then back at the agent beside her. "You think he's moving heroin through Masters County?"

Simmons pursed her lips. "We don't think— we know. The problem is, we're not exactly sure how to catch him doing it."

Ben cleared his throat and Lori swung her attention back to him. "Alicia's going to be moving here for a while. The agency has arranged for her to rent a house. We're setting up a cover that the house belonged to her grandmother and she's inherited it. It will actually be one of the Timber Masters homes," he said with a shrug.

"It's that serious? I mean, for you to move here," Lori asked, unable to mask her surprise.

Alicia Simmons smirked. "I hear all the cool kids are doing it. Ben, Simon Wingate—"

"You know Simon?" Lori interrupted.

"I have heard of Simon," the agent clarified. "We didn't exactly run in the same circles, you understand."

"Right." Lori felt the tension seep from her body. She did understand. Because anywhere other than here in Pine Bluff, she and Simon would not be running in the same circles either.

"I think it would be good if you and Alicia worked together on this." Ben interrupted her line of thinking. "You're both ex-military. Maybe we can say the two of you go back to your time in the service."

Lori glanced over at the other woman. "You were in the army?"

Simmons shrugged. "Navy, but close enough for our purposes."

"True." Lori swung her attention back to Ben. "I don't think you can sell the grandmother story. We don't have many strangers up and move to town, and familial ties run deep in these parts. If you mess with them, someone will uncover the lie whether they mean to or not." She turned the idea over in her mind. "If you're using one of the Timber Masters houses, you'd be better off saying Marlee recruited you to come work for the company."

"Good point," Ben conceded. "I'll talk to Marlee. I'm sure she'd be on board."

For her part, Alicia Simmons simply held up her hand to indicate she was open to anything. "Whatever you think is best. This is your town."

Lori looked from one to the other. They were serious. And they were right. This was her town, even if she never fit in. She wasn't the insecure young girl she'd once been. In truth, she wasn't sure she wanted to fit in.

Either way, of the three of them sitting in this room, she was the one who was the expert on Pine Bluff and the rest of Masters County.

She wasn't being conceited when she realized they were right to leave it up to her to lead the charge on this. Small towns were insular, and whether she thought the town's residents looked at her and her family as being different due to their ethnicity, they were locals. She was going to be able to get better answers from them than any stranger would. Particularly strangers who carried badges and credentials issued by anyone whose authority they did not inherently respect.

The DEA's sweeps of the area, while justified, left a mess in their wake. A mess the residents of Masters County had to clean up. Not everyone had a particularly favorable view of the federal agency regardless of their stance on drug trafficking in the area. Most of the county's citizens understood and appreciated the need to shut those operations down, but they did not appreciate the economic hardships and familial destruction that followed.

"Yes, I think it would be best to use Timber Masters for cover. Almost everybody in the county has a connection to the company either directly or indirectly. You wouldn't necessarily be undercover…more like hidden in plain sight."

Lori tugged at her lower lip as she mulled over possible complications. She saw no downside. Though her own personal agenda may have had more to do with apprehending any of the men involved in possibly abusing young girls, she wasn't at all sad to help disrupt any supply line of illegal narcotics from flowing into the country.

"How are you thinking you'll be able to breach his

security to catch him with the heroin?" she asked Special Agent Simmons.

The other woman sat up in her chair, her posture alert and engaged. "We're not entirely sure yet, but we are sure it's coming through him." She paused and cast a glance at Ben. At his nod of encouragement, she spoke more freely. "I think it has something to do with the snakes."

"The snakes?"

Lori shook her head. She didn't want to appear dim, but she couldn't see how snakes could have anything to do with the transportation of the world's most dangerous opiate.

"Heroin is smuggled in more ways than you can imagine," Alicia said gravely. "We find people smuggling in every body cavity you can imagine, and not only humans." She pulled a face. "The snake trade is one we've been eyeballing for a while. It consists of mainly private breeders and suppliers. They do much of their business online or through mail order. So, yeah, it wouldn't be unheard of for someone to ship a snake stuffed with packets of narcotics. They used them in cocaine trafficking back in the day."

Lori gaped at the other woman in disbelief. Her brain had gotten hung up somewhere around the time body cavities were mentioned, and stalled out entirely when the possibility of smuggling drugs inside of live snakes was mentioned. She was about to say something about how outlandish it all sounded when she remembered the mysterious package Coulter had had delivered to Simon Wingate's office.

Her heart gave a dull thump. Simon Wingate couldn't possibly be involved in this situation, she assured herself. Simon Wingate had plans for a political career. He wouldn't jeopardize his future for anyone, client or no.

At least, she didn't think he would.

The truth was, Simon could be in on the whole thing. Could this be how a future politician planned to finance his campaign? Samuel Coulter and everyone and everything associated with him seemed too seedy for Simon Wingate. Or so she consoled herself.

The package delivery bothered her, though.

Lori ducked her head, racking her brain for every single memory of Saturday night's cookout. Had he mentioned receiving a box on his client's behalf? No, she was fairly sure he hadn't. If it had been something simple and innocent like accepting the delivery while his client was out of town, wouldn't he have said so? Wouldn't he have complained about having to go into the office on a Saturday to receive this mysterious package? She would have, if she were Simon.

"What are you thinking?"

Ben's question jarred her from the depths of her thoughts. "I was wondering how it all works," she said with a wary half smile. Ben narrowed his eyes, but Special Agent Simmons was more than happy to jump in.

"It's pretty common. Most carriers, including the US Postal Service and United Parcel Service, have stopped allowing live animals to be shipped, but there are private couriers and other express services willing to handle the packages. Federal law requires live animals are labeled with the common as well as scientific names for the contents, but it's all legal." She pursed her lips. "You can ship anything from a long baby boa to a full-grown snake. Oh, and they can only ship nonvenomous species."

"Nonvenomous," Lori repeated in a daze.

"Of course, they ship the venomous ones too, though." The special agent gave a wan smile.

"I can't believe there's no oversight," Lori said, aghast.

"There is, but if you were inspecting or getting paid an hourly rate, would you open every box of snakes?" She sank into her chair again and let out a heavy sigh. "I can't blame them. The problem is, they start to believe those are sources deemed reliable based on past inspections. But we know they are the most dangerous kind of all."

SINCE THEY WERE agreed Lori would be point person with the locals, the next morning she made Rinker's Pharmacy her first stop. Chet Rinker's place had long served as the town's express package pickup and drop-off point. If Samuel Coulter had shipped any parcel containing live animals, it would have gone through Mr. Rinker's store. Lori wasn't sure how these things worked, but it was possible the man had a record of deliveries made in the area.

She hung back, sipping a cup of coffee from the bakery and waiting for the line in front of the cash register to dwindle. Marjorie Rinker, Chet's wife, was working the line while he bustled around behind her filling orders without making eye contact with the people at the counter.

Lori waited patiently, enjoying her coffee and letting her speculation run wild. She was so lost in thought she jumped when the bell above the door jingled behind her. She did a double take when she realized the woman bustling into the store was her own—"Mama?"

Sophia Castillo-Cabrera whirled, her expression a mixture of surprise and mortification. "*Mija?* What are you doing here?"

Lori nodded toward the counter. "I need to ask Mr. Rinker some questions, but I was waiting for the line to die down. What are you doing here?"

"Me?" With her hand pressed to her chest and her eyes wide, Lori's mother was the picture of innocence.

Unfortunately, she'd oversold it with her delivery. "I'm here to pick up odds and ends."

Lori frowned at her mother. Sophia was many things, but a good liar was not on the list. "Mama, is everything okay?"

Her mother's mouth pinched into a tight line and her dark eyes narrowed to slits. When she was younger, Lori would have quavered at what she termed her mother's angry face. Now, studying her up close, she could honestly say her expression was more agitated than aggravated.

"The doctor gave me a prescription to help with some...personal issues," she said at last.

Lori swallowed a scoff. Her mother didn't appear to be in the mood for jokes. "What kind of medication?"

"I'm starting to have hormonal changes, not that it's any of your business. The doctor called in a prescription for me, but I'm fine." With a flick of her wrist, her mother dismissed any possible discussion of what Lori could only assume was the onset of menopause. "What do you need to talk to Mr. Chet about?" She moved closer and pitched her voice low. "Are you in trouble?"

The conversation shifted from menopause to pregnancy so fast Lori felt the whiplash. "No, Mama. I have to talk to him about police business."

"Ah." Her mother's hand flew to her chest again, but this time she gave herself a comforting pat. "Okay. Okay, good."

Lori shook her head. "I can't believe you thought— It would be an actual miracle, Mama," she said gravely. "I'm sorry to disappoint you."

Sophia sniffed, clearly miffed. "I'm not disappointed." Her expression softened. "I'm never disappointed in you, *mija*. I just miss you sometimes."

"I miss you too, Mama."

Lori was tempted to confide in her mother, tell her that sometimes she wished her life were exciting enough to make that kind of trouble a possibility. She wanted to tell her about Simon Wingate and the almost kiss. Confess that sometimes she mourned the loss of Jeff Masters and what they might have had. Mostly, she wanted to talk to her mother in the openhearted way they had spoken with one another in the years before the military tore her down and rebuilt her.

The bell above the door rang again.

They spun in unison, and Lori saw Julianne panting in the open doorway, her eyes darting from Lori to her mother and back. She looked scared and remained uncharacteristically silent.

"Is everything okay?" Lori asked, taking a step closer to the door.

"I, uh…" Her gaze slid toward Lori's mother. "I need to speak to you. Official business."

Sophia took the hint. "Don't mind me." She gave Lori's arm a reassuring pat and moved past her. "I'll go get in line. We'll talk later."

When her mother was gone, Lori gave her full attention to Julianne. Lowering her voice, she asked, "What's wrong?"

"Lena is in the office," she whispered, nervously glancing at Sophia's back.

"What?" Reflexively, Lori raised her wrist to glance at her watch. "She should be in school."

Julianne swallowed hard. "She cut. Obviously." Then, taking Lori's elbow, she drew her out the door. "You need to come. She's upset."

Lori's heart began to pound and she quickened her step. "Upset about what? Did she say?"

Julianne huffed and puffed, trying to keep pace. "She only wanted to talk to you, but since I was the only one in the office at the time, I was able to get her to calm down and talk to me. I guess some friend of hers wasn't at school and she called the girl's house and her parents thought she was with Lena—"

"Jasmine!" Lori broke into a run.

She burst into the office and found her sister sitting at Julianne's desk, a can of soda clasped between her hands. Ben stood near Lori's desk, close enough to keep tabs on the teenager, but not so close as to loom over her. He was holding her sister's glitter-cased phone in his big hands.

"What is it? What's happening?" Lori demanded, dropping down to look her sister in the eyes. "Is it Jas?"

Lena nodded mutely, her fingertips pressing into the aluminum can as tears spilled over the edge of her lashes.

Lori glanced up at Julianne before pressing on with her questions. "She wasn't at school today?"

"No. And when I called her cell, it kept going to voice mail, so I called her mom to see if she was sick or something," Lena said, her voice creaky from crying. "She said she was supposed to be at our house."

Lori nodded to show she was following. "But she hasn't been to our house," she prompted, oddly heartened that her sister still considered her a member of the household, whether she lived there or not.

"No. And when I looked at her PicturSpam account, all I saw were pictures of that guy," Lena said, anger and frustration starting to overtake her fear.

Lori cast a quick look in Ben's direction before pushing for more. "The guy from Reptile Rendezvous?"

"Yeah. Rick," Lena confirmed.

"Rick Dale, according to his profile," Ben added.

Lori's head jerked up. When she'd spoken to Jasmine's

mother about what Lena had told her, Keely insisted that they kept a close eye on their daughter's accounts and hadn't seen anything about any guy in particular in her feed. "Is he on there? On Jasmine's page?"

Ben nodded. "All over it."

She stretched a hand toward Ben, gesturing for the phone. "I talked to her mom. Keely Jones said they hadn't seen anything about a guy on her pages."

"You talked to her mom?" Lena demanded, redirecting some of her anger Lori's way. "When? What did you say?"

He shot a look at Lena, then held the phone out to Lori. Unperturbed by Lena's adolescent outrage, she took it and began to scroll. "I talked to her that day. She needed to know what was up. Jas has no business hanging around guys that much older than her." She swiped back to the top of the feed, then frowned as she noted the username showing there. "Le-Le? Does Jas have more than one PicturSpam account?"

She looked up just in time to see the lightning bolt of guilt cross her sister's face. Thankfully, the Cabrera stubborn streak kicked in. Lena jutted her jaw, then shrugged. "I don't know. Maybe."

Heaving a sigh, Lori shoved to her feet. Meeting Ben's gaze, she translated. "That's teenager for 'Yeah. Duh.' In case you don't speak the language."

Turning to Julianne, she said, "Call Keely. She has to be beside herself with worry. We can solve the mystery of the multiple accounts and start piecing together info for an Amber Alert."

Focusing on Ben again, she tipped her chin up exactly as her sister had a moment before. "I'm going across the hall to see about getting a warrant to search Coulter's property. You coming?"

Chapter Eleven

"You cannot issue a warrant to search my client's property based on a hunch," Simon Wingate stated flatly. He couldn't believe he'd actually managed to get the words out. His tongue felt thick. His head buzzed with questions he wasn't entirely sure he wanted answered.

The Amber Alert had come across his phone while he was pouring his second cup of coffee. The first cup he'd downed transformed into a burbling sludge in his gut. He scanned the alert. The scant few facts he saw made his knees go weak.

Jasmine Jones. Sixteen. Last seen in a silver Toyota Corolla. Florida plates.

Jasmine. Lori Cabrera's little sister had a best friend named Jasmine. He'd barely absorbed the information when Dora popped her head into the office kitchenette to inform him he was needed in Judge Nichols's chambers concerning a search warrant. He didn't have to ask what the summons was about or who was likely leading the charge to have his client's property turned upside down and shaken until young Jasmine fell out.

Now here he was, standing opposite Harrison Hayes, Ben Kinsella and Lori Cabrera, and hating the position he was in. Hated opposing people he wanted to call friends. He was duty bound to argue against the issuance of a search warrant for Samuel Coulter's property. It didn't matter if he personally thought the request was reasonable. His opinion didn't count.

Neither did the "evidence" Lori's sister had produced. In the end, they had some screenshots of a social media profile of a young man named Rick Dale, who claimed he worked at the Reptile Rendezvous, and Marialena Cabrera's word that the missing girl, Jasmine Jones, was likely with this Dale character.

While he understood the fire fueling Lori's insistence on obtaining a search warrant, Simon could tell Hayes was aware they didn't have a leg to stand on. His job, his only job, was to make sure nobody trampled on his client's right to privacy. Part of him shuddered to think too hard about what they might find if they had free access to Coulter's property.

"Your Honor, they don't have a shred of evidence connecting my client directly to the disappearance of this young woman—"

"She's not a woman. She's sixteen," Lori interjected.

"Deputy, please," Judge Nichols admonished mildly. "You're only here as a courtesy. Don't make me ask you to leave."

Simon picked up where he'd been cut off. "While I understand time is of the essence, and admittedly there may be some connection between my client and the young man Jasmine Jones was allegedly seeing socially, there's no just cause for my client's premises to be searched."

"Your Honor, the courts generally grant the authorities some leeway when the safety of a minor is involved," Hayes argued.

"We have no evidence anyone was abducted, and absolutely nothing connecting her disappearance directly to my client." Simon chanced a glance at Ben, not daring to look directly at Lori. "There are no legal grounds to search Mr. Coulter's property."

"Your Honor, last week we had another young woman claim—" Lori began.

Judge Nichols held up his hand to stop her. "While I appreciate your dedication, Deputy, Mr. Coulter was not charged in that instance, so I cannot allow it to have any bearing here," he reminded her.

Simon homed in on Lori, imploring her to see reason. "A search warrant grants you too much opportunity to infringe on my client's right to privacy on his own property." He raised both hands to indicate his own frustration, then tried to reframe the sheriff's department's request into something more reasonable. "Can you set up surveillance? You can watch for them from the highway. I don't believe Mr. Coulter's employees live on-site. You might catch Rick Dale coming or going."

"I don't have unlimited resources, Simon," Ben Kinsella said dryly. "We're not exactly staffed for stakeouts."

"Listen, I want Jasmine safe with her family too, but I feel compelled to state for the record even seeking a search warrant for my client's property could be seen as a gross overreach. My client is already feeling put on the spot. I'd hate for him to feel he needs to go on the offensive."

He locked eyes with Hayes. "Which is why I appreciate you calling me in here for this—" he shifted his gaze to the judge "—informal discussion about a missing girl's possible whereabouts."

Heaving a heavy sigh, Judge Nichols ran a gnarled hand over his face, pulling at his jowls. When he opened his eyes, he looked directly at Simon. "November can't come soon enough for me," he said flatly. "Whoever wins the seat is more than welcome to it."

Simon inclined his head. "I understand, Your Honor."

The judge shook his head. "No, I don't think you *do* understand. This kind of stuff might be commonplace up in the city, but these past few years here—" He broke off, shaking his head in disbelief. "I can't for the life of me imagine why your grandfather wants this job."

"Your Honor…" Lori began again.

The judge only shook his head. "Unfortunately, Deputy Cabrera, Mr. Wingate is correct. I need evidence Mr. Coulter had something to do with this young lady's disappearance." Sliding his gaze to Hayes, he added, "Bring me one shred of evidence connecting him to her, and we'll continue this 'informal conversation' about search warrants."

When they shuffled from the judge's chambers, the sheriff was careful to place himself between Simon and Lori, but there was no hiding the deputy's chagrin.

"Well, that went about as expected," Hayes said when they entered the larger office space that housed the district attorney's offices.

"I can't believe you took such weak evidence to him," Simon said, shaking his head.

Hayes shrugged. "I came up against an immovable object."

Steps ahead of them, Lori led the charge. She didn't look back. She didn't speak to anyone. She just made a beeline for the door leading to the municipal building's atrium, no doubt anxious to get back on her own turf.

"Lori, wait," he called after her.

She didn't break stride. Instead, she raised one hand in a rude gesture and kept walking forward, her other palm extended to push open the door.

"Give her some time," Ben advised. "This is hitting close to home for her."

"I understand," Simon snapped. "I'm not the enemy here."

Both the sheriff and the district attorney looked at him, their expressions curious. "No," Ben began slowly. "She only sees you defending her enemy, which puts you squarely on the wrong team."

"Ben, I'm not—"

"I know," Ben said succinctly. "It's not an easy pill to swallow. Not for any of us."

Simon stood rooted to the spot as Ben disappeared into the offices across the hall. Through the glass walls, he saw him stop and speak to Lori, who was clearly agitated. He wanted to go over there and try to reason with her, but there wasn't any point. He might have the law on his side, but working within the law didn't necessarily mean he was right.

"She'll cool off." Hayes spoke quietly.

When Simon glanced over his shoulder, he saw the district attorney staring across the fishbowl atrium into the law's side of the Masters County law and justice center.

"I hope so," Simon murmured. Facing the other man, he asked, "Why'd you even take it in there? There was no way Nichols was going to approve a warrant."

Hayes nodded. "She came storming in here while Judge Nichols was hitting the coffeepot." He shrugged. "He heard her and the judge thought he might save a lot of running around if we got everyone in the room and hashed it out."

Simon nodded, and his gaze strayed back to the woman across the hall. Even through multiple panes of glass, he could see the anger shimmering off her like heat rising from a sunbaked road. "I should never have mentioned a stakeout. She'll park her car right outside those gates every day and every night," he grumbled.

"Yes, she probably will." Hayes peered at him. "You have three options."

Simon jerked, startled by the man's blunt assessment. He tore his attention from Lori. "Oh, yeah? What are those?"

"One, you walk away knowing you did everything legally necessary to save your client a hassle, to heck with a sixteen-year-old girl—"

"I'm not a monster, Harry," he growled.

"Okay, so option two would be to maybe put the bug in your client's ear about how this girl's disappearance is, uh, reflecting on him, and see if he is willing to voluntarily allow the sheriff's department to ease their minds about her being at his place."

"Yeah, I don't think he's feeling overly friendly to the people on our side of the building these days."

"With good reason." Hayes nodded to the sheriff's offices. "One of Ben's friends from the DEA came to call yesterday."

"Are you insinuating they might be coming here to investigate my client for some reason?"

"I'm saying it seems your client has a reputation."

Simon's gaze narrowed. "I'm representing him, not dating him."

"No, your tastes run more to curvy brunettes," Hayes answered, darting a meaningful glance at the windows.

"You don't know what you're talking about."

"You do, but for the life of me, I can't see how you'll ever get over the Coulter-shaped hurdle."

Tiring of Hayes's lecturing, he spun to face the other man head-on. "You said three things."

"Help her," Hayes answered with a shrug.

"Help her how? I have an obligation to my client."

"Help her by helping your client avoid another entanglement with the law," the other man said patiently. "She's not worried the girl has taken off with Coulter. She's worried she's with one of the guys who works for him. Coulter's employees are not your clients. I'd lay odds if your client gets wind the sheriff suspects there's another underage girl hiding out in his refuge, he'll turn the place upside down to get her out of there." He paused, and they both glanced to where Lori sat hunched over her desk, her phone pressed to her ear. "Try helping her in other ways."

Simon let his head fall forward and rubbed the back of his neck. "Okay," he said quietly, his mind racing through all the ways he could broach the topic with Coulter. "Okay. I'll see what I can find out about this Rick guy." He gave his head a shake, his expression grim. "I'm pretty sure I saw him at the Daisy the other day."

"Oh?" Hayes look intrigued.

"I can't say for sure. Mostly I remember the car." He grimaced. "You know how kids take a perfectly good subcompact and trick it out with the popping exhaust and the big wings on the back? It was one of those."

The other man fixed him with a pointed look. The kind that said Simon was missing something by a mile. "Maybe you should share your information with Deputy Cabrera."

Simon rolled his eyes at the man's deliberate enunciation. "Maybe, but I'm not sure she wants to hear anything I have to say."

"The only thing we're certain of right now is a sixteen-year-old girl has not been seen by her parents since Sunday morning." He paused to let the assertion sink in. "We've lost almost forty-eight hours and the clock is ticking."

Swallowing the hard lump of truth, Simon headed for the door himself. "Right." When he was halfway out into the atrium, he remembered his manners. "Thanks, Harry. I'll talk to you later."

Simon didn't look back to see if Hayes was watching when he crossed the lobby; he didn't need to. He could feel the man's gaze trained on the back of his head. Hayes was right. Rick Dale was not his client. Coulter was. Simon was free to share what little information he had on the guy without violating his client's privilege.

When he stepped through the door to the sheriff's department, the occupants fell quiet. Ben even glowered at him, his arms crossed over his chest.

"Can we help you, Simon?" the sheriff asked, cool and controlled. His calm helped counter some of the heat in Lori's dark eyes.

"Yeah, I, uh…" Simon leaned to the side, hoping to make eye contact with the fuming woman behind her gatekeeper. "I wanted to tell you I think I've seen this Dale guy around town."

"Great," she said sarcastically. "Thanks for the intel."

"Actually, it *is* great," Ben interrupted. "If Simon remembers him, maybe other people will too. We can start canvassing."

"I'm also pretty sure I've seen his car." Reaching into his pocket, Simon extracted his cell and swiped at the screen until the information contained in the Amber Alert came up again. He frowned at the information and searched his memory. "It was a Toyota. Older model. I don't remember looking at the plates."

"Thanks for confirming what we already know," Lori

said drolly. "We'll contact your office if we need you to be even more unhelpful than you already are."

Tired of being the target of her ire, Simon switched his attention to Ben. "You don't think it would be helpful to note that the car was more primer gray than silver? Or about the oversize airfoil wing?"

Ben dug into his shirt pocket and extracted a small notebook with a golf pencil jammed through the binding rings. "Airfoil wing? A spoiler?"

"For the sake of simplicity, yes. They're technically different, but you get what I mean."

Ben frowned. "What's the difference?"

"A spoiler creates better airflow and decreases drag, but a wing deflects airflow to add drag."

"Why would you add drag?" Ben asked, his pencil poised.

"Well, on actual race cars, to improve stability and cornering at high speed. These guys probably just think it looks cool."

"Could you two make a date to play *Grand Theft Auto* some other time?" Lori asked, agitation pitching her voice higher than usual. "It's got a wing thing on the back. Anything else you care to share, Counselor?"

Simon resisted the urge to roll his eyes. "The usual aftermarket tricks, taillight covers and I'd guess xenon headlights. The exhaust was modified."

"Roar or popper?" Ben asked.

"More of a popper, but they had a whistle effect in there, I think."

Lori rose from the desk, dividing an incredulous look between Ben and himself. "How is the sound of his muffler supposed to help us find Jasmine?"

"Because people notice noisy cars," Ben murmured, jotting a few more notes. "Anything else?"

Simon shook his head. "If I think of anything more, I'll be in touch."

Nodding, Ben pivoted on his heel and headed for his own desk. "I'll send the information to the state coordinator and they can distribute it to surrounding areas. Thanks, Simon."

"Yeah, anything I can do." His response had been automatic, but he regretted the words. Not because he didn't mean them, but because they sounded trite.

"Yes, thank you so much, Simon," Lori said with a sneer. "You threw us a Froot Loop when we need a life preserver, but hey, you're still a great guy."

"Hey, now," Ben chided from his office.

"Lori," Julianne gasped at the same time.

Lori stared at him, practically daring him to protest her treatment of him. He wouldn't give her the satisfaction. He would do everything he could do—legally and ethically—to help find the missing girl, but he wasn't going to open his client up to an abuse of power because he wanted to make nice with the pretty deputy with the giant chip on her shoulder.

At last, Lori plucked a business card from the holder on the desk and handed it to him. "Please feel free to pass along any other information you would like to share, Counselor."

He took the card and nodded to Julianne as he passed her desk. "I'll call if I come across anything useful."

He hit the push bar on the glass door hard and had one foot in the atrium before he heard Julianne call after him, "Thank you, Simon."

Looking back through the glass, he saw Julianne's hand lowering slowly to her side, her expression anxious and guilt stricken. Lori stood with her arms crossed over her chest and her gaze locked on him. He shouldn't care.

What did it matter to him if a Hicksville sheriff's deputy looked at him like he was something she'd scraped off her shoe?

He did care.

Because he did, Simon shoved his way out of the Masters County Municipal Center, hell-bent on proving himself innocent, though presumed guilty by association.

Back in his office, Simon closed the door and dialed his father's number. It went immediately to voice mail. Sighing because he was all too aware he was letting himself in for a lecture on legal ethics, he swiped the screen again and hit the speed dial for his grandfather. Wendell answered on the second ring.

"Have you burned my office down?" he asked in lieu of a hello.

"Not yet," Simon replied. "The day is young."

"Two phone calls in one week," Wendell commented. "Why do I get the feeling you're not calling simply because you enjoy talking to your dear old granddad?"

"I do enjoy talking to you," Simon retorted.

"We've never talked this much," Wendell challenged. "I'm not complaining, mind you."

"Sounds like complaining."

"If I were to complain about anything, it would be the godforsaken rubber-chicken lunch I have coming up. Why don't you tell me what it is you need?" his grandfather suggested.

"Absolution?"

The whoosh of a heavy exhalation rushed through the line. "Hoo-boy. What have you done?"

"Nothing yet."

"What are you thinking about doing?" his grandfather pressed.

"Firing Samuel Coulter," Simon answered honestly.

There was a prolonged silence on the other end. Finally, his grandfather asked, "Okay. Why?"

"Why?" Simon gave a short laugh. "Because the guy's creepy?" he said, only half joking.

"Creepiness isn't reason enough. You took the man's retainer. You need a genuine conflict or cause in order to sever the relationship."

"I don't think I'm capable of giving the man an unbiased defense."

"If he's willing to accept your reason, good for you. I have to warn you, you're never going to make it through a life in law or politics without having to deal with some real scumbags," Wendell said bluntly. "If you can't get over feeling squeamish from time to time, you'd better start thinking about an alternative career plan."

"To be honest, I'm starting to think so too," Simon said quietly.

"Are you considering giving up the law entirely?" his grandfather asked, a note of worry in his question.

"No," Simon answered without a thought. "I'm not into handling the criminal stuff—I can tell you that. I don't mind doing the wills and probate, real-estate transactions, normal kind of stuff."

"Son, if we could all choose to deal only with the tidier aspects of the law, we would, but in a small-town practice, you take what comes to you."

"Even if the people coming to you are flat-out wrong?"

"Do you know for a fact your client is actively engaged in breaking the law or making you a party to his alleged illegal activities?"

"No." Simon couldn't keep the sulky note out of his admission. "I know there's something wrong about this guy and I don't want anything to do with him."

"Your opinion wouldn't be influenced by Deputy Lori Cabrera, would it?"

"Lori?" Simon tried to sound amused but was pretty sure he came off defensive.

"I hear the two of you were chatting it up at your cook-out the other night," Wendell commented mildly.

Simon snorted but sat up straighter in his seat. "Your informants passed along faulty information."

"Were you, or were you not, seen speaking with Ms. Cabrera in an intimate manner?" his grandfather asked, his careful but unwavering delivery making it abundantly clear how he'd managed to win over so many juries. It made Simon wonder if he could go after a witness with the same steady and undaunted determination.

Instead, he did a fair rendition of the politician shuffle step. "I had a conversation with Ms. Cabrera Saturday evening. We ate some chips and salsa," he said snidely. "Hardly what I would call intimate."

"Mmm. Miss Sophia's salsa, I imagine," he murmured. Then, clearing his throat, he pressed on. "Simon, I understand you and Lori are on opposite sides when it comes to dealing with Coulter's issues, but I would caution you to think long and hard about making an enemy of this man. I understand you may feel a—" he paused, searching for the right word "—fondness for Lori. She's an easy young woman to like. Last I heard, you had no intention of making Pine Bluff your home on a permanent basis, and because *I'm* fond of her, I would hate to hear of Miss Lori being misled or ill-treated in any way."

Simon hissed his frustration through clenched teeth, but his grandfather continued.

"I thought you had aspirations of the political nature," he reminded Simon. "People who have such aspirations need to think twice about alienating the multimillionaire in their backyard."

Simon propped his elbow on the arm of the chair and ran his index finger over his top lip, allowing his grandfather's warning to sink in. "I'm aware of all this."

"And you want to fire him?" Wendell prompted. "Clients with his bank balance and messy legal needs are not going to come along every day. A defense attorney makes a good living off a man who can't seem to keep himself out of trouble."

"Maybe I'm not meant to be a defense attorney," Simon admitted.

"You've certainly mastered the art of the circular argument," Wendell said dryly. "The best I can tell you is to talk to the man. Be frank and honest with him. Get a good feeling for how he might respond."

"Right," Simon said, nodding. "I will."

"And if you *are* interested in Lori Cabrera, I suggest you do the same with her," he added. "She's a bright young woman. Strong-minded too. She responds well to people who are direct with her. If you're looking for a distraction while you're there in town, I suggest you look elsewhere."

"Granddad—"

"The woman's a sharpshooter, Simon. I care about her, but in the end, I'm more concerned with keeping you alive. Not only can she pick you off, but she's clever enough to stage it like an accident."

Simon laughed. "Thanks. I've already been warned."

"No doubt by the woman herself," Wendell added with a chuckle.

Chapter Twelve

Lori sat slumped in her patrol car silently fuming.

A stakeout.

She gave her head a slow shake and repositioned her left arm on the sill of the open driver's-side window. The radar gun she held was sadly outdated, but the latest and greatest the county had to offer. She figured it was worth the taxpayers' time and money to sit out on Highway 19 for a while, watching to see if she could pick off any speeders heading toward Pine Bluff. If she happened to see a silver or gray Toyota Corolla with or without one of those ridiculous wing things stuck to the back, well, good.

True to his word, Ben had relayed the additional information Simon had given them to the coordinator so the other law enforcement agencies in the area had it too. A few of the details had been held back from what was being released to the general public, a precaution frequently used to be sure they were dealing with the possible perpetrator rather than one of the many "hot tips" they gathered by the bushel.

She sank down deeper into her seat. The conversation she'd had with Lena had left her feeling frayed at the edges, but speaking recently to Mr. and Mrs. Jones about their missing daughter shredded her heart.

When she had originally spoken with Keely, Lori discovered Jasmine's parents had no idea she'd even been speaking to any boy, much less an older one. A stranger. Say what you would about small towns, but there was a comfort in knowing all the kids who went to school with your kid. Most of the time, you also knew their parents, where they lived and what teams they played on. The thought of their daughter running off with a guy who was a complete unknown was incomprehensible to them.

Lori could understand their bewilderment. She had known Jasmine since she and Lena had met in kindergarten and become fast friends. The girl wasn't some impulsive rebel. She wasn't a hardheaded teenager who defied her parents' every wish. She was a sensible girl. Jas was exactly the kind of girl most parents wouldn't worry about, which made this all so much more troubling.

A sleek black sports car stuck its nose out from one of the farm access roads. She narrowed her eyes when the driver turned onto the highway heading for town. Lori slumped low and instinctively reached for the radar gun. Sports cars were not the preferred mode of transportation in this neck of the woods. Pickup trucks were more practical. Heck, her own mother drove an SUV. Only one man in this area drove a Dodge Viper. Coulter.

She clocked him at a sedate three miles per hour over the posted limit. He was keeping his speed under tight rein for her benefit. The man had the cojones to lift a hand and wave at his rearview mirror.

"Of all the times to become a law-abiding citizen," she grumbled, watching the car slink by at a modest pace.

She did her best to ignore the man and his ridiculous car. The rip of a powerful motor split the air. He'd gunned it the second he was out of range. Lori scowled in his direction. Even if she flipped on her lights and floored the accelerator, there was no way she could catch up to a car built for speed. Though she loathed the man, Coulter was not her prey on this day.

The man wasn't above the law, was he?

She picked up the radio microphone and toggled the key. "Base, do you read me?"

Julianne's voice came across. "Ten-four, number three. Go ahead."

"If Ben has a mind to hop into his car, a certain gentleman in a Dodge Viper is heading to town at an unsafe speed."

Julianne chuckled. "You didn't try to give pursuit?"

"He didn't punch it until I was well out of range."

Julianne came back on the channel. "Chief says to tell you he's saddling up."

Lori pressed the button on the side of the mic again. "Ten-four. Happy hunting."

Feeling better, she stretched her neck and let her head roll from side to side. She'd let Ben and Alicia from the DEA deal with Coulter. For now. All she wanted was to get Jasmine home safe and sound.

She watched and waited. If people who wrote the scripts for television cop shows were only keyed in to how much of her day was spent simply watching and waiting, they'd opt for a life of crime simply to break up the monotony. The back of her uniform shirt stuck to her skin. A fine film of perspiration formed on her upper lip. Then the radio crackled to life, rattling her out of her rumination.

Lori smiled when Ben's deep voice came through the speaker. "The county coffers should be about three to five hundred dollars richer soon," he said, his voice hearty with pride.

Lori chuckled but didn't pick up the mic to respond.

There was no need. They'd been reduced to harassment rather than action, and the knowledge irked. Gnats. That was all they were to men like Coulter. Pesky and annoying. If the county could occasionally profit off the man's hubris, who was she to pass it up?

"Heading back to the ranch," Ben said gruffly. "Thanks for the heads-up."

Lori grabbed the mic and keyed it. "Ten-four. Believe me when I tell you it was my pleasure."

"Oh, I believe you," Ben returned. "Over."

Lori placed the mic back on the hook and started the engine. Sitting here was only making her feel more helpless than ever. She'd visit Simon, see if she could coax some information out of him about his client. After all, a girl's life depended on it.

SIMON WAS SETTLED in at one of the rickety picnic tables the Daisy Drive-In had to offer, wishing he was anywhere else. The couple who'd been eating there jumped up and scurried away when Coulter fixed his dead-eyed stare on them. So here he was.

"I bet you're used to fancier business lunches than this," Coulter said, unwrapping a greasy cheeseburger loaded with everything.

Simon sat carefully, hoping to avoid picking up a splinter anywhere delicate. "This seems to be where I take most of my lunches these days."

Coulter took a huge bite of the sloppy burger. He spoke around the mouthful of food. "There aren't a lot of options."

Simon watched the man swipe a thin paper napkin across his mouth and keep chewing.

"I hear there used to be a hole-in-the-wall Mexican

place. They tell me the lady who ran it died." Coulter shook his head. "Shame. I love me some Mexican food."

Simon stiffened when the information registered. A Mexican restaurant. The salsa he'd bought was labeled Bonita Anita. Must be a family recipe. The comments Wendell had made about the disposition of Lori's aunt's house all clicked into place.

"Too bad," he managed to reply, keeping his tone detached and unconcerned. The last thing he wanted was Coulter picking up a vibe on how much he was into the town deputy. "This town could use another place to eat. It's either here, or I pick up one of the prepared salads from the Piggly Wiggly."

Coulter took a giant slurp from his disposable cup of sweet tea. He raised the burger, eyeing the dripping mass for where to strike next. "Never could be a salad guy," Coulter said with a wrinkle of his nose. "Rabbit food."

The man took another enormous bite out of the burger, and miraculously, not one speckle of wayward condiment marred the pristine white linen of his shirt. Simon wanted to hate him for aesthetic reasons alone.

"There's a bar out on the highway past my place. Gotta go beyond the interstate ramp to see it. They have a barbecue joint attached," Coulter offered. "They do burnt ends."

Simon inclined his head. "I'll keep it in mind. Thanks." He pulled one of the frilled toothpicks from a triangle of sandwich, took a deep breath and plunged in. "I'm sure you're wondering why I wanted to meet today," he began tentatively.

Coulter shrugged and continued chomping down on his burger. "No problem," he said through stuffed cheeks. "I was going to come see you anyway."

Simon straightened, his senses on high alert. A part

of him hoped Coulter was coming to see him to fire him. "Oh? How come?"

Coulter gulped down his food. "Yeah, well, first of all, I got a ticket on the way into town. I'll need you to take care of it for me. Illegal speed trap or something along those lines," he said dismissively. "I saw the pretty lady deputy sitting out by my place, and sure enough, the sheriff was waiting for me the minute I hit the city limits."

"A ticket?"

He took another sip from his cup, flashing Simon a wide, engaging smile. "I guess I didn't take my foot off the accelerator in time to slow down to the posted in-town speed limit." He shrugged. "I'm pretty sure they were tag teaming me. Surely you can find some technicality to get me out of it. I don't mind paying the ticket, but I do mind being trapped."

Simon's heart sank. He had no doubt he could argue his way out of a traffic ticket for the man, even if he didn't particularly want to. "I'll see what I can do. Listen, I wanted to talk to you about one of the guys who works for you."

"Who?" Coulter asked, unconcerned.

"A guy named Rick Dale?"

Coulter pulled a paper sleeve of french fries from his bag. "What about him?"

"He's, uh, a person of interest in the search for a missing girl." Simon watched the other man carefully, scanning for any flicker of complicity.

Coulter's eyes narrowed. "Why do I have a feeling this is going to come back around on me?"

Not wanting to get the man's back up, Simon raised both hands to placate him. "Nope. Not at all. You can't be held responsible for your employee's actions. Does he live on your property?"

"No."

Simon nodded. "Didn't think so." As Coulter's attorney, he was glad to confirm there was no probable cause to search the man's property. As a human being, he was terrified for a sixteen-year-old girl named Jasmine.

"Can you give me an address for him? The girl is underage and—"

To his utter surprise, Coulter dropped his burger and pulled out his phone. "I'll do you one better." Pressing his phone to his ear, he scowled at his cheeseburger. "Dale? It's Coulter. Listen, I don't want to nose around in your life, but I have a half-dozen people who can't seem to find anything better to do but snoop into mine, so I'm only gonna say this once. If there's a girl named Jasmine with you, you need to haul her behind straight home. The girl is jailbait, and if you aren't smart enough to know what that means, I don't need you workin' for me anymore. Got it?" There was a pause. Coulter shook his head hard. "Nope. Don't wanna hear a word. If she's there with you, take her home now and pray her daddy doesn't press charges. Or worse, come after you with a shotgun."

He ended the call. "There. Done." He tucked his phone back into his pocket, shaking his head in disgust. "Man, these kids. They have no idea there's a world of difference between the age of seventeen and eighteen."

Simon gaped at him. "She was there?"

"I have no idea," Coulter said, opening his eyes wide in a parody of innocence. "I didn't ask."

Buoyed by the initial success, Simon straightened and braced himself to approach the next thing he wanted to discuss. "Listen, I've been thinking—"

Coulter held up a hand to stop him. "Wait. I almost forgot the other thing I wanted to tell you. I have another box coming tomorrow. You need to sign for it."

"Tomorrow?" Simon repeated stupidly. "Why are you having a box delivered to me tomorrow? Won't you be in town?"

"I have to be up in Atlanta for a meeting." He plucked a fry from the paper sleeve, bit the end off, then used the rest of the potato to point at Simon. "I told my guy it was okay to direct it to you."

Simon didn't even want to ask who his guy was or what his guy did. "I shouldn't be accepting packages for you."

"I think it's the least you can do for all the money I'm paying you. How hard is it to sign your name?" he asked, giving Simon a hard stare.

There was something sinister in the way the man spoke the words *sign your name*. It made Simon's skin crawl. It gave him the courage to forge ahead. "I'm afraid I won't be able to continue as your attorney. I'm not comfortable with signing for parcels for you, and don't feel I can provide you with an adequate and unbiased defense," he said stiffly. "I'm hoping we can part ways amicably. I'm happy to give you some referrals to other attorneys in nearby towns, or even in Atlanta."

When Simon dared to meet the man's eyes, he realized this was not going to be a simple matter of a frank discussion.

Coulter smiled while he picked up a napkin and meticulously wiped his fingertips. It was the closed-lipped curve of the mouth. The smile of a snake. Simon wanted to look away from his disturbing amber eyes. He didn't want to be ensnared by this man's insidious charm. He feared being crushed by him inch by inch. He'd never been big on the outdoorsy stuff, but he'd hunted enough to sense when something dangerous was coming at you, you didn't dare look away.

"You think I don't know attorneys in Atlanta?" the man asked, clearly amused.

Simon willed himself not to react.

"You think I didn't come to you, Simon Wingate, on purpose?" Coulter said, enunciating every syllable of Simon's name with disdain. "You think I did an internet search for 'attorneys near me' and your name popped up?"

Simon spotted the flat calculation in the man's eyes and dropped his gaze, preparing himself to receive a good lashing from Coulter's forked tongue. What he should have been anticipating were the man's fangs.

"I know who you are, Simon. I know who your daddy is, and your granddaddy too." Coulter picked up another fry and popped it into his mouth, rocking back as he chewed. "I know your hopes and dreams. I know where and when you failed. I know about every mistake you've made, Wingate. Particularly every time you've tripped over the line onto the wrong side of the law," he drawled. "So you got off with a slap on the wrist and a suggestion you leave town for a while. Doesn't mean your past screwups just disappear." He snapped his fingers. "How's your granddaddy's campaign coming? You funnel any of that committee money into it before they caught you tossing out contributions like candy?"

"Listen—"

"No, you listen," Coulter hissed.

Simon steeled himself to meet the man's disturbing gaze.

"I. Picked. You."

A cold flash of horror raced through Simon's blood-stream as the man's words sank in.

"I picked you because you're the man I need on my

side. A man with ambition and aspirations. A man with much to lose."

Simon refused to react to the man's implication. "What do you mean? Whether I choose to represent you or not has nothing to do with my father or my grandfather or whatever aspirations I may have in the future."

Coulter simply laughed. "You have absolutely no idea who you're dealing with, do you?"

Simon played the innocent. "I don't understand why we're going down this road at all. It's not like we've had a long-standing relationship. We're not friends. What's your attachment to having me be your attorney?"

Cool and collected, Coulter picked up another fry and dredged it through the small mountain of ketchup he'd squirted onto a pile of napkins. "Missing the point, Wingate. I chose you," he repeated.

Frustrated, Simon shook his head. "I didn't have to take you on."

"But you did." Coulter popped the fry into his mouth and chewed, his gaze impenetrable.

"You're acting like I had no option. I could've said no."

"You could have, but I knew you wouldn't." Coulter plucked a fresh napkin off the pile by his elbow. He wiped his fingers, balled it up and tossed it at Simon's chest.

Simon stared down at the wadded napkin, wondering how the hell he'd stepped into this mess. He'd never been the kid who was picked on in school, nor had he been the bully. He'd been the one who stood on the sidelines disapproving, but doing nothing to stop things from happening to other kids.

Simon wasn't a man inclined to allow himself to be pushed around. He'd never thought himself to be complicit in his silence, but now he felt it. Wiping his damp palms on his pants, he focused on keeping his breaths slow and even. He was too smart to pick a fight with a bully. Coulter's resources far outstripped his, and if he were prepared to make good on his veiled threats, there could be repercussions from this confrontation and they would impact more than himself. So Simon chose to stand down. He wasn't about to be run over.

Holding up his hands in mock surrender, he said, "Whoa. This conversation is escalating to a place it doesn't need to go. I'm only saying I don't intend to keep practicing law here in Pine Bluff for much longer, and I think it might be better for you to find somebody who can handle your needs on a more long-term basis."

Coulter picked up his burger, peeled back the wrapper to expose more of the loaded sandwich and smirked at Simon. "I understand you're only here temporarily, but our relationship can go on even after you leave Pine Bluff. You see, my business interests are wide and varied, and I pay well to have those interests…protected. Seems the occasional favor shouldn't be too much to ask."

He paused long enough to take another outsize bite. Simon waited patiently while the man chomped the food into submission. When he swallowed, he looked across the table, his expression once again flat and unflinching.

"I'm having a box delivered to your office tomorrow, Simon. Express, early delivery. You'll sign for it, and I'll pick it up when I get back to town tomorrow evening." He tapped the table with two fingers, commanding Simon's attention. "Oh, and this is definitely one package you're not going to want to handle."

Without another word, Coulter balled up the remainder of his burger and tossed it into the paper sack. Snagging his fries and tea in one hand, he climbed off the picnic bench and pulled his keys from the pocket of his pants.

"Thanks for lunch. I'll call you when I'm ready to swing by tomorrow."

Simon sat frozen while the man walked away without a backward glance. He flinched when the Viper's powerful engine roared to life. Feeling gut-punched, he stared at the trash Coulter had left strewed across the table.

Another mess for Simon to clean up.

He sat still, waiting for Coulter to pull out and take off. When the roar of the engine faded, Simon closed the lid on his box and swallowed a pang of regret. He'd never order one of the Daisy's mile-high clubs again. And he'd forever resent Samuel Coulter for ruining the silly joke for him.

BACK IN HIS office five minutes later, Simon put a call through to his father. This time when it went to voice mail, he left a message. "Dad, it's me. I need to schedule some time to talk to you tonight. It's important. We may need to conference granddad in on the call too." He paused a minute, trying to think of what else he might need to say. At last, he settled on a simple "I'm sorry. I think I may have screwed up again."

Ending the call, Simon rocked back in the oversize leather executive chair and covered his eyes with crossed forearms. His whole life, he'd wanted to stand out. To not be the third Wendell but to be the only Simon. Now he was coming to realize if he was going to distinguish himself in any way among the Wingate men, it would probably be as the family screwup.

The realization gnawed him. He was not a stupid man. He had ambition, and sometimes it blinded him. He was competent in his skills and comfortable in his own world. Were those bad things? No. If he could remember them here, where he was a fish out of water. Maybe he could figure out a way to snare Samuel Coulter without compromising his own ethics.

Lifting his phone again, he scrolled until he found the contact information he'd taken from Lori's business card. When the call connected, he spoke with a quiet urgency.

"Will you come to my house tonight?" he asked when she answered. There was a pause on the other end, and he threw himself into it. "I need to talk to you."

"Why me?" Lori Cabrera asked.

"Because we want the same thing."

"We do?"

"Yes." He decided he needed to put forth something in a show of good faith. "And, Lori?"

"Yes?"

"I think… I mean, I hope, uh… Jasmine should be home soon."

"What? How? What are you saying?"

Simon shook his head. "I can't answer those questions. All I can tell you is—"

"Hang on. I have another call," she interrupted. "It's Lena. Hang on."

Simon gripped his phone hard. He was about to disconnect when a breathless Lori came back on the line. "Simon?"

"I'm here."

"Jas is home."

"I'm glad," he said, the words flowing out of him on an exhalation.

"I don't know what you did, but—"

"I didn't do anything," he insisted.

There was a beat of silence. "I'll be over at five thirty," Lori said at last.

Chapter Thirteen

She strode up his front walkway, unsure exactly what she was going to say to Simon. She'd spent two hours at the Joneses' house. At first, Jasmine had been unspeakably sassy and belligerent. Lori had hardly recognized the girl. She was glad she'd refused Lena's request to go along. Lori wasn't sure she wanted her baby sister to witness the rapidly escalating power struggle between Jasmine and her parents.

Rick Dale had been smart enough to drop the girl in front of her house before he hightailed. Smart thinking, as Jasmine's daddy was a former University of Georgia lineman. The scrawny guy she'd seen at the Reptile Rendezvous would be the equivalent of snapping a toothpick. The Joneses were so relieved to see their precious girl they hardly noticed Jasmine's sour attitude.

At first.

Lori followed Jasmine to her bedroom. There, she heard all the expected complaints. They were in love. No one understood. She wasn't a baby.

It took Lori a full thirty minutes and a whole lot of nodding and humming her sympathy. She graciously refrained from pointing out how quickly her beloved had bailed on her. Finally, the girl worked herself around to admitting she'd been scared to stay with Rick overnight.

In talking it all through, Lori was able to ascertain the couple hadn't "gone all the way." Jasmine claimed she told him she wasn't ready, and he loved her enough to respect her wishes. Plus, his bed kind of stank. And his apartment was "gross." He had a roommate named Justin who gave her the creeps, and she didn't mind coming home much. But she loved Rick, and Rick loved her, and she was only staying at her parents' house because the sheets and towels smelled better.

In the end, Lori was convinced Jasmine had scared herself.

Now she was anxious to see Simon Wingate. Maybe even a little scared. She wanted to talk with him, maybe try to talk some sense into him in regard to Samuel Coulter if she could. She wanted to stop sparring with him and air out all this unspoken tension between them once and for all.

"Hi," he said as he answered the doorbell. "Come in."

"Hi. I was surprised to get your call, but I guess you heard that Jasmine is home again," she said, shoving her fingers into her jeans pockets and giving a lopsided shrug. "I heard your client made a phone call. Thank you."

"Don't thank me yet," he said, his expression grim. "I need to talk to you."

Lori heard the apprehension in his statement and proceeded with equal caution. "Okay. What do you need to talk to me about?"

"Please sit."

They chose seats on opposite ends of the sofa, but Lori noted how he turned his body to face her directly, and she liked it. She wanted to put all their bickering aside. She didn't know him well, but, aside from his tastes in clientele, what she did know, she liked. Probably more than she wanted to admit.

Simon inhaled deeply and he tipped his head back to stare at the ceiling. "I need you to bear with me while I talk this out in a way which won't get me disbarred," he said quietly.

"Disbarred?"

"I'm having some issues with a few things about a client," he said, choosing each word carefully. "Of course, most of my interactions with this client are bound by attorney-client privilege." He paused and cast his eyes to the ceiling. "Hey, did I tell you I'm also being subtly blackmailed?" he asked, keeping his tone light and casual.

His eyes met hers and held. She sucked in a short breath, but played along. "No. Are you? I didn't think people were blackmailed outside of the movies."

He nodded. "All the time. You see it a lot in politics." He stared, prompting her to read between the lines.

Politics. Someone was threatening to hurt his family politically. Someone who was a client. A client with enough money and clout to hurt the Wingate family's political prospects in some way.

Samuel Coulter.

Lori pressed the tips of her fingers to her lips to keep from speaking the man's name aloud. She didn't want to do anything to cause Simon to shut down their conversation. She offered a wobbly smile as she parsed through various ways of approaching the problem.

"Okay, well, wow. Puts a new spin on things, does it?"

"Yes, it does."

"So, uh, I'm not sure what the bounds of attorney-client privilege are exactly," she began.

"They cover pretty much everything, unless, of

course, a client decides to tell someone who is not their attorney, or the client uses the attorney's services to commit a crime or fraud."

"Has your client done either of those things?"

"Not to my knowledge," he responded, speaking with enough deliberate care to make it clear something may have been done without his explicit knowledge.

"Wow. Okay. Complicated. How about I ask some questions and maybe you can answer them if you can or tell me if you can't?"

Simon nodded. "Might work."

"Okay." She gave a laugh. "I never thought I'd be the one asking questions. You're the lawyer, not me."

He gave a wry smile. "I bet you're pretty good at asking questions all on your own."

"All right. I guess we'll kind of begin with some random stuff to warm up." She paused and tried to come up with the most innocuous question she could think up. "Is your first name actually Wendell?"

He laughed. "Absolutely. Telling women my name is Wendell does nothing to benefit my cause."

"It has a certain nerdish charm," she allowed. "Tell me, are you presently retained to represent a man named Samuel Coulter?"

"Yes." Simon punctuated the admission with a brisk nod.

"Does this conversation have anything to do with a particular client?"

He pursed his lips, considering the question from all angles. "I don't think I can answer one way or another."

"Fair enough." Lori ticked the yes column on her mental score sheet.

"Do you believe one of your clients may be engaged in criminal activity?"

Simon beamed a smile at her, but he shook his head. "I can't answer directly. Calls for speculation. I have seen no evidence of criminal activity, but I think we can make a general assumption at least one of my clients has allegedly engaged in some questionable, if not criminal, behavior."

"Okay, so if I were to invite Ben over here for a beer, and he and I were to have a conversation about all of our suspicions about all of the people who may or may not be doing things of a criminal nature here in Masters County, is there any way you could point us in the right direction?"

This time Simon laughed. "You went way too broad in your questioning. Granddad used to say, 'You catch a lot of little fish with a big net, but you need a strong hook to snag the big ones.' You were on track. Stick with specifics where you can."

"Okay, well, I'm not the one who wanted to talk without doing any talking," she retorted tartly.

He inclined his head in acquiescence. "Understood." He tapped his fingers on his denim-clad knee. "I hear Ben had a friend from the DEA visit," he asked in a studiedly casual tone that made the fine hairs on her arm ripple.

She hesitated, watching him carefully. "Yes. Why do you ask?"

He shrugged. "Curious, is all. Were they stopping by to say hello, or was there a purpose in coming here?"

Lori frowned, uncertain how much she should disclose to this man. After all, he was representing the man Special Agent Simmons had come to Masters County to investigate. Maybe his whole come-over-and-talk thing was a ruse. Perhaps she'd read the situation tragically wrong.

Her mind racing with possibilities, she answered, "I can't comment on that."

Simon blew out a breath. "Okay, so we both have things we can't talk about." He studied her intently. "I am going to assume if the DEA has business in Pine Bluff, it has nothing to do with any of my clients."

She gave an overly hearty laugh to signal he was way off base without saying the words.

"Or maybe it does," he amended, speaking slowly. "Only one of my clients has had any difficulty lately, and nothing I am aware of would fall under the purview of the Drug Enforcement Administration. Unless you're going to try to convince me Timmy Showalter is a bigger fish than I thought."

"No. Timmy's nothing more than a kid who doesn't make good choices."

"I'm trying to figure out what the issue might be," he pressed.

"The issue is, you can't talk about whatever it is that's eating at you, so we're sitting here talking in circles." She tossed up her hands in frustration. "What am I doing here?"

Moving closer to her on the sofa, he said, "Lori, I'm not the bad guy here."

"I know," she whispered, touched by the raw vulnerability in his plea.

"Do you?" he asked, leaning in closer to peer into her eyes. "I really want you to believe me."

"I do."

"Okay," he whispered, almost to himself. "I have a lot of thinking to do, and I need to talk to my dad and Wendell about some stuff, but I wanted you to—" he slanted her a rueful smile "—keep an open mind about me."

"Okay," she agreed, breathless.

"I wish this was easier."

The rasp in his voice was enough to make her believe him. "You wish what was easier?"

"You and me."

"You and me?" she asked, stunned, but pleased by his directness.

"Yes. I want things to be easier between you and me."

She found herself caught up in his intense stare. "You do?"

"Yes. I want to be…with you, but I also want to feel like a man who deserves to be with you."

"And you don't think you are?"

His laugh was short but genuine. "You've spent the past couple of weeks reminding me I'm slime like my client."

"True," she murmured.

She gave him a playful once-over, mainly because she was unable to look him straight in the eye. Her entire life, she'd been taught there were only two sides to every coin. Right and wrong. Truth or lies. Grace and sin. Now she found herself seated on a squishy sofa across from a man she wanted more than she cared to admit, and staring into a giant gray abyss. She wanted him. He wanted her. That was the truth.

"Lori—"

"You're right. This is complicated."

"I'm working on uncomplicating things. The problem is, there's more at stake here than me or you or what either of us might want."

"Okay," she replied. Her desire to push or cajole him into stepping out of the dark and into the light was immediately subdued by the earnest appeal. So she asked the only question she had left. "Then what can I do to help?"

Chapter Fourteen

After extracting a promise from Lori not to give up on him and asking her to stand by as he figured out a way to wriggle out from under Coulter's thumb, Simon showed Lori to the door.

Thirty minutes later, he had both his father and grandfather conferenced in on a call. Once he brought his father up to speed regarding Samuel Coulter, Simon told them about their lunch meeting and the not-so-veiled threats Coulter issued.

His grandfather broke in. "So he's implying he has the means to damage your political prospects."

"Not only mine," Simon said morosely. "All of ours."

There was a beat of silence. At last, his father spoke up. "The man can't possibly have anything on me. I've done nothing wrong." Dell paused and Simon could conjure his earnest, thoughtful expression in his mind's eye. "To the best of my knowledge, I've never met him. I think it's an empty threat. The man is operating under the general impression all politicians have something to hide."

"I concur," Wendell said gravely. "I did handle the sale of his land, but I was the seller's attorney. He used some fellow out of Miami, Florida, for his end of the transaction."

"He seems to have a lot of ties to Miami," Simon

mused. "I've looked into his business ventures, but they appear to be on the up-and-up. At least, on the surface. Made his initial fortune day-trading and expanded from there. Owns real estate all over Florida, a few small businesses, but nothing to bring in the big money. From what I can see, he made the bulk of it in the stock market."

"At least the part of it that's aboveboard." Wendell gave a dismissive sniff. "You wouldn't find any evidence of illegal activities online, would you?"

"No," Simon admitted. "The snake thing is pretty out there. People with money can sometimes go wacky with it, but this appears to be a lifelong obsession."

"I can go back through whatever wildlife legislation I've voted on in the last couple of sessions, but I honestly can't think of any way in which our mutual interests may have crossed paths," Dell concluded.

"Which leaves Simon," Wendell said gravely. "He said he picked you. I'm with your dad in thinking he threw us into the mix for some extra oomph. Your activities on behalf of the natural gas consortium's political action committee weren't a state secret. He probably thinks he can twist your arm harder by adding us in for good measure."

Though it had been nearly a year since Simon had accidentally jeopardized his entire political future by not doing his due diligence on behalf of his lobbying firm, he couldn't argue with his grandfather's conclusion. What Simon had done hadn't been illegal, but the optics weren't good. He'd taken the fall for the firm, walking away with not much more than an unspoken promise of their future support in his back pocket. Now he wasn't certain he wanted to get into the game at all.

"Yeah." He drew a shaky breath. "I admit he threw me at first, but now I can't help but think he's playing chicken with me."

"Good analogy," Wendell said with a chuckle. "Ye gods, son, what did you think the man could possibly have on your father or me?"

"I have no clue," Simon replied honestly. "You're the one who keeps telling me dangerous creatures lurk in these woods. You're the one who told me I needed to come here and take on some easy lawyering while I waited for people to get forgetful. Now I'm trapped in Pine Bluff with this guy using me."

"I did tell you those things," Wendell admitted ruefully. "I didn't tell you to take Coulter on. You chose him. When something too good to be true drops into your lap, it's because it's too good to be true."

Simon bristled when his father piled on.

"Your ego always trips you up, son. You wanted to make a splash. And you wanted to impress this Coulter fellow because he's sittin' on a pile of cash," Dell concluded.

His grandfather picked up the baton again. "Not saying you've done anything wrong. We've all spent some time cultivating some wealthy and powerful people. The problem is, sometimes you allow yourself to be blinded by flash."

There was a long silence, and in it, Simon read his father's tacit agreement with his grandfather's assessment. It pained him, but Simon couldn't say it wasn't true. His whole life, all he wanted was to step into the Wingate legacy. The problem was, every time he took a chance and tried to set himself apart from his father and grandfather, he ended up tripping and falling flat on his face.

He was ruminating on this when his father spoke up.

"There are ways for you to be able to off-load him, but sacrifices may have to be made on your part. More risk taken."

Simon scoffed. "You mean possibly jeopardizing my entire political future. Let's face it—my chances are already slim. With the campaign contribution mess and whatever it is I've gotten myself into down here aside, no one is going to elect an attorney who has been disbarred."

"There are always ways to spin unsavory items from our past into more palatable chunks for public consumption," Wendell insisted. "It comes back to the best defense being a good offense. We need to figure out a way for you to get out ahead of this guy, if not out from under him."

There was another long pause. He could almost hear the three of them pondering different angles. At last, his grandfather chimed in.

"Dora tells me there's a new lady in town. She's supposedly gone to work at Timber Masters," Wendell commented mildly.

"I clearly need to find more for Dora to do if she has time to report every scrap of local gossip back to you," Simon replied. "Of course, keeping her occupied will be much harder if I ditch my neediest client."

"It's a catch-22," Wendell agreed with a hum. "Aside from her ability to keep an ear to the ground, Dora is an excellent judge of people."

"She is," Dell said. "She told me I was going to propose to your mother five minutes after she met her."

Wendell let loose with a guffaw. "Well, son, anyone with eyes in their head could see you were smitten. The bigger question was whether Bettina would have you."

"Can we get back to the subject at hand?" Simon asked, impatient with the conversational detour.

"We're still on the subject," his grandfather replied mildly. "Dora says this woman looks like a Fed."

The three men fell silent.

After digesting the information, Simon spoke up. "I

was about to ask how Dora might know how to tag a federal agent, but then I remembered where I am."

"Mmm-hmm," Wendell hummed. "If anyone's going to be able to spot a Fed a mile away, it's Dora. She watched me go toe-to-toe with enough of them."

"Funny, Ben Kinsella had a friend from the DEA come to town earlier this week," Simon informed them.

"Did he now?" Wendell mused. "Isn't that interesting. I didn't think he'd left on the best of terms with many of his colleagues there."

"Do you think there's trafficking happening in the area?" Dell asked.

"The only thing I've come across was a teenager caught with some weed," Simon informed them.

"There's worse going on," Wendell said ominously. "I think it may behoove you to have a frank conversation with our friends over in the law and justice center."

"And say what? 'Hey, I think my client might be a bad guy after all'?" Simon demanded.

"Did I say you should speak to them about your client?" Wendell retorted, the question uncharacteristically sharp. "I said you should sit down with some of your friends and neighbors. Be a part of the community. Try having your finger on the pulse rather than one foot out the door."

His grandfather's impatience came through loud and clear. Simon ducked his head, tensing his jaw to keep from snapping back. Because, damn it, the old man was right.

"Your granddad is right," Dell said calmly, ever the peacemaker. "You think my trips back home are duty visits to maintain support, but you're wrong. Chet Rinker and I have been best friends since nursery school. Your mother pretends she's jealous Trudy Skyler and I went steady in the eleventh grade, but I think she does it to make me feel good. I'm on the alumni homecoming committee, and not so I can ride in the parade. Pine Bluff is my home," he said, his voice conveying a depth of feeling microphones never quite got across.

"Your mama is an Atlanta girl. She'd never have been happy living in such a small town full-time, so I made some sacrifices. Maybe I should have put my foot down more when you were coming up, but if you hope to represent those people one day, you need to know who they are and what they need."

The simple truth of what his father and grandfather were saying hit him hard. The thing Lori had said about him thinking he was too cool for this place ping-ponged around in his head. They weren't wrong. He'd been resisting settling in. Refusing to believe his time in Pine Bluff was anything more than a speed bump in his life. His chest felt tight and his head too heavy to hold up. Shame pulsed through his veins and warmed his skin.

"You're right," he said at last.

"What did you say?" Wendell prodded. "Can you repeat that?"

"Dad, don't," Dell said preemptively. When Wendell refrained from further commentary, Simon's father pressed on. "It's a good suggestion, Simon. Maybe something more like a meeting," he mused. "A few key people and some frank discussion."

"Yes. A breakfast meeting," Wendell suggested. "Perhaps around the time your express deliveries usually show up."

"Good idea," Dell chimed in effusively. "Never hurts to have a few witnesses around too."

"Hey, did I tell you I ran into Roy Biddle the other day?" Wendell asked Dell.

While his father and grandfather swapped stories about the people they'd run into on their separate campaigns, Simon tapped out a text message.

I need a favor.

He waited, inserting cursory grunts and the expected laughs at intervals. At last, the ellipses indicating a reply was being typed appeared.

Yes?

Can you convince Ben and Harry to meet with us at my office tomorrow morning around 7 or 7:30?

Lori's reply came less than a minute later.

No problem with Ben, but I'll have to check with Harry. You lawyers keep far more leisurely hours. What's up?

He smiled as he listened to his father complain about the number of Auburn fans who'd shown up at his last town hall meeting. Thumbs flying, he typed.

I need to get some perspective on some things. Tell the guys I'll provide coffee and doughnuts.

Always a good incentive. She added an emoji of someone drooling. See you in the a.m.

Simon grinned and tuned back in to the conversation in time to hear Wendell spout off about the "overopinionated knuckleheads" who called into his favorite sports talk-radio station. He couldn't help thinking things were looking up.

THERE WAS NOTHING but a box of doughnuts between him and the woman he wanted to kiss again. Well, the doughnuts, the massive oak conference table, the district attorney and Sheriff Ben Kinsella, who'd eyed him with wary suspicion when he and Lori exchanged greetings notably warmer than they'd been when they'd convened in the judge's chambers.

Though he had no chance of getting "more kissing" added to the morning's agenda, so far his new friends and neighbors had been nothing but forthcoming in giving him their take on the current state of affairs in Masters County.

"You can probably get actual data from the state agencies," Ben was saying. "I can tell you things on the ground have been shifting." He bit into his second cream-filled doughnut and sighed. "I wish I didn't love these things so much. I hate being a cliché."

Lori snickered, and Ben shot her a warning glance. Simon fought the urge to smile reflexively when she hid her own.

"Opioids," Hayes announced, jerking him back to the conversation at hand. "The stuff that went down last spring with the killings associated with Jared Baker and the Crystal Forest Corporation fronting methamphetamine production slowed some of the meth trade in the area, but nature abhors a vacuum. When the crystal wasn't readily available, people started raiding medicine cabinets."

"Rinker's Pharmacy has been broken into no less than three times in the past year," Lori informed him. "Of course, they can't get to anything valuable. Mr. Rinker has his place fortified better than a Pentagon bunker."

Simon scoffed. "You're kidding."

Without missing a beat, Lori spoke to Ben, her expression completely blank. "Simon thinks I'm the funniest woman he's ever met," she said in a voice devoid of inflection. "Whenever I say something, all he ever says is 'You're kidding.' He thinks everything I say is a joke."

"No. Not at all," Simon interjected, scooting to the edge of his seat, ready to talk his way out of whatever circular argument she wanted to invent. "I was simply using a phrase commonly used to express shock and disbelief."

"He doesn't believe a word I say," she said blandly.

"I believe your every utterance to be the gospel truth. I'm the one with limited capacity," he said dryly.

"Addiction to opiates has been on the rise throughout the country," the DA continued, shooting Ben and Lori an exasperated glance. "I'm sure you've heard on the news," he added. "Rural areas are particularly hardhit because the supply isn't steady. The ebb and flow can lead to people doing some pretty desperate things."

"Tighter restrictions on making prescription meds available for recreational use has led people to look for alternatives," Ben said, his expression grave.

Simon glanced from face to face, slotting all the pieces together. "So you're saying there is a trafficking problem in the area," he concluded.

"We're saying we have reason to believe there is," Ben clarified.

"Now we're not only looking for methamphetamine," Hayes said grimly, "but also heroin."

Simon found himself holding his breath, wondering for the millionth time how he'd stumbled into this predicament. His path had been laid out for him since he was a boy. Okay, so he'd tried to take a shortcut and ended up sidelined, but his push for power hadn't knocked him out of the game completely. Coming to Pine Bluff was supposed to be the safe bet, but he'd rolled snake eyes on his initial pass. Now he had to find a way to indicate he'd be open to helping them find whatever it was they suspected.

"I watched that show everyone's been talking about last night. *Exotic Escapades*? The one on Cineflix about the people who claim to do exotic-animal rescue," Ben said, his conversation casual yet oddly pointed. When their eyes met, the sheriff smiled wide and affably. "Have y'all watched it?"

Lori shook her head and Harry simply snorted, but Ben paid no attention to them. His gaze was locked on Simon.

"No," Simon said, approaching the conversational gambit with caution. "I've heard it's a hot mess, though. Doesn't seem your type of thing."

Ben nodded. "It's not, but Alicia Simmons was telling us all about it at dinner last night."

Simon felt all three sets of eyes boring into him. They were testing him. Or trying to tell him something without actually speaking the words out loud. So he swung at the softball Ben had lobbed at him. "Alicia Simmons? I don't think I've had the pleasure of meeting her yet."

Ben rocked back in his chair, his gaze so steady, Simon was beginning to wonder if there was a red laser dot at the center of his forehead.

"She's new to town. Coming down from Atlanta to work for Marlee in inventory control over at Timber Masters," the man said, the picture of casualness.

"No wonder the name didn't register for me." Simon did his best not to let his confusion show. He suspected Ben was steering this conversation in a particular direction, and he was willing to go along for the ride. "From Atlanta, huh?"

"Yep. I believe she was born and raised in the area," Ben continued.

The silence stretched for a few heartbeats. Simon got the feeling he was supposed to respond to this information, but he didn't have the first clue how or why. "I can't say the name is familiar to me, but Atlanta isn't Pine Bluff, is it? I swear, I can't remember the last time I ran into anyone born and bred up there."

Ben laced his fingers together and rocked forward in his chair until his hands landed on the table with a soft thunk. "I knew her some when I lived there."

Framed as it was, the admission shocked Simon. Was this Alicia Simmons the mysterious friend from the Drug Enforcement Administration? If so, what was she doing coming to work at Timber Masters? Unless—

"From your time with the DEA?" he asked bluntly, tired of the subterfuge.

The corners of Ben's mouth curved upward in a smile. "Yep."

"Wow. Well, talk about an interesting career transition." Simon shifted his gaze between Lori and Hayes. Neither of them seemed to be surprised or impressed by the morning's revelations. "I take it she's here temporarily?"

"I believe so," Ben replied so casually they could have been speculating about the weather.

Simon simply nodded. "Okay."

Another awkward silence descended on the room.

Hayes sat up too, making a show of checking the time on his wristwatch. Ben shifted in his seat. Rumpled and unshaven, the sheriff had clearly come off an overnight shift. "Well, I appreciate the sunrise breakfast, but I—"

"Wait," Simon blurted, startling his three guests.

When they looked at him, puzzlement and suspicion written all over their faces, he felt a hot flash of embarrassment. For a man trained to win oral arguments, he was having a hard time keeping his guests interested enough to hang around until the damn express delivery van got around to him.

"I, uh…" He cast about, hoping to find another topic compelling enough to keep them seated for a few more minutes. "About Coulter…"

He clammed up and stared back at their expectant faces. What the hell was he going to say? They waited, their expressions a tossed salad of wariness, expectation and caution. Thankfully, the front door burst open and Dora bustled into the foyer, speaking loudly enough to draw everyone's attention away from him.

"No. I will not sign my name," she was saying, her voice sharp and precise. "I am not Mr. Coulter's representative… Simon!"

He flinched when she bellowed his name. The other three swiveled in their seats, their attention fixed on the door to the conference room. Launching from his chair, he did his best to keep his voice light and cajoling, hoping a laugh would cover his nerves. What he was about to do could backfire in his face, but he had to do something.

"Yes, ma'am," he said, hurrying toward the reception area. "I'm in a meeting, Dora." He drew to a stop at the conference room door. "What's wrong?"

"You've got another box of snakes." She complained so loudly, Simon wanted to hug her. "I thought you told him you weren't going to accept any more packages on his behalf."

Smirking, Simon stepped into the foyer. A shipping box nearly twice the size of the last one sat at the feet of a uniformed delivery driver. The man practically threw the electronic tablet at Simon.

"I need a signature," he said with a hint of desperation.

"Of course." Simon took the stylus the man offered and scrawled his name in the signature window. "Thank you." The man took his tablet back and scuttled out the front door.

Pitching his voice loud enough for the people in the next room to hear, he said, "I did inform our client we did not wish to accept any additional packages on his behalf, but he told me this one was already in transit and reminded me he has our firm on retainer to act on his behalf."

"Doesn't make you his errand boy," Dora snapped.

"No," Simon replied, dropping his voice to a more intimate level. "It means he has a certain amount of say in the services he expects me to provide for him." He pulled his phone from his pocket and started snapping photos of the box. "You go on and settle in. I'll finish up in here."

Dora jerked her chin toward the conference room. "Who are you meeting with so early?"

"It's Harrison Hayes, Ben Kinsella and Lori Cabrera," he said, slipping the phone back into his pocket. He eyed the box, mentally psyching himself up to lift it.

"You should tell them what he's been shipping in here," she said with a huff.

"It's not illegal," he reminded her, hoisting the box.

Not only was it larger, it was also heavier than the last. Either the man had a dozen or so baby snakes in there or one fairly large one. He grimaced and held the box away from his body as he carried it into the conference room.

"Sorry," he said, placing the box on the credenza situated parallel to the conference table. The box was clearly marked. He made sure the label was facing them, plain as day. Plastering a smile on his face, he nodded to his guests. "Well, I guess we should all get on with our busy days."

Lori shot him an incredulous look. "Seriously? You took delivery of what appears to be a box of snakes and you don't expect us to ask questions about it?"

"You can ask whatever questions you need to ask," he replied, opening his hands in an invitation for them to bring them on. "Whether I can answer them is a different matter."

"Does that box have what I think it has in it?" she persisted.

"I cannot even pretend to be able to read your mind, Deputy," he said with a placid smile.

"You don't have to ask," Harry pointed out. "It says so right there it's a boa constrictor."

"Yes, I believe they have to label all shipments of live reptiles," Simon informed him.

"I guess we don't have to ask who it's for," Ben said, rising from his seat.

"I can't say, anyway," Simon said, keeping his eyes locked on the sheriff.

"Do your clients regularly ship things to you?" Hayes asked, his gaze sharpening.

"No." Simon shook his head. "Only one client, and it's only been a couple of times when he's been away and unable to accept delivery." He made a point of glancing at the box. "Makes Dora uncomfortable, though, so I'll keep the box in here until my client gets back later today."

Hayes exchanged a glance with Ben.

Lori stared at him, her face a mask of stark disbelief. "You know this guy is up to no good. I can't understand how you can continue to defend him, much less sign your name to packages delivered to him. Doesn't that put you at risk?"

Simon caught the note of worry in her admonishment,

and a sort of cool calm washed over him. It was the polar opposite of the heat he felt when he kissed her, but it pleased him all the same. Her worry meant she cared, and if she cared, he could let go of his own worries.

Pulling his phone from his pocket, he waved it at her. "I've taken photos of anything I signed for, so I can show my client the packaging was intact upon delivery and upon transfer to its rightful owner. On the advice of *my* attorney," he added with a sly smile.

"Good thinking." Hayes stood, and Simon watched as the district attorney and the sheriff both made their way around the opposite end of the conference table. They'd pass right by the box on the credenza on their way out, and he wouldn't have to say a word about it.

Lori stayed stubbornly planted, her eyes darting nervously from Simon to Ben and back again when the two men passed by her. Simon wanted to reach out to her, tell her this was all a part of his plan. Then again, it wasn't much of a plan to brag on.

"Ben, I hear you have a friend who's new to town. Boy, that can be rough around here," Simon said, letting out a low whistle.

The sheriff's step slowed, and he glanced over at Lori, surprise and bewilderment written all over his face. Simon leaped in to save her the trouble of having to answer to her boss. "Marlee mentioned it when we had lunch the other day. Then Dora reported back to Wendell the new lady Marlee hired looked like a Fed." He chuckled. "Anyway, you and I know how hard it can be when you're the new kid in town." He shot a pointed glance at the box, then met the sheriff's steady gaze again. "You should bring her by sometime to introduce her. Maybe this afternoon. I don't have anything going on until my client swings by to get his box."

THE MINUTE THEY left Simon's office, Ben unclipped his phone and started thumbing through the screens. Lori shot Hayes a look. "You get what he's doing, don't you?"

Harrison gave a short nod. "Yep."

"He could get in trouble, couldn't he? I mean, big trouble," she said worriedly. "Last night, he said something about being disbarred."

"He won't be disbarred," Harry answered distractedly. "His client might fire him, file a grievance or make things difficult for him, but he won't be disbarred. He's playing this smart."

"Not if he wants to have a career in politics," she answered.

Hayes faced her directly. "Does he? When did he tell you he did? I got the impression the two of you didn't exactly trade confidences."

"Alicia's going to come hang out with me this afternoon," Ben announced, ending the call. "I'll take her around, introduce her to some folks."

"What?" Lori asked, baffled by Ben's willingness to play along in this murky swamp of a situation.

"Like Simon said," the sheriff answered with a shrug.

Lori glowered at him, wondering if the sheriff had lost his mind. "Like Simon said," she hissed, "there's a boa constrictor in there." She pointed to the door. "Your friend was the one who told us the DEA suspected Coulter was smuggling drugs using his stupid snakes," she reminded him, her voice rising.

Ben simply nodded. "Yes, she did. I believe I'll take her by to meet Simon this afternoon. You never know who we'll run into while we're there."

Hayes patted her arm reassuringly. "I'll get with Judge Nichols on the paperwork. We'll need a warrant for the box, once it's in Coulter's custody, and another for his property, if the contents of the box give us enough justification."

She and Ben watched the DA hustling toward the municipal building. "And what am I supposed to do? Nothing?" Lori demanded.

Ben was a step ahead of her. "I need you to interview both Jasmine Jones and Kaylin Bowers, but this time, focus on the snakes. I hate to say this, but I almost think all this stuff he and his guys were pulling with the young girls in the area was sort of a smoke screen. You said yourself Dale didn't do anything with Jasmine Jones sexually."

Lori noted the flush darkening the sheriff's cheeks. "No. She said he didn't try anything."

"Exactly," Ben said, jabbing a finger at her. "What nineteen-year-old guy doesn't try to get it on with the girl he's been flirting with? Those guys knew better. If anyone is good at tightrope walking the law, it's Coulter. Hell, he could have terrorized and dumped Bella Nunes out on the highway hoping someone would pick her up. Like bait."

"Bait?"

"To distract us from what was going on." He paused for a minute. "Maybe call Bella Nunes too. She was the one who got the closest to the snakes themselves."

Lori shuddered, remembering how scared the girl had been the night she'd picked her up on the highway. "Okay, but what do I ask them?"

Ben tipped his head back. "Is this how all the snakes come in? Does he ship any out? You said something about one of the girls meeting a guy at a tent revival. Do they move the snakes in any other way? Do they let people handle them in the park?" He leaned in to look her in the eye. "I need you to lock down your feelings about Simon and Coulter, and think about the bigger picture. Can you do that?"

"Of course I can," she snapped, insulted.

Ben didn't back off. "Good, because I can tell you I wasn't too great about keeping my feelings for Marlee under wraps when her world was blowing up."

Lori could feel Ben's steady gaze boring into her cheekbone. "Okay. Yeah. I get you," she said at last.

"There's no shame in caring about people, Lori, but right now we have an open window and a clear shot," he said gruffly. "We need every scrap of information those girls might have, and you are the best person for extracting it. I need you to look past the smoke screen. We need you sharpshooter focused, because moving or not, the target is the same."

She nodded once. "Right. I'm on it."

Ben clapped her on the shoulder and prodded her toward the office. "Come on."

Lori shook her head. "No. I'm going to have to get parental permission to speak to Kaylin and Jas. I'm going to walk over to the Joneses' right now. They told me they'd be taking a day or two to work things through."

"Okay, good." He hooked his sheriff's department ball cap onto his head and raised a hand in farewell. "Call me with any info. I'll get Alicia in and we'll start going over how we want to approach this."

Lori took about three steps in the opposite direction, then cast a concerned glance at the renovated home where Wendell had long ago established the Wingate Law Firm and Simon fought to keep it alive. She didn't have time to go back in to see him. It peeved her to think she'd been taken in by Samuel Coulter's smoke and mirrors, but she didn't have time for ego indulgence. Simon had given them this opportunity, and she was determined to make the most of it.

but she didn't have time. Are Underwood Simon had given them this opportunity and she was determined to use this moment to protect—

Chapter Fifteen

Simon tried not to fidget under Special Agent Alicia Simmons's unflinching stare, but he was fighting a losing battle. Tall and solid, with a no-nonsense manner, the woman was intimidating.

"I am sure you are aware most of the information Deputy Cabrera collected from the young women who'd been involved with the Reptile Rendezvous or its employees is hearsay and inadmissible, but it does paint a slightly clearer picture. From what we can gather, Coulter uses the reptiles he claims to nurture as little more than snakeskin suitcases."

Simon felt his stomach roll over. "Allegedly," he said quietly.

Special Agent Simmons obligingly added the word. "I'm sorry. Coulter *allegedly* uses his business as a front for moving product coming in from Mexico and Colombia. We believe the primary means of entry to be via cruise ship, but it's not unusual to fly it in." She shared a wan smile with Ben. "Illegal substances coming into the country are usually easier to catch. Distribution, well, that's where we play Whac-A-Mole."

"The DEA believes Samuel Coulter is a much bigger player than his operation here in Georgia would let on," Ben informed him. "He has a number of ways to move product from South Florida. He's sort of a high-level middleman, connecting the larger organizations who import it with existing distribution networks."

Alicia Simmons picked the thread up again. "He has established ties to Jacksonville, Florida, and Atlanta, but we believe he has become the leading supplier feeding the back roads leading up through the Appalachians."

"Doesn't seem there'd be much money in moving it through the mountains," Simon commented with a frown.

"More people get a cut in the cities," Alicia explained with a shrug. "Eastern Tennessee, Kentucky, West Virginia, Ohio… The rural communities in these states have been ravaged by opiate addiction." She leveled a glare at him. "Your client has finally made himself the kingpin he's always wanted to be."

Simon opened his mouth, then closed it again when he felt Ben's hand land heavy on his shoulder.

"You don't have to do a thing, Simon. Let this happen. The plan is in place. The box has been x-rayed, and we know the specimen in it is more than large enough for him to use for transport. When Coulter comes to collect his parcel, the game warden and I will serve him with the warrant and ask him to cut the tape and open the box. If he refuses, we'll ask you to open it as his representative."

A shudder ran through him and Ben must have felt it.

"You only have to cut the tape. Alicia and representatives from the state and US fish and wildlife departments will be on hand. Lori got some good information on the number and kind of snakes coming in and out of there from Kaylin Bowers and Bella Nunes. Enough to persuade Judge Nichols to issue a warrant. Lori and her team are in position to serve the warrant the moment we have Coulter."

Simon hated the thought of Lori charging in armed

with nothing more than a piece of paper and whatever backup Alicia Simmons could scare up on short notice. He couldn't help feeling it would take an army to bring down a man like Samuel Coulter.

Simon's phone lit up and Samuel Coulter's name appeared on the display. "Here he is."

Ben nodded to it. "Go ahead."

Simon answered the call, but put his client on speaker so they could all hear. "Hello?"

"Hey, Simon. Got my package?" Coulter asked, his tone jovial.

Irritated, Simon laid it on thick, hoping to come across as conciliatory and eager to please after the previous day's confrontation. "Your box arrived. Miss Dora took one look at the label and made me put it up in the conference room for safekeeping." He chuckled, hoping to establish camaraderie. "You keep shippin' those things here and I'm gonna have to give her a raise. I can barely afford her now," he complained, pouring on the good-old-boy charm he'd inherited from his father and grandfather.

Coulter chuckled. "Do what you have to do. I honestly don't understand why people get so squeamish around serpents. They are the most amazing creatures."

Simon looked up at Ben and Alicia. "To each his or her own."

"Yes, well, I am less than thirty minutes out. I apologize if I keep you at the office a few minutes after five."

"No problem," Simon said, his fake bonhomie sounding hollow to his own ears. "I can certainly hang around awhile."

"I'll be there shortly," Coulter replied.

Simon exhaled when the beeps indicating the end of the call bounced off his office walls. He double-checked the screen. "Well, okay." He checked his watch and was relieved to see it was well past four o'clock. "Okay, so we have an ETA."

Ben called Lori's cell phone directly to relay the information. When he disconnected, Simon frowned at him. "Is she not wearing a radio?"

Ben frowned. "What? Yeah. Of course she is."

"Why did you call her cell?" Simon asked, nodding to the phone Ben gripped in his hand.

"Because people love to listen in on police band radios." Ben shot him a glance. "You'd think they'd teach that in ambulance-chaser school."

Simon rolled his eyes. "I must have been sick that day."

Ben smiled and dropped down into one of the conference room chairs, stretching his bulky frame to fill the space, seemingly relaxed. Simon envied the man's ability to shrug off the stress of this situation. Right now, he felt his skin fit two sizes too small.

"So, what's going on with you two?" Ben asked.

His tone was so offhand Simon knew the question was anything but casual. He didn't have any answers himself. How was he supposed to come up with some for Ben?

"Who two?" he parried.

"You and my deputy," Ben said pointedly.

"I've only met Mike the one time, but he seemed decent enough," Simon replied evenly, unwilling to give himself or Lori away so easily.

"Lori."

The sheriff spoke her name with such gravity, Simon couldn't bring himself to foist the man off with flippancy. "I don't know," he answered honestly.

"You think something is going on," Ben concluded.

Simon gave a jerky nod. "Something is going on."

Silence hung heavy between them, but Simon refused to say anything more on the matter.

"She's had a rough time of it," Ben said at last.

"I am aware," Simon replied quietly.

"And she's not the type to…"

The other man paused, and Simon wondered which of the many facets of his possible relationship with Lori he would choose to object to first.

"She's rooted here," Ben concluded.

"I get it."

"Do you?" The sheriff looked straight at him.

Simon schooled his expression into something neutral. "Yes."

"Okay," Ben answered at last.

Simon snorted, shocked by the laconic response. "'Okay'? All you have to say is 'okay'?"

Ben shrugged. "You're both adults, and I'm not her daddy. I trust Lori to make good decisions. If she decides on you, then she must have thought it through."

When five o'clock came, Dora stood outside the conference room door with her purse caught in the crook of her arm. She looked from Simon to Ben and back again. The tiny lines on her forehead bunched together into one deep crease of worry. "Do you want me to stay?"

Simon shook his head. "It would be better if you didn't. We need to make everything seem normal when Coulter shows up."

"You take care of yourself," she ordered, wagging a finger at Simon. "Your grandfather will skin me alive if I let anything happen to you on my watch."

Simon laughed, warmed by the thought of his efficient but acerbic assistant standing up to Coulter on his behalf. "We're okay, Dora. Nothing's going to happen. They'll serve the warrant, he'll open the box and we'll deal with whatever we have to deal with. I'll call you when I leave."

"Please do," she ordered. Then, darting a glance at Ben, she added, "You make sure he follows through."

"Yes, ma'am," they answered in unison.

Once Dora left, Ben got up to go check on Alicia, Hayes and the agents holed up in Simon's office. Simon tipped his head back and closed his eyes, breathing deeply to calm his agitation. The urge to text Lori and remind her to be careful roiled inside of him, but the notion was ridiculous. Of the two of them, she was far more capable of taking care of herself. He had one guy to face. She would be facing a group of hostile employees scrambling for what to do when presented with a search warrant.

The sound of the outer door opening jolted him from his thoughts. He rose from the conference room chair and stepped into the foyer to greet his client. Coulter looked cool and tousled. He wore a pair of dark pants cut loose and flowing. His shirt was unbuttoned. Simon couldn't help thinking if the man were not handsome, the look would be retro ridiculous.

"Good afternoon," he said, forcing a note of welcome into his voice. "How was the drive down from Atlanta?"

"Drive?" Coulter accepted Simon's hand and gave it a perfunctory shake, offering his slippery smile. "I never said I drove. A friend of mine has a helicopter. I hitched a ride with him."

"Flying beats driving any day." Simon tried for a chuckle, but almost choked on it.

Ben stepped out of Simon's office, followed closely by an officer from the Georgia Department of Natural Resources Law Enforcement Division. They crossed in front of Dora's desk, and Coulter stiffened. He darted a glance at Simon, but otherwise kept his cool. "Sheriff Kinsella, what brings you here?"

Gesturing to the other man, he said, "This is Terrence Scroggins. He's an officer with the Department of Natural Resources. They received information of a parcel being delivered to this address containing a live animal. Officer Scroggins needs to inspect the parcel."

Coulter's eyes narrowed and sharpened. "How did the Department of Natural Resources hear about this particular delivery?"

"We monitor all shipments under the Lacey Act," Officer Scroggins provided helpfully. "We do random inspections when we see an increase in activity."

Coulter did not look amused. "Two shipments is considered an increase in activity? I hope you're not monitoring my Amazon account. You'd be completely overwhelmed."

Scroggins chuckled at the joke. "No, we're more than happy to leave your shopping to you. We're only concerned about parcels containing creatures."

The man smiled and rested his hands on his hips above his utility belt. Simon couldn't help but notice the wildlife officer seemed to carry much the same equipment Ben and Lori did on theirs. He felt a wave of relief at being on the side of the two men in the room who were armed.

"The tracking is done by recipient, not by address," Officer Scroggins informed him. "We track the number of parcels delivered to your own address, Mr. Coulter. I assure you it is simply a matter of numbers."

Simon gestured to the conference room. "Well, shall we?" He waved an arm toward the door. "I'm not sure about the rest of y'all, but I want to get on with my evening. I'm assuming if this is a matter of routine, it shouldn't take long."

They moved into the conference room, and Officer Scroggins produced an impressive array of tools as he inspected the markings on the box carefully. "Of course, I'll need to measure the specimen to make sure it's within proper regulations." He shot them an open, unassuming smile. "You wouldn't believe the things people try to get away with shipping because they think nobody's paying attention."

Simon watched the man place a pair of gloves, some calipers and a tape measure on the credenza beside the box. "Mr. Coulter, if you'd please open your parcel, I'll inspect the specimen and we'll all be on our way."

Coulter hung back, his gaze traveling from the game warden to the sheriff, then to Simon. "What happens if I refuse?"

"Sir, I assure you it's purely routine," Scroggins interjected.

"I'm speaking to my lawyer," Coulter snapped.

Moving slowly, the game warden stepped to the conference table, pulled his cell phone from his belt and held it up for Coulter to see. "A couple of measurements, a few photos, and we should be all good."

Simon leaned in to talk to his client in a low voice. "Go ahead and open it. Get this over with."

"In all my years of collecting snakes, I've never had an inspection take place after delivery," Coulter said warily. "You'll forgive me if I'm dubious, but my dealings with the Masters County Sheriff's Department so far have not been what I would consider cordial."

Ben pulled an envelope from his back pocket and handed it to Simon. "I will concede your client has a point. You'll find the search warrant in there."

Coulter snorted and cast a derisive look at the envelope. "A search warrant seems extreme for a routine inspection, doesn't it, Sheriff?"

Ben shrugged. "You said it—our relationship hasn't

been particularly smooth up to this point. Officer Scroggins asked me if we would have any difficulty gaining your cooperation, and I advised him I had concerns."

Coulter crossed his arms over his chest. "I'm not opening it."

Ben didn't take his eyes off the man. "Simon, you might want to advise your client to comply."

"Yes," Simon said slowly. "It would be in your best interest to go along with what they're asking." He made a show of opening the envelope and withdrawing the search warrant. He could feel Coulter's gaze creeping over him. He scanned the page, pretending to check every dot on the *i*'s and crossbar on the *t*'s. "This seems to be in order."

There was a protracted silence. Then Coulter gestured to the box. "I didn't sign for this parcel."

The simple statement made Simon's blood boil. "No, of course you didn't."

"I'm not opening anything I did not sign for." Coulter placed a hand squarely in the center of Simon's back and propelled him forward. Simon stared down at the box. The label affixed to the box said it all. Boa Constrictor. Adult Female.

"Mr. Wingate signed for this particular parcel. It was delivered to his address and he took receipt of it."

"Again, we tracked the intended recipient," Officer Scroggins said, keeping his tone genial. "It's addressed to you in care of Mr. Wingate."

"Mr. Wingate is my attorney," Coulter snapped.

Harrison Hayes chose that moment to make his appearance. "Afternoon, Mr. Coulter."

Simon glanced back to see Samuel Coulter sneer at the district attorney. A belligerent set to his jaw, Coulter shoved his hands into the pockets of his pleated pants and fixed them with a stubborn glare.

"Well, now it's a party," he drawled.

"I have an invitation." Harry held up a folded piece of paper. "This is an affidavit signed and sworn before Judge Nichols saying Simon Wingate accepted this package on your behalf as you requested."

He moved to thrust the piece of paper at Coulter, but rather than taking it, the man pulled his hands from his pants pockets and grabbed Simon's left arm in a viselike grip. "You set me up?"

In a flash, Coulter had Simon's wrist twisted up behind his back. Simon bit back a yelp of pain as the man added a little extra torque to his hold on him. "What? They just want you to open the box."

"I'll have your license for this," Coulter hissed.

Simon's brain flashed to Lori. She was about to run onto Samuel Coulter's property with a piece of paper, a firearm and her conviction that she'd been right about Coulter all along. He had to make sure this man was neutralized so she could complete her mission.

Simon saw Ben step closer. "Seriously, Coulter, assaulting your attorney isn't going to help the situation."

Coulter urged Simon to take another step toward the box. "I can buy and sell you all six times over. By the time I'm done with you, you won't be able to get a job sweeping floors in any police department, Sheriff." He drew a ragged breath. "And you..." He jerked on Simon's arm again. "You're finished before you even begin. Any thoughts you had of a career beyond this Podunk town are over. I'll have your law license. I'm gonna—"

"Take the damn box," Simon ordered. "Take it and get out of here. We're done."

Coulter let out a hard bark of laughter. "How stupid do you think I am? My fingerprints aren't on the box, but yours are. I bet you have pictures of it too. I can't help it if people put my name on a mailing label. This isn't my address. I'm not the one who's into this up to his neck."

A shot rang out and they all jumped.

Coulter's grip loosened, and seeing his opening, Simon broke his client's hold on him, grasped the other man's wrist and twisted until he heard a crack. The sound both sickened and energized him. Coulter cried out and dropped to one knee, and the sheriff moved in.

"Hold it right there, Coulter." Simon looked up to find Ben standing over them, his service weapon drawn and trained on Coulter.

"You wanna talk assault," Coulter ground out from between clenched teeth. "I'm pressing charges. I think he broke my wrist."

"We'll see who's pressing charges against who after we open this box," Ben said, signaling for the officer from the state department of natural resources to step forward. "Officer Scroggins, if you wouldn't mind?" he said, tilting his head toward the box.

Officer Scroggins stepped around Coulter, his service weapon trained on the man. "I do believe this is the first opportunity I've had to fire my weapon in almost twenty-two years of service. Well, fire it around humans, I mean," he amended. "Had to put down some animals," he explained as he holstered his sidearm. "Sorry I took a chunk out of your side table here."

Dazed, Simon looked over to see a fresh chunk of wood splintered out of the credenza just beneath where the box sat.

Simon shook his head to clear it. "Yeah, uh, no worries." He pushed himself up onto all fours, then rose shakily, gripping the side of the conference table to get his balance. Then he flopped into the nearest chair, feeling almost boneless in the wake of the adrenaline rush.

When his gaze met the concerned gaze of the DA, he attempted a smile. He was fairly sure it fell short. "I guess all those tae kwon do classes my parents popped for finally paid off."

Hayes's mouth thinned into a line. He watched Coulter grasping his wrist and gritting his teeth. The man gave up on trying to stand, pain and fury etched into every line on his face. No one made any attempt to help the man, and he finally gave up, twisting around to sit on the floor, grumbling threats and cradling his injured hand. "They certainly did."

Special Agent Simmons and a gentleman from the US Department of the Interior skidded to a halt in the foyer. They peered around Hayes, trying to get a handle on the scene.

"What the hell is going on here?" Simmons demanded.

Feeling light-headed, Simon dropped into the nearest chair and blew out a huff of breath. "He didn't want to open the box." He shifted his gaze to the man on the floor. The second their eyes met, he said, "I resign. In light of this…situation, I can no longer be your attorney."

"I'll ruin you," Coulter ground out between clenched teeth.

Simon remembered the confidence his father and grandfather had in his ability to decide what was best for him. And for them all. "Go ahead. Do whatever you think you can do."

"Mr. Coulter refused to open the parcel. Officer Scroggins has agreed to do so for us," Ben informed the newcomers.

Officer Scroggins unfolded a multipurpose tool and slit the tape securing the package with brisk efficiency. Simon held his breath as the man lifted the lid and removed foam insulation. A moment later, he reached in and pulled out a loosely coiled snake Simon figured might stretch as long as the conference table. Everyone but Coulter jumped back when he placed the snake on the table.

"Don't worry—she's dead," Scroggins pronounced flatly.

"She might be hibernating," the man from the US Department of the Interior offered.

Officer Scroggins turned a piercing gaze toward Coulter. "But she isn't hibernating, is she, Mr. Coulter."

"I have no idea what's wrong with that snake. I ordered it from a catalog—"

"You ordered it from your friend Ramon Calderon, in Miami," Alicia interjected.

"And your friend Ramon didn't do a very good job with packing her," Scroggins said grimly.

Simon watched in dazed horror as the wildlife officer turned the limp snake over to show a pattern of irregular lumps and bumps pressing against the scaly skin, and a long, sloppily sewed incision mark. Before Simon could get a closer look, Scroggins used the same tool to reopen the incision, and a handful of tied-off condoms filled with powder spilled out onto the table.

Alicia Simmons didn't miss a beat. "Samuel Coulter, I'm Special Agent Alicia Simmons of the Drug Enforcement Administration. You are under arrest…"

Her words faded in and out. Simon couldn't help staring at the gaping wound in the snake. He'd never been one to embrace God's more slippery creatures, but his stomach twisted at the sight of the poor creature split open. Who came up with this madness? What kind of sociopath—

"Mr. Wingate?" the DEA agent called out to him.

"Huh?" Simon jerked his gaze from the snake and forced himself to refocus. "I'm sorry?"

"You no longer represent Mr. Coulter—is that correct?"

"That's correct," he and Coulter replied, nearly in unison. Finally, they agreed on one thing.

"I called for an ambulance," the officer from the US Department of the Interior announced, shoving his phone back into his pocket. "Two of your guys are on their way over to escort Mr. Coulter to the regional medical center for an X-ray."

Ben shoved his weapon back into its holster, then produced a zip tie. "Cuffs might be hard on a crunchy wrist." He offered the long strip of heavy-duty plastic to Alicia. "He doesn't strike me as the type to fight through the pain, but if you want me to secure his good hand to something until the ambulance arrives, I'm sure Simon won't mind."

Alicia nodded. "Good. Thank you." Turning back to Coulter, she smiled as Ben pulled Coulter's good hand from his lap and lashed it to the arm of one of the massive leather boardroom chairs. "Mr. Coulter, at this moment federal agents are serving a warrant to search your property located on Highway 19. We expect to add additional charges pending the search and seizure there."

At the mention of Coulter's compound, Simon shot from his chair and stepped over Coulter's outstretched arm to get to the door. Harrison caught his arm. "Where do you think you're going?"

"Lori—" He swung around and stared imploringly at Ben. "I have to get out there."

"Listen, I know. I'm worried too, but there's an operation underway. We can't go running into the middle of it all. She has a job to do, and she won't thank you for getting in the way."

"I'm not going to get in the way, but I have to be there."

Ben looked over at Alicia, and the agent gave him a shrug and a small smile. "Go on. I'm sure I can keep this slippery guy in my sights until our transport arrives. I'll meet you out there."

THE SHERIFF'S SUV flew down Highway 19 headed away from Pine Bluff and toward Lori. Toward whatever trouble she was facing at Samuel Coulter's godforsaken Reptile Rendezvous. Simon clung to the handle above the door, not because he wanted Ben to slow down, but more because he needed to feel tethered to something.

They were more than halfway there when the sheriff spoke up. "I'm not gonna be all paternal and ask what your intentions are."

When he paused to draw breath, Simon jumped in. "Good."

"Her father is gone," Ben said, holding up a finger to forestall any of Simon's protests. "So I have to ask…am I gonna have to kick your ass for hurting her?"

"Not if I can help it," Simon said gruffly.

It was the truth. He would do anything he could to keep from hurting her. He couldn't think about his own motivations now. All he could focus on was the possibility of someone hurting her while they had a heart-to-heart in the car.

"Can you go any faster?"

Ben gave a grim shake of his head. "I'm already doing thirty over."

Simon sighed. He knew Ben was right to be careful. There wasn't a lot of traffic on the highway, but it was late afternoon, and people who lived in the outlying areas of the county were heading home from work. Each and every car they'd come upon had yielded to the blue lights and sirens, but they could encounter somebody who didn't see or hear them coming.

"We're going to get there, and she's going to be fine," Ben assured him.

"We haven't even talked about what this thing is," Simon said quietly.

Ben leaned in. "What thing?"

"Lori and me. This *thing* between us." He murmured the last part, unable to work the words past the lump rising in his throat. Propping his elbow on the door, he ran his forefinger over his lip, wiping away the fine sheen of perspiration. "I mean, I can't even name it, and she might not—"

"She does," Ben stated flatly. When Simon glanced over at him, the sheriff shrugged. "When you work closely with someone, you get a gut feeling when something's going on with them. She's still grieving, though. Both for her family and for Jeff Masters. It's made her question a lot of her choices. No doubt she's questioning her feelings for you. You'll just have to be patient and let her find her way back to herself. Can you do that?"

"Yes. Yes, I can do that." Ben's plainspoken words were a balm. Simon leaned forward in the seat, the nylon restraint tightening against his chest. "I just… She was right all along. About Coulter. About me. If something happens to her because of Coulter—"

"If something happens to her, it would be because she's doing her job. A job she's damn good at, I might add." The two men shared a glance, and Ben refocused on the road. "She's essentially been a cop since she was nineteen years old. Her job is her life, which is what makes her so good at it."

Ben let up on the accelerator and they cruised up a rise in the road. They crested the hill. Below, flashes of blue light cut through the smoke filling the late-afternoon sky.

"She's going in after the girls, right?"

Ben nodded. "The Feds will handle the search and seizure on any drugs found on the premises. Lori has strict instructions to get in there, check the barracks at the back of the lot to see if there are any young women being held in there and get them out without interfering with the rest of the operation."

"I hate that she's going in there alone," Simon muttered.

Ben ran a hand over his forehead, then spoke gruffly. "I do too. She was going to try to round up Deputy Wasson from Prescott County to see if he'd back her up."

Simon tightened his grip on the handle. "Has anyone heard from her?"

The sheriff shrugged. "She's not going to stop and make a phone call in the middle of an operation."

"What about the radio?" Simon asked, gesturing to the unit mounted into the dash.

"I explained about the police band thing earlier."

"Yeah, but the thing's in motion now. Shouldn't y'all be in communication?"

Simon saw the corner of the sheriff's mouth tighten. It was a tell. Ben was worried too. They should've heard something by now.

The sheriff let up on the gas. "Why are you slowing down?"

"Red lights." He pointed to the rearview mirror, and Simon twisted in his seat. Sure enough, two trucks from the volunteer fire department zoomed past.

"We're never going to get there," Simon complained.

Ben snorted and peeled away from the shoulder with

a spray of gravel. "Keep your pants on. I'm not going to let you go in there after her," he pointed out.

"But—"

"No buts. You are a civilian, Counselor. The only reason I brought you on this ride-along is because you'd probably try to hitch a skateboard to my back bumper if I didn't. I need you to stay in the car."

Simon was about to protest, but a sudden crackle of static burst from the radio. He stared at the dashboard, willing it to come to life again.

Ben applied the brakes once more, and this time he hooked a sharp right into the field used as a parking lot. Police and other emergency services vehicles sat parked in a haphazard fashion. Ben pressed the lock button and held it. With his other hand, he cut the engine. "Am I gonna have to put you in the back seat to keep you safe?"

Simon simply stared back at him. "No. I know my place here."

Ben nodded and reached for the door handle. "Sit tight. I'll get you an update as soon as I can."

Simon waited until Ben disappeared into a small knot of people gathered at the side of a black van. The moment the sight line was broken, he opened the car door and slipped out. The flattened grass muffled his footsteps as he headed away from Ben and the other law enforcement types. He had one mission in mind—get to Lori and help however he could.

Chapter Sixteen

Lori signaled to Deputy Steve Wasson of Prescott County to follow her. To his credit, the older man did so without hesitation. When she filled Steve in on the plan to get in and get whatever girls Coulter might have stashed on the property out, the Prescott County deputy had been all for it. The discovery of Kaylin Bowers on Samuel Coulter's property had helped them form a bond over a common enemy.

They'd entered the woods far away from the commotion the federal agents made at the front entrance. Instead, they hopped the fence that ran along the side of the property. Staying low, she wound her way through the trees and scrubby underbrush, following the main footpath but staying off it in case she came across any resistance. Her mission was technically to secure and collect any of Coulter's employees, but she wanted to get to the building undetected first. In case there were people trapped there who might need help.

Bella Nunes had told her she'd stayed in a sort of dormitory at the far end of the grounds, and that other young women were staying there too. Kaylin Bowers's parents claimed their daughter had been tight-lipped and belligerent since her return home, but she had agreed to talk to Lori. Briefly. Kaylin confirmed the existence of such a building and mentioned there were a few other girls staying there at the time she'd been there. She claimed they locked the door from the outside at night to prevent people from wandering the park and to keep the female members of the staff "safe."

Making her way through the wooded area, Lori carefully moved aside branches and pointed out fallen tree trunks to Wasson. Though she had her service weapon holstered at her hip, Lori was more comforted by the rifle in her hand. These woods were her home. This was her backyard.

The path widened beside her, and she slowed her steps. The canopy of leaves and needles trapped the worst of the smoke from the nearby fires. She moved in a crouch. The trunks of the young pines were inadequate cover, but since she was dressed in her tactical gear, someone would have to be looking hard to find her.

When they'd studied the aerial shots of Coulter's property, Lori had been the one to point out the large Quonset hut–style building at the rear of the property. She had to give Special Agent Simmons credit. She didn't bat an eye when Lori told her she wanted to run straight into the remote area of the compound. Nor did the special agent try to stand in her way.

Less than a quarter mile up the fire road, the roof of the building came into sight. They slowed, creeping toward the low barracks on silent feet. About fifty yards out, still hidden in the cover of the tree line, Lori held up a hand signaling Wasson to stop.

Cupping her hands around her mouth, she shouted, "Masters County Sheriff's Department. Is anyone in there?"

When there was no reply, she faced the other deputy. "I'm gonna need you to circle around to the end and cover the other door, but let me try to get them out on this end. They may respond better to a female voice." Wasson simply nodded. "We need to get into the building without fuss or firepower. Get me?"

"I'm with you."

"If my intel is right, there are likely teenage girls in there. I figure they are unarmed and definitely freaking out. We need to proceed with extreme caution."

"Got you," Wasson replied.

"Radio check," she whispered into her mic. When she heard his clipped response of "Check," they split up.

Moving in a wide circle, Lori approached the door on the far end from behind the hinges. If someone came bursting out, she could use the door as cover. She settled into position against the building's wall. Inspecting the door on their side, she spotted the padlock holding a large metal hasp closed.

"Crud," she muttered. Then she whispered into her mic. "Far door padlocked."

The reply from Wasson came through the earpiece. "Same." There was a crackle of static. Then he asked, "Shoot it off?"

She scoffed, then keyed the mic. "Negative. That only works in movies." She eyed the padlock, then continued. "Stay put. I'm going to bust it off. No shooting unless someone shoots at us first."

She sprang forward and used the butt end of her rifle to pound the hasp three times in rapid succession. A cacophony of high-pitched screams came from inside the building, and Lori dropped to the ground, waiting to see if anyone inside attempted to fire on her.

From her low vantage point, she could see the screws securing the hasp to the ancient building were giving way, but the lock held.

Then a trembling voice pleaded, "Help us."

Lori sprang to her feet and slammed the stock down on the rusted metal again. On her second blow, one side popped loose. "Hang on," she called to them.

Using her bare hands, she peeled the whole thing back enough to open the door, then stepped aside for cover. "Sheriff's department," she shouted again. "We have the building surrounded. Drop your weapons!"

"We don't have any weapons," a young woman cried. "I swear!"

Lori took a deep breath and swung the door open wide, praying the occupants were telling the truth. Lori squatted low and tipped her head around the edge of the door to sneak a peek.

Three girls who appeared to be in their midteens huddled together on one of the narrow beds at the center of the room, their arms wrapped tightly around one another. Exhaling heavily, Lori let the relief wash over her.

"Come out now. Keep your hands high where we can see them." When the girls failed to move, she barked, "Now!"

They untangled themselves in a flurry of long, coltish limbs. Sobbing and staggering, the girls stumbled toward the door, their hands held high.

"Coming out on my end," she said into the radio.

"Ten-four," came Wasson's reply.

Her breathing returned to something approximating normal when Wasson came trotting around the side of the building, weapon raised and ready.

"They're unarmed," Lori called to him.

"We should secure them," he said, his voice pitched low. "As a precaution. At least until they've cleared all the personnel from the grounds."

The impulse to argue was strong, but the man was

right. Until they had these girls processed, there was no way to know if and how they were involved in Coulter's operations. Reluctantly, she and Wasson started to zip-tie the sobbing girls' wrists to one another, all the while trying to reassure them that they were just being careful.

"What the hell are you doing?"

The breathless demand shot up Lori's spine. Wasson pivoted in the blink of an eye, his sidearm unholstered and aimed directly at Simon Wingate.

Lori exhaled in a whoosh, then placed a calming hand on the deputy's arm. "Ease up. He's one of the good guys."

At least, she thought he was.

He stood there with his arms raised in surrender. She saw his suit jacket was torn at the shoulder, his matching pin-striped pants were covered in dust and grime, and his polished shoes were caked with mud and leaves.

"I'm going to turn that question back on you, Counselor. What do you think you're doing here?"

"Helping you," he replied, still a little out of breath but unapologetic. "I thought you came up here alone."

Lori shook her head, then gestured to the man beside her. "Deputy Steve Wasson, Prescott County, meet Samuel Coulter's attorney, Simon Wingate."

"Former attorney," Simon corrected quickly. "Samuel Coulter's former attorney."

"They have him in custody?" They wouldn't have gotten the go-ahead on the compound if they didn't, so it was more a statement than a question, but Lori craved the eyewitness confirmation. Particularly from this particular witness.

"Yes. He's in custody." Simon flashed her a shaky but reassuring smile. "But why are you cuffing these young ladies? They haven't done anything wrong, have they?"

"That's yet to be determined," Deputy Wasson replied. "But we don't believe so," he added, raising his voice to be heard over the fresh round of sobs rising around him.

"We're just securing them until we can be sure everything has gone off as expected." She craned her neck and looked up at the fog of smoke trapped in the treetops. "What's on fire?"

Simon shrugged. "From what I can gather, random structures."

"Literally a smoke screen," Lori murmured. Glancing over her shoulder at the three girls strapped hand to hand, she gave them as reassuring a smile as she could muster. "Deputy Wasson is going to take you down to base via the fire lane," she told them. "There will be officers there to take your statements." She picked up the rifle she'd set against the building. "Mr. Wingate will go with you. He's an attorney, and no doubt looking for some new clients."

"Hey," Simon objected.

She heard the injury in his tone and softened a little. "A joke," she said, raising a hand.

"Where are you going?" he asked as she shooed them away.

"I'm going back through the woods. I want to make sure none of Coulter's guys go slithering off under cover of smoke."

"But—"

Ignoring the fleeting impulse to hurl herself at him and thank him for caring enough to come after her, she lifted her rifle into ready position, then jerked her chin toward Wasson. "But nothing. Go with him."

"Lori, I—"

"Simon, I appreciate your concern, but this is what I am trained for. This is what I do. And I can't do what I need to do and cover you too. Go. We'll talk when I get down there."

To her relief, he clamped his mouth shut, took the arm of the girl closest to him, and they started walking from the far end of the Quonset hut to the dirt road beyond the tree line. Lori watched until they were out of sight, then pulled her own disappearing act.

The woods were eerily quiet. There was no birdsong or chirruping of insects. No doubt the smoke from the fires and commotion down below had sent all the wildlife to ground. Which meant the only creatures stirring in these woods would be up to no good.

The trail she'd been following spilled into a single-lane gravel road. She crept closer, crouching low and scanning the length of the road until she spotted a pre-fabricated building near where the road intersected with the fire lane.

Lori frowned, trying to recall whether she'd seen the road on the aerial photographs the DEA had provided. Probably not. A car was backed up to the door. The late-afternoon sun blazed off the windshield. Lifting her rifle, she peered through the scope for a better look. It was a dull gray Toyota, more primer than paint, with a large wing attached to its open trunk. This was Rick Dale's car. Seeing the ridiculous spoiler attached to the compact car made her think of Simon.

"Wasson, hold up," she whispered into the mic. "Take cover for a minute."

A second later, the reply came. "Ten-four."

Raising the rifle, she used the scope to scan the area. The car was backed in close to the building. The rear bumper nearly touched the door. A light shone from the inside, slicing out into the smoky haze settling over the area. She hunched down and watched. A thin, tattooed man in a black concert T-shirt carried two duffel bags from the building and deposited them into the open trunk.

Opening her mic, she called for the special agent heading up the ground operations. "Ruggalo?" she whispered into her mic.

Special Agent Mark Ruggalo, a man nicknamed Hulk and who could have been used for a recruiting poster, answered. "I read you."

"Do you have eyes on Rick Dale?"

A second later, his gruff "Negative" came through her earpiece.

"I do."

"What's your twenty?"

"There's a metal building on the fire lane that runs the east side of the property. Closer to the rear than front."

"Stick a pin in him if he moves. We're coming."

Lori watched as the guy disappeared back into the building. Then she lowered the muzzle of her rifle. She keyed the switch on her radio again. "Wasson, hold your cover. I'm going to take out his tires, try to slow him down."

Without waiting for any response, she aimed her rifle at the left front tire and put a bullet clean through the sidewall. If Dale heard the crack of her rifle, it didn't deter him from his mission. He appeared again, seemingly oblivious to the deflating tire. She watched him load two more bags into the trunk, then hustle back into the building. Shifting her position, she took aim at the other front tire and put a bullet-sized hole in it too.

Opening her mic, she said, "Flat front tires should hobble him, but you'll want backup, Ruggalo. He's loading something out of here, and I'm betting it's what you're hunting."

The monitor in her ear hissed and crackled. "Ten-four. Almost there," Ruggalo replied.

Lori held her breath, watching Dale's every move and hoping she didn't have to take a shot at him, as well. She'd do it if she had to, but she much preferred not to.

A rustle in the leaves behind her alerted her to someone's approach. Rolling to her side, she drew her sidearm in case there was a close-range confrontation. She'd barely had a chance to aim when Simon Wingate dropped onto the leafy mulch beside her.

"What are you doing? I almost shot you," she hissed.

"Wasson and the girls are hunkered down right over there." He pointed slightly up the slope and to the east. "I saw the sun glint off your scope when you were calling things in."

"Simon, this isn't a game of backyard cops and robbers. I'm not toting a water gun here," she said, exasperated.

He raised both brows, affronted. "I'm aware of that." He scooted his elbows under his chest and lifted his head. "I thought you would like to know that Cassidy—that's one of the girls you rescued—says that's where they keep the 'superexpensive and rare' snakes," he said, squinching to approximate the use of air quotes. "She says only Coulter and his main man have keys."

"Looks like Dale is his main man," she said. Sighing, she set her handgun down in the space between her and Simon and took up her rifle again. Sighting on the door, she growled. "Keep your head down."

She heard a twig crack somewhere off to her left, swung the gun around and blew out a breath of relief when she spotted Ruggalo and his team approaching. Opening her mic, she whispered, "I see you. I'm at two o'clock. Deputy Wasson and the girls from the Quonset hut are somewhere between your three and four. He's loading up, but I don't know how much more that tiny trunk can hold."

Ahead of her, Ruggalo's team moved into position, using hand signals to fan out and surround the building. "What have we got?"

Lori raised her scope and scanned the area and the building. The door stood ajar, but Dale had not reappeared with any more bags. "So far, I've witnessed him placing four large black duffel bags into the trunk of the car. I have no idea what they contain. He's inside."

Ruggalo held up an okay signal to let her know he'd heard her.

"I believe there's only one way in or out. I'll cover your six."

As Ruggalo and his team advanced on the small building, she turned to Simon. He was so close she could feel the moist heat of his breath on her lips. "I'm moving down behind them. I will stay back, but I need you to promise to stay here."

She waited for an argument. After all, the man was a lawyer. She couldn't expect anything different from him, could she? But rather than speaking, he leaned in and pressed his mouth to hers.

Instead of tasting of desperation, fear or impatience, his kiss was soft and sweet. A promise of things to come rather than a last-ditch effort.

When they parted, he pressed his dirt-streaked forehead to her cheekbone near the nylon strap of her tactical helmet and whispered, "Go get 'em."

Her lips still tingling from his kiss, Lori skittered down a slight incline and took up a position well behind the team of federal agents. She settled in, her gun sighted on the open doorway as the men scoped the area and conveyed information to one another using the tactical gestures she knew as well as she knew the alphabet.

Ruggalo dispatched his men with swift efficiency. She wrapped her finger around the trigger as the agent nearest to the door shouted their identification and warned the occupant that they had the building surrounded.

Thankfully, Rick Dale seemed to have a well-developed sense of self-preservation. Or he knew damn good and well he wasn't the one who would bear the brunt of whatever the Feds were about to rain down on Samuel Coulter. That was the thing with drug busts. There was usually someone higher up in the food chain to squeal on.

After a tense minute, they heard the man inside the building call out, "Don't shoot. Okay?"

He came out of the building with his hands held above his head. They instructed him to stand facing the side of the shed, his hands pressed high on the wall. One agent held him at gunpoint and barked questions while another patted him down. Dale claimed he was alone. Within minutes, they had confirmed his story and cleared the area. The Toyota's trunk and doors stood wide open.

Ruggalo stood up from his position between Lori and the rest of his team. "What's in the bags?"

Dale simply shook his head. "I'm not talking until I get a lawyer, but I wouldn't open them if I was you, man."

For a split second, Lori was afraid Simon would jump up out of the leaf mulch and volunteer his services, but to her immense relief, he held his silence.

One of the agents walked over to the trunk and nudged one of the duffel bags with the barrel of his gun. Lori stared through the scope, her stomach roiling as she watched the bag undulate.

She pressed the button on her mic and said to Ruggalo, "Snakes. No telling what else he has in there, but he definitely has snakes."

"Ten-four," Ruggalo called back.

Three more agents trotted into the clearing. They wore windbreakers rather than the full tactical gear the others had, but they were carrying assault weapons. Ruggalo waved them over to the building. Lori rose to her knees as Ruggalo called their progress to the base. He was just nodding at Alicia Simmons's response of "Ten-four. Return to base" when the crack of rifle fire made them jump.

Lori watched in horror as Ruggalo stumbled backward and fell to the ground. But then her entire world squeezed down to a pinpoint. Falling back to her belly, she marked the agent's position and calculated possible trajectories. Lori instinctively swung her rifle into position, using the scope to scan the woods to her left.

She saw the glint of another scope and fired on instinct.

Her weapon's report seemed to echo back at her. She heard the telltale thud of a body landing hard on the soft forest floor and exhaled in a whoosh. She pushed up and rocked back onto her knees. Using the scope, she found a thin young man stretched out prone on a bed of pine needles and crunchy leaves.

Behind her, Simon bellowed her name. She turned to find him running toward her, her own service weapon extended in front of him. The moment he was within reach, she grabbed a handful of his suit coat and yanked him down beside her.

"What do you think you're doing?" She snatched her gun from his grasp. "Do you even know anything about guns?"

"I don't need to," he said, panting. "You do."

"Well, the first thing you need to know is that a handgun isn't going to do you any good at long range," she said, checking the weapon. Thankfully, he hadn't been foolish enough to discharge it.

"I'd do it, though. I'd do it to protect you," he said fervently.

"It's a good thing I don't need protecting," she shot back.

She tore her eyes off the handsome idiot beside her as she spotted two of the backup team sprinting across to check on the shooter. To her relief, she saw Ruggalo work himself up onto one elbow. She watched as the agent probed the front of the Kevlar vest that had saved his life.

"You okay?" Lori asked into the radio.

"Yeah. Knocked the wind out of me," he responded weakly. "Good shootin', Deputy. You're an ace."

Glancing over at her ragtag group covered in the dust of the day, she keyed her mic and said, "Base, this is Cabrera. We had a situation, but the threat has been neutralized. Send medical and backup."

THE SCENE IN the parking lot had grown exponentially in the time since he'd slipped out of Ben Kinsella's SUV. Simon knew there'd be hell to pay for that, but he was too busy getting an earful from the diminutive deputy walking down the dirt track beside him to care.

"Wow. Look at this," he said, gesturing to the carnival of flashing lights atop nearly every vehicle.

While they were in the woods, a command center had popped up. Almost every foot of the field was covered with emergency vehicles. He noted at least three counties other than Masters present. Then there were the black panel vans and unmarked cars used by the Feds. His hands shook with unspent adrenaline.

Personnel scurried from group to group. Firemen in full turnout gear clumped back and forth and up and down trails shouting instructions to one another. Lori raised a hand to Deputy Wasson as he herded the three young women they found toward a black van parked beside an ambulance.

Special Agent Ruggalo sat in the open back door of an ambulance, medics crawling all over him as he spoke into a mobile phone. Lori raised her hand in a wave and he responded with a salute and a thumbs-up.

Simon spotted Ben Kinsella standing with the sheriff from Prescott County, their heads bent together in conversation. "Guess I'd better go let Ben get his shots in on me."

Lori grabbed his arm and spun him around to face her beside a Prescott County cruiser. "That was probably the most harebrained thing a person could possibly do. What were you thinking?" she demanded.

"I was thinking I needed to get to you." He waved an all-encompassing hand at the scene around them. "I knew your mission was not the DEA's mission. I didn't know if you had backup and I couldn't let you run off into the woods alone."

"Stop there," she advised. "Simon, I was doing my job."

"I know—"

"A job I've had since I was nineteen. A job I'm damn good at doing."

"I know you are. But I was worried sick. What if you went in there and I never got a chance to tell you—"

He stopped abruptly and took a moment to search her eyes. "Give me... I just need to..." He stopped, then gripped her upper arms gently and turned her away from him.

"What are you doing?" she demanded.

He found the catch for her chin strap and popped it open. Lifting the helmet from her head, he sighed when he caught sight of the thick, heavy knot of hair coiled at her nape. Ducking his head, he pressed his lips to the spot he'd ached to kiss since the moment he first laid eyes on her. Her skin was damp and dusty, but he didn't care. She was alive and warm and everything he needed.

"I have been aching to do this." She shivered and he pressed another gentle kiss to the sensitive spot. "The first time I saw you, all I could do was think about kissing you right here," he whispered. "Taking your hair down. Sliding my fingers through it."

"Simon—"

"I know this isn't the time or place, but, Lori, I need you to know I am not sorry I went in after you. I'd have done anything I needed to do to save you, because I am on your side, Lori. I want to be by your side.

"And, logically, yes, I know what I did today was boneheaded." He chuckled and squeezed her arms tight as he pressed his cheek to her hair. "But logic doesn't work when it comes to how I feel about you."

He felt the breath rush out of her and gathered her close, pulling her back against him. "You were right about me at the start. I wasn't giving Pine Bluff a chance," he said with a wry smile. "I didn't plan on staying here one minute longer than I had to."

She stiffened. "And now?"

Drawing a bracing breath, he loosened his hold and urged her to turn to face him. "To be honest, I've never sat down and thought long and hard about what I want to do or where I want to be." He blew out a breath. "I took the path laid out in front of me the minute I was born."

"It's what most of us do."

"Not you," he countered.

Lori wet her lips. "Not me."

"All my life, I've been trying to find shortcuts. Why bother paying dues or taking time to think about whether I might actually want something different, right?"

"Right," she whispered.

"I was wrong," he said, holding her gaze. "I was so wrong. I had no idea everything I ever wanted might be right here."

"Simon—"

"Listen, this is new. You and me. And I told Ben, I'm not even sure you actually think it's a thing, but... My parents are so in love with each other," he whispered, looking straight into her eyes. "I'm supposed to want all the other stuff. The power, ambition, adulation, but in truth, all I ever wanted was someone who simply wanted me. Was happy with me just the way I am."

She swallowed the lump in her throat. "I get you."

"I haven't done anything to make you believe in me, but I—"

"I haven't been nice to you," she interrupted. "I haven't given you much of a chance, and I'm sorry."

He gave her a lopsided smile. "You've been a challenge. And believe it or not, I don't mind a challenge."

"I guess we're a better match than I thought," she said with a laugh.

"We are," Simon replied, but he wasn't laughing. "You challenge me, Lori, and in doing so, you make me think about what I want to accomplish. Who I want to be. And I think I'm starting to figure it out."

"Are you?"

"Yes."

"And who do you want to be?"

"I want to be the guy who gets to kiss you. More than that, I want to be the guy who *deserves* to kiss you."

Lori licked her lips, pressed the heels of her hands to the corners of her eyes and stomped her booted foot as she looked away from him. "Don't make me cry. I'm in uniform," she said in a low rush.

Simon's smile came slowly, but when it ramped up to full strength, it was dazzling. "Well, I certainly don't want to make you cry out of uniform."

"Cocky," she admonished, her voice husky with emotion.

"Hopeful," he corrected. "Hopeful you'll give me a chance. Hopeful you'll show me how good small-town life can be."

She whipped her head up and her gaze met his. "You're staying here?"

"I think so," he said, the idea solidifying in his mind. "Something about this place feels like home. And don't think it doesn't pain me to admit it."

"I know it does," she said, a smile tugging at her lips.

"Speaking of pain, did I tell you I took Coulter down in more ways than one?"

"Did you? How's that?"

"Turns out I've retained some pretty slick martial arts skills. Remind me to show you my moves later."

She tugged his head down and her smile blossomed as his lips grazed hers. "Oh, I will, Counselor. I definitely will."

* * * * *

COMING SOON!

We really hope you enjoyed reading this book.
If you're looking for more romance, be sure to
head to the shops when new books are
available on

Thursday 2nd September

To see which titles are coming soon, please visit
millsandboon.co.uk/nextmonth

MILLS & BOON

THE HEART OF ROMANCE

A ROMANCE FOR EVERY READER

MODERN

Prepare to be swept off your feet by sophisticated, sexy and seductive heroes, in some of the world's most glamourous and romantic locations, where power and passion collide.

HISTORICAL

Escape with historical heroes from time gone by. Whether your passion is for wicked Regency Rakes, muscled Vikings or rugged Highlanders, awaken the romance of the past.

MEDICAL

Set your pulse racing with dedicated, delectable doctors in the high-pressure world of medicine, where emotions run high and passion, comfort and love are the best medicine.

True Love

Celebrate true love with tender stories of heartfelt romance, from the rush of falling in love to the joy a new baby can bring, and a focus on the emotional heart of a relationship.

Desire

Indulge in secrets and scandal, intense drama and plenty of sizzling hot action with powerful and passionate heroes who have it all: wealth, status, good looks…everything but the right woman.

HEROES

Experience all the excitement of a gripping thriller, with an intense romance at its heart. Resourceful, true-to-life women and strong, fearless men face danger and desire - a killer combination!

To see which titles are coming soon, please visit

millsandboon.co.uk/nextmonth

LET'S TALK

Romance

For exclusive extracts, competitions
and special offers, find us online:

 facebook.com/millsandboon

🐦 @MillsandBoon

📷 @MillsandBoonUK

Get in touch on 01413 063232

JOIN US ON SOCIAL MEDIA!

Stay up to date with our latest releases, author
news and gossip, special offers and discounts, and
all the behind-the-scenes action
from Mills & Boon...

 millsandboon

 millsandboonuk

 millsandboon

It might just be true love...

MILLS & BOON
MEDICAL
Pulse-Racing Passion

Set your pulse racing with dedicated, delectable doctors in the high-pressure world of medicine, where emotions run high and passion, comfort and love are the best medicine.